whispers OF YOU

THE LOST & FOUND SERIES

CATHERINE COWLES

Editor: Margo Lipschultz
Copy Editor: Chelle Olson
Proofreading: Julie Deaton and Jaime Ryter
Paperback Formatting: Stacey Blake, Champagne Book Design
Cover Design: Hang Le
Cover Photography: Braadyn Penrod

Dedication

For Megan.
Thank you for believing in me and my stories from day one. For reading each and always encouraging and supporting. I love you to the moon and back, dearest cuz, and I'm so lucky to have you in my life.

whispers
OF YOU

Prologue

Wren
PAST

M Y EYES NARROWED AS I TOOK IN MY NEMESIS. MY HEAD lowered as if I were dipping my hat in one of those old Westerns. I swore the beast was mocking me. "Please, for the love of all that's holy, don't burn."

The chicken and vegetables in the roasting pan didn't respond. They never did. They made their displeasure known by blackening to a crisp, no matter what I tried.

I'd been practicing for weeks. Every time I showed up at the meat market again, Sal would give me a sympathetic smile and move to the back to get me another chicken. He'd tried time and time again to give me tips. He'd even printed out recipes and removed the giblets for me.

I was getting better. But the results, while edible, still didn't taste all that good. Whispering a barely audible prayer, I opened the oven and slid the roasting pan inside. I closed the door and pressed my hand to it as I shut my eyes. "Please, please, *please.*"

Roasted chicken and mashed potatoes were Holt's favorite

meal. When I'd asked his mom for the recipe, she'd given me a soft smile, her eyes glowing. *It's a family recipe. Passed down from my great-grandmother. But I know it'll be in good hands with you.*

I worried the side of my lip as I stared at the oven. The familiar squeeze around my lungs took root. I wanted so badly to get it right. Perfect.

If Holt were here right now, he'd probably press his lips to the top of my head and tell me to breathe. That the intention behind the action was what mattered, not the outcome. Then he'd eat the worst blackened bird if it meant a smile stretching across my face.

As if I'd conjured him with my thoughts alone, my phone rang on the counter—a tone that was only his. It wasn't as if I needed a special one for Holt. I could count on one hand the number of people who called me on a regular basis.

Holt. His sister, Grae. Two other friends from school. My grandma.

Certainly not my parents, who took off every chance they got, traveling to so many places I couldn't keep track. As I reached for my phone, I tried to remember if it was a conference in Cincinnati or Chicago they'd gone off to this weekend.

My mouth curved as I lifted my phone. The photo that flashed on the screen was my favorite—Holt's arms wrapped around me, his lips pressed to my temple, and his deep blue eyes shining. The cheesy grin on my face said it all: My happiest place was always in his arms.

I slid my thumb across the screen. "I hope you're not calling because you had to rescue a kitten in a tree, and now you're going to be late."

Holt's chuckle skated across the line. It was deeper than it had been when we'd gotten together two years ago. A sound that sent a pleasant shiver skating across my skin.

That was the gift of knowing someone all your life. You got to see every incarnation of them. I had a lifetime of chuckles to play over and over—from little boy to teenager to man. I got to hear the way age sank into that sound and made it husky.

"Not gonna be late, Cricket. I'm just calling to see if you needed me to pick up anything at the store on my way over."

I scanned the kitchen. It was a wreck, but I had time to set it back to rights. "I think I'm good. Just need you."

"That's the way it'll always be."

There was a warmth in his voice that soothed so many of my rough edges. The ones caused by missing-in-action parents and living all but alone in an empty house. The ones of never feeling good enough, no matter how high my grades were or how many extracurriculars I participated in. With Holt, I could simply *be*.

"I like the sound of that," I said softly.

Voices sounded in the background. "That's Nash. I told him I'd help him with his bike."

The voices grew. It was the typical cacophony of the Hartley household. With four brothers and one sister, their house was always barely contained chaos. I loved it. It was so different from the sterile silence of mine.

"Tell him hey."

"Little Williams, release my brother's balls for ten minutes, would you?" Nash called.

There was a scuffle and a grunt.

"Shit, Holt. That hurt."

Holt let out a low growl. "That's what happens when you're an ass."

I couldn't help the laugh that escaped my lips.

"Heard that, Wren," Nash shot back. "And I won't forget that you laughed at my pain."

"Sorry, Nash Bash," I said, loudly enough for him to hear across the line.

"Don't apologize to that moron," Holt said.

"Loveable moron," Nash yelled, his voice moving away from the phone.

Another laugh bubbled out of me.

Holt sighed. "Sorry about that."

"He's harmless." The truth was, I loved feeling like I was a part of the Hartley clan. Nash's teasing. Grae's steadfast friendship.

Lawson's protective big-brother act. Even Roan's scowls in my direction. I loved that they treated me as one of theirs.

"As harmless as a two-by-four to the head," Holt grumbled. "I'd better go help him, or I'll never get to my girl."

That warmth was back. Spreading. Sinking deep into the places that were only his. I pitched my voice low. "Holt?"

"Hmm?" His footsteps told me he was already moving toward the massive garage on the Hartleys' property.

"This is one night you don't want to be late." My voice held a husky promise.

Holt's steps halted. "Cricket..."

A flutter took root in my belly. "Just don't be late."

The list of things that typically kept Holt from running on time was endless. A mama duck was trying to cross the street, and he had to stop traffic so she and her babies could get there safely. He couldn't find his keys. He'd searched high and low until he found them in the door to his truck. But the most common was that he'd gone out with his dad on a search and rescue call. He'd forget to text, and Grae would inevitably have to let me know where he'd gone.

I couldn't begrudge him any of it because his reasons were always so good. *He* was so good. That was Holt. Easily distracted but with the best heart. And I'd love that heart until the day I died.

"I won't be late." Holt's voice was low and full of promise.

That heat inside me sparked and twisted. "See you soon."

"Soon, Cricket."

The line went silent, but I kept the phone pressed to my ear as if I could still hear the strains of the voice I knew better than my own curling around me. There was little I loved more than my nickname slipping from his lips.

My mouth curved at the memories of him picking it up. We'd been playing Ghost in the Graveyard, and I'd been scared out of my mind when it was my turn to hide, my heart hammering so hard against my ribs that I'd trembled.

When Holt had snuck up on me, I'd let out the most pitiful chirping noise—not even a scream or a shriek. He'd pulled me into a hug, his warm, strong body cocooning mine, and said, *"Don't worry, Cricket. I'll scare the ghosts away."*

He'd come to mean safety to me long before we ever became a couple. Looked out for me since before I could walk. But it was more than that. There was no place I felt more at peace than with Holt by my side.

I gripped the phone tighter, holding it to my chest as a million memories ran through my mind. I was ready. I didn't want the cliché of losing my virginity to Holt in a hotel room after his senior prom next month. I didn't want our first time to be in his dorm room when he left Cedar Ridge for the University of Washington next fall, worried his roommate might come home at any moment. I wanted special. Him and me.

Pushing off the counter, I started for the stairs and took them two at a time. As I rounded the corner and moved into my room, I studied the space with new eyes, assessing if it was too juvenile.

I'd never felt the two-year gap between Holt and me more than now that he was headed to school. He would only be a few hours away, but it felt like he'd be on another planet. I let out a shaky breath.

The distance didn't matter. What Holt and I had? It was made to last. We'd been through too much together—the highs and the lows, the everyday and the extraordinary. Birthdays and holidays. Issues with parents and almost losing Grae. Campouts and Hartley family dinners. Our whole lives were forever entwined.

I had all the incarnations of his chuckle, and I wasn't letting go.

With that thought, I moved to the shower. I didn't put on music like I usually did. I let the memories of Holt cascade over me as I washed my hair and then dried it. As I painstakingly put on makeup that accentuated my hazel eyes, making them seem greener. As I slipped into my favorite sundress—the one I knew Holt loved.

I grabbed my phone and checked the time. A soft laugh bubbled out of me. Fifteen minutes late. But I knew Holt—sometimes better than I knew myself. So, I'd accounted for that. The chicken still had thirty minutes left to cook.

A car door slammed, and a flurry of sensations skittered through my chest. I hurried to my window, looking down through the gauzy curtains. But it wasn't Holt's silver truck in the driveway. Instead, I saw a familiar SUV—a newish one that already had a slew of dents.

My gut tightened as Randy Sullivan and Paul Matthews climbed out. What were they doing here? I quickly glanced around the street, mentally assessing if they'd somehow ended up at the wrong house. If it were after dark, I'd guess they were here to toilet paper my house—because tripping me in the halls and mocking me in class apparently weren't enough.

Their laughter had me returning my focus to them. Paul lifted his hand, thumb and forefinger making the shape of a gun as he pointed it at my window. A chill skated down my spine.

Randy laughed and jogged up the steps, ringing the bell.

The sound echoed through my quiet house. But I didn't move.

The bell rang again.

"Wren," Randy singsonged. "Come on down."

Something about his voice had always grated against my skin and set my nerves on edge. My grandma always said we had intuition for a reason, and we were fools if we didn't listen to it. So, I stayed exactly where I was.

As they continued pressing the bell, I could just make out the two boys. A grade ahead of me, they looked just like the rest of the kids in our high school: T-shirts and jeans, hair a little bit askew. But there was cruelty in them. There always had been.

I wasn't the only person they picked on, but it was always those physically weaker than they were. Maybe because they'd been given such a hard time in middle school. Maybe that meanness was just in them. Whatever the reason, I gave them a wide berth whenever I could.

"Maybe she isn't home," Paul said, looking through the side window.

Randy shook his head. "Car's here."

"So she's out with Holt."

Randy pointed at the lights illuminating the dining room and kitchen. "She's home. Bet lover boy will be here any minute."

An ugly smile twisted Paul's lips. "What's wrong, Wren?" he called. "Don't want to see us?"

"Oh, she'll see us," Randy shot back. His hand slipped under his T-shirt, fingers closing around something I couldn't quite make out as he pulled it from his waistband.

My mind put together the individual pieces before the whole picture. Black handle gripped tightly in Randy's fingers, silver barrel glinting in the low light. A gun.

A buzzing started in my ears. It wasn't that I'd never seen a gun before. Our town was far off the beaten path in Eastern Washington, nestled between mountains that meant reaching Cedar Ridge by car in winter was sometimes impossible. We had bears, cougars, and coyotes. Shotguns and rifles were typical, especially for folks farther out.

But I didn't think I'd ever seen a handgun before, and certainly not in the grasp of a classmate on my doorstep.

Paul laughed and pulled a gun from his waistband, as well. "Did you try the door? It's probably unlocked."

It was true that most residents around town didn't concern themselves with that sort of thing. But I could always hear Holt's voice in my head. *"Want to hear that lock click."*

He hated that my parents left me alone so much. Had drilled it into my head time and again to check all the doors and windows before going to bed. Over time, it had become a habit. A compulsion. I locked every door after I entered. Drove Grae crazy that she couldn't waltz right in—until I'd eventually given her a key.

My heart hammered against my ribs as my fingers skittered across my phone's screen. It took four tries to hit those three little numbers. Nine. One. One.

"Cedar Ridge police, fire, and medical. What's your emergency?"

"T-there are two guys trying to get into my house. They have guns," I whispered.

"Damn. It's locked." I heard Randy mutter.

Paul sighed and bent over, searching the stoop. "There has to be a key hidden somewhere."

"Who am I speaking to, and where are you located?"

"Wren Williams." I rattled off my address.

"Wren, it's Abel. I'm gonna get you some help. You just stick with me. Are you somewhere safe?"

I gripped the curtains as I watched Paul and Randy making their way around the house. Each step brought them closer to that damn ceramic frog my mom kept on the back deck, the one with the key underneath *just for emergencies.*

"They're looking for the key." My voice trembled as they disappeared from sight. Maybe I should make a run for it. But my closest neighbor was half a mile away. It would only take one lucky shot to make me regret taking that chance.

"Is there one outside?"

"Yes," I breathed.

"I want you to hide, Wren. The place they'd be least likely to look."

My mind spun. How many times had Grae and I played hide-and-seek in this house as kids? Too many to count. I knew every nook and cranny. Yet I couldn't get my brain to cooperate.

"Wren?" Abel pressed.

"I-I don't know where to go."

"How about an attic or crawl space? A closet? Or under a bed?"

A series of images flashed through my mind. Options. Not the attic. The door was too obvious. The entrance to the crawl space was downstairs. I couldn't risk it. The thought of shoving myself under a bed had my chest constricting.

It had to be a closet. I started moving. Mine would be one of the first places they'd look. I wanted to go to my parents' and surround myself with their familiar scents, but I forced myself to go the other way to the second guest room.

Panic licked through my veins as I scanned the space. None of the closets provided much protection or disguise. They would be too easy to search.

I darted back into the hall and went to the guest bathroom. I pulled open the cabinet under the sink. Setting the phone down, I hurried to empty it of its smattering of contents. I quickly shoved them into one of the drawers.

Grabbing my phone, I crawled under the sink. I'd always been of average height and glad of it, thankful that I blended into the background. But right then, I would've given anything to be petite like Grae.

I pulled the doors closed, but they didn't quite make it. I shoved myself harder against the back wall.

Abel's voice cut across the line. "Wren, where are you?"

"The bathroom. The guest bathroom. In the hall. Under the sink. How long till the police get here?"

Part of me hoped it would be Holt's oldest brother, Lawson, who responded to the call. The other half wanted him nowhere near this.

The dispatcher was quiet on the other end of the line for a moment.

My heart dropped. "Abel?"

"There have been three shootings tonight. All available officers are out on calls. I've got two coming to you, but they're up the mountain. It's gonna be a minute."

Three shootings. It wasn't possible. Not in a town as small as ours. The worst thing to happen here was a bad car accident that had killed two people. Shootings happened in big cities. Not here.

The buzzing in my ears intensified and infiltrated my entire body. It had to be them. Randy and Paul. A million things ran through my head. Questions of why and who had been targeted. Had anyone been killed?

A knock sounded on the back door, and I jumped, hitting my head.

"Wreeeeeeen, I can see the food on the counter. We know you're home," Randy called.

"Could you see them, Wren? Did you recognize them?"

"Yes. R-Randy Sullivan and Paul Matthews. They go to my school."

"And you saw their weapons?"

"Yes. Handguns." I was going numb now as if this were all happening to someone else, and I was watching from above.

"Do you have a weapon?"

"No." My voice cracked.

Holt's dad, Nathan, had been adamant about teaching us all gun safety, but to this day, that had been the only time I'd ever held a weapon—unless you counted a kitchen knife.

"Officers are fifteen minutes out. They'll be there soon."

"Found it!" Paul called.

I heard the key in the lock, the cylinder turning and bolt sliding. Or maybe it was my imagination that made it sound as if a bomb had just gone off at my back door.

"They're in the house." My words were barely audible as footsteps pounded up the stairs. "Don't talk."

Abel didn't say a word, but a click sounded across the line. A barely discernable agreement.

Chaos erupted down the hall—from my room. Crashing furniture, and the closet door banging.

"Where the hell is that tight-assed bitch?" Randy growled. "Lover boy isn't here to protect you now, is he?"

Oh, God. Holt. My mind warred with itself. Part of me wanted him here to rescue me from this nightmare. But another part wanted him as far away from this house as possible.

Randy's twisted face flashed in my mind. The anger that had etched itself there after he'd asked me out in the seventh grade, and I'd declined.

My breaths came in quick pants as Randy and Paul moved from room to room. The air stilled in my lungs as footsteps sounded in the bathroom. Someone tore back the shower curtain.

A shot sounded, and then I heard shattered glass.

"Save your bullets for things that matter," Paul said.

"She's here somewhere," Randy gritted out.

"And we'll find her."

Faint footsteps sounded downstairs, and relief and fear warred inside me. Holt or the police? Holt would've rung the bell. It was the police. It had to be.

The cabinet doors flew open, and Paul hooted with glee. "Look what I found, Ran. If it's not a Goody Two-shoes hiding under the sink."

A sneer twisted Randy's face as Paul hauled me out. "Get on your knees."

Paul shoved me to the floor. I hit the tile with a force that jarred my spine, and my phone tumbled to the bathmat.

Randy snatched it up, glaring at the screen. His finger punched the end icon. "Stupid bitch was on with 9-1-1. You tell the cops who was here?"

"N-no."

"Fuckin' liar." Randy slapped me so hard my head snapped back, and I tasted blood.

Footsteps sounded in the entryway. I prayed for the officers to hurry.

Paul stomped on my phone, the screen making a crunching sound. The only thing I could see was the now-fractured image of me and Holt, shattered into a million tiny pieces. "We gotta get out of here. The cops will be on the way."

Randy's eyes flashed. "No. I'm having my fun with her first."

A siren sounded in the distance. More help.

Hurry.

I chanted the word over and over in my mind as if the two syllables could save me.

"We gotta go *now*," Paul snapped.

"Then help me get her ass in the car. I'm taking my time with this one."

My stomach roiled as the metallic taste in my mouth intensified.

Paul raised his gun. I couldn't look away from the muzzle pointed straight at me. Memories flashed within the darkness of the barrel. Laughing as I sailed through the air after Holt threw me into the lake. The buzz beneath my skin the first time his lips touched mine. Holt holding me tightly as I let the tears flow when my parents had forgotten my birthday. Again. Planning that big, beautiful future that would be ours.

All my best moments had been with Holt. But I hadn't had nearly enough.

I opened my mouth to scream. To beg. I wasn't even sure which.

But I didn't get the chance.

I heard a pop, like the sound of a single firecracker slicing through the air.

Heat bloomed in my chest. Then fire. And I was sliding down.

The tile was so cold, frigid compared to the inferno blazing in my torso. I wanted to sink into that coldness to escape the heat. But most of all, I wanted Holt.

"What the fuck?" Randy bellowed.

"She's not worth getting arrested over, man. We gotta run!"

The ceiling above me melted into a cascade of colors, the pastels swirling together until it almost looked like my favorite time of day. Twilight. How many times had I made Holt sit with me past the sunset so that I could watch nighttime take hold? So the sky could soothe my soul.

I almost felt Holt's lips pressed to my temple. *I'll watch every twilight with you. Every moonrise, too.*

Footsteps pounded on the stairs. "Where the hell is Holt? We need them both."

I tried to get my brain to place that voice. But I couldn't quite… *Don't worry, Cricket. I'll scare the ghosts away.*

The twilight ceiling darkened, and the only thing I could think then was that I was glad Holt was late.

But I would've given anything to feel his arms around me one more time.

Chapter One

Holt
PRESENT

TEN YEARS.

I couldn't help but circle the number in my head. Three thousand, six hundred, and fifty days. Yet I still knew these mountain passes like the back of my hand. The ones that got so packed with snow during the winter months they became impassible, the only ways in and out of town by air or taking the ferry to the opposite end of the lake, assuming things weren't frozen.

The feeling of being mostly cut off from the world had always been something I'd relished. Cedar Ridge felt like a place the evil of the world hadn't touched. We all knew better now. Evil was just better at hiding sometimes.

My gut tightened as I took the final curve that would deposit me across the border of the town limits, my Mercedes G63 hugging the road like a dream. On any other day, I would've gotten a thrill out of taking these mountain passes, testing my reflexes, and feeling that hit of adrenaline that reminded me I was still alive. But not today.

The bend in the road straightened, and I caught sight of the same sign I'd passed too many times to count. *Welcome to Cedar Ridge. Population 2163.* The number was higher than it had been ten years ago, and the appearances I'd made since leaving had always been by air—in and out as quickly as humanly possible.

Not tempting fate. No chance of seeing familiar faces other than my family. No risk of seeing *her*.

Memories slammed against the walls I'd erected in my mind, brick by painstaking brick. Blood. The feel of her thready pulse beneath my fingers. My palms desperately trying to shove life back into her chest.

The leather on the wheel creaked with audible protest as I reinforced those mental walls. Hell. I needed better defenses if I were cracking after only seconds.

Then again, maybe I didn't. I deserved every painful memory that swirled and wreaked havoc on my brain.

I glanced at my dashboard clock. Eleven thirteen. My gaze shifted to my watch. Eleven fourteen.

A muscle in my jaw ticked as I quickly took in the screen of my satellite cell phone. Eleven fourteen. My fingers moved deftly to the console, adjusting the clock to match the correct time.

One minute.

To some people, it would be nothing. But I knew that lives could be lost in mere seconds. A whole minute was the difference between safety and catastrophe.

My cell rang through my SUV's speakers, and Jack's name flashed on the console. My thumb hit the button on the steering wheel to accept.

"Everything okay?"

"If I told you the team was falling apart without you, would you get your ass back here?"

I didn't say anything for a moment. The team was falling apart *with* me. I wasn't sure whether it was my dad's heart attack or the past finally coming back around for payback.

Jack let out an audible breath. "I know we've been hit with one tough case after another. But what happened to Castille wasn't your fault."

"My mission, my responsibility." A single second and another person on my watch had almost lost their life. Months of rehab were helping, but he still had a long road to a complete recovery.

"Every single one of us knows that this job comes with risks."

We did. Working private security around the world could mean anything: Working for private contractors in the Middle East, wealthy families in Europe, celebrities in Los Angeles, CEOs anywhere you could imagine—people whose lives were at risk for any number of reasons. Greed. Obsession. A hunger for power.

Between that and the war zones where I'd served my tours, I'd seen unparalleled levels of darkness. But nothing would ever touch what I'd seen in my sleepy hometown.

My gaze tracked the storefronts that had barely changed in my decade away—the rustic cabin-like shops and restaurants with their huge windows that beckoned you inside. I caught quick glimpses of the lake between the buildings. A little girl running down the street, her braids flying, laughing as her father chased her.

You would think that nothing bad could happen here, but you would be wrong.

"Holt?"

I jerked my focus back to my second-in-command, my brother in all the ways that mattered. "You know I didn't leave because of Castille." I could've lived with the guilt eating me alive. I was no stranger to that. "My family needs me." And it was time for me to suck it up and be here.

"How's the old man doing?" Jack asked.

"Nash said he's grumpy as hell and driving my mom up the wall."

Jack chuckled. "Doesn't surprise me. He doesn't strike me as the type to sit still for long."

My dad had come to train my security team in search and rescue a few years ago and had left an impression on just about everyone. "No, sitting still is not his forte."

The sound of a chair squeaking came across the line, and I pictured Jack in his office in Portland, staring out over the Hawthorne Bridge. "Have you seen her yet?"

A phantom fist gave my heart a vicious squeeze. "Who?"

Jack sighed. "Oh, I don't know, maybe the girl you won't shut up about every time you drink a little too much whiskey."

I let a slew of silent curses fly. Overindulging didn't happen often, but it was unavoidable at times. Anniversaries—the good and the bad. Birthdays—hers and mine. The time Grae had thought she was helping by telling me all about the *amazing guy* Wren was dating.

Just thinking her name lit a fire in my gut. The burn was a mixture of good and bad. Desire and destruction. Love and a soul-shredding guilt.

Jack kept pushing, not sensing the war playing out in my head. "Let me know when you have your run-in. I have a feeling it will be interesting."

"We aren't teenaged girls. I'm not feeding you gossip."

"I'll call Nash then. He'll keep me in the loop."

A curse slipped free, and Jack chuckled. I'd regret introducing my walking trouble of a younger brother to Jack for the rest of my days. "Piss off. And don't sink my company while I'm gone."

"Will do, Sarge. Let me know how long you're thinking once you're settled."

"You got it." I hadn't given the team a timeframe for my absence. Simply told them I needed indefinite leave. I had to get the lay of the land here. See how my family was.

If I were honest, the call about Dad's heart attack three months ago had scared the hell out of me. I'd met them at the hospital in

Seattle where they'd airlifted him. My mom's pale face, flashed in my mind, so ashen it was almost translucent.

It had been a hell of a wake-up call. I was missing out on my family's lives, and I didn't know how long I'd have them. And all because I'd let my demons rule my life for far too long. I knew better than anyone that second chances rarely came around.

I was about to end the call when Jack spoke again.

"If you get a shot, take it."

My gaze bored into the road in front of me and the forest that leapt up around it with pines so tall I had to look through my sunroof to see their tops. "You telling me to take a hit out on someone while I'm here?"

I'd thought the quip would make my ex-sniper friend laugh, but only silence greeted me.

"Don't leave things left unsaid. Even if you're scared as hell to say them."

The muscles in the back of my neck tightened, knitting themselves into intricate knots. "It isn't words she needs from me." It was atonement. But I couldn't give Wren anything that would heal the wounds I'd caused for not being there during the one moment she'd needed me the most.

"That's bullshit. A damn cop-out if I've ever heard one."

"You don't know," I growled. No one did—to hold the girl you loved more than anything as the life bled from her body.

"Maybe I don't. At least not exactly what happened. But I *do* know what it's like to have regrets. To live with ghosts. I don't want that for you."

A little of the pissed off seeped out of me at that. "I hear you." It was all I could give Jack. I sure as hell couldn't give him a promise to make things right because that was impossible.

"All right, man. You know I'm here if you need me. Call anytime. And if shit gets bad, I'll take our chopper."

That was friendship. The kind born of battle and bloodshed. Of being in hellish situations with only the other to get you out. We had each other's backs. Always.

"Thanks. Tell the team not to blow anything up while I'm gone."

Jack chuckled. "You never want us to have any fun."

I shook my head and ended the call.

I'd made it to the center of town during the phone call. Just a couple of blocks left. But they were brutal ones. Wildfire Pizza, where I'd taken Wren on our first date. Cones, where she and Grae always begged me to stop on the way home from school.

But the damned dock was the worst. I swore I could still taste the hint of mint from the lip balm Wren always wore. Feel the hesitant press of her mouth to mine. See how she looked up at me with so much trust.

And I'd destroyed it all.

Chapter Two

Wren

"LITTLE WILLIAMS," NASH CALLED AS HE MANEUVERED the bullpen, headed toward dispatch city. He held up a hand for a high five.

I shook my head but smacked his palm. "There's no Big Williams." But no matter how many times I made that point, he kept calling me that. For so long, it had been like an ice pick to the chest every time he leveled the nickname at me, conjuring memories of all the outings I'd had with Holt and the Hartley clan. But over time, it had lessened to a dull ache.

Lawson came up behind his brother, clapping him on the back. "You know you'll never get Nash to call you by your actual name."

Nash patted Lawson's chest. "Damn straight, boss man."

The eldest Hartley scowled. "Stop calling me that."

Nash's lips twitched. "*Chief* better? Big man? Head honcho?"

"I'm gonna start making you call me sir."

I choked on a laugh and gave Lawson a mock salute. "I think it works."

"Sir. Yes, sir," Nash snapped out.

Lawson gave his younger brother a shove. "Get back to work before I have to fire your ass."

Nash started jogging backward, his green eyes twinkling. "Never. Who would catch all the bad guys?"

I couldn't help the roll of my eyes. "Single-handedly taking down drug cartels and terrorist outfits every single week."

"And don't you forget it." He waggled his eyebrows. "The rest of the ladies certainly don't."

"Nash…" Lawson warned.

"Don't worry, boss. I'm on the case."

Lawson pinched the bridge of his nose. "I don't even want to know what case that is."

I leaned back in my chair. "Probably the case of some cougar's missing bra."

Lawson's face screwed up. "I really don't need that mental image in my head."

I pressed my mouth into a hard line to keep from laughing.

"Yeah, yeah, yuck it up."

I held up both hands. "I didn't say a word."

"Your eyes did," he griped.

The smile wouldn't stay off my face, no matter how hard I tried. "Nash is like the station mascot. Keeps things light."

"I guess that's worth the chaos he leaves in his wake."

There was fatigue in Lawson's voice that was more than the typical exasperation I heard when it came to his brother. I straightened in my chair. "Everything okay?"

He waved me off. "Fine. Just a lot going on. Not getting as much sleep as I should."

The dark circles around Lawson's eyes told me that much was true. Between being Chief of Police in a tourist town with not enough officers, raising three boys on his own, and his father's recent heart attack, it was no wonder he was exhausted.

"Want me to take the boys for a few hours later?"

Lawson shook his head. "No, we're okay. I just need to turn in a little earlier tonight."

"Let me know if you change your mind. Or if Kerry needs any help with your dad."

The corner of Lawson's mouth pulled up. "You might regret that offer. He's been a bear lately."

Empathy washed through me. "He's not used to being laid up like this." Nathan had mostly healed from the bypass surgery, but rehab for the leg he'd broken when he fell was taking a little more time. I knew better than most how frustrating it could be to have your body hold you back from what you knew your soul needed.

My fingers twitched at my side, itching to circle the raised scar over my heart and trace the line that bisected my chest. I fisted my hand instead.

Concern filled Lawson's features. "Sorry. I didn't mean—"

"You're fine." But I felt a flicker of annoyance rise. It didn't matter how much time had passed; the people around me still had this deep need to tread carefully.

On my good days, I could remind myself that it was because they cared. On the bad ones, I was a pitying smile away from biting someone's head off.

"You distracting my dispatcher from doing her job?" Abel asked as he strode up. Salt and pepper laced his hair now, and his dark skin crinkled around his eyes.

Lawson shot him a grin. "Never."

"Abel," I said in a stage whisper. "You're not allowed to criticize the *boss*."

Lawson chuckled. "Everyone knows it's really Abel who runs the show."

"Damn straight, and don't you ever forget it."

His voice was the same as it had always been, that even tone with just a bit of grit that had seen me through what I'd thought were my darkest moments. And he'd never given up on me. He'd gotten me help as soon as he could and had given me a sense of purpose that I'd desperately needed when my world had crumbled around me.

Lawson gave Abel a salute. "Keep manning the ship. I'll go push some paper around."

Abel harrumphed, which only made Lawson grin wider as he headed to his office.

"Give me the lay of the land."

"Pretty quiet today." Day shifts were either silent as a mouse or total bedlam. As more and more tourists descended, it would tend toward the latter. Teenagers being stupid. Boaters having too much to drink and thinking a DWI only applied to cars. Lost hikers.

Abel lowered himself into the chair at the cubicle next to mine. "I'll cover you when you leave for lunch."

"Thanks. I've still got a bit."

Two officers passed our desks. Clint Anderson lifted his chin. "You in for poker this weekend, Williams?"

"Only if you're ready to get cleaned out."

He shook his head, glancing at his partner. "She's brutal. Shows no mercy."

Amber Raymond smiled in my direction, but it was forced— and it always would be. I didn't blame her. On a night we'd all seen the face of evil, her younger brother had died, and I hadn't. My wounds should've meant me being in the ground, too, but something had kept me holding on.

Not something. Holt.

Invisible claws dug into my chest, ones of grief and rage. But I'd mastered not letting that show. I could be in agony on the inside, and no one would know.

"Hey, Amber." I smiled, but it was strained. I didn't want to be a reminder of all she'd lost. But I wouldn't look away from her grief either.

"Hi, Wren."

My phone rang, and I instantly swiveled toward my computer monitors as I positioned my headset. "Cedar Ridge police, fire, and medical. What's your emergency?"

"T-there's someone here. I think they're trying to break in."

My stomach dropped, but I kept my breathing in check as I

glanced at the computer readout. "Is this Marion Simpson at five-two-two Huckleberry Court?"

"It's me, Wren. They're scratching at the door like they're trying to pick the lock. Please send someone."

"Stay on the line. I'm going to get someone out to you right now." I clicked over to our radio system. "Reported 10-62 at 522 Huckleberry Court. Possible B and E in progress. Requesting officer response."

A familiar voice cut across the line. "Officers Hartley and Vera responding. Let us know what we're walking into."

I switched back over to the call. "Ms. Simpson, are you home alone?"

"Y-yes."

"Can you see who's at your door?"

"No. I'm in my bedroom. I didn't want to go down there."

A loud banging sounded across the line, and my stomach twisted. "Stay where you are. I have two officers en route. They should be there momentarily." If Nash was driving, they'd be there in under two minutes. But this was one circumstance where I didn't mind his daredevil ways.

"Thank you, Wren."

There was still a slight tremble in her voice, but it wasn't nearly as bad as it had been earlier.

"Of course. Do you have any weapons in the house?"

"Just my shotgun, but it's downstairs in the gun safe."

"Okay. Hold on for me. I'm going to give the officers a little more information." I moved to the radio. "Marion Simpson is the only person in residence. The only reported weapon is a shotgun in a gun safe downstairs. She's located upstairs in her bedroom."

"Thanks, Little Williams. We're less than a minute out. Stay on the line with her."

"Will do." I went back to the phone line. "Ms. Simpson, two officers will be there in less than a minute."

"I've told you, Wren. Call me Marion."

"Okay, Marion. What do you hear now?"

"I'm not sure… Rustling, I think. Is he getting in?"

God, I hoped not. "The officers are almost to your house."

"I hear sirens," Marion said, the line crackling. "They're here."

"That's good. Just stay on the line with me."

Shouts sounded from far off. I focused on keeping my breathing even, controlled. In for two, out for two.

"Oh, dear," Marion mumbled.

"What's wrong?"

"I need to go."

"Marion, don't—" But the line had already clicked off. I called her back, but she didn't answer. Then I opted to turn up the radio.

"Little Williams, you might want to call my brother."

"Law?"

"Roan."

I was already dialing his cell. "What's going on?"

"I just tranqued a bear. Apparently, Ms. Simpson's been feeding them."

From his chair next to me, Abel cursed. "Is she a moron?"

"Oh, no!" Marion wailed. "Did you kill Yogi?"

"I gotta go," Nash muttered.

My anxiety left me on the flood of an exhale. Then laughter bubbled up. "Keep feeding them, and they'll be really annoyed when you stop."

Abel took the phone from me. "I'll call Roan and get Fish and Wildlife on it. You take your lunch."

I glanced down at my watch. Only five minutes late. I pushed out of my chair and pressed a kiss to Abel's cheek. "Thanks."

He waved me off with a grumble, and I moved toward the front doors and sunlight. As I stepped outside, I took in a lungful of mountain air and the scent that would always mean home.

"Hey, girl," Gretchen said with a big smile. My old classmate had a reusable shopping bag slung over her shoulder, currently stuffed full of produce.

I returned her grin. "Coming from the farmers market?"

She nodded. "Told Mom I'd make her favorite pasta primavera."

"How's she doing?"

Gretchen's smile faltered for a moment. "She's hanging in there, but her heart's still struggling. We're just making the most of all the days we have together."

God, Gretchen had been through enough. Targeted the same night I was, she lived with those nightmares every day. But she never let them skew her outlook on life.

"Why don't I bring you guys dinner next week? We can have a real catch-up," I suggested.

Gretchen beamed. "That would be great, and Mom would love to see you."

"Wren," Grae called from across the street, holding up a take-out bag from the deli.

"I'd better run," I told Gretchen. "I'm meeting that one for lunch." I hitched a thumb in Grae's direction.

"Have fun."

I waved and then looked for traffic before darting across the street. I pulled my best friend into a hug. "I thought we were going to Wildfire."

An expression passed across her face so quickly that if I hadn't known her all my life, I likely would've missed it.

"Grae…"

She started walking. "I thought we could do sandwiches in the park instead."

I hurried to catch up with her. "What's going on?"

"Nothing." Her pace quickened. "Just hungry."

I grabbed Grae's elbow, slowing her to a stop. "Grae Hartley, I've known you for my entire life, and I know when you're lying to me."

She shuffled her feet as I studied her. "We need to talk about Holt."

I dropped Grae's arm as if it were a branding iron. "We shall not speak his name. That's the rule, remember?"

She'd tried at first, wanting so badly to fix what had been ir-revocably broken. Then I'd started avoiding my best friend of forever, not answering her calls, making excuses for ducking out of plans. We'd finally been forced to come up with a ceasefire of sorts, and this was what we'd settled on.

Holt didn't exist for me. I knew his family talked to him. Saw him, even. But they never mentioned his name in my presence. Until today.

Grae worried her bottom lip. "Emergency exemption requested."

A lead weight settled in my stomach. "Did something happen to him?" The words came out in a rush of barely audible breath. I knew what he'd done when he left Cedar Ridge. He'd gone into the military. Then private security. Throwing himself into one risky situation after another, and all of them as far from home as he could get.

My heart hammered against my ribs as blood roared in my ears. Even though I hadn't seen Holt in nine years and seven months, I still knew that he was here. On this Earth. Breathing. I'd have known if he weren't. Some part of my soul would've registered it.

Grae blanched. "Oh, God, no. I'm sorry. It's nothing like that."

Relief blazed through me like an ice bath after third-degree burns. "What is it?" There was a snap of annoyance to my words. Anger surged at the reminder that no matter how much time had passed, I still cared.

Grae met my gaze, uncertainty filling hers. "He's back."

Chapter Three

Holt

"HOOOOLT," A FEMININE VOICE SINGSONGED.

I froze in the entryway of the bed and breakfast. I'd known it was a risk to stay here, but I hadn't wanted to stay at my parents' place, and my siblings all had their own lives; they didn't need me crowding their space.

I slowly turned around and forced a smile as I took in the woman in her early sixties. "Ms. Peabody. Nice to see you."

She clasped her hands in front of her and practically vibrated with excitement. "You're grown now. You know you can call me Janice."

Her nickname growing up had been Ms. Busybody, and with good reason.

"All right, Janice."

Her shoulders gave a little shimmy. "I was so excited when I saw your name on the roster. I knew you'd come home eventually. All good sons do." She leaned in a little closer, a look of exaggerated sympathy on her face. "How is it being back? I know there has to be a lot of memories…"

Janice let the sentence hang, waiting for me to finish it. She'd be waiting a hell of a long time.

I locked down my expression. I'd had years to master my blank mask. She wasn't getting any tidbits of information to gossip over with her cronies.

"It's good to be back, but I need to head out. Wouldn't want to be late to my parents.'"

"Oh, of course not. Tell your mom hi for me."

I didn't miss the disappointment in her voice. I'd continue being a disappointment every time she tried one of these ambushes. I'd tried to snag one of the vacation rentals in town, but they were all booked up for the season. Still, it might be worth trying again in case someone had canceled.

Giving Janice a nod, I headed for the door.

"Wren's working across the street. I'm sure your brothers told you, but just in case they didn't…I'm sure she'd love to see you."

My gait hitched in mid-step. So much for that blank mask. But I didn't say a word, just kept walking.

My pulse beat harder in my neck, the rapid rhythm of trying to fight off the memories. The sticky feeling of her blood between my fingers. Her fading heartbeat. The knowledge that I'd failed her. She'd almost died because of me. Because I'd let Nash distract me. I might as well have been holding the gun myself.

I sucked in the mountain air as I stepped outside onto Main Street. There was nothing like it. It didn't matter how many places I'd been, none of them smelled quite like this—a blend of pine and fresh water and something unique to Cedar Ridge. I let it fill my nostrils and swirl around, praying it would cleanse the nightmare images from my brain.

"Holt?"

My head jerked up at the familiar voice—older now, deeper, and a little raw with age.

I forced another of those fake-as-hell smiles. "Jude. Good to see you, man."

He strode forward to take my hand in a hard grasp. "Thought I was looking at a ghost."

Maybe he was. There were times I thought my life had ended the day I almost lost Wren. I moved through the world differently now and saw everything through an entirely new lens.

Motion behind Jude caught my attention as another of my high school friends stepped forward. Chris gave me a chin lift, but there wasn't a whole lot of welcome in his dark gaze. "Holt."

I didn't blame him for that lack of warmth. When I'd bailed on Cedar Ridge, I'd bailed on everyone. It had felt like the only way to keep from drowning was to pretend that I was an entirely different person—without friends or family I talked to more than once a week.

Without *her.*

"Hey, Chris."

I extended a hand, and he waited for a beat before accepting it.

"What are you doing in town?" Jude asked. His face looked the same, but he'd bulked up since high school, his shoulders broader. And he'd gained a good fifteen pounds of muscle.

"Wanted to spend some time with my dad and the rest of the family." To try to mend some of the hurt I'd caused. Maybe find a new normal.

Chris shifted his lanky frame, begrudgingly turning his gaze to me. "How's he doing?"

"Better. Just ornery."

The corner of Jude's mouth kicked up. "Not shocked about that. I've been meaning to stop by this week, but work's been kicking my ass."

"It gets worse every tourist season," Chris muttered.

"What are you guys doing these days?" I hated that I had to ask the question. We'd been the three musketeers while growing up until Wren and I had gotten together, and my world's axis had shifted. But even then, we remained close. It wasn't until I'd left that things changed.

Jude grinned. "Went into business together. Mountainview Construction."

"That's great. Building houses?" I'd seen that company name on a build on my way into town, and it had looked amazing. Pride swelled inside me for my friends. Chris had always fought against pressure from his father to go into medicine, and Jude's dad had been an asshole who'd told him he'd amount to nothing. The fact that they'd gone out on their own and built something was incredible.

Chris nodded. "Started with small cabins and grew from there."

"He's being modest, but I'll brag. We're building some of those behemoths for the tourists who fall in love with it up here."

My lips twitched. "The ones who use their places for all of two weeks out of the year?"

"Those would be the ones," Jude said, shaking his head.

We were quiet for a moment as if there was nothing else for us to talk about. That cut. I used to be able to shoot the shit with these guys about anything.

Chris swung his keys around a finger. "How long are you in town for?"

"Not sure yet. Trying to get the lay of the land with my family."

"Gotta be hard to take time away from that fancy security gig you've got," Jude said.

Apparently, even though I wasn't up to date on town news, they were current on mine. "We're making it work."

Chris grunted.

Jude sent him a quelling look. "I'm sure your family appreciates it."

I wasn't quite so sure. I hadn't been able to get a read on things when I'd dropped the bomb that I was coming home in the sibs' text chain. Maybe they thought I wouldn't follow through, or maybe they'd simply gotten used to life without me.

I glanced down at my watch. "I should head out. I'm supposed to be over there for an early family dinner. Let's grab a beer while I'm in town." Pulling out my wallet, I handed each of them a card.

Jude let out a low whistle. "Even his business cards are fancy. You feel this cardstock? Someone went and found himself the high life."

Chris smirked. "Holt has always been fancy. You're just losing your memory in your old age."

Jude socked him with a half-force punch. "Watch who you're calling old, grandpa."

I'd missed this, the good-natured ribbing. Giving each other a hard time. I had it with the guys on my team, but they didn't know me as well. Because the truth was, I hadn't let a single soul in since that night ten years ago.

"Text me if you geezers want to grab a drink."

"Will do," Jude called as they walked on.

Chris simply gave me another chin lift.

It was better than nothing. A start.

I picked up to a jog, heading to my SUV in the lot on the side of the B&B, but I couldn't help my gaze from traveling to the police station across the street. A few buildings down from the inn, it looked just how I remembered. Yet, somehow, it was entirely different. Likely because I knew it was where *she* went most days.

My eyes bored into the brick structure as if I could see through the walls by sheer force of will alone. Was she in there? I wondered if I would even recognize her if she walked down the street. I'd kept tabs on her. I didn't have a right to, yet I did it anyway. But I'd stayed away from pictures.

I couldn't handle seeing those hazel eyes. The way the flecks of green blazed like emeralds in the sun when she laughed. Or was mad. Or when I kissed her.

Chris gave me a shove as we headed down Main Street. "Screw off. That three-pointer would've been nothing but net if you hadn't gotten in my way."

I rolled my eyes. "Sure. You're basically LeBron."

Jude snorted. "He's just waiting to get drafted straight out of high school."

"You both suck," Chris shot back.

"Hey, isn't that Wren?" Jude asked.

Just her name had something deep inside me tightening. As I turned and caught sight of the form at the end of the dock, my steps faltered. It was something about the slope of her shoulders and how they curved inward as if she were hiding from the world.

Like that would work. Wren was the kind of stunning that had all the guys at school taking notice—just waiting until fall when she was a freshman.

I slapped Jude on the back. "I'm gonna go check on her. I'll catch up with you later."

"Seriously?" Chris complained.

Jude chuckled. "Guy's got it bad. Let him shoot his shot."

I ignored them and headed off in a jog. It didn't take me long to reach her, but Wren didn't look up, not even when I lowered myself onto the dock next to her.

The breeze picked up, blowing her light brown hair out of her face. That was when I saw it. The tracks tears had left behind on her cheeks.

Everything in me twisted as panic lanced through me. A million possibilities for her tears ran through my head, each one worse than the one before. "What happened, Cricket?"

She stared out at the lake. The sun had set, but there was still a glow in the air. "I love the twilight. Even after the sun's gone, no one can forget that it was there."

An ache took root in my chest. "Your parents?"

"They forgot my birthday's tomorrow. They decided to leave on a trip. Asked your parents if I could stay with Grae for the week."

God, I wanted to rip her parents a new one. They were always taking off on her. They'd ask her grandma to stay or send her to a friend's house. The only thing they cared about was her getting straight As. They didn't give a damn about anything else.

They didn't see how amazing their daughter was. Didn't see that she had an empathy which meant she saw things the rest of the world missed. Had a kindness that meant she welcomed everyone into her circle. And a loyalty that meant she'd always have your back.

I wrapped an arm around Wren's shoulders, pulling her into my side. She felt right there. As if it was where she always belonged.

Wren burrowed her face in my chest. "I don't want to care. It's not like this is the first time. But I keep thinking that if I'm good enough, get my grades higher, join more clubs—something—that I'll be worthy of their love."

My hand cupped her cheek, lifting her face so I could stare into her eyes. My thumb swiped at the fresh tears that had started to spill. "You're worthy, Cricket. Beyond worthy."

Those hazel eyes sparked as Wren's breath hitched.

"You're the most amazing, kind, beautiful person I've ever known. If they can't see that, then it's their loss."

Her gaze dropped to my mouth as if she were memorizing the words that fell from it.

Some invisible force pulled me in, closer than I'd ever dared. I stopped just shy of those bee-stung lips. But Wren closed the distance and made that final leap.

When she made contact, the flavor of her mint lip balm bursting on my tongue, I knew I'd never be the same.

My fingers closed around my keys, squeezing tightly as I ripped myself out of the memory. I didn't need thoughts of those eyes dancing in my head or her taste on my tongue. They already haunted my nightmares. I didn't need them taunting my days, too.

Beeping the locks, I climbed behind the wheel and continued out of town. The tightness in my chest eased a little. I wasn't as much at risk now. A chance run-in was far less likely.

I knew from my check-ins that she lived in a small cabin on the opposite side of town. It was remote. No roommate. No live-in boyfriend, as far as I could tell. I hated the idea of her being out there. Cut off. And given how cell service worked here, I doubted she had any out there. I just prayed to God she had a landline.

My SUV hugged the curves of the mountain road, taking me higher. My dad had bought the property just out of college when the land was cheap. Then built a small cabin for Mom and him to live in. It still stood on the same land today, but when he'd started his outdoor gear company, and it had taken off, he'd built something bigger—something they could grow into—and they'd needed the space with five kids.

I turned off the main road onto a private drive marked only by a small street sign. My gut tightened as my SUV climbed and slowed in front of a gate. It fit with the property, made of rustic wood with *Hartley* burned into a crossbeam.

When I rolled down my window, my finger paused for the briefest moment before pressing the intercom.

My mom's voice came across the line a second later, and the gate was already opening. "Holt, get up here! Didn't you have the code?"

I didn't because I'd never driven in before. When I came for Thanksgiving or Christmas, I took a chopper from Portland and landed on the helipad my dad had installed for emergencies—and those visits had been few and far between. "I guess not."

"It's ten twenty-four. Now you have it whenever you want to stop by."

I groaned. "Mom. You can't use your anniversary as a password."

"Why not?"

"Because it's one of the first guesses someone would make."

"You can give me your lecture once you get up here. I need to pull the chicken out of the oven."

My throat tightened. How many times had I forced that meal down when all it did was make me want to choke? But I couldn't bring myself to tell my mother that my favorite meal had been ruined. I could still smell the scent of chicken cooking as I searched the house, trying to find Wren.

I needed a session with a heavy bag, stat. Or, even better, a round with Gomez, the best mixed martial artist on our team. I needed someone to beat the hell out of me so the pain I felt wasn't *this*.

Instead, I moved my foot from the brake to the accelerator and started for home. The paved drive wove between the tall pines, and I knew it must have cost a fortune when my dad had the asphalt laid. But when the snow came, it was a million times easier to plow when you weren't fighting against gravel.

The trees thinned as I climbed, and the house came into view—a mountain lodge with a blend of glass and stone and wood, though the glass dominated. It was almost as if you could see through the whole house.

Dad had always said that he wanted to feel like he was living in the wild. That there was nothing between him and nature. Dark wood beams framed the glass in a way that made the structure feel like it was part of the forest. And the stone tied it to the ground beneath.

The home spread across the mountainside, an enclosed walkway joining the two halves. My mom had always called the farther part *the kids' side* when we were growing up. We could run wild in an epic game of hide-and-seek, and she got her peace when she needed it.

The memories that battled for supremacy now were good ones: laughter and teasing, epic pranks and water gun fights, pizza feasts and monster movie marathons. But they left a trail of guilt in their wake—one that burned as it dug in deep.

I pulled my car to a stop in the circular driveway behind four other vehicles. I realized that I wasn't sure which belonged to whom. The Fish and Wildlife logo on the side of a white SUV told me that it was Roan's, but other than that, I had no clue.

Shutting off the engine, I climbed out and headed for the house. The front door opened, and I caught a blaze of movement. A second later, a petite body hit me with a force that was shocking for her size.

"You're here!"

I grinned as I lifted Grae into the air. "Missed you, too, G. How are you feeling?"

She growled in my ear, ignoring the question but hugging me tighter. "I still can't believe it. Have you decided how long you're staying? Are you sure you want to be shacked up at the B&B? I bet Mom and Dad would let you stay in the cabin—"

"Let the man breathe," Lawson said with a chuckle.

I set Grae down and moved to my eldest brother, pulling him in for a hard hug. "Damn good to see you, Law."

He thumped me on the back. "Wasn't sure your ugly mug was really gonna make it."

His words stung, but it wasn't anything I didn't deserve. Lawson merely meant it as a gentle jibe. He didn't know how deep the sentiment cut.

"Fam bam back together again," Nash called, throwing himself around us and pulling Grae into the huddle.

She hit my back with an oomph. "Nash…"

Roan approached our group as Nash reached out for him. "Don't even think about it."

Nash gave an exaggerated pout. "Come on, grumpy cat."

Roan scowled, keeping his distance.

Nash sighed. "Fine, ruin the family reunion."

Roan lifted his chin in my direction. "Hey."

That was him. No welcoming me back because he knew how hard it was for me to be here. More than once, I'd wondered why he hadn't taken off, too. The night of the shooting had scarred him, as well—in some ways worse than the rest of us. Maybe he'd stayed to prove people wrong.

"Good to see you."

Roan simply grunted. "Mom said dinner's ready." With that, he turned and headed back toward the house.

"As you can see, not a lot has changed," Grae mumbled.

It was on the tip of my tongue to ask if Wren had changed. Did her laugh still have that husky edge? Did her nose crinkle when she smiled? I shoved that down and started for the front door. "Sometimes, things staying the same is a good thing."

"Dad!" Drew called from the steps. "Luke's hogging the Xbox."

Lawson sighed. "I can tell you what *has* changed. Full-fledged teen angst." He lifted his gaze to his middle son. "Not for long.

Dinner's ready. Say hello to your uncle so he doesn't think I raised a bunch of heathens."

Drew gave me a lopsided grin. "Hey, Uncle Holt. It's sick you're back."

I glanced down at Grae. "Sick?"

Nash clapped me on the shoulder. "It means cool. You need to brush up on your lingo."

A small boy dodged around Drew and rushed toward me. "Uncle Holt."

I caught him on the fly, lifting him into the air. "Hey, Charlie. How'd you grow so much since I saw you last?"

Guilt dug in deeper. It had only been a few months, but Charlie and Drew seemed like they were each a head taller.

He grinned down at me, showing a gap where two front teeth should've been. "'Cause you're never freaking here."

Lawson groaned. "You know your grandma doesn't like you saying freaking."

"It's not even a swear," Drew muttered.

"Maybe not, but this is her house, so we play by her rules. Right?"

"We play by her rules because she makes cookies," Charlie chimed in.

"Smart man," I whispered, setting him down in the entryway.

"Luke," Lawson called.

"What?" a voice snapped back—one deeper than I remembered.

Lawson pinched the bridge of his nose. "God save me from teenagers."

"I'm not a teenager," Charlie said helpfully.

"And I thank my lucky stars for that every single day."

Drew rolled his eyes. "We're not that bad."

Lawson lifted his brows. "Paintballing the side of the house? Luke taking my car for a joyride when he doesn't have a license? The yelling at decibels not fit for human ears?"

Drew gave his dad a sheepish smile. "We're keeping you young."

"You're giving me gray hair."

There was humor in Lawson's voice, but there was also bone-deep fatigue. I had no idea how he kept up with it all, but maybe I could help lessen his load while I was here.

"Luke, get your butt out here. It's time for dinner," Lawson called.

There was nothing for a good minute, and then a teen I barely recognized emerged from the basement. Luke was only fifteen, but he looked older. His dark hair curled around his ears, and he had a scowl on his face that resembled Roan more than it did Lawson.

"Hey, Luke."

He lifted his chin in my direction. "Hey." Then, just as quickly, he dismissed me as he started toward the open-concept kitchen and living space.

Lawson's mouth pressed into a hard line. "Sure you don't want to stay with us? You could get the cold shoulder twenty-four-seven. It's a dream."

I chuckled. "I think there was a season *we* were all pretty surly with Mom and Dad. I'd say that's normal."

He grimaced. "I'm being punished for my misspent youth."

Nash leaned in to whisper in Lawson's ear. "But it was worth it."

Lawson shook his head as we all started for the kitchen. "You haven't gotten your payback yet. Just wait until you're raising a handful of hell-raisers just like you."

Nash's head jerked. "Bite your tongue. I'm not going down that road anytime soon."

Grae grinned. "I can't wait until someone takes you down."

"Me? Never. I'm way too practical."

It wasn't that. It was that Nash had only ever cared for one girl. And when he screwed that all to hell, he'd built and kept those walls sky-high.

"Holt!" Mom hurried from the kitchen and pulled me into a hug. "I'm so glad you're home."

"Thanks for making dinner."

"Your favorite."

I tried to hide my wince with another fake smile. "Thanks, Mom."

She released me, and I started toward my dad, who sat on the couch, his leg propped up on an oversized ottoman. It was out of the cast, but he was clearly still nursing it. "Hey, Dad. How are you feeling?"

His lips pursed, the lines on his face deepening. "You didn't have to come check on me. I told you I was fine."

My brows rose. *Ornery was right.*

"Thought it was time I came for a visit that lasted longer than a few days."

Dad's eyes narrowed on me. "Why? That sure as hell never mattered to you before."

My mom gasped. "Nathan."

I held up a hand. "It's okay."

"No, it's not," Grae said, glaring at our father.

"She's right," Nash chimed in. "Not cool, old man."

Dad swung his leg off the ottoman and stood, limping toward the dining table. "I'm just speaking the truth. I'm not going to run around preparing some feast for the prodigal son when I know he'll probably take off tomorrow."

Grae squeezed my arm. "He doesn't mean it. He's hurting and throwing himself a pity party."

"He does mean it," I said quietly. I just didn't know how I'd let things get this bad.

Chapter Four

Wren

I SAT IN MY TRUCK, STARING AT THE RESTAURANT. MY GAZE tracked the script on the sign: *The Warf*. I needed to go in. I was already five minutes late. If I let it drag to ten, I'd be firmly in the rude category. That wasn't who I was.

But when I'd said yes to dinner with some real estate guy on vacation from Seattle, I hadn't known what today would hold. The thought had anger flooding my system. He didn't get to do this.

It was bad enough that I measured every guy I ever went on a date with against Holt. A mental tally that always left the new guy coming up short. But now he was invading my physical space, too?

I'd thought we had a silent agreement. He didn't show up around town, and I didn't drunkenly call him, begging to know why he'd left. At least that was the agreement in my mind. And now that was all shot to hell.

"Looks like you're staring pretty hard there."

I jolted, sending up a million curses in my head as Chris stepped up to my open window. I didn't let people sneak up on me. I was always aware of my surroundings. "Hey."

"You okay?"

I blew out a long breath. "Want to go on my date for me?"

He let out a low, familiar chuckle, one I'd heard a million times. At first, that laugh had killed me. It didn't sound right because I was used to hearing it mixed with Holt's. But Chris and Jude had stuck it out, not letting me push them away.

They were the ones I called when I couldn't fix the leak under my sink. Or when I needed furniture moved around that I couldn't wrestle myself. They checked in on the regular and made sure I always knew I had help if I needed it.

Chris shook his head. "I think whoever's in there waiting for you would probably be damn disappointed if I showed up."

I leaned back in my seat, still staring at the restaurant as if I could make it disappear. "He's back."

Chris stiffened. I felt the shift in the air as his muscles tensed, but it took him a moment to speak. "I know."

I looked at him then, studying the way that tension had etched itself into Chris's face. "You see him?"

He nodded. "Ran into him outside the B&B. I think he's staying there."

My stomach twisted like someone wringing water out of a towel. Way too close. I'd thought for sure he'd stay with Lawson or Nash. Maybe in the cabin. But less than a block from where I worked every day? That felt like a slap in the face.

"You okay?"

"No," I answered honestly. "Are you?"

I wasn't the only one Holt had left in the wreckage. Chris, Jude, the Hartleys. Who knew who else? We had all been hurt when he took off. It was almost worse that he'd stuck around all through my rehab after the shooting. That he'd held my hand as I regained enough strength to move my body again. It was as if he'd built me back up only to level the death blow.

A muscle in Chris's jaw ticked. "He's an ass."

My lips twitched. "That's the truth."

"I can't just forget that he blew us all off like we were nothing."

Nothing. It ricocheted around my body just like that damn bullet had.

"But I also know that what happened twisted him up good. I know that's why he made stupid-ass decisions that hurt a lot of people—people who didn't deserve it."

I swallowed against the burn creeping up my throat. It was as if the fire the bullet had started in my chest had never been fully extinguished. It flared up again without warning to take me out at the knees.

It wasn't that I thought Holt was malicious. I knew him too well for that. It was that our love hadn't been enough. I had always thought it was a force that could move mountains. But at the end of the day, he had been able to leave with nothing more than a letter slipped under my door.

"I'd better get in there."

Concern flashed in Chris's green eyes. "I could go in and tell this dude you're sick."

I shook my head.

"You slipped and fell, got amnesia, and don't remember your name?"

A laugh bubbled out of me, and I climbed out of my truck. I pulled Chris into a quick hug. "Thanks."

"Always, Little Williams."

I groaned as I released him. "Not you, too."

He grinned. "Nash's nicknames are catchy as hell."

I shook my head and started for the restaurant, even though it was the last thing I wanted to do.

"That one dump of a building in an up-and-coming neighborhood was my breakthrough. All of a sudden, the big players were taking notice. They wanted *me* hunting for opportunities for them. Not anyone else."

I made a humming voice as William droned on. It wasn't like

he cared about what I had to say anyway. All he wanted was to think he had a captive audience as he relived his *many* corporate victories.

"From then on, I was running with the big dogs. One client introduced me to another, and before I knew it, I was buying that Maserati."

The urge to roll my eyes was so strong I had to bite the inside of my cheek. I did my best to tune out his voice in my head, but I still studied the man opposite me. There was no denying that he was handsome. He had dark brown hair, expertly cut and styled, but it didn't swoop down over his forehead the way Holt's did. And my fingers didn't itch to run through the strands.

My fingers curled into fists under the table, my nails biting into my palms. Chris had joked about amnesia, but sometimes, I wondered if something like that would be a kindness. Not to remember how Holt's smile pulled to one side a little more than the other. The way he ran his thumb under his bottom lip when he was thinking hard about something. How his blue eyes went soft when he told me he loved me.

I burrowed deeper into Holt's side as we stared up at the night sky. He'd created a cozy nest in the bed of his truck, one perfect for stargazing. It was my favorite thing in the world: Holt, me, and the peace of nature around us.

His fingers trailed up and down my arm. "I say a place with a view of the lake. Far enough outside of town that things are quiet but not as far as my parents' place."

I grinned into the dark as warmth spread through me. I loved dreaming about the future with Holt, all the endless possibilities of what our life could be. "That sounds perfect. I only have one requirement."

Holt chuckled, the new, deeper sound wrapping around me and creating a cascade of shivers over my skin. "Wraparound porch with a swing."

I turned into him more, nipping at his pec. "Are you suggesting that I'm predictable?"

His chest shook with silent laughter. "Asks the girl who re-reads Little Women *every single year and can recite the movie by heart."*

I let out a huff of air. "I know what I like. Is that so bad?"

Holt brushed the hair out of my eyes and tipped my face up to meet his. "Not if I'm one of those things."

My stomach dipped and rolled, three little words playing on my tongue, begging to be set free. "I like you, Holt Hartley."

His eyes sparked with intensity. "I love you, Cricket. With everything I have."

Everything in me soared. "I love you, too. I always have."

He grinned, the devastating kind that always took me out at the knees. "We're gonna have a beautiful life."

He said it with such certainty that I believed every word.

"Dessert?" Frannie asked as she approached the table, pulling me out of my memories.

"I couldn't eat another bite," I hurried to say before William could say otherwise.

"How about an after-dinner drink?" he prodded.

"I shouldn't. Driving those mountain roads."

A devilish smile stretched William's face, but it was smarmy and forced, not authentic and wild how Holt's had been. "You could come back to my rental with me."

Frannie's brows rose as she pressed her lips together to keep from laughing.

"I think I'm just going to head home." I looked up at Frannie. "Could you split the check for us?"

William whipped out a credit card. "I'd never let a lady pay."

I guessed he wasn't a jerk, offering to pay, even knowing he wasn't getting laid. But it didn't change the fact that he was a pretentious cheeseball. "Thanks."

"I'll get your receipt right out to you," Frannie said, hurrying away.

"What about dinner tomorrow night? I'm here for two more days."

"I've got plans the next two nights." It wasn't a total lie. I was going to take Shadow for a hike after work tomorrow, and Grae and I usually had a movie night at least once a week, and we were due.

A flicker of annoyance flashed in William's eyes, but he reined it in. "Text me if you change your mind."

"Sure."

Frannie hurried back to the table. "Here you are, sir. Make sure you come back and see us."

He nodded as he filled in the tip, signed, and handed the slip back to her. "Walk you to your car?"

Oh, hell no. I wasn't giving this guy an opening for a kiss. "You know, I see a friend I need to say hi to. Thank you so much for dinner. I hope you have an amazing rest of your trip."

William grumbled something under his breath as he got to his feet and headed for the door. As he grabbed the handle, Frannie dissolved into laughter, the lines on her face deepening with the action. "That poor guy."

"What about poor me? I had to listen to a play-by-play of every real estate deal he's ever closed, and every car he's bought. I'm sure he was moving on to his investment portfolio next."

She snorted and then pulled out a bag from behind her back. "This should soothe the soul."

I grabbed the sack. "Lava cake?"

"Like I'd give you anything less."

I stood and kissed her cheek. "You're an angel."

"Don't you forget it."

"I gotta get home to let Shadow out. See you later this week?"

She shooed me off. "You know it. Go kiss that girl for me and give her lots of belly rubs."

"I will."

I moved through the restaurant, waving to people I knew and taking note of the unfamiliar faces, wondering what their stories were. Pushing open the front door, I stepped into the night air. Even though it was spring, it had a bite to it, that little bit of an edge that made you sit up and pay attention. It was the perfect night to sit out on my deck wrapped in a blanket.

I started toward my truck, but a voice stopped me dead in my tracks.

"Hey, Cricket."

Chapter Five

Holt

I KNEW NOW WHY I'D STAYED AWAY FROM PHOTOS OF WREN. She'd been beautiful when I'd fallen in love with her. But now? It was the kind of beauty that branded you. Looking at her and truly seeing? You'd never be the same.

Heading back to the B&B, I'd frozen as I saw her stepping out of the restaurant. I'd stood in the shadows like a creep, just watching her, drinking in every detail like a man burning from thirst. She'd tipped her face up to the sky and breathed deeply as if taking the whole world into her lungs, not wanting to take a single thing for granted.

Her long hair cascaded down her back. The soft brown had hints of blond woven through it that hadn't been there before. I hated that I didn't know when they'd appeared. Recently? In the weeks after I'd left?

The moonlight hit the swells of her cheeks, her skin picking up the rosy glow, even in the darkness. But the lack of light stole that mix of brown and green in her eyes from me. I would've given anything to see just how much green danced in them tonight.

Wren's nickname had slipped from my tongue so easily that it was like I'd never stopped saying it. As if my mouth knew its shape better than any other word.

She froze, her muscles locking with a force that should've cracked bones, and then her head lowered to face me. "Holt."

Everything about this was wrong: the cool expression on her face, the absence of emotion in her tone. A million questions played in my head; things I'd been dying to know the answer to for years—things I didn't have a right to know.

"How are you?" It was the only thing I could allow myself to ask, and even that answer wasn't something I deserved. But I craved it anyway.

"Good. I'm sure your parents are happy to have you home."

The words came with a careful politeness that I'd never heard from Wren before. A flatness. An indifference.

Anything would've been better. Screaming. Crying. Slapping me across the damn face. Not staring at me like I was no one. A stranger.

I twisted my keys around my finger. "One of them is."

I thought I might've seen a flicker of reaction, a little emotion bleeding through. But when I blinked, it was gone, and I wondered if it had simply been the moon and wishful thinking.

"I need to get home. Nice to see you, Holt. Hope you enjoy your stay."

Wren was moving before I had a chance to say another word. She cut through the parking lot to a red truck that looked as if it had seen better days. I wanted to know the last time a mechanic had looked it over, and if the brakes were still sound. All the tiny details I didn't have any right to. Things that had always given me a sense of purpose and pride.

Wren's hair lifted in the breeze as she climbed behind the wheel. Her eyes never once strayed in my direction, instead remaining focused only on the parking lot around her.

I stayed frozen to the spot as she backed out and pulled onto the road. I didn't breathe until her taillights disappeared altogether.

I'd been an idiot to think that I could handle seeing her. Even now, I swore I smelled a hint of gardenia on the breeze. Just like that perfume her grandma had gifted her all those years ago.

I wanted to roll around in it and burn it out of me all at the same time. I pulled my cell from my pocket and hit a contact. Two rings later, Lawson answered.

"Everything okay?"

Big brother, through and through.

"Is there somewhere around here I could hit a heavy bag tonight?"

Lawson was quiet for a moment. "I'm taking that as a no. Everything isn't okay."

"Just need a bag, Law."

"Go to the station. We had a gym installed in the back. I'll tell the officer on duty you're approved to use it."

"Thanks, man."

He was silent again. "I'm here if you ever *do* want to talk about it."

I swallowed the urge to snap at him. "Thanks."

I hit end on the call before he could get another word in. I didn't trust myself to hold it together any longer. Jogging up to the B&B, I prayed that Janice had already called it a night. I couldn't be responsible for my actions if she started nosing around right now.

The reception area was blissfully silent as I moved through and took the stairs two at a time to the second floor. My hand trembled slightly as I moved to unlock the door to my room. I only gripped the key harder. A second later, I was inside.

I grabbed shorts, a tee, and some sneakers from my suitcase and quickly changed. Moments later, I was jogging down the block toward the police station. The door was locked, but as soon as the woman behind the desk saw me, she pressed a button, and I heard a buzz.

Pulling the door open, I stepped inside. "I'm Holt. My brother, Lawson, should have called about me using the gym."

The woman swallowed, her jaw working. "I remember you. I'm Amber Raymond."

A flash of memory lanced through me. A sea of black after a week of black. Her brother's funeral had been the last one. And we'd all been so damn tired of grieving.

Five funerals. Six people in the hospital. Two assailants in jail. The possibility of a third never identified, leaving the town to question everyone around them. It was more than we could take. But I knew it was the worst for people like Amber—those left behind.

"Of course. Good to see you."

"You, too. Gym's down that hall." She pointed.

"Thanks." I was already moving, taking my opening to escape additional ghosts.

The room was dark when I stepped inside. I tried the lights one by one until I illuminated the heavy bag and nothing else. As I strode toward it, I pulled the hand wraps from my pocket and began weaving them through my fingers in a familiar rhythm.

It didn't take long to get them in place. I pressed a fist to the bag, testing the weight and the feel. Even if a bag was an exact duplicate of the one you typically used, it was never the same. The people who laid into it each and every day shaped it. How many? Were they short or tall? How hard did they hit?

Each testing jab was an introduction to the bag—a get-to-know-you between leather and fist.

I shifted my weight to my toes and picked up my pace. With speed came force. Wren's face flashed in my mind. The expression that said I was nothing to her.

My hook slammed into the leather, making my bones rattle.

Flecks of emerald, the ones that blazed when I kissed her, teased and taunted.

My fists flew, each one hitting harder than the last. The sound had me hurtling back in time before I could do anything to stop it.

I slammed my truck's door and jogged around the front, heading for the walkway. Wren would give me hell for this. I adjusted my grip on the flowers, hoping they would buy me a little goodwill—the peonies were hard as hell to find in Cedar Ridge. I'd had to beg the florist to order them special.

The sound of tires screeching had me glancing down the road. I caught sight of a dark SUV taking off like a bat out of hell. Idiots. I swore I heard sirens in the distance. Maybe someone would pull the assholes over and ruin their joyride.

I turned back to the house, picking up my pace. My steps faltered as I reached the door. It stood ajar, just a few inches.

"Cricket?"

I pushed it open with two fingers. "You in here?"

No answer. I turned around, wondering if she'd headed outside for some reason, but I didn't see any sign of her anywhere.

The scent of garlic roasted chicken filled the space as I stepped inside. I couldn't help my chuckle. I hoped like hell we didn't get food poisoning. My girl had mastered many things, but cooking wasn't at the top of the list.

I caught sight of the dining table and stilled. It looked like it should've been in one of those home décor magazines: tablecloth without a single wrinkle, greenery woven around candles and flowers, the good china—the kind Wren's mom only used for special occasions.

A grin pulled at my lips. She'd told me that she wanted tonight to be special. I shook my head as I climbed the stairs. Didn't Wren know by now that she made every damn moment special just by breathing? My favorite moments were just her and me in the bed of my truck, staring up at the stars.

As I reached the top of the stairs, I listened for the shower, thinking that must've been why I hadn't heard her. But there was nothing but silence.

I jogged toward her bedroom and stopped dead. It looked as if a hurricane had torn through the space. Pictures were smashed, the bedding was all askew, and feathers from her pillows lay scattered everywhere.

"Wren," I called louder, panic digging in its claws.

There was no answer.

I swallowed, pulling my phone out of my pocket. Her house was one of the lucky ones that got cell service around here, and I was damn glad for it right then. I hit the first contact in my favorites. Cricket flashed on the screen, along with my favorite photo of her.

Wren's head was tipped back as she took in the tail end of the sunset, a look of bliss on her face at knowing that her favorite time of day was coming—the twilight hour. She'd had no idea I'd snapped the photo, but that just made it sweeter.

A ringing started, first through my speaker and then down the hall. But the sound from down the hall was off somehow. Garbled.

Blood roared in my ears as I started toward the sound, a million brutal what-ifs playing in my mind. I looked in the guest room, but as soon as I stepped in, the sound got farther away. Hurrying out of there, I skidded to a stop outside the hall bath. As I stepped inside, everything in me froze.

My brain couldn't compute the sight in front of me. It was something out of a horror movie, not real life.

Wren's body lay crumpled at an unnatural angle, her torso twisted as if she'd been trying to protect herself. And the blood... so much of it. I swore it was everywhere. Too much for someone to still be breathing.

That thought jerked me into action. I sank to my knees, the bones hitting the tile with a crack.

"Wren. Can you hear me?"

The first-aid class I'd taken to go on search and rescue calls with my dad came back to me in fits and starts. I pressed my fingers to her neck as I leaned down.

No breath tickled my face. How often had I felt Wren's soft exhales against my skin as she cuddled close? All I wanted was one of those right now. But there was nothing.

I strained to feel the flutter of movement against my fingertips. I felt a staggered, faint beat, each too far apart for anything good.

Sirens sounded as I rolled Wren to her back, but they weren't close enough. I prayed I was making the right call. I had no idea what damage had been done to her chest. A bullet? A stab wound? I could make it worse with CPR, but she wouldn't make it either way if she wasn't breathing.

I tipped her head back and gave two quick rescue breaths before positioning my hands over her chest and plunging down. She wasn't short, but Wren had always seemed delicate, her wrists so tiny her bones seemed easily breakable. I could hurt her. And that was the last thing I ever wanted to do. Still, I forced myself to press on.

As I continued the rhythm, I stared down at her, my heart outside my body. I searched for any signs of life, but I didn't see a damn one.

My fist slammed into the bag at an angle that had pain searing through me. I stumbled backward, falling to the floor, my body shaking in violent waves. The memories were too raw and real to escape.

An anguished sound tore free from my throat. I could still feel her heart beneath my hands, willing it to beat again. I would've made a deal with the devil for Wren to live. And I guessed I had in a way.

Because Wren had gotten her miracle. And when she healed and was whole, I did the only thing I could, the only *right* thing. I walked away so she could find someone worthy of her.

Chapter Six

Wren

PUSHING OPEN ONE OF THE FRENCH DOORS, I STEPPED OUT onto the deck. My slippers padded against the wood boards as I wrapped the blanket tighter around myself, my hand trembling with the movement. Shadow moved quietly at my side, the silver in her Husky coloring catching the moonlight as she raised her head to sniff the air.

"Don't go running after any critters."

She let out a huff of air as if to say, *"You never want me to have any fun."*

I lowered myself into the half-moon-style chair, slipping my feet out of my slippers and curling my legs under me. Shadow circled and then lay down on her dog bed as I wrapped my hands around my mug of tea.

Breathing deeply, I took in my little corner of the lake. It was remote. In winter, I had to plow the driveway if I had any hope of getting out, but it was peaceful—my small cabin built on a tiny piece of land that jutted into the water.

It made me feel as if I lived on my own private island. There were no prying eyes, no searching questions from nosy tourists. Cedar Ridge had always been known for its majestic landscapes and as the perfect escape. But after that night, it was known for a whole other reason.

Two guys had shown up last year, looking to get interviews for a podcast they were making for the tenth anniversary of the shootings. *Anniversary.* They weren't the only ones to use the word, but I hated it. Anniversaries were for happy things, not darkness like that night.

The two guys in their early twenties had walked right up to my door and told me they were going to be the ones to figure out if there really was a third shooter. One who got away. All I had to do was rip open my traumatized psyche and tell them every detail about that night.

Just the memory had me gripping my mug tighter. Like I hadn't tried to remember. I'd replayed those words—the last thing I'd heard before the world went dark—over and over in my head. *"Where the hell is Holt? We need them both."* But it sounded different every time. Sometimes, male. Other times, female. Old, then young. Occasionally, it was Randy or Paul.

It was a special kind of torture when I heard it in the tones of people I knew—those I loved. I woke up at night in a cold sweat, shaking.

Most people thought I had imagined the third person. None of the other survivors had seen anyone else. Only Paul and Randy. And they had sworn they'd done it alone. That they'd been on a mission to make all those who had supposedly wronged them pay.

Some days, I wondered if the third person had only been in my mind. But those words were burned into my memory and haunted my dreams.

The cops had interviewed me, time and time again. The town had been on edge, thinking someone could strike at any moment. Parents didn't let their children walk to school, didn't leave them with babysitters. People only went out in groups.

But days turned to weeks, and nothing happened. Finally, one of the state police suggested that, in my altered state, I'd only *thought* someone else had been there. I'd fought it at first, but it wasn't long before I gave in and agreed.

The town wanted to go back to normal. To pretend that the ugly business had never happened. That they were safe.

It wasn't that easy for those of us marked by that night. We bore the scars in every way. We felt them every time we moved, from the ghosts haunting us to the need to be wary of everyone around us.

Only my ghost was still alive. He'd just vanished from my life.

Pain lanced my chest, that burning fire that a single bullet had started but was kept alive by the torture of missing the person I could never have.

Holt's face flashed in my mind, torturing me just a little more. His hair was different. That same light brown shade but more closely cropped on the sides. I couldn't help but wonder if that stray lock still swooped across his forehead.

I wanted it to. But maybe he'd found a way to tame it as he'd grown into a man. Nothing about the person I saw tonight read: *boy*. Broad shoulders and a muscular chest, defined arms and thighs that told me he was still running every day.

All it had taken was a single second for his image to burn itself into my mind—into my bones. To leave a scar just like so many others that ravaged me.

I'd never be able to clear it. My hand lifted of its own volition, slipping under my sweatshirt and finding the raised flesh. Some part of me had thought a bullet hole would be perfectly symmetrical, but mine certainly hadn't healed that way—lopsided and with fraying edges.

I closed my eyes, breathing deeply. The mountain air soothed the shattered parts of my body and soul. I reminded myself that this was evidence of just how strong I was. That I could make it through anything. Because I'd done it before.

My eyes opened, and I let my hand drop to Shadow's head, scratching behind her ears. My life was good—better than good. I had a home to call mine, beauty all around me, and a job that kept the lights on and gave me a sense of purpose I hadn't been sure I'd ever have. I also had a dog that stuck by my side, and friends who were family. It was why I would never leave Cedar Ridge, and why I hadn't left even when I was at my worst.

I had an embarrassment of riches. And Holt wouldn't make me lose sight of that just because I didn't have *him*. He'd be here for a few days and then be off again to parts unknown. I wouldn't hear his name on anyone's lips for years to come.

I'd taken comfort in that before, felt safe in the walls I'd built around my existence—ones that he didn't exist within. But something about that didn't sit quite right now. Maybe because I'd seen him as a real, live, breathing human.

Maybe because I'd seen the hollow look in his eyes, the one that told me he'd turned something off within himself. I knew how that went. You thought you'd pay any price if you could just make the pain stop.

But when you turned off the pain, you turned off the pleasure. You couldn't appreciate the way the moon glimmered on the lake. Or how a piece of chocolate tasted as it melted on your tongue. You missed the joy of friends wrapping you in so much love you thought you might drown in it.

You weren't truly living.

I gave those thoughts a healthy shove. Holt hadn't earned my empathy and understanding. And he'd made it clear that he hadn't wanted my worry.

The best I could do was wish him nothing but good, even if that meant knowing he had a life that would never involve me.

Invisible claws of grief dug into my heart, but the pain was worth it to stop myself from drowning in anger and resentment. I would send him hope for a happy life, but I would do it from a distance.

Shadow's head snapped up, her gaze cutting to the woods behind my cabin.

I grinned down at her. "Hear something you want to chase? Sorry, girl. Not tonight."

My gaze flicked to the trees where a light glimmered for the briefest moment before extinguishing. The hair along Shadow's spine rose as she let out a low growl.

I blinked a few times, wondering if my mind had conjured the light with all my reminiscing about the past. Bringing nightmares out into the light was never a good thing. I strained to see through the trees and swore I saw a flicker of movement.

A chill skittered across my skin. No one should've been out this way. The person who owned the property that butted up to mine had never built on it. The nearest house was a good mile away.

My eyes strained harder, but Shadow settled back on her dog bed. It was nothing and no one. I shook my head. Apparently, I was seeing ghosts everywhere now.

Chapter Seven

Holt

THE DOOR OPENED WITH A FAINT CREAK AS I STEPPED inside Dockside Bar & Grill. My wrist ached with the motion—just another reminder of last night's shitshow.

"I'll be damned. Holt Hartley? Is that you?"

Jeanie's voice carried enough that half a dozen patrons turned in their seats. An older couple I remembered as parents of a classmate bent their heads to whisper. A woman I thought had been a couple of years older than me blatantly stared.

I had to fight the grimace that pulled at my mouth, turning it into another of those damned forced smiles. "Good to see you, Jeanie."

She pulled me into a back-slapping hug. "It's good to see you. It's been way too long."

"Chris and Jude here?"

"The three musketeers back together again. Pleased as punch to see it. They're at that booth in the corner." She pointed her notepad toward a table by the windows.

"Thanks."

"You want something to drink? I'll grab it for you while I'm getting the boys theirs."

I guessed we'd always be *boys* in her eyes. The same ones who stopped after school for french fries and root beer floats. My smile came a little more genuinely this time. "Still got root beer on tap?"

"Is the sky blue?"

I chuckled. "I'll take one of those."

"Coming right up."

I maneuvered through tables, trying to avoid any questioning stares. I didn't have the answers they were looking for.

"Always were Jeanie's favorite. She gave you extra french fries every single time," Chris grumbled.

"She gave you extra ice cream in your root beer float."

Jude's lips twitched. "So much for keeping a low profile, huh?"

"Guess so," I said, sliding into one end of the semi-circular booth. "It wasn't like that was going to last anyway."

Chris took a sip of his water. "Not in Cedar Ridge."

Gossip spread like a wildfire in the dead of summer. And since things had been relatively calm over the last several years, I qualified as news.

I rubbed the back of my neck. "I hate feeling watched."

"People are just bored," Jude said. "Before long, someone'll have an affair, or a kid will shoplift, and you'll be old news."

The tightness in my chest eased a fraction. I'd known that. It had just been so long since I'd experienced small-town rhythms that I'd forgotten. In Portland, I could disappear into the crowd. I didn't know the neighbors in my high rise beyond a polite hello in the elevator. I didn't have friends beyond the guys on my team. My social life consisted of knocking back a few beers at the bar around the corner from our office. Suddenly, that all seemed a little empty.

Jeanie sidled up to the table with a tray. "Two Cokes and a root beer. You boys know what you'd like to order?"

"Usual, Miss J," Chris said.

Jude handed her his menu. "I'll do the fish and chips."

"You need a minute, honey?" she asked me.

That *honey* hit somewhere deep—the familiarity of it. An honorary mother in a town full of them, always looking out for their chicks.

"I'll take the turkey melt. Haven't had one worth a damn since I left."

She tapped her notepad on my shoulder. "We'll get you squared away. Don't you fear."

"Thanks."

Jude leaned back in his seat and took me in, searching. "So, how's it feel being back?"

"Weird." It was the only thing I could give him at the moment. I wasn't about to open my mess of a head to friends I hadn't seen in a decade. They didn't need to know how I'd lost it last night or that I hadn't slept a wink because every time I started to drop off, my dreams were filled with blood.

"I bet." Jude's eyes flashed with a mischievous glint. "How's the B&B?"

He accentuated each letter as he spoke, and I scowled in his direction. "How do you think?"

Jude burst into laughter, and Chris let out a begrudging chuckle.

Jude shot me a devilish grin. "We've already heard that you requested no maid service on your room and that you had oatmeal and fruit for breakfast. Janice is worried that you're not getting enough to eat, tortured soul that you are."

I groaned, pinching the bridge of my nose. "What is wrong with that woman?"

"Too many years of watching the daytime soaps. Now, everything's a saga to her," Jude shot back.

I let my hand drop. "Either of you know of a vacation rental that would take a tenant for a couple of months?"

Chris's brows rose. "You're staying that long?"

"That's the plan right now. But if my dad's welcome was any indication, I'm not sure it's the best idea."

Jude studied me for a minute. "He missed you."

My throat burned. "I talked to him every week." There'd been increased tension in the conversations over the past year, but I'd had no idea my dad was that upset with me.

"It's not the same as being here. He's struggling to get back on his feet, and he's taking that out on you because he's hurt, not because he doesn't care."

I grabbed my root beer and took a healthy drink. "Well, I'm here now. I'm trying to make things right."

Chris sent Jude a sidelong glance. "It'll take time for people to see that. You can't just expect them to fall in line because you said you're staying."

"I know that," I clipped.

Chris held up both hands. "I'm just trying to explain where folks might be coming from."

Air hissed from between my teeth. "I know. I didn't handle things well." I met the gazes of the two men at the table. "I'm sorry I bailed on our friendship. Neither of you deserved that."

Jude stared in my direction. "You were going through a lot. It couldn't have been easy."

"I was just trying to keep my head above water. A clean slate seemed like the best thing for everyone at the time. But I know I hurt a lot of people in the process. Handled things in a messed-up way."

Chris studied me. "Wren know how you feel?"

Her name was like fire in my veins, washing through me and leaving a trail of ash in its wake. "I don't think Wren cares much how I feel. And I get it."

Jude scoffed. "I really thought a decade away would make you less of a moron."

My head snapped in his direction. "Excuse me?"

"The girl's still in love with you. Never stopped for a damn second. I don't think I've ever seen her go on more than a handful of dates with someone. Won't let anyone in her life even utter your name."

There weren't words for the riot of emotions going to war in my chest. Half of the sensations couldn't be defined, but the few that could were dangerous. Hope. Grief. Want. Anguish.

"Just because she hasn't met the right person yet doesn't mean she won't." Each word shredded my throat on the way out. But it was a pain I deserved. And one I would experience time and again if it meant that Cricket was happy. Safe.

A straw pelted me in the face. "What the hell, man?"

Chris shook his head. "Jude's right. You *are* more of a moron than when you left. Woman like that? She's once-in-a-lifetime."

"I know that," I growled. I'd already concluded a long time ago that I would never love someone the way I'd loved Wren—the way I *still* loved her. Because it didn't matter if it had been ten days or ten years. A love like that ruined you for all others.

Jude's eyes narrowed on me. "A woman like that who still loves you after you walked out of her life at the worst possible time? That's a damn miracle. You don't appreciate it, and I'm pretty sure God is going to strike you down."

He was welcome to do it. There was a reason I always took the riskiest jobs. The worst assignments on those jobs. I'd made a habit of tempting fate, giving it plenty of chances to take me out. To pay the price for all the ways I'd let down the person who mattered the most.

"You should talk to her," Jude said quietly.

"Don't think that would go over too well. What we had... It's gone."

Jude's eyes flashed. "You don't know that. And if you've got a second chance, don't waste it." His cell buzzed on the table, and he picked it up. A second later, his fingers were flying across the screen. "I gotta bail. Missing hikers."

"You on the team?" I asked as I stood to let him out of the booth.

Jude and Chris had both volunteered for search and rescue in high school, but for some reason, I thought they would've moved on to other things by now, and that maybe I'd been the one tethering them to that endeavor.

He nodded. "We've got a good crew. You should requalify. Come out with us sometime."

A flicker of something lit inside me. Excitement, I realized. Not the false kind that came from an adrenaline dump on a job but the kind that came from purpose and helping others. I'd never let my certification lapse, but I hadn't been on a team either. "I'll talk to my dad about it."

Jude clapped me on the shoulder. "Good. Glad you're back."

"Thanks." It was all I could say, but his words meant more than he would ever know.

I slid back into the booth, glancing at Chris. His gaze was fixed on Jude.

"You okay?"

"Huh? Yeah." He zeroed back in on me. He was quiet for a moment and then sighed as if giving in. "So, tell me about your coolest client. Please tell me you had some hot-as-hell affair with a Hollywood starlet."

I choked on a laugh. "Sorry to disappoint." But I told him my best stories from the job, and Chris caught me up on all the happenings in Cedar Ridge, studiously leaving Wren out of it. It didn't exactly feel like old times—the conversation was stilted and awkward in a few places—but it was progress.

I snatched the bill, pulling some cash from my wallet. "Buying lunch is the least I can do as a thank you for giving me the time of day."

"You don't have to do that, man."

"I want to."

Chris slid out of the booth. "Then I won't argue with you because that lunch was damned good."

"I missed that turkey melt."

He chuckled as we started for the door. "Nothing like the food you were raised on."

"You're so right."

I collided with someone in the entryway. "Sorry—"

"Watch where you're fuckin' going," the guy hissed as he wobbled a little.

I froze. It was like being hurtled back in time. The face was one of the few that haunted my nightmares.

"Keep moving, Joe," Chris clipped.

"How 'bout you assholes watch where you're going?"

"Joseph Sullivan, you will watch your language in this establishment, or you'll get your food elsewhere," Jeanie said as she strode over.

"Whatever," the teen muttered and headed for the door.

I still hadn't moved. He looked just like him—the spitting image if it weren't for the dyed black hair and a million facial piercings. And he certainly had Randy's rage.

Jeanie made a tsking noise. "What that boy needs is some good parents in his life."

"He's not going to find them at home," Chris murmured.

Much had been said in court about Randy's alcoholic father and his missing-in-action mother, but in the end, it hadn't helped with the sentencing. He and Paul were currently serving consecutive life sentences with no chance of parole.

"He's angry, and I don't blame him. This whole town looks at him like they're waiting for him to turn into his brother," Jeanie said.

My gut twisted with a combination of sympathy and unease. That kid was staying alive on rage and fear. I'd seen that kind of combination before.

And it was deadly.

Chapter Eight

Wren

"GUARD MY DONUTS FOR ME WHILE I'M OUT ON THIS call, Little Williams?" Nash asked, lowering a bakery box in front of me.

Abel snorted from the cubicle next to us. "They'll be gone before you're even out the door."

"Hey," I said, tossing a paper clip.

He leaned back in his chair. "You know she's got a thing for sweets."

"Life is uncertain. Eat dessert first. It's a good life motto."

Nash tightened his grip on his donuts, raising the box away from my desk. "Will you watch my donuts, Abel?"

I rolled my eyes. "You're just like—" My words cut off. *Holt.* He was just like Holt with his obsession with food—pie, in particular. But food of all kinds was worthy of devotion.

Nash shifted uncomfortably and then opened the box. "You can have one. Just not the Boston cream."

How pathetic must I have looked for Nash to offer me one of

his precious confections? I forced a grin as I nabbed the strawberry one. "Works every time."

Nash gaped at me. "You faked emotional distress to steal my donuts?"

The laugh that came was real, and it felt good. The sound hadn't passed my lips since before I'd met Grae for lunch yesterday. "Hasn't anyone ever told you it's a cliché for cops to eat donuts?"

Lawson swooped in and stole a glazed one. "I'll take that cliché every single time."

Nash snapped the lid of the bakery box closed. "My donuts. Mine."

"Did someone say donuts?" Jude asked as he strode up, pack slung over one shoulder.

Nash let out a pathetic moan. "Next time, I'm getting two dozen."

I pressed my lips together to stifle my laughter. "Might want to go for three."

Jude leaned on the half partition to my cubicle, scanning my face. "You hanging in there?"

I fought the curse that wanted to surface. It wasn't that I didn't appreciate Jude and Chris looking out for me. I did. But asking that in front of two of Holt's brothers? Not freaking cool. The last thing I wanted was one of them telling Holt that his presence hurt me. Holt didn't get to know that he affected me at all.

I took a large bite of the donut, speaking around the fluffy dough. "Perfect now that I've got this strawberry goodness."

Nash grinned. "Donuts make everything right with the world."

Lawson didn't buy my act quite so easily. His eyes narrowed a fraction as he studied me. I'd tried to cover the dark circles the best I could, but I was no makeup artist. And I couldn't do anything about the red streaks in the whites of my eyes.

So, I opted to shift my chair, turning back to my screen and willing my phone to ring. That was an awful thing to hope for. That someone was in enough distress to call nine-one-one. But that was where I was at.

Lawson cleared his throat, shifting his focus to Abel. "The team's meeting at the trailhead. We should have enough officers left to cover incoming calls, but will you call in reinforcements if things look thin?"

Lawson and Nash served on the volunteer search and rescue team for the county with a couple of other officers. Having a law enforcement presence on the team was helpful but could leave us short-staffed.

"Will do," Abel said.

"Let's head out," Lawson ordered.

Nash held his donuts out to Abel. "Guard them with your life. I'm trusting you."

Abel snatched the box, shoving it onto his desk. "Get out of here before I toss your damn donuts in the trash."

Nash glared at him but reluctantly followed his brother toward the parking lot.

Jude lingered, his broad frame leaning over the cubicle partition. "Sorry, Wren. I didn't mean to put you in an awkward spot—"

"It's okay. I just don't want Nash and Law going back to Holt with any stories. He'll be gone before we know it, and I'll be fine."

Jude's eyes shifted to the street.

Unease trickled through me. "What?"

"Nothing. It just sounded to me like Holt might be sticking around for a bit."

The sweet pastry in my stomach suddenly made me feel a little ill. "He might be saying that, but I doubt he'll follow through."

Jude leveled me with one of his patented stares. One that screamed: *Don't bullshit me*. I fought the urge to squirm in my chair. "What? It's not like he's ever stuck around before."

"Wren. This could be good for you both. A chance to clear the air. Then, maybe both of you can move on."

His words were like an ice pick to the chest, each one a carefully placed blow. He didn't mean to inflict the pain, but he had.

"I *have* moved on. Holt didn't give me any other choice. And he sure as hell didn't give me a chance to *clear the air* when he bolted with nothing but a half-assed letter. So, excuse me if I'm not eager to rehash how he crushed my damn heart when I needed him the most."

I spun to face my computer screen.

"Wren—"

"I'm working, and you have some lost hikers to find."

Jude was quiet for a moment. "Okay."

I heard his footsteps retreat, each one shoving the guilt swirling inside me a little deeper. Jude didn't deserve my anger. He, Chris, and the Hartleys had stayed. Were there for me through it all. Gran, too.

An ache spread in my chest as her face flashed in my mind. How she'd forced me out of bed for long walks each day when all I'd wanted was to let the covers swallow me whole. She'd never wavered, and I'd eventually started to get better. But it hadn't changed the fact that I was walking around like some hollow half person. Because the life I'd thought would be mine, the one I wanted more than anything, had been ripped out from under me.

"Bit that boy's head off," Abel said, staring at his computer monitor.

"I know."

"You're gonna have to face him at some point. And Jude's right about one thing. It's time for you to move on."

I bit the inside of my cheek to keep from snapping at Abel. "I have moved on. I have friends. A job I love. The perfect house."

"What about someone to share your life with?"

"I date. I just haven't found the right person yet." My entire body revolted at the idea. I'd told myself time and time again that it was because I'd spent so many years planning that life with Holt. But that when the right person came along, I wouldn't feel that way.

Abel turned to face me, arching a brow. "You pick apart every man who's ever taken you out. The ones who might be a match? You won't even look their way."

"What are you talking about?"

"I'm old but I'm not dead. I notice how Clint includes you in every poker night and after-work beers."

I stiffened. "Clint would get frustrated with me the moment he realized I would never give up this job."

"What about Chris? Anyone can see how he looks at you."

I swung around in my chair. "Chris is a *friend*. Just like Law, Jude, and Nash. It is possible to have male friends, Abel. You've never made a pass at me."

He chortled. "If I was a few years younger, I'd be sweeping you off your feet."

Warmth spread through me, easing a bit of the anxiety of the conversation. "The curse of my birth time."

The amusement fell from Abel's expression in the quiet that followed. "You should talk to him—"

The phone rang, and I rushed to answer. I would've picked up a live wire if it got me out of the conversation with Abel. "Cedar Ridge police, fire, and medical. What's your emergency?"

"W-Wren?"

The tremble in the teen girl's voice had me snapping upright, my gaze flashing to the screen to check the readout. "What's wrong, Jane?"

"Someone's here. They're trying to get into the house."

Ice slid through my veins as my heart rate picked up. I focused on my breathing. In for two. Out for two.

"You're at home?"

"Yes."

"Is anyone else there?"

"No. Mom's at work, and Dad's on duty. We have a teacher in-service day today."

Dale Clemmons was a firefighter, and he would've lost his mind if he'd heard his baby girl's voice sounding this terrified.

"I hear it again," Jane whispered. "It's like they're scratching at the door."

That had my brow furrowing, and I brought up a map. The

Clemmons family's home wasn't too far from Marion Simpson's place. "Hold on, Jane. Let me get some officers dispatched."

I switched over to the radio. "Reported 10-62 at 27 Mountain View Way. Sixteen-year-old girl is home alone. Jane Clemmons."

Amber responded in less than a second. "Anderson and Raymond en route. Keep her on the line and keep us updated."

"Will do. Be advised of a bear in the vicinity that Marion Simpson was feeding. That could be the culprit."

"Understood."

I switched back over to my phone line. "Officers are on their way, Jane. We've had reports of a bear in the area, so it could be as simple as that."

Roan had taken the guy deeper into the forest while he was tranqued, but once bears knew there was food someplace, they would always come back.

Jane let out a half breath, half laugh. "My friends are going to give me so much shit if I called nine-one-one on a bear."

I grinned. "At least you'll have a story to tell."

The sound of glass shattering had any hint of amusement slipping from my face. "Tell me what's happening, Jane."

"I-I don't think it's a bear."

"Tell me where you are and what you can see and hear."

Her breaths came out in soft pants across the line. "I'm in the den. I think he broke the glass next to the door. Oh, God, Wren. He's trying to get in."

"Hide, Jane. Find a closet or trunk. Anywhere they won't think to look."

My pulse thrummed in my neck as memories flashed in my mind. I shoved them down, focusing on the here and now. I could hear Jane moving as I switched over to the radio. "Window next to the door has been broken. She thinks they're trying to get in that way."

The sirens were already on when Amber came across the line. "Less than a minute out."

But I knew anything could happen in a minute. It could destroy someone's whole world.

I moved back to the phone line. "Where are you hiding?"

"In the back of the coat closet. There's a panel in the back wall that leads to our crawl space."

"Smart, Jane."

I quickly typed her location into our computer system, knowing Amber or Clint would see it.

"Oh, God."

Fear spiked through my system. "What is it?"

"He's in the house," Jane whispered.

"Did you see who it was? Is it someone you know?"

"I only saw them from the back. I think it's a guy. He was wearing a hoodie. It sounds like he's searching for something."

Everything around me slowed, the world tunneling for a moment. I bit the inside of my cheek, hard. The pain was what I needed to stay in the here and now and not let the similarities pull me under to a decade ago.

"Hold on, Jane. I'm going to mute myself, but I'll still be on the line. Stay quiet and keep breathing."

I clicked on the radio. "The intruder's in the house. Male suspect, wearing a hoodie."

Amber bit out a curse as the sirens blared. "We're here. We'll get him."

Empathy swept through me at Amber having to be the one to answer the call. She was just as tortured by these memories as I was.

I listened to Jane's staccato breaths with one ear while I kept the other trained on the radio. The officers maintained an open line as they moved through the house, clearing rooms.

"Shit, he's running out the back. I'm in pursuit," Clint clipped.

Footsteps sounded.

"I'll get to Jane," Amber said.

I struggled to keep my voice even as I unmuted myself on

the phone. "Jane, he ran out the back. Amber is coming to the closet now."

A knock sounded.

"Y-you're sure it's her?"

"Jane, it's Amber. I'm going to open the closet door. Think you can climb out of the crawl space?"

Tears filled the line. "I-I can get out."

Shuffling filled the line, and then the sound of tears as Amber let out an *oof*. "It's okay, Jane. I've got you."

The girl only cried harder.

Abel motioned to me. "Tell Jane her dad's on his way."

"Did you hear that? Your dad's on his way."

I could barely make out the *"thank you"* as she continued to sob. "I've got her now. You can disconnect, Wren."

My finger hovered over the button to end the call as if I couldn't be sure that Jane would really be all right.

Abel leaned over and hit it for me, startling me out of my frozen state. Concern filled his eyes. "You okay?"

I nodded as I jerked to my feet, tearing off my headset. "Gonna take my ten."

"Wren—"

But I was already moving. Everything blurred around me as I wove through the desks, desperate for a hit of mountain air and to not feel as if the walls were closing in around me.

My lungs burned as visions of faces twisted with hatred whirled in my mind. The sound of taunting and destruction filled my ears—the feeling of white-hot pain in my chest.

I tore through the front doors and onto the sidewalk, colliding with a tall, broad form. Arms came around to steady me. It wasn't the body I recognized or even the hands. Those were so different from all those years ago.

It was the scent—pine with a hint of spice and a little something else that I'd never been able to identify but had always meant *Holt* to me. One that always felt like home.

Chapter Nine

Holt

I T SHOULDN'T HAVE FELT THIS GOOD TO HAVE WREN IN MY arms—not when I could feel the panic rolling off her in waves.

The moment she realized that I was the one holding her, she jerked out of my grasp. It cut. I deserved it, but I felt the bite of it anyway.

Worry quickly replaced the hurt. I had trained for a decade in ways that guaranteed my ability to take in a scene and process it in a split second. Wren's face was so pale it was almost translucent, her hands trembled as she wrapped them around herself, and her breathing was far too quick.

"What happened, Cricket?"

"Don't call me that," she snapped.

It might've been anger, but at least it was something. It wasn't the cool indifference of last night, or the anxious panic of mere seconds ago. I'd take anger over those two any day.

I stared at the face I still knew by heart. I would've known Wren anywhere—even with fuller cheeks and lighter hair. She could've looked completely different, and my soul would've some-how managed to pick her out of a crowd.

"Tell me what happened." It wasn't a question, but it was still spoken with as much softness as I could manage with the need to know what had caused this fear in her pulsing through me.

"Doesn't matter."

Wren turned to go, but I grabbed her wrist to stop her. My grasp was gentle, but it didn't matter, the feel of her skin against mine burned through me—a wildfire of want and grief, mixing into a deadly concoction.

She tugged her hand free of my hold. "You can drop the good-guy act. It's just me. You don't have to pretend to care."

My back molars ground together. "I'm not trying to put on any act." The idea that I was a good man had long since dissipated. I had too much blood on my hands. "Just because I left doesn't mean I stopped caring."

Wren looked as if I'd slapped her. Then, a second later, her mask was back in place. "Sure as hell could've fooled me."

She took off down the street as if the hounds of hell were on her heels.

But the look on her face was still so vivid in my mind. A brand-ing iron of betrayal.

I moved to the station. Wren might hate me, but I still needed to know what had spooked her so badly.

Pushing open the door, I stepped inside to a cacophony of sound. A handful of officers were scattered around, talking to each other in raised voices. My gaze scanned the room, searching for a familiar face, one who might tell me *something*.

"Holt."

I turned at Nash's voice, not missing the lack of easygoing amusement on his face. "Aren't you supposed to be out with search and rescue?"

Nash's jaw tensed. "Law and I had to turn back. Call in town."

"What kind of call?" It must have been bad to get them to leave their SAR team down two men.

He inclined his head to the side, and we moved down the hall. "Break-in at Dale Clemmons' place. Their teenaged daughter was home alone."

Everything in me stilled. "She okay?"

"Thankfully, yes. The intruder took off into the woods. We're organizing a search now."

I swallowed the bile crawling up my throat. "Wren take the call?"

Nash's eyes flashed. "Yeah."

I muttered a slew of curses.

Nash punched me in the arm, bringing my focus back to him. "Wren can handle herself. She's been doing this job for a long time. This isn't the first time she's gotten a call that triggered her. Won't be the last, either. It's part of what makes her uniquely qualified to be a dispatcher. She has an understanding that very few people have."

That fire inside me burned again, turning everything in its wake to painful ash. "She shouldn't have to *have* that understanding."

"No, she shouldn't. But she does. That's life. It's messed-up and rarely fair."

I turned back to the doors, staring out them as if I could somehow track where Wren had gone. I had a deep urge to run after her, to try to take away a little of that pain. But that would be the last thing she wanted.

"It wasn't your fault, Holt."

I jerked around to face Nash.

"It wasn't," he pushed. "It was two sick teenagers who never should've had access to weapons."

My nostrils flared, and my breathing turned ragged. "I. Was. Late."

"And I made you late. Do you think I wanted Wren to get shot? That I wanted her to almost die?"

I shook my head in a rough movement. "*I* made her a promise. Me. If I'd been there—"

"Then they would've shot you, too."

"I could've protected her."

Nash lifted his brows. "Did you have a concealed carry permit at eighteen that I didn't know about?"

I slammed my mouth closed.

"That's what I thought." He shook his head. "You saved her life, Holt. You got her breathing again. You stayed with her until the paramedics got there."

"Stop," I barked.

Images assailed my mind. Skin so pale, going cold. Life slipping away under my fingertips.

Nash stared at me. "You need to let this go or it's going to kill you. You've already been trying to kill yourself for a decade. Get a clue. The reaper doesn't want you. Maybe this is your shot to make things right, here and now."

"You don't know what you're talking about."

But he did. Nash and I had been the closest in age—Irish twins, my mom had always said. We'd been attached at the hip since the moment he was born. He knew me too damn well.

He leveled that knowing stare on me now. "You think I don't see you? First the military, war zone after war zone. And then when that calmed down, you had to go private sector so you could choose the riskiest jobs. I bet you took the most dangerous assignments on those missions, too."

"It's called being a leader."

"No, it's called being reckless." Anger flared in Nash's eyes. "Did you ever stop to think what it would do to us if we lost you?"

I jolted at his question.

"That's what I thought. It's time to grow up, Holt. Take responsibility for the things that are yours and let go of the ones that aren't."

"I'm sorry." I didn't have any other words for him. I'd screwed up time and time again when it came to my family. All I could do now was be here and make different choices.

A little of the anger bled out of Nash's expression at my apology. "You have to deal with this. You need to stop running."

"I'm here, aren't I?"

"There's more than one way to run."

God, did I know that.

Wren's face flashed in my mind—the panic embedded there. I could see the little tremor in her hands as if she were still standing right in front of me.

I'd thought that if I left, she'd be able to heal. That she'd be safe.

And the truth was, I hadn't wanted to face what I'd done to her. Hadn't wanted to see that betrayal in her eyes as she'd finally come to terms with the truth—that I hadn't been there the moment she needed me the most. But it was time for me to face it. I needed to let myself drown in the pain and not hide from it by taking mission after mission.

Because Wren still lived with that pain. Every. Damn. Day.

Chapter Ten

Wren

THE ECHO OF FOOTSTEPS ON THE LINOLEUM FLOOR ROSE above the low din of the station. I shifted my gaze to the computer screen in front of me, trying to get a read on the reflection. Man or woman? Size? Shape?

It didn't really matter who it was, just as long as it wasn't Holt's broad-shouldered form. His words echoed in my head. *"Just because I left doesn't mean I stopped caring."*

That phantom rasp in my mind had anger pooling deep. He wanted to come back? Fine. He wanted to start showing his face around town? I could deal. But he did not get to tell me he *cared*.

People who cared didn't vanish the moment you were well enough to leave rehab and go home. I'd replayed those months between the shooting and Holt bolting over and over in my head. Looking back on it, I could see that something had shifted in him. But at the time, I'd been in too much mental and emotional pain to see it.

The deadness in his voice should've been my first sign. He would hold my hand and kiss my temple, but never did his mouth meet mine. He was a fierce defender, keeping away the reporters and the morbidly curious, but was never truly alone with me.

It was embarrassing now—how clear it had been that he'd wanted nothing to do with me. Yet I'd been stunned as I'd read the damn letter.

"Wren."

I breathed a sigh of relief at the sound of Chris's voice, then spun in my chair. "Hey."

The planes of his face were etched with concern. "I heard what happened. You okay?"

Annoyance sparked and flickered under my skin. "Why wouldn't I be?"

He was quiet for a moment. "The, uh, break-in call. It would make sense if it brought back memories."

"My house wasn't broken into. We should be worried about Jane." And I'd make sure I went by her place sometime in the next few days to talk to her. It helped to have someone who'd been there.

The survivors of the shooting and I had formed a sort of club—the type that none of us wanted to be a member of. Those we'd lost held honorary membership. Five dead. Six injured. Students. Teachers. A coach. Innocent bystanders who had gotten in the way. Randy and Paul had made a hit list of every person they thought had ever wronged them and had ticked them off one by one.

Chris stared at me for a moment. "It's okay to not *always* have it together. It's normal. What you went through—"

"Don't," I bit out. "I've done the therapy thing. I don't need my head shrunk by my friends, too."

He winced, and I instantly felt like the worst kind of jerk.

"I'm sorry. I didn't mean—"

Chris waved me off. "I get it. I just want you to know that I'm there for you if you ever need to talk. Or not talk. I'm also good with takeout and beer."

The corner of my mouth lifted. "Only if it's a pepperoni and pineapple from Wildfire."

Chris's face screwed up. "That's just wrong, and you know it."

"Don't judge my culinary choices."

"You mean your culinary *crimes*."

I only grinned wider. "You've never even tried it."

He shuddered. "I'll get you your pizza crime. I'll stick with meat lovers."

"Fine."

"How about tonight?"

I pulled my phone out to check my calendar and froze. In big letters was *Family Dinner at the Hartleys'*. I was over there at least once a month but had made these plans with Grae last week—before everything had changed.

"You got plans?" Chris prodded.

"Uh, yeah."

"With who?"

"Grae," I said, still staring at my phone. Maybe she'd meet me in town instead.

Chris nodded. "Later this week then. Tell G hi."

"Yeah, sure."

"Wren."

My head snapped up at Lawson's voice. Chris had left, and I hadn't even realized it. I'd still been staring at that tiny calendar square on my phone like it was a cobra poised to strike.

I shoved my cell into my desk drawer so the damn thing couldn't taunt me. "Can you come to my office for a minute?"

Dread pooled in my stomach. "No one else is on duty. Abel went to lunch and—"

"I'm back," he grumbled, sliding into the cubicle next to mine. "Go talk to Lawson so he isn't hovering over me."

"I love you, too, Abel," Lawson said with a chuckle.

"Holler if you need me," I told Abel as I rose from my chair.

"Who do you think you're talking to, missy? I was the only dispatcher on duty for almost a decade."

His indignant response had my lips curving. "Of course. And you walked to school in four feet of snow, uphill both ways."

"Damn straight. Now, get out of my space and let me focus."

I shook my head and followed Lawson toward his office. But the moment we stepped inside, and he'd shut the door, any flickers of amusement fled.

"Have a seat," Lawson said as he moved to his chair.

I worried the side of my lip as I followed his order. "Am I about to get fired?"

Lawson's eyes flared. "I sure as hell hope not because you're the best dispatcher I have."

"Abel's the best dispatcher you have."

"He's good in a crisis, but he's ornery on a good day. He doesn't have even a smidge of the empathy you do."

I leaned back against the chair, a little of the worry draining out of me. "Abel has all the empathy in the world. He just hides it under crankiness."

A grin pulled at Lawson's mouth. "You may be right there. Either way, you're my number one."

I arched a brow. "You sure that's not because you've been looking out for me basically since I was born?"

The twelve years separating him from Grae and me had meant that he was always protective, but over his younger brothers, too. He shrugged. "Maybe. But who says I can't have favorites?"

"I have a feeling human resources might frown on that."

"Good thing HR is Anderson, and he's already drowning in his police work."

I snickered. "Guess you're safe."

Lawson leaned back, his chair squeaking. "You okay?"

I rolled my lips over my teeth as if that would keep me from giving him the truth. "You asking as my boss or as my friend?"

"I'm asking as your surrogate big brother."

In so many ways, that married the two. Lawson had a calm steadiness about him that made people want to leave their burdens at his feet. He had that quality that I missed in Holt so damn much—that silent assurance that nothing I told him would ever freak him out.

He didn't *see* me the same way Holt had. Holt knew what I was thinking or how I was feeling before I could even find the words. But there was comfort in knowing that I could still keep the worst of my torture to myself around Lawson.

"The call rattled me. It isn't the first one that has, and it won't be the last. I can handle it."

Lawson nodded. "I know you *can*, but you're also allowed to take care of yourself when you get rattled. If you need to take the rest of the day, do it."

I shook my head. "That would just make things worse. I took a walk around the block. Cleared my head. I'm good."

"All right. How's everything else?"

I arched a brow. "Are you digging, Chief Hartley?"

He had the decency to look a little sheepish. "I've been known to, time and again." The hint of humor slipped from his face. "He's a mess, Wren."

My fingers curved around the arms of the chair, but I didn't say a word.

Lawson let his statement hang heavy in the air for a moment. "I know he hurt you, but he was a kid, too. What happened to him, finding you like he did…it can twist a person up."

"So it's *my* fault he bailed?"

"Of course, not. I'm just saying there are as many sides to a story as those who've lived it."

My back teeth ground together. The fact that Lawson made a perfectly reasonable point just stoked my mad. But I breathed through it. "I get it. He was struggling. You think I don't hate that? But I can't just forget that he left me when I needed him the most. That what we had wasn't enough for him to fight through whatever bullshit was swirling in his head."

I met Lawson's gaze dead-on. "He broke me, Law. Worse than that bullet. Worse than the agony of waking up after open-heart surgery. Worse than the torture of months of rehab. I can't just magically forget that happened."

I stared down at my phone, my gaze tracking over the text again and again.

Grae: *My best friend isn't a pansy-a biznatch.*

I couldn't help the flutter of my lips. Grae had always had a foul mouth. Probably because she had four older brothers. But when Lawson's first son was born, she'd done her best to clean up her act. The results were these ridiculous non-cussing curse words.

And she'd been using them to taunt me all afternoon. To bait me into coming tonight.

I tossed my phone into the cupholder and stared up at the house. I knew every nook and cranny of it like the back of my hand. How many times had I wished I could live here growing up? Too many to count.

And then there were the times when I'd picture it—building a house on the land that would be close enough that Kerry and Nathan would be in their grandbabies' lives every single day. Those invisible claws dug deep, and I shoved the memories down.

I was good at that. Shoving away things that I didn't want to look at. I was a master at it, really. But I could never burn the memories out altogether.

And we had half a lifetime of them. Grae and I had been in the same playgroup as infants. And Kerry often told this story of two-year-old Holt toddling over, transfixed by the baby with the hazel eyes. She said he used to stand guard over me, not letting anyone close until they proved their good intentions.

That had never changed over the years. Always my protector. The one who picked me up when I took a tumble off my bike and tended to my skinned knees. The one who insisted his brothers let Grae and me play whatever they were doing. The one who decked a jerk in the third grade for making a habit of taunting me, thus getting suspended for a whole week.

I'd been half in love with Holt Hartley since I could walk. But it took some time for him to come around to the idea. He'd said that he'd always loved me but that the love just looked different at each point in our lives. I'd thought that would continue forever, never realizing he could simply walk away.

I tugged the keys out of my ignition and wrapped my fingers around them, the metal teeth biting into my flesh. I wished the flash of pain were stronger. I needed so much worse if I were going to make it through the next few hours.

Climbing the steps to the front door, I took one last lungful of mountain air. My steps paused, and I almost lifted my hand to knock as if Holt's presence had turned this place into a stranger's home. I shoved the impulse down and opened the door.

The sounds of muted chaos came from the living area. I followed its strains. Grae leapt from the couch the moment she saw me. "Wren!" She engulfed me in a hug. "I was worried you were going to bail," she whispered.

"Your thirty-two texts might have given me a clue to that."

She sent me a sheepish smile. "Was pansy-a biznatch too much?"

I grinned. "That was my favorite one."

"Come on. Let's get a drink."

She ushered me to the kitchen, and I was proud that my steps only faltered slightly as my eyes locked with deep blue ones. Holt's stare was like a force field I had to fight against to make any forward progress.

"Hey, Cricket."

A flash of agony ripped through me, but I simply nodded. "Holt."

"My girl's here," Kerry crooned, pulling me into a hug. "Now all is right with the world."

"I didn't bring anything, but I've got two hands that can help."

"All I need is you in this space, and I'm happy as can be."

Warmth filtered through me, easing the worst of the pain of hearing my nickname on Holt's lips.

"What's up, Little Williams?" Nash asked, popping a cherry tomato into his mouth.

Kerry smacked his hand with a towel. "Wren, you can help me by guarding the food from these two heathens."

Holt's lips twitched into that devilish smile I'd always loved as he snagged a roll off the cooling rack. "It's a compliment, Mom." He popped a bite into his mouth. "I never eat as well as I do here."

Nathan shifted in his seat. "If that's the case, you'd think you would've made it home for more than twenty-four hours once a year."

Pain lashed Holt's face. It was there one second and gone the next. But the depth of it was so intense, I'd never forget the image.

"Nathan…" Kerry said in a low voice.

"Not holding my tongue in my own house," he grumbled.

I sent Grae a sidelong look, and she gave a small shake of her head. My gaze shifted back to Nathan, the man who had been nothing but an overgrown teddy bear to me. He'd occasionally been hard on his kids, but it was always when they'd done something boneheaded. And he always ended every lecture or punishment by telling them how loved they were.

Sure, Nathan had gotten more cantankerous as his recovery dragged on, but this was harsh—even to my ears.

Holt shifted on the stool at the counter. "You can say whatever you need to, Dad."

Nathan snapped his mouth closed and turned back to the TV.

Roan stared at his father. His eyes darkened as he took the man in, but he didn't say a word either.

Lawson's jaw worked back and forth as he stared at his boots.

What had happened to this family I loved so much? Had I been oblivious to them falling apart right under my nose? I knew that I wouldn't let any of them talk to me about Holt, but they told me about their holidays, ones I knew Holt was present for, and

I'd heard nothing but happiness and hilarious stories afterward. This tension had to be new.

Kerry threaded the towel through her fingers, casting a worried look in her husband's direction. I gave her arm a quick squeeze and started for the couch. Looking down at Nathan, I inclined my head toward the hall. "Take a spin with me."

"Haven't you heard? I broke my leg."

"Please," I huffed. "That was months ago. And I know for a fact that your physical therapist wants you taking loops on solid ground several times a day. You going soft on me?"

Nash covered his laugh with a cough.

Nathan arched a brow. "You checkin' up on me?"

"You're more of a father than I've ever had. So sue me if I'd like to keep you around a little longer and stop you from biting everyone's head off. It's gonna be real cramped quarters if Kerry kicks your butt out, and you have to come stay with me."

He tried to glare but it was no use, his lips twitched. It was so similar to how Holt's fluttered it made my chest ache.

Nathan reached out a hand. "Help an old man up."

I wrapped my fingers around his, but he really didn't need my help.

"Seriously, Dad?" Nash gaped. "I've only asked you three times to walk with me since I got here."

Nathan shrugged. "She's better company than you."

Grae chuckled. "I could've told you that."

"Come on," I urged.

Nathan and I moved down the hall, away from the soft sounds of some sports game on the television and the muted conversation. It would take us all the way to the opposite side of the house.

"They're all talking behind my back now," Nathan grumbled.

"Only because you gave them a reason."

His jaw tightened.

"What gives? I'd think you'd be happy to have Holt back."

"I am."

His voice was gruff like he'd been a smoker in another life.

"You weren't acting like a man thrilled to see his son."

Nathan was quiet for a moment as we walked, his gait labored but better than the last time I'd been here. "He won't stay."

"So what?"

His head jerked up. "I want time with my son. I put up with him chasing every life-threatening situation he could find all over the globe, but I'm done with it. I don't know how much time I've got left on this Earth, and I'd like to actually get to know my boy before I'm gone."

My steps faltered, and I gaped at Nathan. "So, you're...what? Trying to heckle him into staying?"

Nathan flushed. "Hey, it's worked so far. He's made it to the seventy-two-hour mark. That's the longest he's been home in a decade."

My chest ached as I turned to Nathan, my hands reaching up to his shoulders. "What you two have is precious. Just because it's rusty doesn't mean the root of it isn't still there. If you want to find your footing again, be honest. Tell him you want him to stay. That you want a chance to know the man he's grown into."

It was a measure of how much I loved this family that I encouraged the very thing that would cut me open and pour acid into the wound. But I knew what it was like to live with pain. Over time, I could deal with this, too. The pain would become normal, and I could take it if it meant the Hartleys finding their peace.

Nathan pressed his lips together. "I'll think about it."

I looped my arm through his and guided us back toward the living area. "That's all I can ask for."

What sounded like a herd of elephants erupted from the basement, followed by shouts of glee and maybe some video game trash talk.

"We'd better get back there," Nathan said as he picked up his pace, looking way spryer than before. "Those grandsons of mine could eat us out of house and home."

"Like father like sons when it comes to food motivation."

Nathan snorted. "I didn't raise no fools."

A grin pulled at my lips as we stepped back into the living area. But that curve of my mouth slipped away as I took in the sight in front of me.

"Put me down, Uncle Holt," Charlie giggled.

Holt tickled the little boy's side and held him upside down by one ankle. "What'll you promise me?"

"You get the first slice of pie! I promise!"

Holt lifted him higher, tickling his other side. "I don't know if I believe you…"

Charlie shrieked and laughed, making a grab for the pie sitting on the counter.

Holt swung him into the air and then caught him in his arms as Charlie begged for him to do it again.

Our gazes locked. An entire lifetime passed in a matter of heartbeats—years full of how Holt would've teased our babies, tossing them high and letting the giggles rain down around us. Years full of watching them grow and making that football team of a family we'd always wanted.

I'd been wrong earlier. I'd never learn to live with pain like this. It would swallow me whole first.

Chapter Eleven

Holt

THE COLOR DRAINED FROM WREN'S FACE, THE GREEN extinguishing from those gorgeous hazel eyes. She was already backing away. Her head swiveled, looking for a way out like a cornered wild animal.

I cursed, setting Charlie down.

"Uncle Holt," he hissed. "Grandma's gonna be really mad. That's a *bad* one."

I couldn't pause to assure the kid it didn't matter because I was already moving, eating up the space between Wren and me. Her eyes widened, and she bolted with a whisper to my dad as she took off for the door.

I picked up to a jog, but my dad grabbed my arm. I tried to jerk it free, but his grip was shockingly strong for a man still supposedly recovering from a heart attack and a broken leg.

"Don't," he said in a low voice. "Let her go."

I jerked my arm out of his grasp. "I know you've finally realized what a garbage human I am and that I never deserved her, but do me a favor and back off for just a damned second."

His jaw dropped as my mom gasped. "You're not a garbage human."

"We both know that's not true. But I'm not going to let Wren suffer for it. So, give me one fucking minute to try to make this right."

"Holt."

My dad's voice had a slight tremor, one that made me hate myself even more—a task I would've thought impossible a couple of seconds ago. But I didn't let that hatred stop me from moving and doing what I had to do.

I jogged to the entryway and threw the door open, searching for her—the person I'd know anywhere.

The image that greeted me shredded whatever was left in my chest. Wren, dropped to the asphalt next to her truck, arms locked around her legs, rocking back and forth.

My legs started moving before I gave them the command, muscles pushing harder as I ran to her. My Cricket. The woman I'd loved all my life.

I dropped to the ground in front of her, hands going to her knees. "Wren—"

"Don't!" She jerked away. "You'll make it worse."

My hands hovered just shy of making contact. "I'll make what worse?"

"It'll hurt so much more if you touch me." Tears streamed down her face as she struggled for breath. "I can't. I thought I could, but I can't. I can't see what we could've had. I can't watch you move back here, fall in love with another woman, and give her all my dreams. I can't."

My eyes burned as if someone had poured a bucket of acid over my head. "Cricket."

Her nickname only made Wren cry harder. "Don't. I know I wasn't enough, but I can't be reminded of that every day. I can't do it."

I reeled back. I'd been stabbed before. Shot. Had my arm

broken by a particularly massive guy in the Russian mob. And none of that hurt even a fraction as much as this did.

The fire inside me burned impossibly brighter. The one that told me time and again just what a failure I was. Because I should've seen this coming.

My girl had always doubted. Struggled to see just how amazing she was. That she was more than enough. That she was everything.

Probably because those assholes who called themselves her parents never bothered to stick around long enough to make her think that she was worth their time. But I'd gone and let her believe the same brutal lie.

"I'm the one who's not enough."

Wren's breath hitched in her throat, and her face lifted. Her eyes were swollen and red, her expression ravaged. "Liar."

I wanted so badly to take her hands, pull her into my arms, and spill every truth. "I fucked up."

Her eyes blazed. But the anger filling them was a welcome relief.

I held up both hands, silently begging for her to let me continue. "I was drowning in guilt, and I didn't know how to face you. You were hurting so much, and it was all because of me."

Wren reared back as if I'd struck her. "You didn't shoot me."

"I was late." The words were barely audible as if dragged from my throat by sheer force of will alone. "I told you I'd be there. Promised you I wouldn't be late."

"You were always late."

That only made it worse. I'd treated so many things in my life with such casual disregard, thinking that I could stroll in any damn moment I pleased. My throat tightened, putting a stranglehold on everything I wanted to tell her. "I should've been there."

It wasn't nearly enough, but it encompassed the truth. I should've been at Wren's side. I'd given her my word. And I might as well have been a million miles away.

Wren stared at me as if trying to put together a puzzle when she'd lost the cover of the box. "The only thing that would've happened if you were there is that they would've shot you, too. Do you honestly believe *that's* what I wanted?"

I shook my head manically as if that might get her to understand. "You were *everything* to me. It was my job to keep you safe. To take care of you."

"We were supposed to take care of each other. That doesn't mean it was your job to be my human shield."

My jaw went hard as granite. "Five minutes difference and I would've been there."

Wren leapt to her feet, green fire burning in her hazel eyes. "I don't give a damn about the five minutes you missed that night. I give a damn about the last ten years you threw away."

Chapter Twelve

Wren

TREMORS ROCKED THROUGH ME AS I GRIPPED THE steering wheel harder, taking each mountain curve quicker than the last. I'd capitalized on the brief reprieve of Holt's stunned silence to slip behind the wheel of my truck and head for freedom.

Only freedom didn't ease any of the pain. I'd thought if I didn't have to see the look of devastation on his face—the true agony—that it would make it better. It didn't.

Everything hurt. The pressure behind my eyes pulsed in a way that I knew meant a killer headache was on its way. My throat burned with the aftermath of my sobs. But that was nothing compared to the brutal tearing sensation deep inside my chest.

A riot of emotions sailed through me and moved so fast that I could barely identify one before the next steamrolled over it. Anger. Hurt. Bone-deep grief.

My vision blurred as I made it to town, and I had to blink to keep on the road. The moment the shops and restaurants started popping up, my phone began to ring. I didn't bother looking down at it. The caller didn't matter, and the last thing I needed was to get in a wreck on my way home.

My knuckles ached as I held onto the steering wheel, treating it as if it were my lifeline. And maybe it was. It gave me distance that had to help eventually.

The stranglehold my ribs had on my lungs eased a fraction as the town melted into my rearview mirror. I took the turnoff onto the gravel road that would take me home.

As the small cabin came into view, I breathed a little deeper. The glow of lights beckoned. This was my haven. My safe place.

A refuge I'd created for myself. Somewhere I could let down my walls and just be. There was no feeling of eyes on me. No pressure to keep it all together when I was falling apart.

My fingers shook as I pulled the keys from the ignition. I gripped them tightly and started for the door. As soon as I was within range of the cabin, my cell started ringing again. And for the first time, I cursed the cell signal amplifier that Chris and Jude had put in for me. They'd intended it for safety, but now it felt intrusive, like maybe I wasn't so free of those eyes after all.

I struggled to get the key into the lock as Shadow let out a happy bark behind the door. Finally, I succeeded, and the door opened. Shadow danced and twirled in circles in the entryway.

I let out a laugh that turned into a sob, and she immediately stilled. Shoving the door closed, I slid to the floor. Shadow moved to me instantly, burrowing against my side. My arms came around her, and I pressed my face to her neck as I let my tears fall freely.

All the pain; the destruction of a life that had been so beautiful and held such promise. And for what? Because of five minutes. Three hundred seconds. Because Holt took the world on his shoulders and couldn't release that Superman mentality.

Five minutes had cost me a lifetime of happiness—or maybe Holt's stubborn bullheadedness had.

As livid as I was with him, my heart broke for Holt, too. The weight he carried was clearly crushing him. It had cost him his home, his family. Me. And for what? So he could play the noble, tortured hero?

My phone rang again. Grae's face lit up the screen. When the ringing stopped, a text popped up.

Grae: *If you don't answer the next time, I'm coming over there.*

My cell instantly started ringing again, and I slid my finger across the screen. "I'm fine."

"You've always been a horrible liar."

I laughed, but the sound was hoarse. "Okay, I'm not fine, but I will be."

She was quiet for a moment. "Want some company? We can watch *Little Women* for the eighty millionth time and eat our weight in popcorn."

"Thanks, G, but I think I'm just going to take a shower and go to bed."

"I'm sorry I pushed you to come. It was selfish. I just kept thinking that maybe I could have all my favorite people together again. But I hurt you, and that makes me a carp friend."

"Carp?"

"Gotta keep it clean for the little monsters."

I snorted. "You're not a carp friend. Not a crap one, either. I get you want things to go back to the way they were. But that's impossible. Tell me you see that."

The other end of the call was silent. She'd loved when Holt and I got together. Said it just meant I'd *officially* be her sister one day. And it wasn't easy for her to give up on that dream.

"G, I love you. Soul sister for life. But I can't give you this." My throat clogged, and tears filled my eyes for the millionth time tonight. "It hurts too much."

"Wren—"

"I don't hate him. I want nothing but good things for him. But I can't have him in my life the way you want me to." If he moved back for good, I might be able to see him in town occasionally and wave. Have a polite, surface conversation, even. But I couldn't watch him move on. I couldn't see him every day, watch him with Lawson's kids—maybe even *his*—knowing that we were too broken to ever find our way back to each other.

"Okay," Grae said softly. "No more meddling. I promise."

I let out a silent breath. "Thank you."

"Love you to the ends of the Earth, sister."

"And to the moon and the stars."

"Lunch tomorrow?" she asked hopefully.

"Sure. Wildfire?"

"Yes, please."

My fingers sifted through Shadow's fur. "I'll text you when I figure out my break."

"Sounds like a plan, Stan."

"'Night, G."

"Sweet dreams."

I hit end on the call. I doubted my dreams would be anything resembling sweet.

Shadow let out a low whine.

I climbed to my feet. "Sorry, girl. Let's take you out."

The snap of a twig outside my window had my movements slowing. Shadow's whine turned to a low growl.

"Probably just a curious critter." But I moved to the table in the entryway, my fingers searching the bowl of odds and ends until it closed around my Taser.

I hooked a leash to Shadow's collar and wrapped it around my wrist, then turned on the flashlight app on my phone. I listened for a moment. Nothing. Opening the door, I stepped outside.

The usual sounds greeted me. Wind rustling the pines. The scurrying of nocturnal animals.

I tightened my grip on the Taser as I moved around the house to where I'd heard the sound. The beam of my flashlight didn't land on any creatures, but as I got closer to the window that gave the best vantage point of my entire downstairs, my gaze caught on something.

A depression in the soft soil that would soon be my flower beds. A smudged shoe print.

My fingers numbly skated over my cell's screen as I stared out at the woods. It rang twice before Lawson answered.

"Everything okay, Wren?"

"I think someone was outside my house. Watching me."

Chapter Thirteen

Holt

EVERYTHING IN ME WENT WIRED AT LAWSON'S WORDS. I moved in closer, trying to make out the other end of the conversation, but he shoved me away.

"What makes you think that?" He was silent for a moment but nodded. "Get back inside. Lock the doors and windows. I'll be over in ten."

That was how long it would take to make the journey from here to Wren's cabin.

"What happened?" I barked the second he got off the phone.

Lawson held up a hand. "She's fine, but she thinks someone's been nosing around her place."

Everything in me tightened at his words. "Press?"

The tenth anniversary of the shooting was this year. My office had fielded so many inquiries for interviews I'd lost track. The media had a sick fascination with what had happened in Cedar Ridge, and thanks to some since-fired deputy, the fact that I had been the one to find Wren had gone public.

Everyone wanted a piece of that story—teenage love ripped apart by hate.

But they didn't get a piece of us. Never.

Lawson's jaw worked back and forth as he pulled his keys from his pocket. "Maybe. Kinda late for a reporter to be sniffing around. She thought she heard someone outside. Went to check it out and found a shoe print."

"She went to check it out? Why the hell didn't she call nine-one-one?"

"She probably thought it was an animal, and it might've been."

I didn't give a damn about might've beens. I cared about making sure that Wren was safe. My feet were already moving, taking me toward my SUV parked at the end of the row of vehicles.

"Where the hell do you think you're going?" Lawson clipped.

"To make sure she's okay."

"I don't think that's such a good idea."

But I was already behind the wheel and sliding my keys into the ignition.

Lawson cursed and jogged toward his SUV.

I didn't waste any time tearing down the drive. My fingers tapped the wheel as I waited for the gate to open—too damn slowly.

The second they opened wide enough, I floored it. The lights on Lawson's police SUV flashed, but I ignored him. When we reached the two-lane road that led to town, he swerved around me, forcing me to dial back my speed.

A litany of curses streamed from my lips as Lawson slowed even further on the stretch through town. The moment the buildings died away, he picked up speed again, swinging down a side road that took us toward the lake.

My gaze shifted to the clock on my dashboard. How many minutes had it been since Wren called? Lawson had promised her that he'd be there in ten. We were at eight now.

Lawson slowed as the road made a Y. The ground was rutted

and needed some serious maintenance. I hated the thought of Wren driving it in the winter.

I pulled in next to my brother as he cut his lights and was out of my SUV in a flash. He cut me off on the way to the door, giving me a hard shove. "Back off. You go up there amped up and ready to take someone's head off, and Wren is just going to get more freaked out."

My back molars ground together. "If someone's been creeping around her property, she *should* be freaked out."

"No. She should be *cautious*. There's a difference. Her being scared won't help anything."

My gut twisted at that. I hated the idea of Wren trembling, jumping at every noise. I wanted her safe, but she shouldn't have to be terrified to get there. Slowly, I let out the air my lungs had been holding prisoner and took a step back.

The tension eased from Lawson's shoulders. "Thank you." He started up the walkway. "You shouldn't even be here, you know. Unless you became law enforcement without telling me."

"I consult with law enforcement all the time."

"Not the same thing."

"So, make me a consultant."

He shook his head and rapped on the door. "It's me, Wren."

A low growl came from the other side of the door.

I arched a brow. "She got a dog?"

Wren had begged her parents her whole childhood for a pet. She'd asked for everything from a puppy to a gerbil. The most she'd ever been allowed was a goldfish. Her parents probably didn't want anything else they were supposed to take care of. *Supposed to* being the operative part of that sentence.

"Heel, Shadow. It's just Lawson."

Wren opened the door to reveal a massive Husky with the most piercing blue eyes standing guard in front of her. The dog's gaze went from Lawson to me and back again.

Wren's head jerked in my direction. "What are you doing here?"

Lawson winced. "Sorry. He overheard the call. There was no stopping him."

My eyes traced the trails that tears had left on Wren's cheeks. Some ended on her chin, while others streaked down her neck. Marks that I had put there.

"I just wanted to make sure you were okay."

Wren stared at me for the count of three. "I'm fine. Really."

Lawson cleared his throat. "Can you show me where you found the shoe print?"

She nodded, motioning around the house. "I was in the hall with Shadow. I had just hung up with Grae and heard what I thought was a twig snap. Shadow growled, which she doesn't usually do unless she's warning me that she heard something."

"Did you hear anything other than the twig snapping? Voices? Footsteps?" Lawson asked.

Wren shook her head. "Nothing…"

Her voice trailed off in a way that had me picking up my pace. "What is it?"

"Last night. Shadow growled then, too. And I thought I saw a light in the woods."

My gaze instantly went to the trees that engulfed the hillside. "Who lives up there?"

Lawson had his eyes trained there, too. "No one. The property hasn't been built on."

I turned toward Wren. "Why didn't you call Lawson then?"

Those flecks of green in her hazel eyes sparked, even in the darkness surrounding us. "I wasn't aware that I was required to call Lawson every time something went bump in the night."

A muscle in my jaw ticked. "It's reasonable to call the police if there's an intruder on your property in the middle of the night."

"It was probably teenagers looking for a place to party."

"Guys. Enough," Lawson snapped. He pulled a flashlight from his pocket and shined it along the side of the cabin.

"It was under that window," Wren said.

His beam of light stilled on a smudged footprint. Everything in me went rigid. I forced myself to step closer. "There's another one." I pointed to another less-than-perfect print. One that said whoever this was had been in a hurry to get away.

"I'm gonna grab my kit from the SUV. I'll take some photos, impressions, and measurements." Lawson looked at Wren. "You should think about staying with Grae for a few days."

"I'm not sleeping on G's couch because some nosy jerk is coming around my place. If someone wanted to hurt me, they would've done it when I pulled in tonight."

The thought had my stomach roiling. I swept the area with my gaze. The cabin. The forest. The lake—and instantly started making plans for security. She was too damn exposed in her cabin out in the open like this.

"You could stay at the guest cabin at our parents'. You know they'd love to have you," Lawson offered.

"Kerry and Nathan don't need me in their space. They have enough going on right now. I'm not letting someone scare me out of my home."

I turned back to my brother and Wren. "And you shouldn't have to."

Shock flared in her eyes. "Thanks."

"I'll stay with you."

Chapter Fourteen

Wren

"**W**HAT?" IT WAS MORE OF A SQUEAK THAN AN actual word, and I didn't miss the twitch of Holt's lips.

I scowled. "You have to be invited into someone's home. Otherwise, you might end up arrested. Right, Law?"

Lawson's eyes ping-ponged back and forth between the two of us. "I really don't want to be in the middle of this. I'm gonna get my kit." A second later, he was ducking his head and making a beeline for his SUV.

"Coward!" I yelled.

Holt snorted.

"Don't laugh," I snapped.

"Wren," he said quietly in that same soft tone that always had me caving to whatever he wanted.

I bit the inside of my cheek and forced myself not to look away. Maybe that voice had made me weak-kneed in the past, but that wasn't me anymore.

Holt moved in my direction, and Shadow stiffened. Holt

seemed to sense it more than see and dropped to a crouch. He held out a hand for her to sniff.

Shadow stretched her neck so she could take a whiff. A second later, she was taking two steps in his direction. The second after that, his fingers were sifting through her fur.

Shadow leaned into his touch, seeking more of his attention. I couldn't help but feel a little betrayed. Shadow was friendly, but she was also protective. On a night where she'd thought there was a threat to me, she shouldn't have been anywhere but by my side.

Holt tipped his head back so he could meet my gaze. "I know I don't deserve it. For a million different reasons. But let me stay anyway. I'll leave first thing in the morning. I just don't want you out here alone when someone's been skulking around."

I stared into those deep blue eyes I once thought I knew so well. "I've been out here alone for a long time."

The flicker of movement was so tiny I would've missed it if I hadn't been so attuned to everything about Holt. And that little hint of motion was nothing but pain.

"I know you have. I'm not trying to say you're incapable of taking care of yourself, just that sometimes it's nice for someone to have your back."

I'd always loved that about Holt. He was on my team first. Always. My number one fan and star pitching coach. It was one of the things I'd missed the most when he left—the feeling of not being alone in the difficulties that life could bring.

Part of me wanted to rake him over the coals for even asking. To take whatever knife he'd plunged into his chest and push it deeper. Know that he was hurting the way I was.

But when I looked into the face I'd known for all my life, I couldn't do it. Because I saw the lines that grief had carved into his features.

Holt's gaze shifted to my dog as he continued scratching her head. "I'd never be able to live with myself if something happened to you."

But something *had* happened to me. And it wasn't the bullet that had done the most damage; it was the aftermath. That had destroyed us both.

As I stared at Holt, I wondered if it had been even worse for him than it had been for me. I cursed myself to high heaven as my resolve wavered. Because as angry at him as I was, I couldn't stop myself from caring. From wanting to soothe those hurts and ease his burdens.

"One night."

Holt's eyes flew back to me. "One night."

I snapped my fingers, motioning for Shadow to follow me. She hesitated for a second and then obeyed. "I'm going to go make sure the guest room's made up."

It was. I'd changed the sheets the last time Grae had slept over after our movie night. But I needed distance. Had to breathe.

I hurried inside, ducking into the guest room the first moment I could. My legs shook as I lowered myself to the bed. "What did I do?"

I'd sat in this house less than an hour ago, telling Grae that I couldn't have this man in my life. And here I was, telling him he could stay the night?

Shadow pushed her head into my hand.

"Like you were any help. Just throw yourself at him, why don't you?"

She huffed out a breath and licked my palm.

I focused on my breathing. In for two. Out for two.

I could handle anything for one night. I wouldn't even know he was here. And by morning, Holt would be gone.

A deep ache settled in my chest at the thought.

"Nope. Nope. Nope." I pushed to my feet. "Come on." I moved around the room like a drill sergeant, checking the barracks—sheets clean and perfectly tucked in, a comforter covering the bed, and one of my grandmother's quilts at the foot of it.

As my fingers ghosted over the patchwork blanket, I could hear her voice in my head. *"I know it hurts, Birdie. And you've got a right to that pain. But think how much he must have cut himself when he walked away from you. Now, he's out there alone, half a world away, with nothing but ghosts to keep him company."*

I'd never believed her that he'd felt the sting of walking away. But I saw it now.

He lived with that pain every single day. That didn't erase what he'd done, though. To me. To us. But I didn't feel quite so alone.

As I stared down at the puzzle of colors that my grandmother had pieced together by hand, a little more of my anger bled away. I made a half-hearted attempt to hold onto it. That anger made it easier not to feel the hurt quite so deeply.

If I could distract myself by being pissed off, the longing for what might have been couldn't take me out at the knees. But I'd have to let it. Because I couldn't look into those haunted blue eyes and make Holt feel worse.

A knock sounded on my front door, and then it opened.

"Wren," Lawson called, stepping inside.

I moved to the entryway, Shadow on my heels. "Get everything you needed?"

Lawson nodded. "Dusted the windowsill for prints, too, but didn't get anything." He glanced toward the vehicles. "Holt said you were okay with him staying."

"*Okay* might be a stretch."

"I can make him leave," Lawson said. "You don't have to deal with him."

I felt a twisting sensation somewhere deep. "I can't put him through that."

Lawson stared at me for a moment. "I've never known two people who loved each other more. Not even my parents. The way you two always were around each other… Like you could sense where the other was at all times and if they needed something,"—he took a breath—"you were giving it to the other before anyone else could blink."

"Law," I croaked.

"I'm not saying you need to run off and get married, but it seems a shame that you can't at least figure out a way to be friends.

That kind of care. Seems like you should at least find your way back to that."

Footsteps sounded on the walkway, and my gaze lifted to dark blue eyes. Holt had a duffel bag slung over one shoulder as he moved toward us. I drank in everything about him as he moved.

Took in the way his white tee clung to his chest muscles, how his dark-wash jeans hugged his hips and thighs, and the way the scruff along his jaw made my fingers itch to feel the prickle of it.

No. There was no chance I could find my way to friendship with Holt. Because he still set my blood on fire.

Chapter Fifteen

Holt

THE FLOORBOARDS CREAKED BENEATH MY FEET AS I rounded the edge of the living room, peering out into the night. It had only taken an hour for me to memorize the location of each troublesome plank. I could move through this entire cabin without making a sound.

But sometimes those sounds were a comfort, a reminder that the world still registered our presence.

I slowed by the window and then stopped. I'd stood outside with Lawson earlier, putting myself in the lurker's shoes. From that position, you could see just about everywhere in the house other than the two bedrooms and the single bathroom. They would have a clear shot of the entryway, hall, and living room. Most of the kitchen and a good chunk of the loft upstairs, too.

My eyes moved to each spot, and even as tension thrummed through me at how exposed Wren would've been, the corner of my mouth kicked up as I took in the loft. Wren had turned it into an open-air screening room of sorts. A deep sectional lined two walls, bean bags were scattered on the floor, and she had a projection screen set up where everyone had a good vantage point.

I wondered how many times that room had seen *Little Women*. I swore I still knew the whole thing by heart, simply from how often Wren and Grae had forced me to watch it. But I would've viewed it a million times more—anything to have Wren's body curled around mine. To hear the soft whispers of her breath and how it hitched in certain parts and whooshed out in others.

Those memories were burned into my brain. And as painful as they were, I wouldn't have had it any other way.

I forced myself to keep moving, one more loop of the tiny cabin. As I did, I checked the lock on each window and door. Almost all of them needed replacing.

Crossing to the couch, I sank onto it and grabbed the notebook from my go bag. I pawed through the contents until I found a pencil. For the next hour, I drew diagrams of each room, marking where I'd place cameras and alarm sensors. I had a friend who lived not too far from here who owned a security systems company and could send me the gear.

My pencil scratched across the pages as I listed everything Wren would need to secure this place. I swiped my thumb back and forth under my bottom lip as I studied the drawings, the list. Something was missing.

I twisted my head to the side, cracking my neck. The answer still didn't come. I tossed the notebook onto the coffee table and returned to my duffel, searching for the smaller bag I had inside.

It didn't look like much, just a small canvas pouch. But it had been my salvation more than once as my brain tortured me night after night. It gave me something to focus on. And I'd learned that it was a great way to puzzle through jobs or problems. My team had learned that whenever we were on a tough case and got stuck, they should leave me holed up in a room with my watches.

Unzipping the bag, I carefully dumped the contents onto the table. I always had a few different watches to choose from. Different eras and issues.

Tonight, I grabbed the one I'd picked up at a flea market in London. The timepieces came from anywhere and everywhere. Some had extravagant names like Rolex and Patek Philippe. Others were classics like Timex and Swatch.

This one looked as if it had been a kid's first watch, maybe from the eighties. The art deco face held splashes of bright colors only slightly muted by the passage of time. The second hand ticked in a steady rhythm but stuck in the same spot.

I grabbed the set of tiny screwdrivers from my kit and set to work opening the back of the watch. Before long, I had it taken apart so I could assess the damage.

A floorboard creaked. I was on my feet in a flash, pulling the gun from the holster at my back.

A second later, Wren emerged from the hallway. Her eyes zeroed in on the weapon in my hand, and she swallowed hard.

Slowly, I moved to holster it again. "Did I wake you?"

She shook her head, making her hair cascade over her shoulders in waves that I wanted to trace with my fingers. "No."

"Sleep not coming easy?"

Wren huffed out a laugh. "Can't imagine why. Triggering dispatch call, creepy lurker, oh, and my ex-boyfriend deciding to take up residence in my living room."

"Hell of a day. Decide which of the three is the worst?"

She made a humming sound. "Still figuring that out." Her gaze traveled to the coffee table. "What are you doing?"

I glanced down at the hobby that had become a lifeline. "Fixing a watch."

Wren's brows rose. "You can do that?"

"Fix clocks, too." I inclined my head to the antique timepiece on her wall. "That's four and a half minutes off, you know."

"I don't really use it to tell the time. That's what my phone is for."

I shrugged, but my fingers itched to grab it off the wall and get it running smoothly again. "Wouldn't hurt to fix it anyway."

"Who taught you how to do this?"

I sat back down on the couch. "No one, really. The internet is a beautiful thing sometimes."

Wren eased forward a couple of steps. It wasn't much, but to me, it felt like the world's greatest victory.

"It's a cool thing to teach yourself to do."

I lifted my gaze to hers. "Want to see?"

Wren stilled, tension grabbing hold of her muscles. My lungs had a stranglehold on the air inside them, refusing to let go until I got her answer. She worried the side of her lip, that familiar little tell taking root in my chest.

"Okay."

Chapter Sixteen

Wren

WHAT THE HELL WAS I DOING? THIS WAS THE definition of a dumb-girl move. Like when the heroine of a slasher movie runs back into the house instead of going to her neighbor's for help.

Yet here I was, sending myself into the killer's den to get sliced and diced. And I couldn't help but think that it would be worth it, just for a little more of that hopeful gleam in Holt's eyes.

I lowered myself to the couch, putting as much distance between us as possible. It was a mistake. The second I entered his orbit, the scent of pine with a hint of spice swirled around me— part comforting hug, part brutal slash to my heart.

"What was wrong with this one?" I choked out. I had to focus on something else, anything but the memories warring to get free.

Holt's gaze swept over my face, assessing. Even my best mask wasn't enough because he would always read me like a book. No, it was more than that. He could sense what I was feeling, as if whispers of those same emotions radiated through him.

His eyes held mine for another beat, and then he turned back to the watch currently in pieces on the table. "This one has a sticky second hand."

"So, it's stuck in time?"

Holt nodded. "It ticks but doesn't make any forward progress."

"Like it's living the same moment over and over again." God, I knew how that felt. And it tended to be the worst one possible. The crushing blow of my eyes tracking over the words in Holt's letter. The one that told me he was letting me go.

Holt shifted in his seat, his assessing gaze back to probe all my scars. "It happens more than you might think."

There was a wealth of understanding in those words. And for the first time since Holt had returned, I felt a whisper of his emotions wash over me. He was trapped in the same prison, but his moment was different. Finding me on the bathroom floor. Not knowing if I was alive or dead.

I tried to put myself in his shoes and imagine what it would have been like to walk in on him like that. I'd seen the photos of the aftermath at the trial—the white tile floor smeared with so much blood it seemed impossible for anyone to have lived through it.

An image flashed in my mind. Holt crumpled on the floor, a gaping hole in his chest. I felt the panic coursing through me, the desperation to stop the blood. To help.

I shook my head, trying to rid myself of the nightmare. Holt's hand encircled mine. "Hey, what's going on?"

The burn was back, lighting up my throat and encasing my eyes. "I'm sorry."

His fingers lifted to my face, ghosting over my cheek and brushing the hair out of my eyes. "What do you have to be sorry for?"

"I'm sorry you found me like that."

Holt's hand stilled. "I just wish I had been earlier."

"Don't. Please, don't wish that." My gaze lifted to his, the pull undeniable. "They would've hurt you, too. Could've killed you."

His fingers tightened in my hair. "I don't care. We would've found a way out. A way through."

"You did find that. You kept me breathing. Kept me alive. You think that's nothing?"

A muscle fluttered in Holt's jaw. "It's not nearly enough. You shouldn't have had to face it alone."

My gaze locked on Holt's. "I need you to do something for me."

He didn't say a word.

I looked at the watch. "I haven't asked you for anything, not for almost ten years." Not since he'd left me with only a goodbye scribbled on some notebook paper. "I need you to do just one thing for me."

"What?" The single word was a hoarse whisper.

I lifted my head so I could look into Holt's eyes, our faces just a breath away from each other. "Forgive yourself. Let this go before it destroys you."

It had already cost him so much: our relationship. His bond with his family. It was time to release these demons.

Holt stared at me, and so much emotion swirled in those deep blue depths. "I don't know if I can."

My hand locked around his wrist, squeezing. "If I don't blame you, you sure as hell shouldn't blame yourself. Honestly, it's insulting that you think I would."

"I don't—I just…"

"You what?"

"It tortures me. The thought of you alone and scared. Knowing they were coming and having to hide in a damn cabinet, just praying you'd be safe. Seeing the gun and knowing what was coming. And you were alone. I can't stand that you were alone."

"I wasn't."

Holt's hand flinched as his expression filled with endless questions.

"You were with me. In that moment where I knew what was coming? I pictured you. Imagined what it felt like to have your arms around me."

"Wren." My name was a ravaged sound on his lips.

"So, you didn't leave me alone." Not until he walked away and didn't look back.

Holt's forehead pressed to mine. Our breaths mingled. "Wren..."

It would be so easy to close that distance. To remember what it felt like to lose myself in Holt's arms, instead of having to imagine each night as I fell asleep. But how much worse would it hurt if he walked away again?

I jerked back. "I need to go to bed. I have work tomorrow."

I bolted for my bedroom before Holt had a chance to say another word. But as I climbed beneath the sheets and burrowed against Shadow's side, I knew sleep wouldn't find me tonight.

As I stepped out of the bathroom, I listened. At first, there was nothing. Then I heard a soft hum.

I let a few curses fly under my breath. So much for leaving first thing in the morning. I started for the kitchen, refusing to take the coward's way out and making a run for my truck.

As I rounded the corner, I blinked. The bar counter was set with two placemats and cloth napkins. Little bowls of sliced fruit were on one side, and glasses of orange juice on the other. Shadow let out a happy bark as she danced around the space. And there, looking right at home, was Holt.

"I hope you don't mind. I took her out a little bit ago," Holt said as he slid two scrambles with toast onto the place settings.

"Uh, yeah. That's fine." I stared at the sight in front of me. "What is this?"

That devilish smile spread across Holt's face. "Pretty sure it's breakfast."

I glared at him. "I know that."

His grin only grew. "Breakfast is the most important meal of the day, and from what I remember, cereal was about all you had mastered."

"I know how to cook." I wasn't a chef by any means, but I could handle the basics. I just hated doing it. The memories of that night had ruined all culinary attempts, so I lived on frozen meals and takeout most of the time. The fact that Holt had found enough ingredients to make the feast before us was shocking.

He pulled out one of the stools. "Sit. Please. I want to run something by you."

I eyed him warily but lowered myself to the stool. The scramble smelled amazing.

"Why are you glaring at your breakfast?" Holt asked as he sat next to me.

"Because it smells so good."

He chuckled. "And that's a bad thing?"

I let out a huff of air. I didn't need Holt in here making amazing breakfasts and looking all sexy with his mussed hair and perfectly fitted T-shirt. A pang lanced my heart. How many T-shirts had I stolen from him over the years? Even now, they were shoved in a box in the back of my closet. I didn't want to look at them every day, but I couldn't bear to get rid of them either.

I popped a piece of banana into my mouth. "What did you want to talk to me about?"

He opened the notebook that lay between us. "This is what I'd like to do for a security system for you. Cameras at all the entry points and over a few windows. Motion detectors here, here, and here. Alarm sensors on windows and doors. Panic buttons in each room. We could also think about turning that hall closet into a panic room."

I gaped at Holt. "Have you been drinking the drugs?"

"If you mean coffee, then yes."

"No, I mean some crazy hallucinogenic something that would make you think I'd let you turn my cozy cabin into a superspy lair."

Holt leaned back, taking me in. "I'm not turning your cabin into a superspy lair. I'm making it secure."

"*You're* not doing anything. This is my home. I say what comes into these four walls and what doesn't."

A muscle in his cheek ticked. "Someone was lurking around your house. You need things in place to keep yourself safe."

"There are locks on all my doors and windows, and I use them. I've got a cell signal amplifier so I can always make and receive calls. That's enough."

"I could break those window locks in two seconds, and it would take me less than fifteen to pick the locks on your doors."

I scowled at Holt. "The only thing that proves is that you've picked up some delinquent hobbies in the past ten years."

He scoffed. "It means this place isn't safe. Unless you want me sleeping in your spare room every night—"

"Excuse me? I let you stay for one night. *One.* Because you gave me that damn wounded look. You aren't staying another. And you sure as hell don't get to show up after a decade and try to take over. If I decide I need an alarm system, then I'll call the company in town."

"Wren—"

The doorbell ringing cut Holt off.

"Wren, you okay?" Chris called. "There's a weird SUV in your drive."

I cursed but slid off the stool and headed for the front of the cabin. "I'm fine." I flipped the lock and opened the door.

Chris's concerned gaze went to me and then the hulking figure behind me. His jaw tightened. "Holt."

The behemoth behind me didn't say anything for a moment, simply stared. "Morning."

I made big eyes at Jude, who was behind Chris, trying his damnedest not to laugh. He coughed. "Morning, Little Williams. Just wanted to check on you before we headed to the jobsite."

"Police calls should be confidential."

"Public record, Cricket," Holt said from behind me.

"Well, they shouldn't be."

Chris's eyes ping-ponged from me to Holt and back again. "We ran into Nash at the diner this morning."

"Remind me to *thank* him later," I mumbled.

Chris squeezed my shoulder. "Why didn't you call? You know you could've come to stay with me if you were freaked."

"I was fine. I just had Lawson come check things out as a precaution."

"Which was the smart thing to do," Holt said gruffly.

Chris's gaze shifted to Holt. "And you decided to play bodyguard."

He shrugged. "Just wanted to make sure she was okay."

"That was good of you," Chris said but didn't sound all that convincing. "Wren, why don't you pack a bag and stay with me for a while? Just until Lawson figures out what's going on."

The anger from behind me hit me like a blast. I pinched the bridge of my nose. "I appreciate the help—all of you. But what I need right now is to get ready for work in peace. I'm not staying with anyone. I'm not installing some NASA security system in my house. None of it."

I strode to the living room and grabbed Holt's duffel. "Thank you for looking out for me, but I'm good."

"Wren—"

"Please. Can you all just go?"

Jude sent me a sympathetic look and grabbed the back of Chris's jacket. "Come on. We need to get to work."

"But—" Chris started.

"No buts," Jude cut him off. "Let's leave the lady in peace."

Holt didn't say a word. He simply waited for Chris and Jude to leave and then followed them out. His steps faltered, and he turned to look at me. His mouth opened as if he were about to say something, but he simply shook his head.

The snick of my door shutting echoed around the space, reverberating off my bones. And all I could think about was how easy it had been for Holt to walk out that door.

Chapter Seventeen

Holt

I SUCKED IN A BREATH, AND THE AIR TREMBLED WITH THE force of me trying to keep my temper in check. I glared at Chris. "What's going on with you and Wren?"

"None of your damn business."

My nostrils flared. "She will always be my business. And you know that."

Chris huffed out a breath, his gaze straying to the lake.

It was Jude who spoke. "We're friends. That's it."

Maybe that was true of Jude, but Chris looked at Wren like a man dying of thirst looked at a glass of water.

"Someone had to step in when you bailed," Chris muttered. "She needed someone. Her parents were checked out, and she was a wreck. She was *dying*. Not because of some bullet, but because of *you*."

Each word was a carefully placed blow designed to inflict maximum damage.

Jude clamped a hand on Chris's shoulder. "C'mon, man."

Chris shrugged him off. "It's true. We might be able to get

over the fact that he bailed on us, but Holt destroyed her, and he shouldn't get the chance to do it again."

Chris stormed toward his truck as I stared after him. Wren's words echoed in my ears. *"I don't give a damn about the five minutes you missed that night. I give a damn about the last ten years you threw away."*

I'd thought I was doing the right thing. But all I'd done was inflict more damage on everyone around me.

"Give him some time," Jude said. "He's protective of Wren, but it's more than that. He was hurt when you left."

Because leaving before I told a soul was the only way I could've done it. "I'm sorry. If I'd been stronger, I would've kept in touch. I just knew that if I kept hearing about home, about *her*, I wouldn't have been strong enough to stay away. And I thought staying away was the right thing."

Jude nodded. "I get that. It's still gonna take some time to mend fences."

Understatement of the century. But if I didn't try, I would keep living this half-life that was slowly eating me alive as memories tortured me. I had to make things right and heal what I could— as people would let me.

I met Jude's gaze. "I'm staying. I don't know for how long, but at least for the foreseeable future. I want to make things right." More than that, I wanted to atone.

"Good." Chris's truck started, and Jude glanced over his shoulder. "I'd better go before he leaves my ass."

I nodded, pulling my keys from my pocket and starting for my SUV. "Hey, Jude?"

"Yeah."

"Thanks for not decking me when I showed up."

He barked out a laugh. "Don't think I didn't consider it."

I grinned. "If I offer Chris one free shot, do you think it would help?"

"Couldn't hurt."

I shook my head as I climbed behind the wheel of my SUV. It

would be worth it for a clean slate with the friends I'd had all my life. But they weren't the only ones I needed a fresh start with.

I stared at the cabin. Leaving felt every kind of wrong, but I worried if I pushed too hard now, I'd lose those glimmers of hope I'd found with Wren last night.

I forced myself to start my SUV and hit Lawson's contact on my phone as I headed toward my parents' property. He answered on the third ring. "Everything okay?"

"Do you ever answer the phone any other way?"

Lawson grunted. "When you have two teenage hell-raisers, one accident-prone six-year-old, and you're the chief of police, people tend to call when there's a problem. Wren doing okay?"

"Happily kicked my ass to the curb this morning."

Lawson chuckled. "I think it's a hell of a lot of progress that you lasted almost twelve hours."

It didn't feel like progress; it felt like torture. Two steps forward, one step back. Except each inch I gained was a reminder of everything I'd missed these past years. "Any updates?"

"I submitted the shoe print last night because I knew you'd be hounding me. It came back as a common, unisex work boot. Hard to get an exact size because the prints were smudged."

"Not exactly narrowing things down."

The boys' voices rose in the background, and then the sound of a door closing came across the line. "I can't do much else unless someone shows up again."

Just the thought of that had rage pulsing through my veins. "I drew up security plans for Wren's place."

"And how did she take that?"

"About as well as you can imagine."

Lawson chuckled. "Holt, you two have a shot to find your way. But you'll kill that if you come in after being gone for a decade and start trying to boss her around."

"That's pretty much what she said. Just without the *you-two-have-a-shot* part."

He coughed, and I knew it was to hide outright laughter. "Listen to the woman."

"I need to know she's safe."

"I get that. I'll have officers stopping by Wren's place regularly. But you might try just *talking* to her. Tell her your concerns and ask if it would be okay if you used your contacts to get her a screaming deal on a security system. But you have to listen to her input on it."

"Why'd you have to go and be all logical?" I grumbled.

"Big brother's job."

"Thanks for sticking with me."

"Always. We've all had our struggles, and none of us is perfect. I sure as hell can't claim to be. I'm just happy you're back—for however long you can stay."

I rolled down my window to punch the code Mom had given me into the intercom. "Means more than I can say. And I'm glad I'm back, too." Even if it was the hardest thing in the world.

"Stop by the station later. We can do a little sparring if I'm not too slammed."

"I'd love that." More than that, I needed it. And Law wouldn't pull his punches. He craved the brutal outlet the same way I did.

"See you later."

"Later."

I hung up, pulling through the gates and heading higher up the mountain. There was no large collection of my siblings' vehicles this morning. I just had to hope Dad was home.

I pulled to a stop in front of the house and turned off the engine. Sliding out of my SUV, I glanced up at the home I'd grown up in. My gaze caught on a figure in one of the rocking chairs.

With a deep breath, I started up the steps. "Morning, Dad."

He looked up at me but didn't say a word. He appeared older in that moment. Not sick or frail but tired. As if life had thrown him one too many curveballs.

He patted the rocker next to him. "Take a seat."

Now was as good a time as any to start my atonement journey.

I lowered myself to the chair, the blades of the rocker thumping against the porch in a rhythmic sound. "Dad—"

"Don't," he cut me off.

My rocking stilled.

"I have some things I need to say."

I braced. If I wanted that atonement, I'd have to take whatever the people in my life dished out. "Okay."

"I've been an ass to you since you got home."

My brows rose at that. Factually, I didn't disagree, but it was more complicated than that. "I'd say you were justified."

Dad grunted, staring off at the horizon. The view was breathtaking and the whole reason he'd bought the property to begin with. It had a vantage point that let you look down on Cedar Ridge—the forests, the town, the lake. It was so quiet up here; it was as if the air itself had gone still.

"I didn't know how to help you," he said, still not looking at me. "I knew you were twisted up inside, but I didn't have the tools to make any of it better. When you left, I thought maybe it was what you needed. A fresh start. A purpose."

"That's what I thought, too." I saw now that I had been looking for a way to prove to myself that I could be trusted. That I could protect those who needed it. Some small part of me hoped that if I could do that, then maybe I could find my way back home.

"Your mom always saw it for what it was."

I glanced over at him in question.

"Running from the demons tormenting you."

My grip on the rocker's arms tightened. I hated that she could see that. Hated the worry it must've caused her. "I thought it was the right thing at the time."

Dad turned to face me, his deep blue eyes so much like mine. "And why's that?"

My jaw clamped tight, not wanting to let the words free. "I didn't protect her. She'd been let down so many times, and I promised her I would always be there for her. When she needed me the most, I was nowhere to be found."

He blew out a long breath. "Holt. That shooting wasn't on you. Those kids were sick. Twisted. If they wanted to find a way to hurt her, they would've succeeded. And I'm damn glad they didn't have to go through you to do it."

"Dad—"

He held up a hand. "I hate what Wren went through; it kills me. Neither of you should've had to face what you did. But you can't be with someone twenty-four-seven. It's impossible. Accidents happen. Horrible tragedies. Evil. That's life. What matters is sticking with the people you love through it all."

That fire lit, swirling deep and burning everything in its wake. "And I didn't."

My dad looked me straight in the eye. "You didn't. And you need to face that. It won't be easy. But you have to find a way to take ownership of your actions while having empathy for the boy who was scared out of his mind."

"Not sure you can have both of those things." From a very clinical viewpoint, I saw why I'd made the choices I had. But the self-hatred was such a loud drumbeat in the back of my skull.

"You have to let yourself feel both. Don't run away from it." He leaned back in his chair. "I haven't been great with talking to you kids about that kind of thing. It wasn't what I was taught growing up. But running from it just ends up hurting us all."

"Like running from the fact that you were pissed as hell at me."

The corners of his mouth tipped up. "That might've been building for some years."

"I'm sorry, Dad."

"No. I needed to let myself feel that anger and then tell you about it. Tell you that I was hurt you didn't find a way to spend more time with us. With me. Instead, I let it build. When I had my heart attack, it scared the hell out of me. All I could think about was all the wasted time. How I had this grown son that I barely knew."

Guilt gnawed at my insides. The idea of my father battling this guilt while recovering from two major surgeries had self-hatred flaring to life again. "Dad…"

"There are two people in this relationship. We are both responsible for saying what we want. And what I want is a relationship with my son. A real one. One where we're honest, even if it hurts."

"I'd say you've been honest lately."

My dad winced. "Okay, we're honest but we do it with a little more kindness and grace."

I took him in, reading nothing but honesty in his face. "I'd like that."

He clamped a hand on my shoulder and squeezed. "Good. Now, tell me what the hell is going on with some creep loitering around Wren's house."

Chapter Eighteen

Wren

THE LIGHTS IN THE BREAK ROOM HUMMED AS I STARED at the coffee spilling into my mug. I willed it to magically have more caffeine. Okay, something more than caffeine—maybe just shy of cocaine. Shoving the pot back under the drip, I poured creamer into the inky blackness.

Amber strode in wearing street clothes and grabbed a takeout container from the fridge. She let out a low whistle as she took me in. "Rough night?"

"That obvious?"

She winced. "Just look a little tired."

"Didn't get the best sleep." Understatement of the century. Maybe I could get one of the EMTs to give me an IV and pour the coffee directly into it.

"You didn't have any more incidents at your place, did you?"

I tried to hide my wince. Small town. Working for the department. Nothing was private. "No, nothing like that."

Not unless you counted an overbearing ex-boyfriend and nosy friends.

"Good." Amber idled for a moment. "I'm off the rest of the day and tonight. If you'd feel better with someone at your place tonight, just give me a call."

I had to fight the urge to rear back. It wasn't that Amber was ever rude to me, it was that I could feel her grief every time she was forced to be in my presence. The fact that she would even offer to come and stay said a heck of a lot about her character. "Thanks, Amber. I really appreciate that."

"No problem." She gave me a sort of half wave and headed for the door.

I leaned back against the counter and took a long drink of my coffee. "Please give me a miracle," I whispered into my cup.

"Talking to beverages now? Should I be worried?"

My gaze snapped up at the familiar, raspy tone. But I wished I hadn't looked. Holt wore workout shorts that hung low on his hips and a T-shirt that clung to every ridge of muscle. I swallowed. Hard. "What are you doing here?"

He stepped into the break room, and I fought the urge to flee. "Meeting Lawson for a sparring session, but I was hoping we could talk. Do you have a minute?"

I wondered if I could chug the coffee first. I needed all my synapses firing at full speed for a conversation with Holt. "I've got five minutes left on my break."

He nodded and shut the door behind him.

The room suddenly felt too small—as if the walls were closing in around me and making it hard to breathe. And even though Holt was still feet away, I swore I smelled that blend of pine and spice. Either that or I was having some sort of scent hallucinations now.

Holt twisted his keys around his finger. "I'm sorry I steamrolled you this morning. I'm used to coming into a problem and having people expect me to fix it."

"I'm not a problem," I gritted out.

His eyes flashed. "No, but someone creeping around your place is. I've worked more stalking cases than I can count. I just wanted to help. But, instead, I was overbearing and rude. I'm sorry."

What was I supposed to say to that? It was hard to hold onto my mad when Holt was being all reasonable. "Thanks."

He gripped the keys tighter. "I would like to help if you'd be comfortable with it."

"Holt, it's a bad idea."

"Cricket, there's nothing I can do that will fix the past. There's not much I have to give *now*. But I can give this. It's what I do, and I'm damn good at it."

The sincerity and the deep pain beneath it were too much. I felt those danged walls I'd constructed to keep Holt at a distance crumbling. "No motion detectors, and no cameras inside the house."

A grin stretched across his face. "I can work with that."

"And we need to talk price. It has to be affordable. We come up with a budget before you order anything."

"Totally fair. My friend owns the company I use for alarm components, so he'll get us a good deal."

I arched a brow. "Is this company good?"

"Halo security systems are the best in the business. You know I wouldn't put anything less in your house."

I did know, damn it. And I'd also seen that name before on homes and businesses. "Okay. Let me crunch some numbers, and I'll figure out what I can afford."

Holt's Adam's apple bobbed as he swallowed. "Thanks for letting me do this. For trusting me with it."

There was that dangerous T-word. Did I *trust* Holt? With my life? Yes. Without hesitation. With my traitorous heart? Never again.

"Sure. I need to get back."

A little of the smile slipped from Holt's face. "Of course. Just text me when you have a budget."

I still had Holt's number in my phone. I'd never managed to work up the courage to delete it as if some part of me were still holding onto hope that it would flash on my phone someday.

I forced the memories from my mind and nodded, slipping around him and out the door. I maneuvered through a scattering of desks until I got to the dispatch corner. Abel's gaze lifted to me, surveying. "You okay?"

"Right as rain."

He grunted. "That boy looks like you just stole his last cookie."

I couldn't help taking a quick glance over my shoulder. Holt's focus was zeroed in on me, his thumb skating back and forth under his bottom lip. The move was so familiar it lit an ache in the deepest parts of me. Igniting a wish that things could be different. That I could erase the last ten years somehow and change that day and everything that followed.

I jerked my gaze back to my computer. "Definitely wasn't me."

Abel snorted. "Whatever you say."

The phone rang, and I hurried to slip my headset on. "Cedar Ridge police, fire, and medical. What's your emergency?"

"Oh, God. Oh, God. Oh, God." A woman's voice cut across the line, breathy and staccato.

"Ma'am, can you tell me what's happening?" I quickly scanned the readout as the woman continued her chant. "Ms. Peterson. You need to tell me what's going on so I can help you."

"H-he's dead. I think he's dead."

"Who's dead?" My hands flew across the keyboard as Abel got on the radio to alert officers.

"Albert. I—oh, God. I think someone shot him."

Blood pounded in my ears as the world around me tunneled. Albert Peterson. My sophomore biology and junior chemistry teacher. The man who had always looked at me with kindness. Who had always taken those extra minutes to check in and make sure I was doing okay. One of the members of that club no one wanted to be a member of but were thankful for just the same. A survivor.

"Ms. Peterson. Where are you?"

"I j-just got home, and he was lying on the kitchen floor."

"I need you to check and see if you can feel a pulse or determine if he's breathing."

"There's so much blood."

Flashes of memories cycled in my mind. The fire in my chest. The cool tile beneath me. The sticky substance tracking down my arm.

I bit the inside of my cheek, hard. "I know it's scary, but you can do this. Officers and EMTs are on their way to you now."

The room behind me was in an uproar. I knew everyone but two officers would take this call. Off-duty cops would flood the place in minutes, wanting to offer their help and support. And our community would lose their mind.

"Oh, God. He's breathing."

All the air left me in a whoosh. "That's good. Can you see the wound?"

"It's in his chest or his shoulder." Ms. Peterson struggled to get the words out around her sobs.

"Grab a towel and put pressure on the wound. We want to do everything we can to slow the blood loss."

"I've got one."

A low moan sounded in the background.

"I'm so sorry, Al. I'm so sorry I'm hurting you."

"Ms. Peterson, is anyone else in the house with you? Did you see anyone when you came in?"

"No, no one. Who would do this?" Her words were a hushed plea.

I didn't know. The kind of cruelty it would take to do this to a man who had already been through hell was almost too much to comprehend. "Are there any weapons in the home?"

"No. Nothing like that."

I could hear Abel relaying all this information to the responding officers.

"I hear sirens. They're coming."

"Just stay on the phone with me until they tell you otherwise."

"Don't let him die." Ms. Peterson's voice trembled with the force of her sobs. "Please, don't let him die. I almost lost him once…"

Silent tears streamed down my face. "Keep fighting. For both of you."

"Cedar Ridge police."

I recognized Nash's voice across the line.

Ms. Peterson's sobs just came harder. "Help him. Please, help him."

There were muffled calls of "clear" and then Nash's voice was in my ear. "We've got her, Wren."

"O-okay." It was only then that my voice trembled. Knowing she was safe. That Mr. Peterson had a fighting chance now that help had arrived.

I pulled my headset off in a shaky daze, barely aware as I hung up the call. The world around me had a fuzzy quality to it like an old television set with a weak signal.

Someone swung my chair around. I couldn't make out the face, only a blurry form. It was the scent that told me everything. Pine with a hint of spice.

I didn't think, I simply threw myself at Holt. His arms wrapped around me. I wasn't sure if I was crying or simply shaking but Holt was my anchor. The only way I could stay in the here and now.

He held me, and he didn't let go.

Chapter Nineteen

Holt

I HAD THE BURNING URGE TO PICK UP WREN, RUN, AND NEVER stop. She trembled against me. I didn't know much; had only heard the initial call come over Lawson's radio as we were getting ready to spar.

Shooting victim.

I gripped Wren tighter. How could she do this job? She chanced being reminded of the worst moment of her life every day.

She pushed against my chest, trying to free herself from my hold. It took everything in me to release her.

Wren struggled to get her breathing under control. Her lips formed silent words, and I realized that she was counting. Inhaling for two. Exhaling for two.

"Sorry," she croaked.

I scowled. "You know you don't have to apologize. Not to me."

She stared at me for a moment, and I saw her struggle to put the pieces of her mask back into place—the one made of cool indifference. I wanted to rip the thing to shreds.

"It was a shock. I wasn't expecting"—she took a breath—"I wasn't expecting Mr. Peterson."

Alarm shot through me, that warning signal that had been finely honed over the past decade.

"I should get back to work. Thanks for…" Her voice trailed off as if finishing the sentence was too difficult.

"You can take a minute to breathe."

Her eyes flashed. "No. I can't. Not in this job. It needs my complete focus no matter what the call is."

My jaw clenched, but I nodded. "I'll be in the gym if you need me."

Because I needed to punch the hell out of something.

I leveled a jab, hook, cross combination at the bag. Sweat flew against the leather as I made contact each time. But it wasn't enough. I needed something that would hit back.

A low whistle sounded, and I jerked around. Nash strode into the gym, Lawson on his heels. "You gettin' ready to take on a fight with the devil?"

I grabbed a towel from the rack on the wall and wiped it over my face and chest.

Lawson tossed me a water bottle. "Desk clerk said you've been in here all afternoon."

What else was I supposed to do? I wasn't leaving, and hovering behind Wren's desk seemed like a piss-poor decision. "Needed to work some stuff out. Tell me what happened."

Lawson and Nash shared a look.

"Tell me," I growled.

Lawson sighed. "They think Albert Peterson will make it. Had to be airlifted to Seattle, but he made it through surgery."

A little of the tightness in my chest subsided. "Any suspects?"

Nash shook his head. "Not yet. Shot came through the window into the kitchen. I doubt he ever saw it coming."

"Footprints?"

"No," Lawson said. "Came from the woods behind the house. There's a layer of pine needles an inch thick."

"You search for other trace? Fibers. Skin."

Lawson arched a brow. "I look like a probationary officer to you?"

I let out a huff of air. "Sorry."

Nash waved me off. "We get it. This is a whole other level of messed-up."

I took a pull from the water bottle. "The wife have any insights? Enemies? Threats?"

"He's a high school science teacher. Not exactly a member of the Russian mob," Nash muttered.

My gaze narrowed on him. "Peterson made some enemies before, and he probably didn't even know it. All it took was a couple of bad science grades."

"That was different," Lawson said.

The muscle along my jaw fluttered. "You have to look at every angle."

"And we will. But I don't want to set this community into a panic if I don't have to," Lawson shot back. "We are talking to neighbors, coworkers, students. If someone had it out for him, we'll find them. But his house butts up to the forest. It's possible this was simply a stray bullet from a hunter."

My gut wasn't so sure about that, but I nodded. "Okay."

"Gonna give in just like that and let big brother do his job?" Nash asked with mock shock.

I gave him a shove. "Screw off."

Nash cracked his neck. "Oh, I'd like to do exactly that, but I'm not off for another three hours."

I grabbed my T-shirt and pulled it over my head. "Don't do anything stupid."

When life got serious, Nash did anything to distract himself from the feelings. Raced his motorcycle. Went BASE jumping off a mountain. Got blind, stinking drunk in the name of fun.

Nash's eyes twinkled. "Who, me?"

Lawson glared at him. "You get arrested, and I'm not doing a damn thing to pull you out of trouble."

Nash patted his shoulder. "You've made that abundantly clear, boss man."

"I gotta grab a shower. Will you let me know if there are any updates?"

Lawson's mouth pressed into a firm line, but then he sighed. "Fine."

I met his gaze, making sure he understood the gravity of what I was asking. "Thank you."

He waved me off. "Get outta my gym. You stink."

I chuckled and headed for the door. As I rounded the corner, Jude came striding through reception, worry on his face. "Hey. You and Wren okay?"

I glanced in the direction of dispatch. She was laser-focused as she typed on her computer. "I think everyone's hanging in there."

Jude followed my gaze. "Not like she'd share if there was hell inside her head." He looked back at me. "Keep trying. She'll never let Chris or me in the way she used to talk to you. I don't think she opens up to Grae like that either."

"I'm pretty sure I'm the last person she'd open up to right now."

He shook his head. "You're wrong. It might take time, but you're the person she needs."

"You sound pretty certain."

Jude shrugged. "I've known you both for a long time. Long enough to know that you've been miserable as hell without each other. I don't want that for the people I care about. That regret will eat you up inside."

I studied him for a moment. "Sounds like you're speaking from experience."

Jude's jaw tightened. "Had something good. Let life get in the way of it. Don't want that to happen to you."

"I'm sorry, man."

"Me, too." He squeezed the back of his neck. "Don't be an idiot like me. Fix it."

He didn't give me a chance to reply. He simply turned on his heel and strode out of the station.

Fix it. I didn't have the first idea how I was supposed to do that when the woman in question could barely stand the sight of me. But I knew one thing: I'd need to stick around to have a chance in hell.

Chapter Twenty

Wren

I TRUDGED OUT OF THE STATION AND INTO THE LATE afternoon sun. Typically, that crisp, clean air would be enough to soothe away whatever had happened on shift. Not today.

The latest update from Seattle told us that Mr. Peterson was in serious but stable condition. How many times had he asked me to call him Albert? Too many to count. But he was forever in that teacher spot in my mind, and I couldn't get myself to call him anything that didn't have a *Mr.* before it.

When he was well enough to come home, I'd make myself call him Albert. I'd move us on from that place we'd been frozen in for so many years. That I'd been frozen in. It was time. I had to let it go. The pain. The fear. The grief. I had to if I wanted a shot at a full life.

I started toward the parking lot and my truck, but the thought of having to cook something when I got home had me changing directions and heading across the street to Dockside. A cheese-burger, french fries, and a chocolate milkshake the size of my head. There was no way that couldn't make things better.

As I jogged across the street, my stomach tightened at the sight of the familiar figure. His head was dipped low, a scowl on his face. He looked so similar to his brother that I forced myself to smile whenever I saw Joe Sullivan. But I refused to treat him the way so many others in town did—like he was just as guilty as Randy.

"Hi, Joe."

The teen's head jerked up. There was a flash of something in his eyes, and then the scowl was back in place. "Hey."

Joe lowered his head again, and I couldn't help but turn as he passed, tracking him with my eyes. He was alone every time I saw him. I got the temptation; it was easier than wondering what your *friends* might be saying behind your back.

I'd had a few people that I thought I could trust probe for sordid details about the shooting, only to turn around and share them with anyone who would listen—including the press. That kind of betrayal cut deep.

But I had Grae. My gran. Kerry and Nathan. Lawson and Nash. Even Roan had my back. When he'd heard that a couple of boys were hassling me, they'd shown up the next day with black eyes and busted lips. They didn't bother me again.

Who did Joe have? I knew his parents were basically nonexistent. And they didn't have any other family that I knew of—and I hadn't heard of any other friends.

A heaviness settled in my chest. I hoped that after graduation, Joe got the heck out of here and found somewhere he could start fresh and build a new life.

"Was he bothering you?"

The familiar rasp of Holt's voice had me spinning around on the sidewalk. "What?"

"Was Joe bothering you?"

"No." I shook my head. "I was just spacing out. Long day."

My gaze caught on the duffel slung over Holt's shoulder. It wasn't the small one he'd brought out of his SUV last night. This one was larger. My throat tightened as I struggled to swallow. "Going back to your life?"

Since the moment he'd shown up, I'd wanted nothing more than for Holt to leave so I could go back to the *normal* I'd created for myself. It was safe. But it was also slowly killing me. Like drinking a little bit of poison every day.

Seeing Holt again had reminded me of how I'd used to *live*. How we could find fun in the silliest and simplest things. How at peace I'd once felt. It hurt like hell to remember that, but it was so much worse to pretend that it hadn't existed at all.

Holt's eyes flared. "Actually, I was going to your place. I wanted to see if I could stay in your extra room."

My heart lurched, a painful stutter step in my chest. "Why?"

The corner of his mouth kicked up. "I need a place to stay that isn't run by nosy busybodies."

I glanced over his shoulder and, sure enough, Ms. Peabody had peeked her head out of the front door of the B&B and was even now watching us like a hawk.

I groaned. "Why is she the worst?"

He chuckled. God, that sound—it was just like I imagined it would be. Deeper. Richer. Like a smoky whiskey that heated you from the inside out. I wanted to drown in that chuckle.

"She has taken it as her personal mission to know everything that happens in this town."

"And to disseminate the information to every person she comes across," I grumbled.

"Yeah, I'd like to get out from under that surveillance. Especially since I'm sticking around for a while."

My traitorous heart picked up its pace. "How long?"

Holt's thumb swept back and forth across the stubble below his lip. "For the foreseeable future. I need someplace to stay until I can find a longer-term rental." His deep blue eyes swirled as they bored into mine. "And I hate the idea of you being out at the cabin alone. Especially after today."

A riot of emotions warred inside me. But that seemed my new normal as long as Holt was around. "It's not your job to protect me."

I didn't say it to be cruel, and that much came across in my tone. It was a simple fact. I'd loved how Holt wanted to care for and protect me a decade ago, but he'd given that away when he let me go. In some ways, it had been a good thing. I'd learned to stand on my own two feet and take care of myself. If Holt had stuck around, I wasn't sure I ever would have done that.

He stared at me, not looking away. "I know it's not. But let me do it anyway."

Those eyes that I had gazed into for over half my life pleaded with me now. They were the same ones that had danced with laughter as Grae and I reenacted scenes from *Little Women*, forcing him and Nash to play Amy and Meg in our band of sisters. The same ones that had filled with tears the day we'd almost lost Grae. The same ones that had shone with love the first time he'd said those three little words to me.

There was only one thing I could say now.

"Okay."

My bare feet plodded along the grass as I walked toward the water, Shadow at my side. The sun sank lower in the sky, painting it a beautiful cascade of colors. This time of day usually calmed me, but now my body was strung tight, on alert, listening for any hint of sound.

The crunch of tires on gravel wound my muscles tighter. I didn't turn around. I stayed focused on the horizon.

Shadow let out a bark, and I patted her head. She would have my back always.

A vehicle door opened and shut.

Shadow let out another bark, this one happier, and then took off running. That had me turning. I watched as my dog happily leaped at Holt's arrival.

He let out a laugh that carried on the breeze. That sound had barely changed, a little deeper now maybe, but the sound itself, the way it was shaped, was just the same.

Holt gave my girl a good rubdown and then picked up a stick and tossed it in the direction of the lake. Shadow took off running as if she were on a single-minded mission. Holt grinned. "She might make a good SAR dog."

"Law said the same thing. I keep meaning to do some training with her, but there never seems to be enough time."

He nodded as he moved in my direction. "I could start her on some stuff. I'm rusty, but I bet my dad would help."

My brows lifted at that.

"We talked," Holt said. "It's far from perfect, but it's better."

"I'm glad." And I meant those words. I wanted healing for Holt and his family. Healing for all of us.

"Whatcha got in the bag?" Holt asked hopefully.

I glanced toward where I'd set the takeout bag and an array of drinks on the edge of the firepit. Four Adirondack chairs circled it. This spot had become one of my favorites since buying the cabin. And now I was opening it to him.

"Burgers and fries."

Holt eyed the drinks. "That a root beer float for me?"

My cheeks flushed. When I'd walked into Dockside to order, knowing that Holt was coming here, I couldn't stop myself from placing the order I had done before too many times to count. I hadn't missed the way Jeanie's eyes had flared at hearing the words pass my lips, but she hadn't said a thing.

"It's a preemptive measure. I don't want you trying to steal any of my milkshake."

A smile stretched across Holt's face that hit me right in the stomach. "You're a goddess among mortals."

I rolled my eyes and began pulling food out of the bag as Shadow ran back for another round of fetch with her new best friend. "Just a smart mortal who doesn't want her dessert stolen."

"That, too."

Grabbing Holt's burger and fries, I offered them to him. His hands closed around mine, a brush of skin against skin that I'd felt so many times before. Only now, I didn't take it for granted. I soaked up the buzz of awareness, letting the hum of sensation soak deep into my bones and hoping I'd be able to keep it there forever.

The slight tightening of his fingers around mine told me that Holt felt it, too. "Thank you. I'm starving."

His voice was just a little deeper, huskier.

I hurried to pull my hands away, took the rest of the contents out of the bag, and then retreated to my chair, taking a long pull from my milkshake. "No problem."

I stared out at the lake with intense focus. The rippling water was far better than the temptation of Holt's face.

"It's a beautiful spot."

I pulled my legs onto the chair and crossed them, depositing my food in my lap. "I'm partial to it."

"How long have you lived here?"

Spinning a french fry between my fingers, I fought the urge to look at Holt. "Almost five years now. Gran and I had a place in town before that."

Because she'd dropped everything when she heard about the shooting and moved to Cedar Ridge. When it became obvious that my parents had no plans to stay put, even though I'd been through a horrific trauma, she moved me in with her.

Holt was quiet for a moment. "I'm sorry you lost her."

I jerked, my gaze going to him now. "How'd you know?"

He plucked at his burger bun. "I kept an eye on things from afar."

Those icy claws of grief and rage dug into my heart again. "But you didn't even call when you knew she was gone?"

Holt knew better than anyone how much Gran had meant to me. Other than him, she was my lifeline. When she passed, I wasn't sure I'd be able to keep going.

Pain flashed across his face. "I went to the funeral. I almost talked to you, but you had so many people around you, and I didn't know if my presence would make things worse."

My heart thudded against my ribs. "You were there?"

I searched back to the day of the memorial. A cemetery outside of Seattle where my grandfather was buried, too. It had been gray and dreary—so fitting. And there had been so many people. Because Gran was loved like crazy. Holt could've easily slipped through the crowd without being noticed.

"I loved her, too. Mostly because she loved *you* so damn much."

The ache was almost too much. It was easier to think Holt had stayed away because he hadn't wanted me, not because he'd loved me too much. Easier to think that he hadn't thought about me once since he'd left, not that he'd kept tabs and been a ghost around the edges of my life.

"Why?" I croaked.

A sad smile played on his lips. "Not sure you're ready for that answer, Cricket."

Chapter Twenty-One

Holt

NASH INCLINED HIS HEAD TO THE CUPHOLDER IN THE center of his SUV. "No wonder you asked for an extra-large. You look like crap."

I grunted as I grabbed the cup and took a long drink. "Gee, thanks."

I knew I looked like death warmed over. Even Wren had looked a little worried when she took in my face before leaving for work this morning. But that was what happened when you were being tortured by thoughts of the person who was everything to you lying in a bed just steps away from your room. Sleep had not happened.

Nash chuckled. "At least you know I won't bullshit you."

"At least there's that."

He eased to a stop at the main road, reaching back to scratch Shadow under the chin. "How'd you convince Little Williams to let you take her dog?"

Shadow's tongue lolled out of her mouth as she happily panted.

"I think Shadow might make a good SAR dog. I told Wren I

would try to do some basic training with her. That's why I asked Law to bring Dad today, too."

Nash nodded. "You need Maddie to make real progress with her."

"You talk to her lately?"

Nash's fingers tightened on the wheel. "Yeah, every now and then. Still in Atlanta with that doofus."

I bit the inside of my cheek to keep from grinning. "You thought every guy Maddie dated was either a creep or a doofus."

"Probably because they were," Nash muttered.

Or maybe because my brother had never been able to pull his head out and realize that he was in love with his best friend. "When's the last time you saw her?"

"I dunno. Like two years ago."

My brows rose at that. "That's a long time for her to not come back for a visit." Even though Maddie's family situation had been less than stellar, she had good friends here and deep ties to Cedar Ridge.

That telltale muscle in his jaw started to tick. "I think he keeps her pretty busy with events for his non-profit and stuff."

"That's a bummer."

Nash's knuckles bleached as he gripped the steering wheel even tighter. "Why does everyone have to go off and change things? Our life was good the way it was, wasn't it?"

I looked at my brother. "You miss her."

"I miss the hell out of her, and it pisses me off that she had to go and get engaged to some dude who lives across the country."

I opened my mouth to try to knock some sense into him, and then I thought about how many people had tried to talk to me about Wren—all my siblings except Roan. My parents. My right hand at my company. None of it had done any good. It'd only pissed me off. The only one who could change things for me was me. I had to be ready to come back here and face things.

Maybe *ready* wasn't the right word. Nothing could have

prepared me to face Wren again. But I had to be willing to live through all the pain for a chance to make things right.

Nash glanced over at me. "What's wrong?"

"Nothing. You just made me think about something."

He arched his brow in question as he guided his SUV up the mountain.

"I royally messed up with the way I left things. I was so sure I was doing the right thing, but I hurt so many people when I left."

Nash turned onto a dirt road. "All any of us can do is what we think is right in the moment."

I looked over at him. "And make amends when our actions miss the mark. I'm sorry, Nash. I know I haven't been the best brother to you these last few years."

"Shut up."

I couldn't hold in my bark of laughter. "I'm trying to make amends."

"You don't need to. So you didn't want to come back to a place full of hard memories. Was your door always open to me?"

Nash had been to my place in Portland more times than I could count. And he'd used it as a crash pad whenever he needed some city time.

"Sure, but—"

"And did you always pick up the phone when I called?"

My mouth thinned. "I tried to—"

"I'm pretty sure you answered me on that sat phone in the middle of an op in Afghanistan. I heard gunfire. But there you were, asking if *I* was okay." Nash pulled into a makeshift parking spot and leveled me with a stare. "You've got a messed-up idea of what kind of man you are."

I opened my mouth, but Nash held up a hand to cut me off. "I'm not saying you're perfect or that you haven't hurt people. Don't get me wrong, I would've loved to have you home more. But you aren't a *bad* person, Holt. You've always had a heart of gold. So much so that you put way too much on your shoulders."

His words hurt, but it was the good kind of pain, the kind I'd take time and time again.

"Am I allowed to talk yet?" I asked.

Nash huffed out a breath. "Not if you're going to keep being an idiot."

I grinned and then pulled him in for a hard hug. "Thank you. I love you, brother."

He froze and then gave me a hard thump on the back. "You know Grae is going to give us so much shit if we get out of this SUV crying."

I didn't try to hold in my laughter as I released him. "Can't give her an opening."

"Damn straight."

We climbed out of the vehicle, and I took in the twenty or so people milling around. The team had grown in the past ten years, but it was just as diverse as it had been before—men and women of a variety of ages. People you wouldn't think at first glance could hike up a mountain for ten miles and carry someone down. Others who screamed: outdoorsperson.

I opened the back door of the SUV and grabbed Shadow's leash. She hopped out and immediately began sniffing around.

Grae made a beeline for us, dropping to give Shadow a scratch. "Where's Wren?"

"She's working."

Grae's eyes widened. "And she let you take Shadow?"

"I have taken care of a dog before," I muttered.

She chuckled. "It's just that Shadow is her baby. It's hard for Wren to leave her with anyone."

The smallest flicker of something flared to life in my chest—something that felt a lot like hope.

"Hey, man," Jude called as he walked up. "Glad you decided to come."

I grinned as I looked around at the familiar setup taking shape and breathed in the mountain air. "Me, too."

"All right, everyone, gather around," my dad called. "Who's going to play our victim today?"

"Not Jude," Grae quipped. "I had to carry his oversized butt last practice. My back hurt for a week."

Jude grinned at her. "I could be a lightweight compared to who you might have to carry one of these days."

Dad frowned at Grae. "He's right about that. You've got extra snacks and your Glucagon kit, right?"

The humor that had been dancing on Grae's face fled. "I have done this a time or two before."

"I volunteer Nash for victim," I cut in before the conversation could devolve.

Nash sent me a withering glare. "Gee, thanks."

Dad nodded. "Put these under your shirt to get your scent on them. We'll give them to the dogs."

"You're gonna pay for this, Holt," Nash growled.

Jude choked on a laugh. "Let's give him a fun injury, Nathan. Broken tailbone maybe?"

Nash chased after Jude, trying to give him a good swift kick. "I'll show you a broken tailbone."

I glanced at Grae, hoping for a flicker of a smile, but she stared at the ground. "G."

She looked up and shook her head. "I'm good. I'm gonna go check my pack."

Crap. Grae never took kindly to someone challenging her ability to care for herself just because she had type 1 diabetes. But for those of us who had been there when we almost lost her, it was hard not to check and double-check that she had everything she needed.

Shadow let out a little whine, and I tipped my head down. "Need a potty break?"

She panted, and I led her into the forest a couple of steps so she could do her business. As I came back out of the trees, I caught sight of Roan, leaning against a pine, present with the group but not a part of it.

I started over to him. "Hey."

Roan nodded but didn't say a word. His eyes warmed a fraction as he took in Shadow, though. Dropping to a crouch, he tapped the ground in front of him, and she came right over. Roan gave her a good scratch behind the ears. "Going to train her for SAR?"

"Gonna see if she can pick up the basics."

He dipped his hand into his pocket and pulled out a small treat, offering it to her. "She'll do good with a job. A purpose."

"I think so, too. It has to get lonely out at the cabin while Wren's at work."

Roan nodded, but I knew he didn't agree. My second eldest brother lived for solitude. While we all knew where he lived, I didn't think he'd invited any of us out there. And it wasn't exactly easy to access even if he had.

"How's Fish and Wildlife treating you?"

He glanced over at me, a flicker of annoyance passing over his features at being forced into polite conversation. "Good."

That was it, a single-word answer.

"You should come over to Wren's. We can all have dinner, or you and I can go on a hike." I had to try. It was why I was here. But in so many ways, it would be hardest with Roan. His wounds from a decade ago compounded his aloofness.

"Yeah, when work calms down."

I wasn't an idiot. I knew work would never *calm down*. But I'd let Roan off the hook. "You just let me know."

"Come get your teams," Dad called.

I scanned the group, looking for the county team leader. "Where's Phyllis?"

"She retired last month," Roan said.

Jude fell into step beside me. "They're still looking for her replacement. Your dad is holding us together right now the best he can."

Nash moved into our grouping, grabbing a walkie-talkie from the table and turning back to me. "It's not a fancy security firm, but it's a job you'd be good at. Has benefits. Maybe you should think about applying."

The thought of staying lit a fire in me, but it wasn't completely painful this time. It was a mixture. I'd missed the hell out of doing SAR. I'd missed my family. I'd missed Wren.

But if I stayed, and Wren still wanted nothing to do with me? I'd be signing up for a lifetime of torture.

Chapter Twenty-Two

Wren

"That's the last of them," Abel grumbled.

He'd been muttering and complaining for the last couple of hours as he finished this month's reports. But the annoyed mumbling was almost a comfort at this point.

"You're free."

He glared at me. "Until next danged month."

I grinned. "The price of being the boss."

"Yeah, yeah. Do me a favor and take these to the actual boss?"

"You got it." I pushed to my feet and stretched before I grabbed the stack of papers. It had been slow today. After the events of the past few days, I appreciated the reprieve, but it was also making me go a little stir-crazy.

I wove through the desks, making my way toward Lawson's office. Clint grinned as he slung a duffel over his shoulder. "Hey, Wren."

"Hey. You off shift?"

"Yup. Gonna go grab some grub at Dockside. Want to take your lunch?"

I fought the flinch that wanted to surface as I remembered Abel's words about Clint and Chris. I liked Clint but had zero interest in dating him or anyone else I worked with. "Thanks, but I gotta hang around here."

Disappointment flickered across his face, but he quickly schooled his expression. "Hope it's a good rest of the day."

"For you, too. Enjoy your lunch."

Guilt flickered as I kept moving toward Lawson's office. Clint was a good man. He'd always been kind to me. There were times I just felt broken. Like that internal compass was always pointing in the wrong direction when it came to relationships.

Because it was still pointing firmly toward Holt. I slapped that thought away the second it surfaced. It was the last thing I needed swirling around in my head.

A raised voice had me pulling up short outside Lawson's office.

"It's bullshit, and you know it, Chief. He doesn't have an alibi. We should be arresting him and pushing him hard," Amber said as she paced.

Lawson kept his voice calm and even. "There is absolutely no evidence that Joe had anything to do with this."

"He's got that same hatred his brother did. I've warned you time and again. I didn't want it to go this far, and now it has."

Lawson's face hardened. "I know you've been through hell, but it's skewing your objectivity. We follow the evidence. Not rumors and gossip."

"What about your gut? You trust that, don't you?" she pushed.

Lawson was quiet, but his lack of answer gave Amber everything she needed to keep pressing on.

"My gut has been screaming about Joe Sullivan for years. And I'm not the only one. If you don't do something about him, people will take action on their own."

Lawson stiffened, his back going rigid. "You'd better not be suggesting what I think you are, Raymond. That'll cost you more than your job. You harass that boy, and I'll take you into custody myself."

Redness crept up Amber's throat. "You would protect him over me? I've served with you for *years*. I'm trying to keep the people of this town safe."

"You need to take a break and get some perspective. I'm giving you paid time off tomorrow. Get your head on straight. If you can't, you and I will be having another conversation altogether."

Her cheeks puffed out as Amber struggled to get her breathing under control. Instead of saying anything, she whirled and stormed out of the office, knocking into me on her way past.

My gaze followed her as she charged through the desks and out the front door of the station. My insides twisted themselves into intricate knots. They pulsed and cramped with grief for everyone involved. Joe. Amber. The endless stream of people the shooting had marked.

As I turned back to Lawson's office, I took him in. He leaned over his desk, his head resting on one hand as he pinched the bridge of his nose.

I stepped inside and quietly shut the door. Taking a seat, I studied the man who had been like a brother to me for my entire life. "What can I do?"

Lawson didn't look up. "I wish there was something."

"She's hurting."

"I know. But I can't have her going out and doing something stupid just because she's in pain."

I made a humming noise in the back of my throat. "You're right. And Joe doesn't deserve this town being on his case. He's already torn up because of how people around here treat him."

Lawson straightened, sitting back in his chair. "If you can see that, why the hell can't the rest of Cedar Ridge?"

I let out a long breath. "Because it's easier to think there's a bad guy. An outsider. Someone to look out for. But the truth is we all had a part in what those boys did."

Lawson stared at me, not saying a word.

"They needed help, and they didn't get it. We're supposed to be a community. We look out for each other. People knew they weren't getting the care they needed at home. But no one stepped in." I swallowed hard. "I'll never forget what they did. That terror. But it's not as simple as two rotten apples. People made them that way."

A muscle in Lawson's jaw ticked. "You're right. I've had some minor trouble from Joe, but nothing that would suggest this." Lawson was quiet for a moment and then seemed to come to a conclusion. "I'm gonna have a word with him."

I opened my mouth to argue, but Lawson held up a hand to stop me. "I'll do it out of uniform. Invite him to dinner. Seems like he could use a friend."

My mouth curved. "You're a good man."

He grunted. "Don't go spreading that around."

Laughter bubbled out of me. "I hate to break it to you, but the rumor's already out."

"Yeah, yeah." He motioned for the papers in my hand. "Those for me?"

"Abel's end-of-the-month reports."

Lawson took them from me. "You'd better go tell him to take lunch. If he doesn't get fed after paperwork, he can be a real bear."

I winced and glanced over my shoulder to see Abel muttering to himself. "That ship might've already sailed."

Lawson chuckled. "Hurry. Maybe you can turn it around."

I did exactly what he instructed, all but running back to our cubicles. "Paperwork dropped off. Why don't you take lunch?"

Abel eyed me suspiciously. "I packed a lunch."

"Well, it's a beautiful day. Why don't you eat it outside and enjoy the sunshine while things are quiet?"

"Fine. Text me if things get busy," he huffed.

"Will do."

I held my breath until Abel disappeared into the break room to get his lunch. The air slowly left my lungs as I turned back to my computer screen. Abel could be prickly as a cactus when he wanted to be, but his heart was ooey-gooey goodness through and through. No crankiness could hide that from the world.

Tapping out a rhythm on my desk, I surveyed the area. There really wasn't anything to do. We were all caught up on paperwork. No more reports needed to be filed.

My mind started to drift to last night. To the lake. To Holt. How he'd silently watched over me for the past decade. That familiar war of longing and anger took flight inside me. I never knew which one would win out on any given day. Lately, the anger was hitting hard but in short bursts, while the longing was settling somewhere deep in my bones, showing no signs of leaving.

My hand moved to the mouse, and I clicked on solitaire. Anything to distract me from that stormy sea of emotion. I moved the cards around on the screen in a half-hearted attempt to beat the computer.

The phone on my desk rang. In a split second, I'd minimized the card game and was tapping the button on my headset. "Cedar Ridge police, fire, and medical."

"This is Calvin Dwyer at 65 Alpine Drive. I just heard two shots across the street. I think at the McHenrys."

My blood turned to ice. Gretchen. It was the only thing I could think for a full second. Her smiling face filled my mind. The way she had the ability to see the positive side of everything—even the hell we'd been through ten years ago.

"Hold on, Mr. Dwyer. I'm dispatching officers now. Please make sure your doors and windows are locked."

I hurried to switch over to the radio. "Shots fired at the McHenry home on Alpine Drive. I'm getting an address now."

It was only blocks from the station. Officers could be there in under a minute. Everyone would be okay.

A series of muted pops sounded over the phone line as officers, including Lawson, responded to the call on the radio.

"Did you hear that?" Mr. Dwyer barked. "That was more."

"I heard it, sir. Officers are responding. Can you see anyone at the house?"

"I—I don't think so—wait! Someone's heading out the back door. They're wearing a black hoodie."

I quickly typed the description into our computer system so the officers had it. I could hear the sirens, both leaving the station and near Mr. Dwyer's home.

"I see a squad car. They're here."

"Please stay in your home with the door locked, Mr. Dwyer. An officer will come to speak to you as soon as they're able."

"Okay. Thank you." He didn't hang up. "I'm shaking."

Shock. It was beyond understandable. "Can you get yourself some water and take a seat?"

"Water?"

"Or just take a seat. I don't want you passing out on me." I typed in a request for the EMTs to check out Mr. Dwyer, just to be safe.

Voices sounded over the radio, officers entering the McHenry house.

"I can do that."

I forced myself to focus on Mr. Dwyer. "Nice and easy."

A shuffling sounded in the background, then a cabinet opening and closing before a chair squeaked.

"Slow sips," I instructed.

"That helps."

"I'm glad."

A knock sounded.

"Someone's at my door."

"Mr. Dwyer," a familiar voice called. "This is Officer Jones. I'm here to take your statement and do a medical check."

Jones was one of the police officers with senior medical training, and I let out a breath, knowing Mr. Dwyer would be in good hands. "You can open the door. That's one of my colleagues."

"Thank you—I—thank you."

"Of course. Stay safe, Mr. Dwyer."

I disconnected the call the moment I heard Officer Jones inside the home. My fingers found the volume for the radio, and I clicked it up.

Familiar voices crackled across the line, calling out different rooms as clear.

"I've got a body," someone said. "Downstairs bedroom." A pause. "No pulse. She's gone."

"Hell, she's in a hospital bed connected to oxygen. Who would do something like this?" another voice asked.

Nausea swept through me. Gretchen's mom. The woman with heart failure that Gretchen had been caring for every single day for the past two years.

"Kitchen," a shaky voice came across the radio. "Th-there's no way she's alive. Oh, God. I can't—I think I'm gonna be sick."

The person cut out as someone said the name I'd been dreading.

"It's Gretchen."

Chapter Twenty-Three

Holt

"TOLD YOU THAT YOU WOULDN'T BE AS RUSTY AS YOU thought," Nash said as he pulled out of the parking lot and onto the mountain road.

It had been a rush to be back with the SAR team, using a combination of old instincts paired with the new skills I'd learned in the Marines and running security details. It all came together in a way that almost felt meant to be.

I reached back and scratched Shadow's head. "This here is the real star of the show. She was picking up scents like you wouldn't believe."

Nash threw a grin over his shoulder at the dog. "That's because I'm your favorite, right? You just had to find me."

I chuckled. Shadow hadn't been the one to find Nash first, but she had shown signs of following his trail, which was pretty incredible for her first time out. With a little training, she would be a first-rate SAR dog.

"So…" Nash began. "What do you think about that job opening?"

It had been circling in my brain since the moment he'd mentioned it. I opened my mouth to answer him when the radio in Nash's SUV beeped.

Wren's voice came across the speaker. "Shots fired at the McHenry home on Alpine Drive. I'm getting an address now."

Nash cursed, pulling the radio out of its cradle and pressing a button. "Officer Hartley responding. I'm fifteen minutes out."

McHenry. The name swirled around in my brain as my blood went cold. Gretchen. The girl Randy and Paul had gone after simply for ruining the curve in their chemistry class. She'd had the least severe injuries of all those who'd gotten hurt that night. Because she'd made a run for the lake and hidden under her neighbor's dock for an hour before the police had arrived, and she'd felt safe enough to come out.

She'd had a graze on her shoulder and a mild case of hypothermia but, otherwise, was okay. That might not be the case now.

I waited to hear Wren's voice again, but there was nothing. Only messages I knew she had typed popping up on Nash's dashboard computer. Nothing about them told me if she was okay. If this was wrecking her.

A new array of voices came across the radio. Officers clearing the residence. One victim. Then two.

There was no sign of the typical smile Nash wore. His hands gripped the steering wheel so tightly, it was a wonder it didn't crack in two. "What the hell is going on?"

I stared out the window as the sirens sang into the usually peaceful air, urging the SUV to go faster. "I don't know." Something happening to one of the shooting victims could've been a coincidence. But two? There was no way.

Nash made the trip to the McHenry house in half the time he'd predicted, screeching to a halt outside. "You can't come in."

"I know. I'm going to the station." Because I only had one priority right then—Wren.

I jumped out of the passenger side, opening the back door and grabbing Shadow's leash. Then we were running for the station.

It wasn't far, only a matter of blocks, but the journey felt as if it took a lifetime.

Yanking open the front door, I strode inside. The officer behind the desk looked too young to be wearing a uniform.

"C-can I help you, sir?"

His hand had gone to the butt of his gun, and I realized I must've looked half-feral.

"He's fine, Carl," Abel called as he motioned me over.

I hurried to the cubicles.

Shadow went straight to Wren, nudging at her hands. Wren absentmindedly stroked the dog's head, but it was as if she were on autopilot.

I crouched down next to her. "Wren?"

She jolted at the sound of my voice. "What are you doing here?"

I glanced at Abel, whose brows were furrowed in worry. "Wanted to make sure you were okay."

"I'm fine."

The words weren't pissed off like Wren was furious at me for suggesting that she might be human. They weren't fragile either, like she was on the edge of breaking. It was something so much worse. They were empty. Devoid of any emotion at all.

Abel cleared his throat. "Holt, can you take Wren home?"

"I don't need to go home," she said evenly, but the words were too slow for her normal speech.

Shock setting in.

"I'm afraid that's not up to you," Abel said, letting a little authoritativeness slip into his tone. "You're done for the day. We can talk tomorrow and see where you're at."

She stared up at him but didn't say a word. It was as if she didn't have any fight left in her at all. And that was what broke something deep inside me when I didn't think I had anything left to break. I'd seen Wren in so many incarnations, but I'd never seen her totally and completely defeated—as if she'd given up altogether.

Wren slowly got to her feet and bent to grab her bag from a

desk drawer. She didn't bother picking up Shadow's leash, she simply started for the front door of the station.

Abel and I shared a look, and then I hurried after Wren. I thought for sure when I snagged the bag from her shoulder that Wren would make some sort of protest, but she didn't even flinch, she just kept walking outside and toward the parking lot.

I looped Shadow's leash around my wrist as I dug in Wren's bag for her keys. When she started for the driver's door, I gently guided her to the passenger side as I beeped the locks. She made no protest, simply climbed inside.

I opened the back cab, and Shadow quickly jumped in. She moved to her owner's side, laying her head on Wren's shoulder. Wren didn't react at all.

A million different curses flew through my head as I got behind the wheel and started the engine. I forced myself not to drive more than five miles over the speed limit, knowing the town was crawling with cops looking for anything out of the norm. My gaze kept pulling to the right side of the truck. To Wren.

She was pale. Too pale. And those breathtaking hazel eyes were vacant now, no green fire in them at all.

I hated everything about her demeanor but didn't have the first idea how to fix it. All I could do was get her home. Be there for her. Show her that she wasn't alone.

The drive to Wren's cabin felt as if it took hours, but we finally came to a stop. I turned off the engine and hopped out, rounding the vehicle. But by the time I got to her side, she was already heading toward the house.

I let Shadow out, immediately unhooking her leash, and the dog ran after Wren, who halted in front of the door. She just stood there. Waiting.

I hurried up to the house, finding the key and sliding it into the lock. Wren slid by me as I opened the door, and I didn't miss the way her body vibrated with phantom energy—the shock setting in deeper. Shadow let out a low whine.

Pointing to the dog bed in the living room, I motioned for Shadow to lay down. She seemed to glare at me but did as I asked.

"Let's get you in a shower," I said quietly. It was the only thing I could think of. If I could get Wren warm, she would be okay.

Wren didn't fight me. Didn't tell me to mind my own business. She just followed me to the bathroom.

I turned on the water and held my hand under the spray until it was a soothing warmth. Turning around, I studied the woman who had always owned me, body and soul. "Will you be okay?"

Wren didn't say anything, but she did nod.

I hesitated for a moment and then headed for the door. "I'll be right outside."

Quickly ducking into her bedroom, I searched for the comfiest sweats I could find. Grabbing those, a T-shirt, and some underwear, I headed back into the hall. It was quiet at first, just the steady fall of the water against the shower's tile floor.

Then one guttural sob pierced the air, and my chest cracked right along with it.

Another sounded, a third on its heels.

There was a brokenness to the noise that I'd never heard in all my life. A brokenness that had been living in Wren since that day ten years ago. A brokenness I'd left her alone in.

Chapter Twenty-Four

Wren

IT WAS TOO MUCH. AS IF MY ENTIRE SYSTEM WERE overloaded and short-circuiting.

My legs shook so badly that I had no choice but to slide to the shower floor. Water pelted down on me, but I wanted it to hurt—I wanted my body to hurt the way my soul did. At least after the shooting, after Holt left, my outsides matched my insides.

My fingers found the scar between my breasts, the one where they'd cracked open my chest and rearranged my insides in a bid to save my life. Now, it was like I was in the middle of open-heart surgery but with no anesthesia.

Memory after memory slammed into me. Holt's voice telling me he loved me as I woke up after surgery. Mr. Peterson's kind expression as he asked me how I was holding up. Gretchen's wide smile as she recounted all the ways the shooting had made her grateful for her life.

The sobs came faster. Harder. I couldn't take in any air. It was as if there wasn't any in the room around me.

The shower door jerked open, and the water cut off. I couldn't find it in me to care. All I could do was rock and gasp for the air.

A second later, a towel wrapped around me, and someone lifted me into strong arms. The world around me blurred. I thought there was a blanket then, too. A bed.

And then I was drowning in Holt. He was all around me—that pine and spice.

"I've got you."

I felt the words against my skin as much as I heard them, a gentle brand that sliced to my very core.

"Do you?" I choked out, my voice raw.

Holt held me tighter against him. "I'm so sorry, Cricket. You'll never know how much. I'm here. I'm not going anywhere."

His words only made me cry harder.

"Cricket." My nickname was an anguished plea.

There were no more words. Only soft caresses. His lips ghosting across my forehead. His hands skating up and down my back.

The last of my walls came tumbling down. Because the truth was, the only thing that could bring me comfort right now was Holt—the tender way his fingers moved, the feeling so achingly familiar. The way his mouth uttered nonsensical things in a language that was all ours.

I wanted nothing in this moment but him. Needed to lose myself in the man I had never truly let go of.

I released it all. The what-ifs. The pain. The grief. And I let Holt soothe every wound that had been festering for a decade.

It wasn't just one action or whispered prayer. It was all of it, coming together from the boy he had been to the man he was now.

I gave myself over to it. As the tears subsided and the trembling ceased, I still couldn't get close enough. I was a woman starved. Cut off from the most beautiful thing I'd ever experienced and finally feeling it again for the first time.

"Holt." His name was a hoarse whisper—a rough plea.

His hands brushed my wet hair out of my face. "Tell me what you need, Cricket. Anything."

"I need you." They were the hardest three words I'd ever said. Terrifying and painful, yet full of hope.

His body went rigid. "I don't think that's a good idea—"

I was already pulling away, the sting of rejection too strong. But Holt caught me, bringing me back to him. "Look at me, Cricket. See me. I've thought about you every damn day. Wanted you with every breath. Nothing will change that. Ever. But I won't be able to live with myself if we go there, and you regret it tomorrow. You've been through hell today—"

I pressed my fingers to his lips, stopping the trail of words. "Trust me, Holt. Trust me to know my mind. To know what I need."

Right now, that was to remember that I was alive. Breathing. That even if I didn't have Holt forever, I could have him for this moment. Maybe we could live our forever in this room. In the moments that passed from one breath to the next.

He stared at me. Searching.

Slowly, I pulled my hand away from his mouth and leaned in. My lips hovered a breath away from his. I waited for one beat. Two. Then I closed the distance.

I sank into the familiar heat that was Holt. I'd kissed those lips a thousand times. Felt their coaxing warmth and gentle pressure.

This kiss was different. It was a mix of deepest want and coming home. There was a desperation in it that had never been there before. His fingers tangled in my hair as I sank into the melding of our mouths. I wanted to disappear in the taste of him.

Holt's hand dipped under the blanket, the towel, and then his fingers were on my skin. They danced over my waist, moved to my hip, pulling me flush against him.

I'd always loved the feel of his roughened fingertips against my more delicate flesh. The way they sent waves of pleasant shivers flying through me. That wave was back. Only this was more.

Holt broke away from the kiss, but his mouth still hovered over mine. "Tell me you're sure."

I brought my eyes to his, letting him see the truth burning there. "I'm sure."

"Wren."

I felt my name on his lips, and the vibrations carried through the air and landed on my skin, burrowing deep.

Holt peeled the blanket away from me and then the towel. The blue in his eyes sparked and swirled as he stared down at me. His fingers skated over my skin as if he were imprinting the image in his mind forever.

Then he leaned over me. Holt pressed his lips to the scar over my heart. That heart seized in a stuttering beat. His lips traced the long line over my sternum, trailing down.

"Holt," I breathed, starting to squirm. I wasn't ashamed of the scars or even embarrassed. But here? Like this? I felt exposed. Like one raw nerve ending.

"Your strength only makes you more beautiful," he said hoarsely, his lips still skimming. They followed my rib cage down and then rose to my breast.

I arched into Holt, searching for more. More contact. More *him*.

His tongue flicked out, tracing my nipple. "Your skin is like heaven—silk and you."

My fingers tightened on his shoulders and then moved to the buttons on his flannel. I trembled, struggling to pull the fabric free. The need to feel him against me, all of him, was so strong that I couldn't seem to get my hands to cooperate.

"Wren," Holt whispered, his hands framing my face. "We've got time."

But I wasn't sure we did. None of us was promised forever, and I couldn't expect Holt to stay in a place that held so much pain for him. I didn't tell him any of that. Instead, I gave him another truth. "I need your skin against mine."

His eyes searched mine as if he sensed there was something more. But then he sat up, his fingers deftly undoing the buttons.

As he stood, he shrugged off the flannel and pulled his white tee over his head.

I couldn't help but drink him in. It was my turn to burn an image into my memory. And I knew this one would ruin me for all others. Holt was lean muscle wrapped in lightly tanned skin—the color of the sun on a wheat field, a fading gold.

My fingers tightened around nothing at all. Because they ached to touch. To trail through the dusting of hair on his chest. To slide over the dips and ridges of his abdominals.

Holt's fingers went to his jeans, his boots already removed somewhere along the way. Then his jeans were gone, too. I swallowed hard as Holt tugged at his black boxer briefs.

And then he was standing there, nothing but air in between us. God, he was gorgeous. Not just for this body, but because of the heart I knew beat beneath that muscle.

Holt moved toward the bed, and I couldn't stop myself from reaching up, my fingers ghosting over his chest, letting the sensations wash over me.

Closing his eyes, Holt breathed deeply. "Been dreaming about your hands on me every damn day."

The same dreams had haunted me in sleep. I'd wake tangled in the sheets, restless and too hot. I'd try to take the edge off, but it was almost worse that way somehow.

He brushed the hair out of my face. "You have protection?"

I blinked up at him. "You don't?"

The corner of his mouth kicked up. "Cricket, there hasn't been anyone in a long time. I realized it wasn't fair to go there with a woman when the only one I wanted was you."

His words carved themselves into my heart, ripping me open and searing me with the most beautiful pain. A tear slid down my cheek, and Holt swept it away with his thumb. "Hey. What's that about?"

"There hasn't been anyone for me in a long time. And I'm on the pill." The truth was, there had only been one. A drunken night

I'd regretted with everything in me. But I'd wanted that stigma of virginity gone.

Holt pressed a kiss to one cheek, then the other, before moving to my forehead and finally my lips. "Thank you for trusting me."

My heart cracked, and I found myself wanting to give all the pieces to him.

Instead, I kissed him deeper. I lost myself in his taste and feel.

Holt's hand slid between my legs as I arched into him. I gasped into his mouth as his finger dipped inside and then moved in long, languid strokes as if he were in no hurry at all.

But I was. I didn't want to waste a moment. Not with Holt.

My hand wrapped around his length, and Holt let out a groan as I stroked him, up and down.

"Heaven," he growled.

My finger skated over his tip, feeling a brush of wetness.

Holt's thumb circled that bundle of nerves, and I let out a mewl as sparks lit under my skin. But I forced myself to pull away because this wasn't how I wanted to come apart. I wanted Holt moving inside. Needed to feel him *everywhere*.

"Not like this."

Holt searched my eyes.

"I need all of you."

That blue flashed in understanding, and then Holt was rolling on top of me. He pressed another kiss to the scar above my heart and then his eyes didn't leave mine. Not for a single a second.

Holt's tip bumped my entrance, and then my legs encircled his waist. Everything stretched as he slid inside. A delicious ache, just shy of pain.

His forehead pressed to mine as I struggled to keep my breathing even. "You with me?"

My thumb traced his lips and then trailed down his throat, the stubble there prickling my skin. "I'm with you."

Then Holt began to move. Slowly at first—shallow, testing thrusts.

My hips rose to meet his, finding a rhythm. I didn't worry

about what was right or expected. I trusted my body to find Holt's in whatever was supposed to be ours.

Holt tilted his hips, arching deeper into me. My mouth opened on a silent plea as my fingers pressed into his shoulders, nails digging in.

Something about the move broke Holt's reserve, his worry about how breakable I might be. Some of that earlier desperation found us again. The need to be closer. To remember and to never forget.

Everything in me quivered as Holt hit that spot deep inside. The one that made light dance across my vision and had tears leaking from my eyes. I only wanted more. We met each other again and again, clinging to the need building between us.

"Are you with me?" Holt growled, his hand dipping between us, thumb circling my clit.

"With. You." I had to sneak the words between breaths.

Holt pressed on that bundle of nerves. It was too much. The rightness of Holt moving inside me. The overload of emotion. Sensation.

All it took was one last spark.

Holt arched into me, impossibly deeper, and then I was falling. But there was no fear because he fell with me. Whispers in the air all around us. Whispers of him. Of us. Of the past. Of the present. Of forever.

I let them take me under, embed themselves in my skin, and carry me away.

Wave after wave crashed over me as I held on to Holt. Gripping as if I'd never let go.

A hoarse shout tipped his lips, and then Holt was spiraling, too. A twisting swirl of sensation. Both of us trying not to miss a single thing.

Because a fear still lived down deep; one that told me the whispers of him would be all I ever had.

Chapter Twenty-Five

Holt

MY LIPS TRAILED DOWN WREN'S SPINE. SHE LET OUT A sleepy little moan that had me grinning against her skin. "Morning."

My voice was raspy, etched with exhaustion. Likely because Wren and I had lost ourselves in each other more times than I could count. As if we were trying to make up for all the time we'd lost. And when we'd both been too spent to continue, we'd slept tangled in each other.

"Need sleep," she grumbled.

I couldn't help my chuckle.

Wren flipped onto her back, not bothering to pull the sheet up. "I missed that sound."

"My laugh?"

She nodded, her fingers ghosting over my throat. "I thought I'd have all your chuckles. That I'd know what it sounded like at every stage of life."

Each word carved itself into my chest. I'd stolen so much from her. Those chuckles. Our life—the one we'd planned for so long.

I cupped Wren's face, my thumb sweeping back and forth across her cheek. "Never stopped loving you. Not for a single second."

I didn't give a damn that it might be too soon. That Wren might not be ready to hear these words. Because she needed them. I might've royally screwed up, but it wasn't from a lack of love.

The green in Wren's eyes flashed as her fingers stilled. "You can't say that."

"Whether I say it or not won't make it any less true."

Wren snatched her hand back and pulled the sheet up to cover herself. "Don't, Holt. Please, don't make any promises."

Promises she worried I'd never be able to keep. Maybe she wasn't ready to hear them out loud, but I'd give them to her silently. Inaudible prayers lifted into the air. And I'd give her actions—the strongest words of all.

I pulled Wren into my arms. "Okay. No promises. But no pulling away either."

A little of the tension went out of Wren's muscles at that. "I don't know if I can do whatever this is."

My fingers trailed through her hair, and I relished the silky feel of it. "Can you do it for today?"

She worried the side of her lip. "Yes."

I pressed a kiss to the spot she was nibbling. "One day at a time. It's all any of us can do."

And I would use those days—every single second of each of them. I wouldn't let Wren down. Not this time. I reached over to the nightstand and grabbed a mug of coffee, handing it to her.

She looked surprised for a beat as if she'd expected me to launch my case right then and there. "Thank you," she said, pushing up against the pillows and taking a sip. "This is much better than when I make coffee."

I grinned. "Pretty sure you burn coffee, too, Cricket."

She scowled at me. "I do not."

"Mm-hmm."

Wren grabbed a pillow and smacked me with it. "Rude."

I laughed. I wasn't holding back on any of those chuckles. Not when Wren had been missing the sound. Leaning over, I brushed my lips across her temple. "Sorry. I will repay you with muffins."

I handed her one from the nightstand.

Wren's eyes widened. "This is warm."

"It's just a mix, but they're damn good."

She bit into it and moaned.

My shorts suddenly felt a little too tight.

"Chocolate chip is the best," Wren mumbled around the muffin.

It was her favorite. How many times had I seen something I knew she loved and wished I could beam it to her? Now, I could.

I leaned back against the pillows. "How do you feel?"

She eyed me carefully. "Why do I have the feeling you're not asking if I'm sore?"

I turned on my side, my fingers running up Wren's blanket-covered leg, dipping between her thighs. "I want to know that, too. If I need to be taking care of you."

Wren's cheeks darkened to a deep shade of pink. "I'm fine."

I kissed her softly. "Good. Want to know how your heart is, too."

She was quiet for a moment, staring down at her muffin. "I can't believe she's gone." Wren looked up at me. "This wasn't a coincidence."

My mouth thinned into a hard line. "That would be extremely unlikely."

Grief flared in her hazel eyes. "My mind keeps circling around to why. Who would want to go after the survivors? We've all already been through so much."

God, I wanted the answer to both of those questions. Wanted it so I could wipe that person from the planet. "I don't know, Cricket. I wish I did. Law is working on it, and I'm going to help him in any way I can."

She nodded. "Does he have any leads?"

"I don't think so. I was going to drive you to work and see if I could grab a few minutes with him." I'd checked my phone this morning and there hadn't been anything other than a text reading: *Don't let Wren out of your sight.* Didn't exactly give me the warm fuzzies.

Wren started to get up. "I'll shower. We can go in early—"

I gave her arm a gentle tug, pulling her back to the bed. "We've got time. I need to talk to you first, and you need to eat. The last thing we need is you passing out."

Wren grumbled something under her breath about overbearing alpha males but shoved a piece of muffin into her mouth. "Talk."

I pressed my lips together to keep from grinning. But that smile didn't feel nearly as tempting when I thought about what came next. "We need to talk about your security."

She stiffened. "All right."

"I already ordered some basics from my friend, Cain, to outfit your property."

"I thought you were waiting for my budget."

"I was, but I knew I could send back whatever didn't work with what you were comfortable spending." That much was true. But I also knew that Cain would give me half the stuff for free if I needed it, so I could do some creative accounting.

"Fine. Do whatever you think is necessary. Just no cameras or motion sensors in the house. I really don't need Shadow or me being blown sky-high."

The husky appeared at the sound of her name, panting around a bone.

Wren arched a brow. "I'm not the only one being spoiled, I see."

"Gotta work on both my girls."

Wren's expression softened at that before she forced her gaze back to the muffin. "Anything else?"

"No going anywhere alone right now, okay?"

She was quiet for a moment. "Do you think whoever this is will come after me?"

My chest constricted in a vicious squeeze. "It's a possibility." One I wasn't about to let come to fruition.

"I won't go anywhere alone."

I hated the defeat in Wren's voice. Weaving my fingers through hers, I squeezed. "It's not forever."

"I know. I don't want to be stupid."

I nodded and then released her to pull a few more items from the nightstand. "This is one of the personal alarms we give clients. Pull this pin here, and an alarm will sound that everyone within a two-block radius will hear."

Wren toyed with the tiny key chain. "Handy."

"I know you said you had a Taser, but it would make me feel better if you held onto this for a little while, too."

I dropped the small pocketknife onto her lap. Wren stared at it, not moving an inch. The knife was worn, the engraving on the side practically rubbed off because I'd run my fingers over it so many times. *Holt Hartley. Love you forever. Happy 18th Birthday. Love, Cricket.*

"You kept it."

It wasn't a question, but it *was* begging for an explanation.

"It's been everywhere I have. Wouldn't go on a mission or job without it. It's kept me safe more times than I can count. Now, it's going to keep you safe for a little while."

Wren swallowed as she looked up at me. "I'll keep it for a little while."

But it would be longer than that. Because even when she was safe and placed it back in my hands, *I* would still be here. And sooner or later, she would believe that forever was just a lifetime of a little whiles.

Chapter Twenty-Six

Wren

HOLT PULLED INTO THE PARKING LOT TO THE SIDE OF the station, and I fought the urge to squirm in my seat. I'd had that twitchy feeling ever since we'd gotten in the car. It felt as if Holt's eyes were on me, assessing, surveying each injury and scar so he could sew up every one.

But they hadn't been. His fingers had been linked with mine, but his head was on a swivel, eyes scanning the road and the streets of downtown. Likely looking for a bogeyman that could jump out at any moment.

I breathed deeply. As I let the air out, I imagined pulling on a mask. One where people wouldn't ask me if I was okay a million times today. One where everyone would forget that I'd let shock completely take me under yesterday. As far as I could remember, there had barely been anyone in the office by the time we left. My greatest performance would have to be with Abel.

"What are you doing?"

My gaze snapped to Holt. "What do you mean?"

His finger circled the air in front of my face. "Erasing every-thing you're feeling. Hiding from the world."

Of course, he saw that. He'd always seen it all. Every single time I found myself drowning. Except the one time I needed him the most.

"Sometimes, the world doesn't have the right to your feelings. It doesn't mean you're hiding. Just that some emotions are only for the people you trust most."

A flash of pain streaked across Holt's face. "You did that the first day I saw you."

I didn't look away. Not from Holt or his hurt. "I did. But I didn't keep anything from you yesterday. You saw it all." I'd let my walls tumble to the ground and left myself raw and exposed.

Holt's hands framed my face. "Thank you."

I leaned forward, brushing my lips against his. I couldn't fight the pull to soothe Holt. It was too strong.

His forehead pressed to mine. "We should go in there."

"I know." But it was the last thing I wanted to do. In this mo-ment, I wanted to hide—somewhere there were no shootings or cruelty or pain. Where everything was easy, and life always worked out.

Holt sighed as he let me go, turning off the engine and climb-ing out of his SUV. I reluctantly followed suit. His hand found mine the second I was out of the vehicle. I squeezed his fingers and then tried to let go. He wouldn't release me.

"Holt," I hissed.

He glanced down at me. "You're not hiding us, are you?"

My jaw went slack. "No, but I don't need anyone knowing my business either." Because if he decided to leave, Holt wouldn't have to face countless nosy people around town. I would.

"You're right, it's none of their business." He still didn't let go of my hand.

"Holt…"

"Not going to pretend I'm not in love with you, Wren. Missed touching you. Sometimes, I'd be walking and swear I felt your hand in mine."

Everything inside me jerked as if I were in a car, and the driver had slammed on the brakes. It was a painful lurch that demanded attention.

"Oh."

It was the only thing I could say.

Holt dipped his chin and pressed a kiss to the top of my head. "Yeah."

He held the front door to the station for me but still didn't let go of my hand. I didn't try to shake it free. As we stepped inside, my skin started to itch at the feel of so many eyes on me. I did my best to ignore the sensation as Holt led us toward Lawson's office.

Clint and Amber were talking in hushed tones as we passed. Clint's gaze zeroed in on our joined hands. His eyes flashed, but he didn't say a word.

My stomach churned, but maybe it was better this way. Rip the Band-Aid right off. He could find someone that actually suited him.

Holt came to a stop outside Lawson's closed door and knocked. "Come in."

Holt opened the door and ushered me inside, still not letting go of my hand.

Lawson looked exhausted—stubble coating his face and dark circles rimming his eyes. But when his gaze caught on our hands, his mouth curved. He was polite enough not to say anything, though.

Nash was not.

"Holy shit." Nash let out a hoot from the couch. "It's a Christmas miracle in the middle of spring."

"Nash…" Holt warned.

"What?" Nash asked with mock innocence. "I can't be happy for my brother?"

"You are welcome to your happiness, but you are *not* welcome to give Wren a hard time."

Nash's gaze went from Holt to me, a devilish grin playing on his lips. "Little Williams, you don't look too rested. Could someone have kept you up all—?"

Lawson threw a pen at Nash.

"Ow! That was uncalled for, big brother. I could report you to HR for an abusive work environment."

Lawson shook his head. "Good luck with that. Morning, Wren. Holt."

"Morning," I said, my cheeks still fire engine red.

"We wanted to see if there were any updates," Holt said, bringing us back to the point.

All humor fled Lawson's face. "We don't have much. A figure in a black hoodie, fleeing the McHenry home and heading into the woods."

Holt glanced between Lawson and Nash. "This one's different. The other was through a window. This is up close and personal."

"Someone's getting more comfortable with killing," Nash said, shadows swirling in his eyes.

Nausea swept through me at such callous disregard for human life. "The officers were right? Mrs. McHenry didn't make it?"

Lawson shook his head. "They called it at the scene."

I didn't know if that was a kindness given that Mrs. McHenry wouldn't have had anyone left. I had to hope that she and Gretchen were together somewhere and that they were at peace, even if it was far too soon.

"Who are you bringing in for questioning?" Holt asked.

Lawson and Nash shared a look.

Holt let out a growl.

"You're not police," Lawson said. He turned his focus to me. "And neither are you."

I stared back at him. "Maybe not, but I could be on some asshole's hit list, so I'd say that entitles me to a little information. And it's not like I won't see whoever you bring in."

Holt's hand twitched in mine, holding me tighter.

"Little Williams has a point," Nash said.

Lawson blew out a breath. "We're talking to a lot of different people. Everyone with a connection to the shootings years ago and everyone who was in the vicinity of the recent ones. But we aren't bringing anyone in for an interrogation just yet. We're also contacting all of those who survived the shooting ten years ago and warning them to be cautious. But we're asking them not to spread that around."

I ran that over in my mind. "You don't want to spook anyone."

"No, I don't. I don't want panic in my community, and I don't want whoever did this to cover their tracks any better than they already are," Lawson agreed.

I gripped Holt's hand tighter as I searched for the words I needed. "What if there *was* a third shooter?"

I hadn't talked about my suspicions since that third and final conversation with the police ten years ago. The acting chief then had made me feel like a hysterical child whose mind couldn't be trusted. And I'd started to believe him.

"I know the doctors said that I might have been confused because of the blood loss and trauma, but I swore there was a third person in the house that night."

Lawson leaned forward in his chair. "I thought you said you were mistaken. That it was only two."

"The cops back then… They made me doubt everything I remembered if it didn't fit with their narrative."

"Assholes," Holt muttered.

Lawson sent him a quelling look. "Trust me. I'm not a fan of how they handled things back then either. But they were under a hell of a lot of pressure to lock this one up and throw away the key. That led to them forcing things where they probably shouldn't have. The truth has its own timeline."

But the time it took to get there could sometimes do irreparable harm. They knew that better than most because they'd seen Roan be destroyed by questions over whether he had been involved. It didn't matter that none of us believed it. That suspicion had changed him, and he hadn't been the same since.

Nash studied me. "Randy and Paul always swore up and down that it was only the two of them. No one else. Don't you think they'd want their partner doing time with them?"

I pulled my hand from Holt's, and he let me go this time as if he sensed that I needed freedom to move. I twisted my fingers together as I rocked from the back of my heels to the balls of my feet. "I've played that night over and over in my head—even when it was the last thing I wanted to think about. I heard someone downstairs. Abel had told me the police were on their way, and I thought it was them, that they were sneaking upstairs. I thought I was going to be okay."

A muscle in Holt's jaw ticked wildly as he gripped the back of a chair.

I didn't let it stop me. I had to get it out. "I heard them coming up the stairs and then heard someone say, '*Where the hell is Holt? We need them both.*'"

The room around me went wired. I'd never told anyone but the police exactly what I'd heard. I'd never recounted any of this to Holt. Every time I'd tried to talk about what had happened, he'd shut me down, saying it wasn't good to rehash it all.

I turned to him. "I was glad you weren't there," I whispered. "I never would've made it if something had happened to you."

So many emotions blazed across Holt's face. They moved so quickly, I could barely track one before it morphed into the next. Then he was moving. He pulled me against him, wrapping his arms around me. "I'm right here, Cricket."

Hope flickered to life in my chest. It was a hope that terrified me, but I couldn't pull away. I gripped his shirt, my hands fisting there. "I'm just glad you're okay."

"We need to go back over the original case," Nash said.

I turned in Holt's arms, facing Lawson and Nash, but Holt didn't let me go. The heat of his body seeped into my back and felt far too comforting. "It was ten years ago."

Lawson began typing on his keyboard. "You never know what

we might find. We've still got all the evidence and records filed. I'll have them brought up so we can go over everything."

"Want an extra set of eyes?" Holt asked.

Lawson shook his head. "I'll keep you in the loop, but we can't have you in the room. If we do find something, having you there could call chain of custody into question."

Holt's jaw worked but he nodded. "Call me if you find anything."

"I will."

Holt turned me back to him, brushing the hair out of my face. "I'll pick you up at the end of your shift."

"Thanks."

"Remember, nowhere alone."

I made a face at him. "I know. And I will be surrounded by cops all day. I think I'll be safe."

"We'll make sure Little Williams doesn't get into any trouble," Nash said with a smirk.

Lawson sent Nash a quelling look and then turned back to me. "Holt's right about being careful. We don't know if the footprints outside your place are related to this. But until we know otherwise, we have to assume they are."

My stomach pitched, and Holt sent a glare in Lawson's direction. I worked to keep the worry off my face. "I'll be cautious. I promise. But right now, I need to get to work."

Holt lowered his head to brush his lips across mine. "Call me if you need me."

I swallowed the ball of emotion gathering in my throat. How often had I wanted to do just that? I would've given anything to hear Holt's voice on the other end of the line countless times. "Okay."

I forced myself to take a step back. "I should get to my desk."

Holt nodded. "I'll walk you."

We started out of the room, and all eyes were instantly on us. Only Amber approached. "What did the chief say? Are they bringing in Joe Sullivan?"

My stomach cramped. "I don't think he's any more of a suspect than anyone else is."

Amber glared at me, and her brown eyes sparked with some brighter color. "I thought you of all people would push for justice. Joe Sullivan is just like his brother, and everyone knows it."

"That sounds more like a witch hunt than justice to me. Don't you think Joe has been through enough?"

Redness crept up Amber's throat and stained her cheeks. "You've got to be kidding me. *You'd* defend him?"

"I'm not defending anyone. I'm just saying that Lawson is following the evidence, and so far, nothing points to Joe."

Amber stared daggers at me. "Have you forgotten what they put you through? What they cost you?" Unshed tears glistened in her eyes. "Or maybe you don't give a damn because you didn't die that day. Some people weren't that lucky."

Before I could get another word out, she spun on her heel and tore out of the station. Clint stared after his partner, wincing. "I'm sorry, Wren. She's been torn up lately. These shootings are bringing everything back."

"You need to have a word with your partner," Holt growled.

Clint's gaze hardened as he turned to Holt. "You've been back two minutes. I don't think you have a right to demand that I do anything."

"Guys," I said, trying to stop things before they escalated. "Let's take a breath." I lifted my gaze to Clint. "I know she's hurting. I don't want to make that worse, and I know I usually do. I'll do what I can to keep my distance. But Holt's right, you need to talk to her. This obsession with Joe isn't right."

Clint's focus drifted to the back door that Amber had torn through. "I know. I've tried. She doesn't want to hear me."

"So, keep trying. We all need to be focused on finding the person truly behind these attacks."

Because if we didn't, someone else would die.

Chapter Twenty-Seven

Holt

I PUSHED OPEN THE DOOR AND STEPPED OUTSIDE, FEELING A tug somewhere deep. I didn't want to leave Wren. Even knowing she was in the safest place in town, it still felt wrong.

It didn't help that I knew I was leaving her in the vicinity of Amber's venom. I'd seen the way Wren had gone pale at Amber's words. How her hands had tightened into fists as she struggled to stay in the here and now. And I'd wanted to throttle Amber for it.

I cracked my neck, trying to alleviate some of the tension there. It didn't work. Instead of heading to my SUV, I moved toward the coffee shop down the block. It had obviously changed hands since I'd left. The sign above it now was painted in whimsical letters: *The Brew.*

The inside of the place had the same fanciful look like *Alice in Wonderland.* But the smattering of people inside told me they must have decent coffee.

As I opened the door, a tiny bell jingled overhead. A red-haired woman behind the counter smiled widely at me. "Welcome to The Brew. What can I get for you?"

"Can I get a drip? Black with one sugar?"

She visibly deflated at the unoriginal order.

"And, uh, I'll have one of those scones." I pointed to something in the bakery case.

Her face lit up again. "Those orange-cranberry ones are amazing. You won't regret it."

"Thanks." I handed her a bill. "Keep the change."

"Coming right up." The woman bustled around to ready my order.

I turned to fully take in the space, and my gaze caught on the occupants of a corner table. Jude and Chris sat with what looked like breakfast burritos and large mugs of coffee.

Jude waved me over.

I made a motion for him to give me a minute, but I didn't miss the hard set of Chris's jaw. I wasn't welcome.

"Here you go, sir. I hope you have a wonderful day."

"Thank you. You, too."

I took the to-go cup and bakery bag and moved in the direction of some of my oldest friends. No more running. If Chris was pissed at me, he could let that out to my face, and I'd take whatever he had to say.

"Hey, guys. Late start?"

Construction was usually up and going before nine.

Jude grinned. "Just killing a little time before a client meeting. What are you doing in town?"

"Just dropping Wren at the station."

Chris's expression hardened, but he didn't say a word.

I lowered myself into the empty chair without asking, turning to face him. "Look, I get that you were here for Wren when I wasn't. I'll never be able to repay you for that. Never."

Chris grunted.

"I know I hurt you." I glanced at Jude. "Both of you. I'm so damn sorry. And I'll do what I can to make it right. You want to tell me what a shit friend I was? I'll listen to every word you have to say. You want to deck me? I'll give you one free punch."

Chris's jaw worked back and forth, but he wasn't telling me to get lost. So, I kept pushing on.

"I love Wren. Never stopped. It killed me every single day to be away from her. But I'm here now, and I'm not going anywhere. I'll fight with everything I have for her. And she's giving me a shot. So, I'm taking it."

Pain flashed across Chris's face. I'd hurt him again. But the truth was, if Wren had been interested in him, they'd be together now. I wasn't angry that he'd developed feelings for her. She was a living, breathing miracle and impossible not to love. But they weren't meant to be.

"You're sticking around?" Jude asked.

"I'm staying. Need to figure out what that looks like, but I'm not going anywhere."

A grin stretched across Jude's mouth. "I'm damn glad to hear it. Cedar Ridge hasn't been the same without you."

"Thanks, man." I turned back to Chris. "I'd like for us to find a way back to our friendship."

His jaw clenched. "It's not about me. You didn't see her, Holt. I'm not trying to be an ass, but you need to know. You wrecked that girl. And I'm worried you're gonna do the same thing all over again if things get too hard."

Chris's intention might not have been to hurt me, but he'd succeeded just the same. The idea of how much pain Wren had been in after I left was something I'd never forgive myself for. "I didn't leave because things were hard. I left because I thought I didn't deserve her. That she needed someone better."

It was the first time I'd stated it that plainly. Something about it was freeing.

Chris's gaze met mine. "What makes you think you deserve her now?"

"Oh, I don't. There's no question. She deserves so much better than me. But I'm going to do everything I can to be that man."

Chris studied me, looking for something. "I guess we'll see."

The words weren't exactly full of confidence. But I'd take them anyway. "You will."

Because I had a feeling that proving I could stick would go a long way to smoothing over some of Chris's resentments.

Jude rubbed his hands together. "Gang's all back together now."

Chris let out another grunt.

Maybe we weren't quite back to three-musketeers status. I got to my feet, grabbing my coffee and scone. "I gotta get back to the cabin. Hope you guys have a good meeting."

A little of the humor fled from Jude's face. "Any updates on things?"

I instantly knew what he meant and shook my head. "Nothing yet. But I hope like hell they get something soon."

"Let us know if you hear anything," Chris said.

"I will."

I maneuvered around the tables and headed out into the morning sunshine. It was going to be a beautiful day—perfect weather for working with Shadow on a little training.

My steps faltered as I turned to head back to the station and my SUV. Joe Sullivan stood across the street, staring at me, his eyes blazing. And he was wearing a black hoodie.

Chapter Twenty-Eight

Wren

I PUSHED BACK FROM MY DESK AS LUCILLE LOWERED HERSELF into the chair at the cubicle opposite me.

"How were things today?"

Her tone was even, but her eyes held worry. She'd seen some rough calls in her eight years on the job, but shootings were a whole other level.

"Pretty quiet. Possible heart attack this morning. Minor car accident this afternoon."

While I was grateful there hadn't been anything like yesterday, it had left me with far too much time to think. And remember. Holt's hands on my body. His lips skimming my skin. The way everything had come apart around us.

"You holding up okay?"

Lucille's voice had me snapping back to the present. "Yeah. I'm fine." I forced a smile. "I'll be less so when I have to switch to nights in two days, but that's life."

She chuckled. "Those first two days are the worst. Doesn't matter which direction I'm making the switch."

For me, the nights were always rougher. I needed the sunshine. The four p.m. to two a.m. and two a.m. to nine a.m. shifts were brutal. I had to mainline coffee and do the occasional round of jumping jacks in my cubicle.

"They really should give us extra pay on those switch days."

Lucille snorted. "Run that by the chief."

"I just might."

Lucille let out a low whistle as I bent to grab my bag.

"I think you've got a visitor."

I straightened, turning in the direction she had her gaze pointed. The hard swallow was reflex. There was Holt, eyes zeroed in on me with intensity. He wore a Henley that hinted at the muscles beneath—dips and valleys I'd had my hands on just hours ago. He had the sleeves pushed up, exposing tanned forearms. My gaze trailed to his fingers—long and talented fingers.

Lucille laughed. "Oh, girl. You are so screwed. I just hope it's in a fun way."

"You and me both," I grumbled as I started toward the man in question.

As soon as I was within arm's reach, Holt took the bag from my shoulder. He leaned in to give me a quick kiss. "Good day?"

The normalcy of it all grated, maybe because I'd wanted it for so long. Someone to share my life with. The ups and downs of my day. But it wasn't just *someone* I'd wanted. It was Holt. And now that he was here, acting as if he'd never left, I battled between annoyance and blissful relief. But the emotion eating at me the most was fear.

"It was mellow."

"That's good, right?"

"I think we can all use mellow right about now."

Holt held the door for me, and I stepped through. As soon as we were on the sidewalk, he took my hand in his. The feel of those calluses against my more delicate skin sent a pleasant shiver up my arm. My body was a damn traitor for Holt Hartley.

He opened the passenger door of his SUV, and I climbed in.

Holt rounded the vehicle and got behind the wheel, tossing my bag onto the back seat.

I toyed with my fingernail as Holt pulled out of the parking space and started toward my cabin. This had always been him. He wasn't afraid of a little silence. On the other hand, I felt as if I were crawling out of my skin.

"So, what did you do today?"

He glanced over at me and then back to the road. "Got a coffee and scone at The Brew. The scone was incredible."

I couldn't help the smile that came to my lips. "They have the best baked goods. Did you get the orange-cranberry?"

"Yup. Finished it before I even got home."

My heart jolted at the word *home*, but I shoved it down. "Then what did you do?"

"Worked with Shadow in the morning. She's got great instincts. I really think she'd be an asset to the SAR team."

Pride bloomed. "She's always been too smart for her own good."

Holt chuckled, the sound swirling around me. "That just means we need to keep her busy. Give her a job. She kept me company while I installed your security system."

My brows lifted. "You installed it?"

Holt shrugged as he turned off the main road and onto the dirt lane that would take us to the cabin. "I would've preferred to have Cain's team do it, but they're maxed out right now. It would've taken them at least another week to get up here. Didn't want to wait around."

"No laser beams that will blow me up, right?"

The corner of his mouth kicked up. "No laser beams. I promise."

At least there was that. Holt pulled in next to my truck. "You need a garage."

"Please tell me that your next project isn't to single-handedly build me one."

He grinned. "Not single-handedly. But I thought it might be a good project for me, Jude, and Chris to take on while the weather's good."

Chris had been harping on the fact that I needed a garage for years—pretty much since I bought the place. I was sure that he and Jude would jump at the chance to get that taken care of.

"I don't mind not having one. It's only a pain when it snows."

Holt shook his head as he slid out of the SUV. "Safer for your truck and you to have one. We could put in a mudroom that connects the garage to the house."

I rounded the vehicle and started toward the cabin. "I don't know what you think dispatchers make, but it's not enough for a project like that." Maybe one day, but not anytime soon. The only way I'd gotten this place at all was because of the nest egg Gran had left me. A nest egg my father hadn't been overly pleased about.

"I've got it."

My steps faltered, and I slowly turned to face Holt. "You've got it?"

"I've got plenty of money, Wren. It's just sitting there. Why not use it here?"

"Because it's not your house. It's mine. Gran gave me the money for a down payment, but I worked my butt off to get approved for the loan. And I work my butt off to pay the mortgage every month. That's important to me. I have a place that I earned. That's mine."

Hurt flashed in Holt's eyes but he covered it quickly. "Okay. No garage."

The annoyance seeped right out of me as I took in the man opposite me. "I'm not trying to be a jerk, but after you left, I had to figure out how to stand on my own two feet. And I'm not sorry I did. It's given me a sense of pride that I didn't have before. When we were together, I leaned on you too much."

"I liked you leaning."

Because Holt liked being the problem solver, the one people relied on. It gave him a sense of purpose. That wasn't a bad thing, but he took on things that weren't his to carry.

"We need to find a better balance." The words were out of my mouth before I could stop them. Dangerous words because they spoke of a future—one that was far from guaranteed. "A give and a take."

Holt moved into my space. His hand brushed the hair out of my face and then skated down my neck until he massaged my shoulders. "If you think I didn't lean on you, then you weren't paying attention. Every time I needed an escape from the craziness of my family. When life hit hard, you were the only person I wanted, the only place I wanted to be. You, more than anything, were home."

I let my head fall to his chest. "Okay. Just hold off on any major construction, would you? Whatever this is…it's new. I can't just go back."

"I get it. Come on. Let's get inside. I'm making you dinner tonight."

Holt made my head spin. Making me dinner might not be breaking ground on a new garage, but it was a part of that life I wanted so badly I could taste it. And the more I let myself want it, the worse the fall would be if things didn't work out. I'd barely survived the first time Holt had left. A second time would be too much to bear.

But I couldn't bring myself to say those words aloud. Instead, I followed Holt inside.

Shadow let out a happy bark and ran toward us. I dropped to a crouch, shoving my face in her neck as I stroked her. This was what I needed. Normal. Constant. Grounding.

"I was going to make Pad See Ew. That good with you?"

I pushed to my feet and moved toward the kitchen. "You make Pad See Ew?"

Holt pulled two beers out of the fridge. "One of my clients was in Thailand for a month. I picked up a few things."

And he'd remembered that it was one of my favorite dishes. Every time we'd ventured to Seattle or Portland, I begged to go to a restaurant that featured a cuisine we didn't have in Cedar Ridge. Thai was my favorite. Indian. Lebanese. Ethiopian. Greek. It was the one thing I hated about living in a small town, we missed out on all that food.

"I bet you've been to a lot of cool places."

Holt popped the cap on the bottle and slid it across the bar to me. "Some cool places and some I'd be happy to never see again."

I slid onto the stool, surveying the man opposite me. "What was your favorite?"

He grinned. "Mykonos. We were doing a security detail for a billionaire and his family, but they never left the estate. We basically got a paid vacation for two weeks. And it was gorgeous."

"Sounds like a pretty cushy job."

A little of his smile dimmed. "Sometimes. What about you? Did you ever think about leaving Cedar Ridge?"

I shook my head. "You know I love it here. The people I love are here. My job."

"When did you decide to apply for dispatch?"

I toyed with a napkin. "A couple of months before I graduated. I wanted to be that voice on the other end of the line for someone else. Wanted to be their hope."

Emotion danced in Holt's eyes. "It's incredible that you've taken the worst moment of your life and used it to inspire you to do good."

My gaze locked with his. "Did you do the same? Military, private security, it's all helping people."

A muscle in his cheek ticked. "There was a fair bit of running mixed in there, too."

I studied the man across from me, trying to muster the courage to ask what I needed to. "Do you really think you'd be happy sticking around Cedar Ridge after being used to that life for so long? The travel? The excitement?"

He opened his beer and rounded the bar, leaning against the counter. "Going a lot of places just makes you realize the value of home more. I'm here, Wren. I'll figure out a way to make that stick. Work remotely or sell the company. Whatever it takes."

My breaths started coming faster, panic and hope warring inside me.

Holt's gaze tracked over my face. "I want you to know I'm here for good."

I pushed off the stool, needing to move. I wanted Holt here with everything I had, but I was terrified to let myself actually say the words out loud. To admit it to anyone.

"Wren..."

Something in his voice had my steps halting, but I didn't turn around. "It destroyed me when you left. I'm terrified that if you leave again, I won't recover a second time."

"I'm so sorry. Those words aren't enough but—" Holt's words cut off as his gaze jerked to the window. The sun glinted off it as it sank low in the sky.

The color leached from Holt's face, and it was as if the world around me slowed. "Down!"

But Holt was already moving, throwing himself at me. Glass shattered. Holt's body collided with mine. And then we were falling.

Chapter Twenty-Nine

Holt

BLOOD ROARED IN MY EARS AS I TOOK WREN DOWN, rolling us toward the couch and cover.

Shadow let out a series of loud barks.

"Shadow, bed," I bellowed.

The dog ran to the crate that housed her bed. It would give her cover. Protection.

My hand slid to the holster at the small of my back, pulling my weapon. My gaze jumped from the trees to Wren, moving back and forth as I tried to assess as much of the situation as I could in brief snapshots. "Are you okay? Are you hurt?"

Wren blinked up at me, stunned. "I-I think I'm fine."

My free hand skimmed over her body, looking for any signs of injury. When I found none, I pulled my phone from my pocket and hit Lawson's contact.

"No updates yet, Holt. I told you I'd call when—"

"Someone just shot at me and Wren at the cabin. Rifle shot. Northwest side of the yard." The faint sound of an all-terrain vehicle starting up carried on the air. "Look for an ATV. I can hear the engine."

Lawson was already moving, barking orders to someone. "Are you and Wren hit? You okay?"

The slight hint of panic reminded me just how much my brother loved me. "We're both fine. Can't say the same for her window."

"Keep cover until we get there."

"You got it."

I disconnected the call and looked down at Wren. She wasn't moving. Her eyes were wide, her gaze shifting too quickly as it scanned my body.

"Wren? Talk to me."

Her mouth opened and closed, but no words came out.

I laid my gun on the floor within easy reach and began feeling each of Wren's limbs, trying to lift her to check her back. Had she been hit, and I hadn't realized it?

The moment I tried to get her into a sitting position, Wren threw herself at me. She held on with everything she had, her legs wrapped around my waist, arms gripping me like a vise. A sob tore free from her throat.

"Cricket." I leaned back against the couch, taking her with me. "We're okay."

"You dove in front of a bullet." The words were barely discernable through hiccupped sobs.

"I dove for *you*. I will every time."

Her head shook back and forth frantically. "You can't. Promise me. You can't."

Wren chanted the words over and over as if she could will the vow from me.

"I can't promise you that."

Her fist thumped against my back. "Why?"

"Because I love you too damn much."

Wren only cried harder. "I-I can't lose you, Holt. Don't make me lose you."

I held her tighter, rocking back and forth. "You're not going to lose me. I'm right here, and I'm not going anywhere."

Wren's hands fisted in my shirt as the sound of sirens filled the air.

"See? The cops are coming. Whoever this was is long gone."

"They could come back," she whispered. "They could be faster next time."

She had a point there. I'd be calling Cain tonight to see what their company had for bulletproof glass. Maybe something with a tint that you couldn't see through.

"We're gonna stay safe. I promise." Because we had no other option. I wouldn't lose Wren now. Not when I'd held her in my arms again. Not when I knew now what it meant to lose myself in her—with her. Not when I was finally home.

Three police department vehicles came to a screeching halt outside the cabin. Lawson was the first out of his SUV, running for the house. Nash was hot on his heels, the other officers right behind.

"We need to let them in, Cricket."

Wren simply clung to me.

So, I got up with her still in my arms. She held on tight, her face burrowed in the crook of my neck.

"Holt?" Lawson called.

"Coming." I picked up my weapon, holstering it and starting for the door. I unlocked it and stepped back. "I've got my weapon at the small of my back."

I didn't say it for Lawson and Nash, they'd assume I was armed after everything that had gone down the past few days. I said it as a courtesy for the officers behind them.

Concern creased Nash's face as he took in the scene, noticing Wren, who still held on to me for dear life. "Is she okay?"

I gave my head a small shake. "She's not injured." But Wren was far from okay.

"Why don't we get you sitting down?" Law said and then

instructed the other officers to begin working the perimeter and searching for the shooter's nest.

Moving into the living room, I lowered myself to the couch and positioned Wren so she could curl up in my lap.

Lawson crouched so he could make eye contact with Wren. "You sure you're okay?"

She nodded, starting to come back to herself as she took in Lawson. "I'm okay."

The words were barely audible, but she sat up. Wren started to slide off my lap, but I kept her close, my arm wrapped around her. Instead of fighting me, she snuggled against my side.

"Walk us through what happened," Lawson said.

I held Wren tighter, not wanting her to have to hear this after living through it, but also not able to let her go. "We were standing by the island, and I saw a glint on the window. I knew it wasn't the sun—it was coming from the wrong direction. Instinct took over. I took Wren down and rolled her. The window shattered. A minute later, I heard an ATV while on the phone with you."

"You're sure it was an ATV?" Nash asked.

"Could've been a dirt bike, I guess. It wasn't a car, truck, or SUV, though. Different engine."

Lawson nodded, making a note in his phone. "We've got all available officers looking."

Nash strode to the wall opposite the new opening where the window had been. "There's your bullet."

Wren swallowed hard. "This could've been so bad."

I leaned into her, resting my forehead against her temple. "We're okay."

She shuddered, and I held her closer.

Lawson cleared his throat. "I texted Jude and asked him to bring over some plywood to board up the window. We can get some new glass ordered, and everything will be back to normal before you know it."

"Thanks. I'm actually going to talk to a friend about some specialty glass," I said.

Wren twisted to face me. Relief washed through me as I took in her expression. All wary skepticism. "What kind of special?"

"Something that will keep people from being able to easily see inside."

"And something impossible to shoot through," Nash muttered under his breath.

Wren let out a sigh, pinching the bridge of her nose. "Is it going to launch rockets in a counterattack, too?"

Lawson couldn't contain his chuckle. "If Holt has anything to say about it, I'm sure there will be an entire missile defense system."

"You know it's rude to gang up on someone," I huffed.

She leaned into me, her mouth curving as she pressed it against my arm. "You might be a *tad* overzealous."

If my girl was giving me a hard time, she was coming back to herself. My breaths came a little easier. "You say overzealous. I say prepared."

An officer knocked on the open door and strode inside. "We found the shooter's nest. There are tracks from an ATV, but no one has seen any sign of the vehicle."

Lawson glanced my way. "Good ears." He turned back to the officer I didn't recognize. "The crime scene techs are on their way from county. They should be here in another thirty minutes to process the evidence there and in the house."

I met my brother's gaze. "Have you zeroed in on any suspects?"

He shook his head. "Not yet. Still talking to people."

I glanced at Wren and then back to Lawson. "I saw Joe in town earlier today. He was wearing a black hoodie."

Wren stiffened next to me. "Holt—"

I squeezed her hand. "I'm not saying he did this, but they need to talk to him."

"I'm going to," Lawson assured me and then turned in Wren's direction. "I'll go as easy as I can on him, but Joe's connected to the shooting ten years ago. A lot of people are. I'm going to talk to every single one."

"I hate this," Wren whispered so that only I could hear.

"I'm sorry, Cricket."

She shook her head. "I know they need to do it and that they're only trying to help, but I hate the idea of analyzing everyone in our community. I hate the idea of strangers pulling apart my home, looking for pieces of whoever this is."

Shadow nosed her way out of the crate, and I motioned her to come to Wren's side. The dog nuzzled her owner's hand, and Wren started petting her.

"We'll make this place your home again."

She blinked up at me, unshed tears gathering in her eyes. "It's been my sanctuary for so long. I've always felt safe here."

Fury lit somewhere deep inside me. That someone would terrorize Wren after everything she'd been through... That they'd try to destroy the haven she'd work so hard to build for herself.

"We'll make you safe here again. Whatever it takes."

Chapter Thirty

Wren

"THAT SHOULD HOLD THINGS," JUDE SAID AS HE SHOT the last nail into the plywood that covered the hole. The huge plates of glass had once been one of my favorite parts of the home—a window that looked out at the lake and one that faced the forest. But I wasn't sure I'd be able to look at them the same way again.

Jude shook his head as he surveyed the room. "I'm so damn sorry this happened."

I let out a shuddering breath. "Thank you for helping us deal with the mess."

Not only had Jude covered the window, but he'd also patched the hole in the wall.

"Of course. Chris is going to pick up some paint that matches your walls tomorrow. Before long, you won't be able to tell that any of this happened."

I glanced at Holt, hanging makeshift curtains over my other large window. I'd never bothered with finding anything to cover them before, but now, I guessed it was necessary. It felt as if the walls were closing in around me. I could almost hear the sound of bars clanging closed in my mind.

"Is he okay?" Jude asked quietly.

The concern in Jude's voice had my heart clenching. I studied Holt as he made sure the curtains were secure, checking every possible vantage point. We were both rattled. We just dealt with it in different ways.

"I think so. You know Holt. He'll try to come at this like a problem he can fix. Assessing every possible angle."

But this wasn't something Holt could fix.

"He loves you. It would kill him if anything happened to you," Jude said.

"I can't let anything happen to him either." Some of the panic from earlier found its way back, clawing at my insides. The day's events replayed in my mind: Holt diving for me, the window shattering, not knowing if he'd been hit.

"Nothing's going to happen to Holt," Jude assured me.

I watched as Holt checked the locks on the windows for what seemed like the millionth time. "I don't want him taking my welfare on his shoulders either. I don't want him blaming himself for every little thing that does or doesn't happen to me." Because that hadn't worked out for us very well before.

Jude was quiet for a moment. "I'm not sure that's something you can control. When you care about someone, you don't want anything to happen to them. If it does, it feels like it's your fault—even if that isn't true."

He was right in so many ways. I would've taken that on if something had happened to Holt this afternoon. I blew out a breath. "I guess we'll just have to make sure nothing happens to either of us, then."

"I guess so." Jude ruffled my hair in his familiar move. "I gotta get going, but call if you guys need anything else."

Holt strode across the space, extending a hand. "Thanks, man. Really appreciate you doing all of this."

I knew it meant the world to Holt. I'd seen the hurt on his face when he realized that Chris hadn't shown. Jude had made some excuse, but I was about ready to drop-kick my friend.

"Anytime. Let me know if the cops find out anything."

"We will." Holt walked Jude to the door, locking it behind him.

I didn't move. Suddenly, I was bone-tired. The kind of fatigue that had nothing to do with sleep but soul-deep weariness.

Holt moved toward me, brushing the hair from my face. "Can I make you something to eat?"

The idea of putting anything in my stomach, even my favorite Thai food, had nausea rolling through me. "I think I just want to take a shower and go to bed." It was only nine, but I'd had enough of today.

"Okay," he whispered into my hair. A second later, Holt was leading me to the bathroom.

He opened the door and flicked on the light. After switching on the water, he turned back to me, going for the hem of my blouse and pulling it over my head.

"What are you doing?"

Holt let the garment flutter to the floor, then leaned in and brushed his lips against mine. "Let me take care of you."

There went that skip in my heartbeat again, the one I used to feel every day thanks to Holt Hartley—the one I'd longed for since the day he left.

"Okay."

Holt's fingers went to the button on my jeans, undoing it and pulling down the zipper. Each click of the metal tines sent sparks of sensation dancing across my skin.

I kicked off my shoes, and Holt tugged on my pants, sending them to the floor. His fingers hooked in the lacy underwear I'd put on that day, thinking there was a chance he might be taking them off. I hadn't pictured that event going down quite like this, though.

Holt slid the lace down my thighs, lifting one leg and then the other to free me. I unhooked my bra and tossed it onto the pile of clothes.

It only took Holt a matter of seconds to shed his, and I couldn't help but take him in.

"You're staring, Cricket."

The corner of my mouth lifted. "You're nice to look at."

Holt chuckled as he opened the shower door. "I'm glad you think so."

I stepped inside the tiled space and moved straight for the stream of water. Ducking under the spray, I let the heavenly warmth rush over me.

Holt moved in behind me. His fingers dug into my shoulders, kneading the muscles.

I let out a little moan but didn't move.

It turned out Holt didn't need direction. He grabbed the shampoo from the shelf in the wall and set to work on my hair. His tenderness made my eyes sting, the way he massaged my scalp and made sure every strand was thoroughly washed.

When Holt moved on to conditioner, he combed the substance through my strands with his fingers, doing a far better job than I ever did. He tipped my head back to rinse my hair and pressed a kiss to the hollow of my throat.

A moment later, he filled his hands with body wash. My thighs clenched in anticipation—want.

Now I knew what it was to have Holt's hands on my skin. To have them everywhere.

He ran the soap up and down my arms, over my stomach, and then across my breasts. My nipples peaked as I arched back into him.

"Holt." His name was a barely audible whisper.

His lips skimmed my neck. "Love you, Wren."

My heart cracked. I couldn't give him those words yet, even though I knew they'd never stopped being true. Just the idea of saying them aloud had my throat constricting and my hands shaking.

His mouth hovered near my ear. "Don't say anything. I just need you to know."

I turned in Holt's arms, my mouth seeking his. I might not be able to give him the words, but I could give him my actions. I could give him *me*.

Holt let out a low growl and deepened the kiss as he hardened against my belly.

I felt the vibrations of that growl everywhere. It lit a fire inside me. A desperation to fight off the memories of earlier and the knowledge that I could lose him in any number of ways. It was a deep need to prove to myself that I could hold on.

My hand slid between us, stroking his length, up and down, relishing the feel of him hardening further.

"Wren…"

"Take me."

I needed Holt. Needed the fire we created between us that was ours alone.

Holt lifted me, stepping back out of the spray and lowering us to the tile bench at the back of the stall. His eyes blazed. "Your show, Cricket."

My confidence faltered for a moment. I didn't have the first clue what I was doing. All I knew was how Holt made me come alive beneath his fingertips.

Holt's mouth brushed against mine. "You're all I want. Feel that."

He pressed himself against my core and everything in me tightened in delicious need. His reaction showed how much Holt wanted me. It gave me just enough courage to move.

My knees rested on either side of his thighs, and I slowly sank onto him. My lips parted at the achingly beautiful stretch.

Holt traced my bottom lip with his thumb. "Nothing but beauty."

He rocked against me, and tiny waves of sensation coursed through me, spurring me on. My hips began to move, almost of their own volition. Tiny rises and falls, testing tilts and arcs.

Everything in me turned to liquid heat as I moved. Holt joined me in the dance, his hips lifting to meet mine. We lost ourselves in the rhythm, the pulse that was only ours.

But it wasn't enough. I wanted Holt to let go. To make me his in a way that meant he'd be with me always.

"Holt." I didn't care that I was pleading. "I need more."

He lifted me off him in a flash. I whimpered at the loss, but he spun me around to face the wall a second later. He thrust inside in one long glide, and I nearly wept with relief. I pushed back, seeking more.

Holt thrust deeper, picking up speed. My legs trembled as my inner walls quivered.

My back arched, meeting him for each movement. I braced my hands against the tile as tears of feeling filled my eyes.

Holt's hand slid between my legs and circled that bundle of nerves. The sound that escaped me wasn't anything I'd ever heard fall from my lips.

"Are you with me?"

"With. You."

Holt flicked my clit, and my world tunneled. If it weren't for his quick reflexes, I would've hit the floor. But Holt's arm encircled my waist, and he held me up as he thrust one last time, my name on his lips.

We collapsed onto the bench, trying to catch our breath.

"Too much?" he asked softly.

"No. Perfect."

Because Holt had done just what my soul had cried out for. He'd marked me in a way that I would never forget, no matter what came our way.

Grae sat opposite me in the overstuffed chair in my living room, her legs curled under her. And she was fighting a smile. "You look way too glowy for being shot at last night. Almost like someone got herself some."

My hand stilled as I reached out to hand her a mug of coffee. "I don't know what you're talking about."

I sent up a million tiny thank-yous that Holt currently wasn't on the premises. What we did have were two officers parked outside the cabin. I tried not to let their presence make me feel trapped, but it was hard not to. The sensation was so familiar that it threw me back to a time when reporters had been camped out on my street, and I felt sure the third shooter would show up at any moment.

Grae only grinned wider, oblivious to my spiraling thoughts. "It's not like I want details. That's my brother. Ick! But I do want to know that you're happy."

I tugged on the corner of my lip with my teeth.

The amusement fled Grae's expression. "You're not happy."

"I'm happy," I whispered.

"Then why do you look like someone just stole your puppy?"

Shadow lifted her head at that.

I sank back onto the couch, pulling my knees to my chest. "I'm scared someone's going to steal that happy."

Grae nodded. "Someone like Holt?"

"Or the shooter. Every time I think about letting myself *really* want this..."

"It terrifies you."

I nodded.

Grae blew out a breath as she settled back into her seat and punched something into her insulin pump. "I'm so sorry, Wren."

"I know it's not rational, but I can't stop the fear from taking hold. I have these moments of crazy joy, but in between, all I see are the endless possibilities for how that could all be taken away."

Grae sipped her coffee. "That's the risk we all face. The price for loving deeply. Family, friendships, relationships. The only certain thing is that we'll lose each other."

My mouth went dry at her words.

"We don't have control over that. We can only control how we live until it's our time. Do you want to spend your time worrying yourself sick? Or do you want to *live*?"

So much of the past ten years had been about protecting myself: from pain, disappointment, and grief. I'd created a bubble that was good. Safe. Predictable. But it wasn't what life was with Holt. It let me escape a lot of the heartbreaking lows, but it didn't have the soaring highs that made the world come alive around me.

When I was with Holt, there was this juxtaposition of sensations. He grounded me in a way that made me feel at home yet propelled me into the air for the greatest rush of my life. I'd never met another person who made me feel that way. And I didn't want to lose that. I also didn't want to dull it by pulling back.

I lifted my gaze to Grae's. "If it doesn't work out, it's going to crush me."

She gave me a sad smile. "Sometimes, that's just the price we have to pay for the good stuff."

I stared at my friend. Her words were heavy with experience, but she'd only ever had casual boyfriends as far as I knew. Grae was the one who usually did the dumping.

"Are you okay?"

Her smile brightened. "I'm fine. But I'd be better if we could watch *Little Women*."

A rightness settled in my heart. Not much could be better right now than some time with my bestie, watching a movie we could both recite by heart. Maybe a little of Grae's fearlessness would rub off on me, and I'd be ready to take that final step.

Chapter Thirty-One

Holt

SHERIFF BRUCE JENKINS MOTIONED TO THE SITTING AREA on the side of his office. "Thanks for coming in. I know you've got a lot going on."

"I appreciate you making the time to see me."

Bruce nodded, offering me a bottle of water as I sat. "We're desperate for a search and rescue team leader for the county. Phyllis left some big shoes to fill when she retired, and we haven't had the right candidate come along since."

"It's a job that requires a lot of different skills."

Bruce studied me thoughtfully. "Tell me how you see it."

I nodded. "You've got the organizational piece. You need to run trainings, meetings, and searches. Facilitate schedules."

"Mm-hmm."

"Then there's the morale piece. So much of SAR is making sure your team gels. That they get the support they need if there's a tough callout. That there's an element of fun in it all as much as possible because these people are volunteers."

Bruce nodded. "That's something a lot of the applicants have overlooked. Anything else?"

"The most important piece is that you can give your all to the search. You know I grew up doing this. My dad had us learning how to track before we could read."

A grin stretched across Bruce's face. "That doesn't surprise me."

I chuckled. "He loved what he did. Still loves it. And he passed that on to all of us. You need that love to stay invested. Because there will be times when the outcomes aren't happy ones. And you still have to go. Because families need that closure."

Bruce drummed his fingers on his knee. "I'll be honest. You're overqualified for this job. I looked into your company after Law told me you were interested in the position, and I worry you might get antsy and leave me high and dry."

Annoyance bubbled to the surface. Proving my staying power was becoming a familiar refrain. I shoved the frustration down. "Can I be honest with *you*?"

"I'd appreciate it if you would."

"I left a girl behind when I took off."

Bruce arched a brow.

"And not just any girl. The one who makes everything settle when you're around her. The one who gives you peace and a safe place to let everything go."

"Been married three times." Bruce's eyes flashed as he spoke. "I know better than most that what you're describing there is a once-in-a-lifetime kind of thing. Something you'd be a fool to let go of."

"I was a fool. I hurt her. I'm trying to make it right. Want to prove to her that I'm in it for the long haul. And I missed my family. I missed these mountains. It's time for me to come home for good. And I can't imagine a better job to have while doing that."

Bruce huffed out a breath, leaning back in his chair. "Hell. The job's yours if you want it."

I grinned so widely that I probably looked a little deranged. "Romantic at heart, aren't you?"

He laughed. "I'm going to tell my wife you said that. And I'm going to tell her that little story of yours because it's gonna make her get all nostalgic about our story. Might even convince her to slow dance with me tonight."

"Sounds like you found the right one in the end."

"I did." Bruce stood, extending a hand. "Now you make sure you do, too. I'll email over the paperwork. We'll run your prints and all that jazz, but I don't expect there'll be a problem."

"Been background checked more times than I can count." And the truth was, if I'd wanted to hide anything in my past, I could've done that, too.

"Then you start in two weeks."

My brows lifted at that. I thought for sure he'd want me to start tomorrow.

"It'll give Law a chance to catch the son of a bitch who's terrorizing people in your neck of the woods."

"I appreciate that, sir."

"Call me Bruce. And remind Law that he's got my people whenever he needs them."

I shook his hand. "I know we're both grateful."

We said our goodbyes, and I made my way out of the sheriff's station, texting as I went.

Me: *How's everything at home?*

A reply flashed on my screen as I climbed into my SUV.

Cricket: *Grae and I called for strippers. I wouldn't come home anytime soon.*

I barked out a laugh. Apparently, my every thirty-minute check-ins hadn't gone unnoticed.

Me: *Hope you had the officers check them for weapons first.*

Cricket: *It was a little awkward since the strippers were dressed as cops.*

I shook my head.

Me: *I'll be home in about thirty.*

Cricket: *I'm heading into work. The non-stripper cops are driving me.*

Damn. I'd forgotten that Wren was working the later shift today.

Me: *Okay. I'll pick you up at two. I'm gonna stop by and see my parents on the way home and then I'll take Shadow for a run.*

Cricket: *You don't have to pick me up.*

Me: *I'm picking you up.*

Cricket: *Bossy.*

Me: *You can boss me around later.*

A new text popped up on my screen. It was a group text sent to me and Wren.

Grae: *Would you two stop sexting? Wren and I need to bawl our eyes out for the fifty millionth time as Beth dies, and then she has to go to work.*

Me: *I'd rather come home to strippers than Little Women AGAIN.*

I shoved my phone into the console and pulled out of the parking lot, a smile still pulling at my mouth. God, I'd missed this: the razzing from Grae, the banter with Wren, feeling like I had my family back.

Turning off the main road, I headed in the direction of my parents' place. I hadn't bothered to check if they were in. It was on the way back to Cedar Ridge and just a small detour up the mountain.

In a matter of minutes, I was punching in the code and the gates were opening. By the time I'd parked in front of the house, my mom was pulling open the front door. "This is a pleasant surprise."

But I didn't miss the worry on her face. "Everything's okay. You were on my way home from a meeting, so I thought I'd drop in."

The tension in my mom's face eased into a more genuine smile. "I made you and Wren a pie. Some cookies, too. They're just cooling. Come on in."

"Marionberry?" I asked hopefully.

"Do I look like a fool?"

"No, you certainly do not." I bent and gave her a hug. "What kind of cookies?"

"It isn't always about you, you know," Mom said, leading me into the house. "They're snickerdoodle."

Wren's favorite.

"I've become pretty partial to snickerdoodle over the years."

Her expression softened. "Because you're a smart man."

"Holt," my dad greeted from the dining table where he was working on a puzzle. "Come help me find this danged corner piece."

My mom sighed. "I don't know why he does those things. They only raise his blood pressure."

"I heard you," Dad called.

"I wasn't whispering," my mom singsonged. She carried a plate of cookies over to the table. "Any updates from Lawson?"

I shook my head as I grabbed a cookie. "Not yet." I was beginning to worry that we would need more evidence, and that meant another crime.

Pulling out a chair across from my parents, I sat. "I met with Bruce Jenkins today."

The puzzle piece my dad had been flipping between his fingers stilled. "About the case or something else?"

"About the SAR job."

Mom's face lit up like a kid at Christmas. "About you taking the job?"

"He said it's mine."

My dad was quiet for a moment, and an unsettling feeling swept over me.

"Dad?"

He stared down at the puzzle. "I don't want you taking a job because I laid a guilt trip on you."

"I'm not. I swear. But I won't lie, you're a part of the decision—you all are. I miss my family, this town, SAR. I missed Wren."

Tears gathered in my mother's eyes. "How does Wren feel about all this?"

"She doesn't know about the job yet, but she's coming around to the idea of me."

Dad barked out a laugh as he wrapped an arm around my mom, nuzzling her neck. "I had to talk Kerry around to the idea of me, if I remember correctly."

She swatted at him. "I thought he was nothing but an adrenaline junkie bad boy." She gave him a quick kiss. "But I reined him in right quick."

"I *let* you rein me in."

"Whatever makes you feel better," Mom huffed.

Dad turned back to me, his expression sobering. "I need to say something, and I don't want you to take it the wrong way."

I braced myself as my mom squeezed his hand tightly.

"I've thought of Wren as a daughter from the moment Grae latched on to her, and I realized her parents were selfish wastes of space."

I gripped the edge of my chair, the wood digging into my palms. "I'm glad she has you."

Worry deepened the lines on his face, and I couldn't help the stiffening in my muscles. "What is it?"

Dad shook his head. "You're both finally getting what you've always wanted. I don't want anyone taking that from you."

But I heard the words he really meant. Someone wanted to finish what Randy and Paul had started, and Wren could be next.

Chapter Thirty-Two

Wren

I ROLLED MY CHAIR BACK AND STOOD. ARCHING MY BACK, I twisted to one side. How was it that sitting still was somehow harder once the sun went down? And working alone made me twitchy.

No other dispatcher was on duty tonight, and there were only a couple of officers in the station. It was a ghost town. It was better than the few occasions I'd been in the building with only the officer behind the reception desk, but still too quiet.

One of the things I loved about working here was the constant buzz of noise. I had the officers on the radio, but even they were typically quieter at night. Tourists pulled over for speeding or DUIs, and the occasional party that needed to be broken up for noise complaints would pick up soon.

I'd have given anything for those calls right now. Instead, I waited, muscles tense and ready to spring into action at the first call of trouble.

It seemed everyone else was feeling the same way. Officers were patrolling neighborhoods, looking for anyone who might be up to no good, their windows rolled down, listening for the sound of a bullet.

Heat crept up the back of my neck, along with a prickling sensation. I glanced over my shoulder to meet a glacial stare. Amber didn't make any move to avert her gaze.

I sighed inwardly and lowered myself back into my chair. So much for Clint talking to her.

The phone on my desk beeped. It wasn't that of an incoming call to nine-one-one but an internal call from within the police station. "This is Wren."

"It's Lawson. Can I talk to you for a minute? Route dispatch calls to my office."

My stomach twisted. "Sure."

I hung up and set up call forwarding. Keeping my head high, I made my way to Lawson's office, studiously avoiding Amber's gaze. Why did I feel like I was being called to the principal's office?

I knocked softly on Lawson's door.

"Come in."

Stepping inside, I shut the door behind me. "I didn't know you were still here." It was almost midnight, and Lawson liked to keep his nights free for the boys.

He grimaced. "Too much to look into. I asked the sitter to stay the night."

The dark circles under his eyes looked even more pronounced than a few days ago. "Just make sure you get some sleep at some point."

The corner of his mouth lifted. "You mothering me, Wren?"

I crossed my arms. "Somebody needs to."

"Trust me, Kerry Hartley does plenty of that."

"But you've gotten too good at hiding how much stress you're under from her." Because Lawson didn't want anyone to worry about him. He was always the one who assumed the role of caretaker.

His jaw tightened. "She doesn't need anything else on her plate right now."

I lowered myself to the chair opposite his desk. "It's okay to ask for help now and again. You know that, right? We'd all love to help with the boys. And I know the other officers here would be happy to take some of your load."

"I can handle my responsibilities," Lawson said, an edge slipping into his tone.

I was treading into the no-go zone. "Okay. I'm just saying we're here if you need us."

His expression gentled. "Thank you. I appreciate it."

Unfortunately, he would never take me up on the offered help.

Lawson leaned back in his chair. "I heard you and Amber had a little run-in."

It was the last thing I'd expected to come out of his mouth. I'd thought Lawson might be updating me on the case or checking to see how I was holding up. "Run-in might be too strong a word."

"Not from what I heard."

My eyes narrowed. "Did Holt call you?"

"No, but he should've. I won't have my officers being cruel to each other."

"She's been through a lot."

Lawson sighed. "I know that. It's why I've given her as much lenience as I have. But she's about to cross a line that she can't come back from, and she's not getting the message."

My teeth toyed with the corner of my lip. "She didn't say anything that awful."

Amber had been hurt, grieving, and had needed to let loose some of that pain. It might not have been fair, but I understood.

"Did she throw the shooting in your face?"

My mouth pressed into a hard line.

"That's what I thought."

"Don't get her in trouble over this, Law. I don't want it. And it'll only make things worse between us."

There was a brief moment of hesitation before Lawson shook his head. "I'll make it clear that you didn't want this and weren't the person to report it. But Amber needs to realize the ramifications of her actions. There's no way she'll become the cop she's capable of if she doesn't."

The twisting sensation was back in my stomach. Because I got his point. Lawson did everything he could to create a healthy environment for his officers and the town. He didn't take the trust the town had put in us lightly. Anyone who put that in jeopardy by behaving badly was dealt with swiftly.

"I try to stay out of her way. I know I bring up bad memories for her, and it kills me that I'd cause someone else pain in that way. I know how it feels."

Lawson stared at me for a moment. "The difference is that you haven't let it harden you. You haven't taken that pain out on others. I see how you react to Joe. You make sure to give him a smile and a kind word every time you see him. That can't be easy."

"What his brother did isn't his fault." It made me sick that people in this town would hold that against him.

"No, it's not. And Amber needs to get that through her head."

"I don't know if disciplinary action will get her there."

Lawson shrugged. "It might not. But it's necessary."

I wasn't going to convince him to take it easy on Amber. So, I simply nodded. "Thanks for making it clear that I wasn't the one to report her."

"Of course." He glanced at the clock. "Do you need a ride home when you're off shift?"

"No. Holt's coming to pick me up."

Lawson's lips twitched.

I rolled my eyes as I stood. "Oh, shut up."

"Pretty sure I didn't say a word, Little Williams."

"Your danged smirk says it all."

Lawson held up both hands. "It makes me happy to see the people I care about happy."

"Yeah, yeah."

I started out the door, Lawson's chuckle following behind me. As much as I gave him a hard time, it meant everything to me that he cared. That he was invested. My parents might have been nonexistent in my life, but I'd filled that space with chosen family—those who stuck.

Taking the long way around to avoid Amber, I sought out the break room. Coffee was a no-go this late, and my nerves wouldn't thank me for it anyway. Instead, I went in search of my secret stash.

Opening the fridge, I pawed through to the back and grabbed one of the two caffeine-free Diet Cokes. Cracking it open, I took a long sip as I walked back to my desk. As I sat, I stole a quick look in Amber's direction. Her desk was empty.

Shit. I turned back to my station, ending the call forwarding and trying to focus intently on a game of solitaire, but my body was too aware of every little sound.

A door slammed, and my head jerked up.

Amber stormed to her desk. She ripped open one of the drawers, grabbed a bag, and then slammed that, too. Her eyes cut to mine, and I saw rage blazing there.

Clint grabbed her arm and whispered something in her ear.

She shrugged him off and turned for the back door, but not before sending me one last scathing look.

"What the hell is that all about?"

I jumped at the sound of Abel's voice. "Geez, give a girl a little warning, would you?"

He grunted. "You were too distracted by the death stares."

I winced. He might have a point there. "What are you doing here? You're not on till two."

"Couldn't sleep. Figured I'd come play backup until my shift starts."

Secretly, I was relieved. I could get Abel on a tear about something. The school board's inane rules. How the intersection north of town desperately needed a stoplight. Anything that would take my mind off the silence and give me something to think about other than another shooting call coming in.

"Everything's been pretty quiet."

Abel glanced at me. "Quiet's good."

It was. But it was also killing my nerves.

Clint strode over. "Can I talk to you for a sec, Wren?"

Abel motioned me to go, muttering something about us being worse than his telenovelas.

I pushed to my feet and followed Clint a few steps away. "I didn't report her."

"I know, but you could've convinced Lawson not to bench her."

"I tried, but he's at his wits' end with her."

A muscle in Clint's cheek fluttered. "She's been through a lot. And this is a hard time of year for everyone."

A hard time of year because we were coming up on the date of the shooting. Everything in me pitched as if I were a sailor trying to stay upright on a stormy sea. "Trust me. I know it's a hard time of year."

Clint blanched. "I wasn't trying to suggest that it wasn't—"

I held up a hand. "I know she's your partner. I'm doing what I can to keep the peace. I try to avoid her and be nice when we do see each other."

"It'll be easy to avoid her now. Law suspended her for two weeks. Black mark on her record."

I winced. That wasn't good. But Clint's tone basically insinuated that this whole thing was my fault. I met his stare, not looking away. "I'm not the one who makes Amber's decisions."

"You could've had her back the other day. Supported her."

I gaped at him. "She's going on a witch hunt. We don't know that Joe has anything to do with this."

"We don't know he doesn't."

My back teeth ground together as I shook my head. "I thought better of you."

Turning on my heel, I strode back to dispatch. "Can I take five?"

"Have at it," Abel said. "Might want to take a few swings at the punching bag. You can pretend it's Clint's face." He said the words loud enough for Clint to hear.

I wanted to laugh, could almost get there, but no sound escaped my lips. I didn't need to hit something. I needed to breathe.

Pushing the back door open, I stepped outside. The night air still had a bite to it, and I sucked it in. The slight hint of pain helped ease the anger a bit, and the clean pine scent helped me reach for peace.

Guilt pricked at me as I took in Amber's empty parking space. She needed a friend—someone who could talk her around to sane decisions. Grae had always been that for me, but not everyone was so lucky.

I pulled out my phone and tapped out a text.

Me: *Lucky as hell to have you, G. Love your guts.*

There was no response, but I didn't expect one. Grae had to lead a hike tomorrow, and she needed her rest more than the average person.

I shoved my phone back into my pocket.

Gravel crunched against the asphalt, and I turned. The blow caught me before I could get there, knuckles cracking against my temple in a vicious hit. Lights danced in front of my eyes.

It was all I registered before falling.

I hit the ground with an ugly thud. The pavement tore at my skin, and I let out a moan.

A shoe came flying at my face, but I rolled, my shoulder taking the hit instead. My fingers locked around the keys in my pocket, and I tugged them free.

A hard kick landed on my back, right above my kidneys.

I cried out, frantically searching my keychain for what I needed. A second later, a piercing siren split the air.

I thought I heard someone curse and then footsteps running away. But I couldn't be sure. All I knew was that the darkness was trying to claim me.

Chapter Thirty-Three

Holt

"**Y**OU'RE SURE ABOUT THIS?"

The uncertainty in my second-in-command's voice had me fighting annoyance. "I'm sure."

Jack sighed. "We're gonna miss the hell out of you. Things won't be the same."

I set down the tweezers I'd been using to lift out a watch's face. "I'm not disappearing. I'll be a chopper ride away. I'll still sit in on meetings when you need me. I'll always be a second set of eyes."

"But you won't be in the field with us."

"No." Because what would I prove to Wren if I left every other week to take on some job? And more than that, I didn't feel the pull to take off to parts unknown like I had before. Maybe because I wasn't trying to distract and numb myself any longer. I was facing things for the first time. And as painful as it had been, I couldn't imagine anything more worth it.

"I wanna meet this girl."

I grinned down at Shadow and gave her head a scratch. "You're gonna like her."

"I know I will, which just annoys me because she's stealing my best friend."

I chuckled. "She has an awesome dog, too. I'm training her for SAR."

"You've already got a sidekick."

I leaned down, pressing my forehead to Shadow's. "What do you think? You gonna be my sidekick?"

Shadow let out a low woof, and Jack laughed. "I think that's a yes."

My phone beeped, and I pulled it away from my ear. The name on the screen had dread pooling in my gut. "That's my brother on the other line. I need to take this."

"Sure. Keep me updated and let me know if you need some backup out there."

"Will do." I hit the button on the screen to switch calls. "Law?"

There was a split second of silence before he spoke. "Wren's fine."

Everything in me locked, my muscles turning to stone, heart-beat stilling. "What happened?"

"She was attacked outside the station."

He barely had the third word out before I was moving. My keys were in my hand, and I was jogging toward the door, giving Shadow the command to stay. She obeyed, but I could tell she didn't want to.

I yanked open my SUV's door. "Is she hurt?"

My voice didn't sound like my own. Even. No emotion.

"The doc is taking a look at her right now."

"Station?" I clipped.

"Yes. Drive safe."

I hung up before he could say anything else. Rocks flew as I reversed out of my makeshift parking spot and took off down the dirt road. My pulse pounded in my neck, and images flashed in my mind.

Wren. Too pale. Blood everywhere.

The sickly slow beat of her pulse fluttering beneath my fingertips.

I slammed my fist into the steering wheel, trying to shake the memories free.

"She's fine." I said the two words over and over, a mantra and a prayer. I said them more times than I could count in the five minutes it took me to get to the station—less than half the time it should've taken.

I screeched to a halt in front of the building and threw my vehicle into park. Jumping out, I ran for the door. The officer behind the front desk pushed a button, making the door buzz before I could reach it. It flew open, and I charged inside. "Where is she?"

"They've got her in the gym," Abel called from dispatch.

There was none of his telltale grumpiness in his expression, only concern.

My ribs tightened around my lungs, making it hard to take a full breath, but I forced myself down the hall toward the gym. The door was open, and as I stepped through, I saw a cluster of people huddled around a massage table.

A woman who looked to be in her fifties was bent over, holding a small penlight.

My legs carried me toward the group, but it was as if I were on autopilot. Everything in me had gone numb.

Clint took one look at me and stepped back, clearing the way.

Wren lay on the table, an ice pack pressed to her head. It wasn't until I saw her chest rise and fall that I took a full breath. But as soon as I did, rage filled my lungs.

Wren shifted as she saw me, the ice pack slipping. The side of her face was already turning black and blue. Angry scrapes stood out against her smooth skin, and blood seeped through her long-sleeved white blouse.

Blood.

Wren was bleeding.

In a flash, she stood and moved to me. The ice pack fell to

the floor as she grabbed my hands. "I'm fine. A little banged up. That's all."

I didn't say anything. I couldn't. All I could do was stare at the blood staining her T-shirt.

"Tell him I'm fine, doc."

"Wren will be perfectly all right," the doctor said.

"You're bleeding." The words were raw, as though they were wrapped in barbed wire, and someone had ripped them from my throat.

Lawson cursed. "She scraped her arm when she fell. It's nothing serious."

My head snapped in his direction. "Someone. Attacked. Wren. Outside your damned police station. How is that not serious?" I growled.

Lawson winced. "Bad choice of words."

Wren looked up, wariness seeping into her expression for the first time. "I'm okay. I took a knock on the head. I'll look rough for a couple of days. That's it."

"You promised me."

Her brows furrowed.

"You promised me you wouldn't go anywhere alone."

How could I believe anything she told me? How could I trust her to keep herself safe?

Wren stared at me. "I stepped out our back door in an extremely lit police station parking lot because I needed a second to breathe. There were people right inside."

"He got to you!"

The words vibrated the air as I bellowed them.

A single tear slid from Wren's eye, but she wiped it away quickly. "That's not on me."

I reared back. Of course, it wasn't on her. I squeezed my eyes closed, struggling to breathe evenly. I was screwing this all up. And I couldn't. There was too much at stake.

I moved in a flash, wrapping Wren in my arms. I fought the

urge to tighten my hold, the instinct was so strong, but I didn't want to hurt her. "I can't lose you," I croaked.

"I'm right here," she whispered.

But someone could take her from me at any moment. How could I have forgotten that?

Chapter Thirty-Four

Wren

"It all happened so fast. I don't think I saw anything." My head pounded as I tried to search through my memories. "I heard gravel crunch and started to turn, but whoever it was, hit me before I saw anything."

Holt's hand tightened reflexively around mine.

Lawson gave me a gentle smile. "That's okay. What about after they hit you? Did you hear or see anything?"

"Just a boot. They tried to kick me in the head, but I rolled, and they got my shoulder instead." I glanced at the man beside me. "Holt gave me one of those personal alarm things. I managed to get it from my pocket and pulled the pin. It scared them enough that I heard them running away."

"Probably pierced his eardrum, too," Clint said with a small grin.

Holt scowled at him.

Lawson cleared his throat. "Did you get any sense of the person's size?"

I shook my head and instantly regretted the action; the

throbbing in my skull only intensified. "I don't think so. They hit me before I could see them, and then I was on the ground."

Holt's hand tightened again, and I traced circles on the back of it, trying to soothe the demons that had clearly taken hold.

Lawson typed a few things into his phone. "We'll have an officer pull any security camera footage we can get from the local stores tomorrow."

"I want to see it," Holt said.

Lawson's mouth pressed into a hard line. "I'll see what I can do."

Holt narrowed his eyes as if to say, *you'd better*. "Are you done? I want to get Wren home."

Worry etched itself across Lawson's face. "Sure. We can talk tomorrow, Wren. I'll have patrols going by the cabin."

Holt nodded. "Thanks."

But there was nothing in Holt's voice. No emotion. It sounded dead. I'd heard that tone before. When I was in the hospital and in a rehab clinic. It was the sound of Holt turning off. Of blaming himself.

He turned to me. "Will you be okay to walk?"

I blinked up at him as the blood pounded in my ears. "Of course." I slid off the massage table, ignoring the twinge in my shoulder and along my ribs. Things were going to be black and blue for a while.

"Call if you need anything," Lawson said.

"Thank you," I replied softly.

He reached out and gave my hand a quick squeeze. There was so much in that simple gesture. Lawson was telling me to hang on. To stick with Holt.

But it wasn't me who had a hard time sticking.

Holt led me through the station, and I kept my gaze focused on his back. I didn't want to see the sympathetic looks. The worry. The anger. I wanted to do what Holt had done and turn it all off.

But I wouldn't let myself. I'd made it through hell before. I could do it again. I wouldn't lose all the joys in life just to numb the pain.

Holt held open the passenger door to his SUV and gently helped me inside. He bent, reaching across to buckle me in.

My breath caught. He'd done this before, too. When it still hurt my chest too much to buckle myself.

Holt rounded the vehicle, no sign of any emotion on his face.

We were both quiet on the drive. Each second of silence ticked up my anxiety a little more. The panic and what-ifs swirled around me, weaving a web that grew tighter and tighter.

Holt pulled to a stop in front of the cabin. I unbuckled myself and was out of the SUV before he could come around to my side.

"I was going to help you."

"I didn't need your help."

His brows pulled together. "Let's get you inside and lying down."

His hand pressed against the small of my back, the gentlest pressure urging me onward. I hated that care. Him treating me as if I could break at any moment.

I swallowed hard and started for the house. I moved quickly enough to escape the gentleness of his hand. Pulling my keys from my pocket, I searched for the one to my front door. My fingers stuttered over the personal alarm.

It was something I didn't think I'd ever be without now. I shoved the key into the lock and opened the door.

Shadow was right there, licking my hand and letting out a low whine.

I gave her a good scratch. "Everything's okay."

Holt didn't say anything. He simply stepped inside and locked the door behind him.

I made my way to the kitchen, searching for the Tylenol and filling a glass with water.

"How bad does it hurt?" Holt asked.

"Not great, not awful. I'm sure a good night's sleep will help."

And I was sure it would, but the chances of me getting one were slim to none.

Holt stared at me as I swallowed the pills.

I set the glass down with a clang. "Stop it."

He jolted. "Stop what?"

"Don't do this to me."

Holt blanched.

"This is exactly how you sounded after I was shot. You said all the right words, but your voice was dead. You were holding my hand but putting a million miles between us. Don't do this." My voice cracked on the words, my fear breaking free and spilling out into the open.

He moved in a flash. He was on the other side of the kitchen and then suddenly, he was right there, wrapping himself around me. "I'm not pulling away. I promise."

His pine-and-spice scent swirled around me. "You are. You're here but it's not *you*."

Holt nuzzled my neck, breathing me in. "I didn't want to scare you."

My hands pressed to his chest, giving him a hard shove. "*This* scares me. Nothing could terrify me more than watching you turn yourself off. Watching you fade away in front of my eyes."

Holt's hands fisted, his knuckles bleaching white. "You want to hear that when Law called, my heart stopped? That I want to find this person and end them. Not get them arrested and send them to jail, *end* them."

"Yes, I want to hear it."

His eyes glittered in the low light of the cabin. "You want to hear that I failed you? Again."

I gave his chest another hard shove. "The only time you fail me is when you disappear! When are you going to get that through your thick skull?"

"When are you going to realize that you deserve so much better than me?"

The pain in Holt's voice tore at me with tooth and nail. Tears gathered in my eyes. "How can't you see what an amazing man you are? It doesn't matter what I deserve or don't because I want *you*. You're all I've ever wanted. So let me make up my own mind. Don't steal my choice from me."

Holt moved into my space, wrapping me in his arms again. "I love you, Wren. I can't lose you."

"You have me. But you can't keep worrying our life away. We have to live in the here and now."

"I know. I'm trying. This just scared the hell out of me."

Of course, it had. I leaned into Holt, ignoring the pain it caused. "I'm sorry." I pressed my lips to his throat. "But I'm okay. It scared the hell out of me, too, but I fought. You know why?"

He stared down at me.

"Because I was fighting for you. For us. For all the time we wasted."

Holt's eyes blazed, and his hand slid along my jaw. "I don't want to waste any more time."

"No more hiding from me?"

He leaned down and brushed his lips against mine. "I can't hide from you, Cricket. You're *in* me. In my marrow."

His words buried themselves deep in my heart, and I opened my mouth to tell him. To give Holt those three little words, but his phone let out a series of beeps before I could.

He cursed and pulled the phone from his pocket. In a flash, his expression turned to granite. "Someone's here."

Chapter Thirty-Five

Holt

MY ENTIRE BODY WAS STRUNG TIGHT AS THE VIDEO came into focus—a figure wearing a black hoodie prowling around the tree line of the forest. My jaw locked. "Call 9-1-1, then Law."

"Who is it?"

"I can't tell." I slid the phone back into my pocket and then pulled the gun from the holster at the small of my back. "I want you to stay here. Where would you feel safest?"

There weren't enough good options. I didn't give a damn what Wren had to say about it, I was building a safe room in this cabin as soon as this nightmare was over.

Wren lashed out, grabbing hold of my shirt. "You're not going out there."

My free hand came up to cup her face. "I have to. He'll run the second he hears a vehicle. This is my chance to end this. To give us that freedom."

Tears brimmed in those gorgeous hazel eyes. "I can't lose you either."

I ducked down, bringing us eye-to-eye. "You're not losing me. This is me making sure of that."

Because I was done. Whoever had been terrorizing us and this town would be stopped tonight.

"Holt..."

There was so much in Wren's eyes. Words she hadn't said but that I'd never stopped feeling. Those faint whispers of her that lived in me no matter where I went.

I squeezed the back of her neck. "Tell me when I get back."

"But—"

"When I get back."

Because I wanted those words freely, not in a moment when Wren thought she might lose me.

"When you get back." Her words were soft but filled with steel.

I kissed her quickly. "Go in your bedroom. Lock the door. Call Law."

"Okay." But she didn't move.

"Wren."

More tears filled her eyes. "Come back to me."

"Couldn't keep me away."

Wren turned, Shadow on her heels as she pressed the phone to her ear. I waited until I heard the lock to her door click and then started for the entryway. I checked the camera. The same figure hovered just inside the tree line.

I didn't see a weapon in the person's hands, but that didn't mean they didn't have one. The front door to the cabin was hidden from the figure's view. If I could make it down the incline to the lake without being seen, I could loop up and around and sneak up on them from behind.

It was a risk, and it meant leaving Wren here alone. Unprotected.

I glanced down at my phone. The figure didn't show any signs of movement. They simply stared at the house. Waiting.

I had to hope they were waiting to make their move until someone left. All the curtains in the cabin were drawn, and the broken window was still boarded up. There was no way for anyone to see inside. They'd have to wait.

My ribs tightened around my lungs in a brutal squeeze as I shoved my phone back into my pocket and slipped out the front door. Flipping the lock, I closed the door behind me as quietly as possible. The quiet snick of the latch sounded like a cannon in my ears.

I stood on the stoop for a moment. Waiting. Listening. There was nothing but the expected night sounds and faint breeze in the pines.

It was time. I lowered myself to a crouch as I rounded the side of the cabin. It would be my best chance of cover—that and moving quickly.

Luckily, I'd donned a dark flannel and jeans today. It would help me blend in with the darkness. I moved across the back deck and hopped down into the grass. I made my way across the yard, over by the firepit and chairs, and down the embankment to the lake below.

This would be a happy place for Wren again—her haven. Just as soon as we had this asshole in hand.

I jogged down the beach until I'd put enough distance between us that I didn't think whoever was hanging around would see me. With a quick look at the trees, I ran across the open space. I didn't breathe until I'd made cover.

Pulling out my phone, I checked the camera. Whoever it was, they were still there, and they'd lit a cigarette. I tried to make out any features in the glow. The hands were masculine, but that was all I could tell.

I put my phone back and adjusted my grip on my gun. Moving slower this time and careful to avoid any downed branches that might give me away, I started around to whoever was lying in wait.

The path I carved brought me up behind the cabin and the lurker. As they came into view, everything in me tightened. They were average-sized, their hoodie making them seem broader than they actually were. And they seemed human—not like the monster they were.

I took a step, too distracted with whoever I was about to face, and my foot came down on a twig. The sound was deafening.

The person in front of me whirled around. I caught sight of the side of a face, but it wasn't enough to identify them, and then they ran.

I let out a stream of curses and took off after them. They were fast, jumping over logs and darting around trees.

"Stop!" I yelled.

Like that did any good. I needed backup.

I pulled the phone from my pocket again as I ran, yelling out a voice command to call Lawson. He answered after half a ring. "Where the hell are you?"

"Woods in back of the cabin. Heading northwest on foot. In pursuit of a man in a black hoodie. I need backup."

Lawson cursed. "You're not a damn cop." But then he barked out an order over the radio, and I knew help was coming.

The figure in front of me whirled for a split second, and I saw the flash of metal in the moonlight. I ducked as they fired, the shot going way wide and hitting a tree a few feet away.

"Tell me that was you," Lawson growled.

"I'm afraid not."

"Take cover until backup gets there."

"Can't do that." I raised my gun to return fire, but the figure was too smart, running in a haphazard zigzag that I couldn't pin down.

Instead, I pushed my muscles harder, the burn turning to fire. But I pictured Wren scared and hurt. Let myself feel the terror we'd all experienced since discovering that a shooter was back.

It lit something deep inside, and I charged up the hill. The person in front of me cursed. He pointed his gun in my direction again but wasn't even aiming as he ran. The bullet hit a tree at least ten feet from me.

I was gaining. Just a little bit more. Wren's hazel eyes flashed in my mind—the green in them that shone like emeralds. How she looked up at me with all the love in the world, even if she wasn't ready to say it.

I launched myself at the man, taking him to the ground in a hard tackle. He struggled beneath me, giving me an elbow to the jaw. I cursed but answered with a swift punch to the cheek, stunning him enough for me to wrestle the weapon from his hands.

Pressing my forearm against his throat, I struggled to keep him in place. "Don't move."

The hoodie slipped from his head, and Joe Sullivan stared up at me with fury in his eyes.

Chapter Thirty-Six

Wren

HOLT WRAPPED AN ARM AROUND ME AS I SHIVERED. THE heat from the tea seeped into my hands, but even with that and Holt's body pressed against me, I couldn't get warm. There was a coldness in me that no outside force could remedy.

We leaned against the back wall of the viewing room on the other side of interrogation. I couldn't take my eyes off the person sitting at the table. The boy. Because Joe Sullivan was all of seventeen—too young to be sitting there. Too young to be wrapped up in this. Too young to have caused such suffering.

But I knew that wasn't true. I wished it were. I wanted to believe that kids didn't have to live with this as a reality. But they did. I wished that humans weren't capable of the kind of cruelty necessary to take a life for no good reason—but some of us were.

"I didn't want it to be him," I said quietly.

Holt pulled me tighter against him. "I know, Cricket."

I didn't care that my shoulder and ribs throbbed; I needed the pressure to know that Holt was here. That we were okay. Those minutes in my bedroom might as well have been forever—an eternity where I'd felt what it might be like to live a life without Holt. I'd already gone ten years without him. I wasn't going a second longer.

I turned into him, pressing my face to his chest and breathing him in. "Tell me you're here."

Holt's lips ghosted over my hair. "I'm right here. Not going anywhere."

The door to the viewing room opened, and I forced myself to straighten. A handful of officers piled into the room. I stiffened as Amber entered the space in her street clothes. She sent a self-satisfied smirk in my direction, but it quickly slipped from her face.

I glanced up to see Holt glaring at her. Laying a hand against his stomach, I pressed a kiss to the underside of his jaw. "It's okay."

Nash moved around Clint and Amber, not bothering to hide his annoyance at Amber. "Law's gonna be pissed you're here."

Amber stiffened. "Seeing as I was the one who was right all along, I highly doubt that. I'm guessing I'll get an apology from him after this."

Nash scoffed. "Keep living in dreamland." He moved into my space, dropping a quick kiss on the top of my head. "You holding up okay?"

"Hanging in there." I should've been feeling relief. Instead, I felt ill. Even knowing all the damage Joe had likely caused, my heart ached for him.

Nash lowered his voice as he leaned closer to Holt and me. "We found a rifle in Joe's trunk. They have to run ballistics, but so far, it's a match to the shooting at the Petersons."

My stomach cramped. This was good. It meant the survivors were safe again. Holt and I were safe.

Holt trailed a hand up and down my spine. "How long will it take to run?"

"County's rushing it to the front of the line. We're running the handgun to see if that matches Gretchen and Mrs. McHenry. Hopefully, we'll get a report tomorrow," Nash said.

"Good." Holt's jaw was hard as he stared at Joe. There was no sympathy in his gaze, but it didn't look like there was relief either.

The door to the interrogation room opened, and Lawson stepped inside, a man in an ill-fitting suit trailing behind him. "Joe, this is your court-appointed attorney, Mr. Cushing. Your parents agreed to let us question you—"

"Don't answer anything unless I tell you to," the attorney said.

Joe simply scowled at them both and crossed his arms. "You can both jump off a cliff."

Lawson sighed as he sat. "What were you doing at Wren Williams' cabin tonight?"

"Don't answer that," Mr. Cushing said and then turned to Lawson. "Mr. Sullivan wasn't even on Ms. Williams' property."

"But he was on private property. At the location where a shooting took place recently."

Mr. Cushing arched a brow. "Is Mr. Sullivan under arrest for trespassing then?"

Lawson's jaw hardened. "I can add that to the list."

Mr. Cushing's mouth pulled down in a frown. "That's a fine. Not jail time. Release the boy to his parents."

"I'm afraid that's not possible. I'll be holding Joe for the full seventy-two hours. Or until the ballistics come back on the handgun in his possession and the rifle we found in his trunk."

All the color drained from Joe's face as his gaze jumped back and forth between the two men.

"This interview is over," Mr. Cushing said curtly. "You can hold my client, but he won't be speaking with you. I, however, would like a word with him in private. Please clear the room and observation."

Joe jolted at that, his gaze going to the two-way mirror. I swore those dark eyes looked right into mine as if he could tell that I was there.

A tear slid down my cheek. So many lives destroyed. And for what?

Holt rolled me into him as I burrowed under the covers. I went without protest, craving the warmth that hummed beneath his skin.

"Talk to me," he said, lips skimming over my hair.

"Can't get warm."

"Cricket…" He hauled me gently on top of him so we were front-to-front. More of that warmth, that *life* seeped into me.

"I was so scared something would happen to you tonight."

So scared that I would lose him.

Holt's fingers trailed along the ridges in my spine. "I hate that I put you through that."

"I've been so scared to make that final leap. So terrified that you'd leave, or something would happen."

Holt's hand slipped under my T-shirt, the rough pads of his fingertips sending a cascade of tingles across my skin. "Just because you haven't said the words doesn't mean you haven't made the leap."

But not saying the words was my last wall of protection. The thing I thought would save me if everything fell apart. Only it wouldn't. Grae's voice danced in my mind, talking about missing out because I was too scared of the pain that might come. But that pain would come no matter what. And living my life in half measures would only heap regret on top of it.

I sat up, straddling Holt, my oversized T-shirt pooling around me. I stared down at the man who I'd known in every incarnation growing up. I'd worried there would be too much time lost between us now—that I wouldn't know him anymore. But that couldn't have been further from the truth.

I would always know Holt. Sometimes, better than I knew myself. Because I knew his soul. The very core of him. The trappings of that soul might change, but the soul itself never would.

Pressing a palm to his chest, over his heart, I let down the last of my walls. "I love you. I never stopped loving you. Not for a single breath."

Holt stilled beneath me. Not breathing. I swore his heartbeat even halted.

He rolled me to my back in a flash, hovering over me. "Say it again."

"I love you."

"The next part," he growled, his words sending vibrations across my face.

"I never stopped loving you."

Emotion filled Holt's eyes, the dark blue turning to a color I couldn't identify. A single tear slipped free and landed on my cheek. "Never thought I'd hear those words again."

I reached up, ghosting a hand over his face. I relished the feel of his stubble prickling my palm. His jaw beneath my fingers. Reveled in the knowledge that this man was mine and I was his. "Nothing could keep me from loving you."

Not hurt or logic or an entire world separating us. We were meant to be. We would always find a way back to each other.

Holt dipped his head, his lips a breath from mine. "Are you with me?"

"I'm always with you."

My hands came around his shoulders, skimming over smooth skin until I reached the worn flannel pajama bottoms he wore. My fingers hooked in the band.

"Wren, you have to be hurting."

"The only thing that will hurt me is if I can't be with you right now."

It was the truth. I needed him more than oxygen. Had to cement this forever with flesh and bone.

Holt pressed his forehead against mine. "Promise me you'll tell me if it's too much."

"I promise." But I knew it wouldn't be. Because it was Holt and me.

His hand slipped over my hip, his eyes flaring. "No panties?"

I grinned up at him. "Seemed like a waste."

He chuckled.

I lifted a hand to his throat. "Do it again."

Emotion filled Holt's gaze, but he did as I asked. I closed my eyes and let the sound wash over me. I'd never take a single chuckle for granted.

"Wren."

My eyes fluttered open. There was such reverence there. So much it almost hurt to take it in.

My legs encircled Holt's waist, a silent request for my deepest need. His tip bumped my entrance, and then he was sliding inside. My lips parted with the barest sound, one Holt swallowed with his mouth.

The kiss was long and slow and deep. Holt poured everything into it that there weren't words for. A language that was only ours.

He began to move in slow, lazy thrusts, ones that took their time and let me feel *everything*.

My fingers dug into Holt's back as my hips rose to meet his. There wasn't desperation this time because I knew Holt was mine. That he was staying. That this was our second chance at a life we would always cherish.

His hips angled him deeper, and I let out a gasp. Warmth spread through me, the kind that had escaped me all night. And I held on as Holt picked up speed.

Rolling waves quaked through me as each thrust landed. Holt sucked in air. "Love you, Wren. Every moment of every day."

Tears filled my eyes as I let his words hit me—no walls or defenses. I let myself feel Holt's love. It hurt in the best way. The kind that branded and would be with me forever.

I gripped his shoulders tighter as my muscles shuddered, and I edged toward the precipice that would change everything. "Every moment of every day."

I let myself fall, spiraling with Holt, knowing we were losing control together and that nothing would ever be the same. But knowing that it would be better. It would be us.

Chapter Thirty-Seven

Holt

MY HAND SKIMMED ALONG WREN'S HIP AS I SLID THE plate of poached eggs and toast in front of her. My lips ghosted her hair as I breathed in the scent I loved above all others—mountain air and a hint of gardenia. I'd never get tired of it.

Wren tipped her head back to look up at me, a smile teasing her lips. "Are you gonna sit?"

I gave her a long, slow kiss, my tongue seeking hers. "I'm having a hard time not touching you."

She smiled wider against my mouth, then reached over and pulled the second stool so that it was practically flush with hers. "Problem solved."

"I like the way you think." I slid onto the stool, and my thigh pressed against Wren's. "How do you feel?" I hadn't missed the ibuprofen and Tylenol next to her plate.

Wren made a face. "Like I took a tumble. But nothing too bad."

My eyes narrowed on her.

She rolled hers. "Calm yourself, oh, overprotective one."

With everything we'd been through lately, that would take time. The deepening bruise on the side of Wren's face didn't help.

"You know, it could give a girl a complex if you keep scowling at her like that."

I circled a finger around Wren's face. "I hate this."

Wren burst out laughing. "Gee, thanks."

The sound was the best thing I'd ever heard. She'd chuckled in my presence since I'd been back, even laughed some, but I hadn't heard that full-out, from-the-soul laughter in ten years. God, it was heaven.

I leaned over and took her mouth. "You laughing at me?"

She nipped my lip. "Definitely. Your romanticism knows no bounds."

I skimmed my fingers gently over the darkening skin. "This is what I hate. I'm so sorry, Wren."

Her hand curved around my arm, squeezing. "The bruises will fade. My ribs will heal. I'd pay that price a million times over if it meant ending up here."

My chest gave a painful squeeze. The good kind. "Love you, Cricket."

"Love you, too."

"Gonna need you to say that at least ten times a day for a while."

She chuckled. "Don't you think ten is a little extreme?"

"You're right. Twenty is better."

Wren's laughter filled the air as my phone rang. I reached for it on the counter. "It's Law."

The laughter died on Wren's lips. "Answer."

"Hey. Everything okay?"

"That's my line, isn't it?" Lawson asked.

"Just trying to spread the concern around."

"Fair enough. Got two things for you."

My fingers tightened around my phone as I lowered it and tapped a button. "All right. You're on speaker with me and Wren."

Lawson let out a long breath, and I heard the bone-deep fatigue in it. "County techs came in early this morning so they could run ballistics."

"And?" I pressed.

"The handgun wasn't a match. But the rifle we pulled from Joe's trunk is the same one used in the Peterson shooting."

"Prints?"

"Looks like it was wiped clean, or Joe was using gloves. But our chain of custody is tight, so we should be good."

Sorrow etched itself in Wren's face. "Is he talking to you?"

That was my Cricket. She needed to understand the why. Her empathy was so ingrained, she felt for those who had done the worst to her.

Lawson sighed. "Not a word. To us or his lawyer."

We would likely never know the why. We might get pieces but never the whole picture. Sometimes, a person's mind simply twisted. And Joe had been living with the derision of so many in this town for too long. The fact that we were coming up on the tenth anniversary only added to it all.

"What's the second thing?" I asked.

"Got a favor."

"Name it."

After everything Lawson had done for us, I'd give him anything.

The sound of shuffling papers came across the line. "We got a call from out of state. A girl who's been backpacking up here didn't check in with her parents when she was supposed to. They have the coordinates for where she would have likely been over the past twenty-four hours. Asked if someone could go look for her. They're sick with worry."

"Backpacking alone?"

Lawson let out a huff. "Don't get me started. It was some walk-about after she broke up with a boyfriend."

It was beyond reckless. Anything could happen in these mountains, and if you weren't prepared, it could be deadly. "What do you need from me?"

"It's a wide area, and it needs to be searched. With everything going on down here, I can't leave to help. A few others on the team can't get off work today either. Can you go with Nash?"

My gaze automatically pulled to Wren. The last thing I wanted to do was leave her. She'd been through too much in the past twenty-four hours. "I don't think—"

"He'll meet Nash at the station," Wren cut in.

"Cricket…"

She smiled at me. "Grae's been blowing up my phone like crazy. I told her I'd meet her in town for lunch. She won't rest until she sees for herself that I'm in one piece." Wren leaned over and kissed me. "Go help this girl."

Lawson's voice intruded on the moment. "It's gonna be your ship soon anyway."

Wren's brows lifted. "Your ship?"

"Way to spill the beans," I said.

"You haven't told her?"

"Told me what?" Wren asked, a little annoyance slipping into her tone. My Cricket didn't like being left out of the loop.

I grinned. "Got a new gig. Team leader for Harrison County Search and Rescue."

Wren's jaw went slack. "But your company…"

"Jack's taking the helm there. He's buying me out for a sixty-percent stake. I'll still help with strategy and higher-level planning, but I won't be in the day-to-day business."

A hint of worry swept over her face. "But you worked so hard to build it. You guys are at the top of the industry."

"You been checking up on me?"

Wren huffed out a breath. "It doesn't take a superspy to google in a moment of weakness."

I leaned over and kissed her, drowning in her taste. "Love you." My hand slipped under her hair, squeezing her neck. "I'm proud of what I built. But so much of that urge to push for more, to reach for the best, was because I was running. From memories. From demons. I don't want that anymore. I don't need it. What I do need is a life here. With you. With my family."

"Holt..."

"I love you, Wren. I want this life with you. That means living it each and every day. Not running around the globe whenever a call comes in."

She searched my face. "You're sure?"

"Never been more sure of anything in my life."

Wren's mouth stretched into a wide smile, and she let out a squeal as she launched herself at me. I knew the move had hurt her when she winced.

"Careful, Cricket."

Lawson cleared his throat. "Uh, guys. Love you both, but I really don't need to hear you going at it over the phone."

Wren's face flamed. "Sorry about that."

"Shove it, Law."

He chuckled. "Nash is headed to your place right now. Dad's with him to run comms from the SUV."

I shook my head. "You were so sure I'd say yes?"

"I know my brother," Lawson said. "You always come through when we need you."

My chest burned as Wren burrowed deeper into my side. "Love you, too, Law."

My throat was so tight I could barely get the words out. Emotion pressed down on me, an avalanche of gratitude for this second chance—with my family, with Wren, and with the life that was always meant to be mine.

Chapter Thirty-Eight

Wren

"LOOKING LIKE A PRIZEFIGHTER, LITTLE WILLIAMS," Nash said as he climbed out of his SUV, Nathan following behind.

Holt glared at him. "Nash…"

He only rolled his eyes. "I'm just saying our girl's a badass. That's all."

I padded across the drive and wrapped my arms around him in a hug. "Thanks, Nash Bash."

His smile widened, taking on a more authentic air. "Been a while since you called me that."

Too long.

"I'm feeling more like myself lately."

Nash gently ruffled my hair. "Couldn't think of better news."

Nathan surveyed my face, his mouth going tight.

I let go of Nash and turned my hug on Nathan. "I'm fine. I promise."

"You don't look fine. Maybe you should go up to the house. Kerry can take care of you today. You can rest and—"

I stretched up on my toes to kiss his cheek. "I'm fine. I need to clean up around the house, and I'm meeting G for lunch."

Nathan frowned at me. "You're sure?"

I patted his chest. "I'm sure."

When I turned around, Holt had a tender smile on his face. I crossed to him, wrapping my arms around his waist. "What's that about?"

He brushed the hair back from my face. "I'm glad you've had them in your corner."

My heart squeezed. This was the bittersweet truth. If Holt hadn't left, I might never have forged quite this deep of a bond with his family. It had happened because I was mostly alone in the world. Because Holt was gone. But life was rarely simple and never perfect. It was like the land around us, full of jagged edges and pieces askew. But it was beautiful in its imperfections—more so because of them.

I wrapped a hand around Holt's neck, pulling him down to me. "I love you."

"I'm totally getting twenty today."

I snorted. "Cocky much?"

"Confident. There's a difference." He closed the distance, his lips dancing across mine in the gentlest of touches. "Love you always."

The words wrapped around me like the sweetest music I'd never tire of hearing. "Okay, I'm on board with twenty."

He chuckled, giving me another kiss.

Nash made a gagging noise. "Seriously? She's like my sister, and I really don't need to see you two making out."

Nathan gave a swift elbow to Nash's gut, and he let out a wheezing cough.

"I'd think you'd take my side, Dad."

Nathan grinned, the smile so similar to his son's. "Nothing makes me happier than seeing these two right where they're supposed to be."

The warmth of his words wrapped around me. The Hartleys

had always made me feel like a part of their family. But something about letting down my walls with Holt and giving him everything deepened that connection. And to have Nathan and Nash accept it all so readily was a balm to my soul.

Holt searched his father's face as if looking for any hint of disingenuousness. "Thanks, Dad."

"Okay, enough with the emo lovefest. We need to hit the road if we want to log some miles today," Nash said.

Holt nodded, letting out a whistle. Shadow came running from the lake. He bent and latched the leash to her collar.

"You sure you'll be good with her all day?" I asked.

"I've got water and food. You said she's good with long hikes, right?"

I gave my girl a rub. "She lasts a hell of a lot longer than I do."

"It's the sled dog in her. This will be good."

I linked my fingers with Holt's and squeezed. "Be safe. Promise?"

"Always. Be home before dark."

"Call on your way."

Holt pressed a kiss to my forehead as he released my hand. "Will do."

The guys and Shadow piled into Nash's SUV. I stood in the drive until they disappeared from sight.

I didn't rush back into the cabin. Closing my eyes, I breathed deeply, letting the crisp, clean air sweep through me. It was a reclaiming of sorts. Of this refuge I'd built. It was mine again.

A smile teased my lips. No, it was ours. Because I knew I'd never ask Holt to find his own place. After being without him for so long, all I wanted was him in every way I could have him. Cooking breakfast in the mornings. Playing fetch with Shadow after dinner. Curling up in bed with me every night.

I opened my eyes and started for the cabin. The minute I got inside, I went around to every window and pulled the curtains and blinds. I was done living in the dark.

The morning light made the wood in the cabin glow an almost

gold. I'd always loved that but being without it for the past several days had made me appreciate it even more—just like having Holt here with me now after missing him for so long.

I hummed as I moved around the space, tidying as I went. I cleaned up the dishes from breakfast and moved into the bedroom. My mouth curved as I took in the bed, the sheets rumpled, and pillows scattered.

As I put things back to rights, I nibbled the corner of my lip. Holt's duffel bag sat against the room's far wall. He'd put a couple of things in the bathroom, but that was it.

Holt was pushy in a lot of ways. When it came to my safety. With letting me know he was here to stay. But not when it came to this.

The permanence of having him here was something that Holt had left entirely up to me. I loved him all the more for it. He'd taken a choice away from me once, but he was giving it back to me now.

Tossing the final pillow into place, I turned to the dresser opposite the bed. It was an antique that had been my grandmother's, and I loved having it here now. I crossed to it and ran my fingers over the wood. It was worn and showed its age in the grooves and gashes. But they only gave the dresser more character.

That was how I wanted my life to be. I might have scars, but that only meant I had lived this life fully. I'd stopped doing that for a while. But I was changing that now.

My fingers curled around one of the brass pulls, and I slid a drawer open. Carefully, I rearranged my socks and underwear so they could fit in half the space. Then I opened the one next to it and removed all my pajamas, refolding them so they fit next to my undergarments. I did the same thing with the middle two drawers. Then the bottom two.

I went for Holt's duffel, laying it on the bed. I paused for a moment and wondered if I was overstepping. I had to hope Holt would see the beauty of the gesture and not be annoyed that I was pawing through his stuff.

He didn't have much: boxer briefs and workout gear, a few pairs of jeans, tees and flannels, his jacket and boots he'd already stored in the hall closet.

I made quick work of arranging his belongings in the drawers, and the corners of my mouth kicked up as I thought about making this place truly *ours*. Of having more of Holt's belongings mixed with mine. Of picking out art for the walls or painting the rooms a different color.

My hands skimmed the inside of the duffel. I pulled out his watch repair kit, placing it on the top of the dresser. My gaze caught on something at the bottom of the bag. It was so thin that I'd almost missed it.

The flash of color had caught my attention—a tiny glimpse of pink in the sea of black that was the bag's interior. My fingers curled around what felt like plastic.

Lifting it, my heart stuttered in my chest. It was a photo. One laminated for protection but worn by the years. The corner was peeling back, and some of the plastic had been rubbed away in places.

It was the two of us. When I took in the image, it was like looking at babies—so young, with no idea what would come our way. But so unbelievably happy.

Holt had his arms wrapped around me while I had my face pressed to his neck. I wore a coral sundress that I'd bought just for the barbecue at his parents' house. This had been only days before the attack.

I'd never seen the photo, but it was *us*, Holt making me safe and at peace in his hold, and me grounding him and assuring him of just how amazing he was. I loved that us. But I thought I'd love the us we were now even more. Because I'd found a strength I hadn't known I possessed when I had to face life alone. And it only made me love Holt more. *Appreciate* him more.

And Holt could see that new strength in me. I recognized it in the glint of respect that shone in his eyes. It would never change that he wanted to shield me from the worst life had to offer, but that was who Holt was. I loved that he was the kind of man who wanted to protect everyone he cared about.

A knock sounded on the front door, pulling me out of my sappy thoughts. I started down the hall, but my steps faltered. I slid my phone from my back pocket and opened the camera app Holt had set up for me. A familiar SUV sat in my drive, and I sighed as I took in the person on my front step.

Forcing myself forward, I opened the front door. "Hey, Amber."

She smiled at me, but the curve of her mouth was anything but genuine. "Wren. Can I come in?"

Normally, I would've taken whatever punches she felt the need to dole out, but I was done with it. "That depends on why you're here."

The fake smile slipped from her mouth. "That's rude."

I shrugged. "I'm all about protecting my peace these days."

A hardness slid into Amber's gaze, and she moved so fast I didn't have a chance to brace. She shoved me hard, pushing me inside the house, then pulling a gun and leveling it at my chest. "You know what, Wren? I don't really give a damn about your peace."

The gun swung out in a flash, cracking across my temple and sending me hurtling into the dark.

Chapter Thirty-Nine

Holt

SHADOW SHOVED HER HEAD OUT THE WINDOW AS NASH guided his SUV up the mountain roads. Her tongue lolled out of her mouth, and she let out a bark.

"I think someone's happy," my dad said.

I turned in the back seat, taking Shadow and giving her a rub. "It's good for her to get out a little more. Wren had someone walking her in the middle of her shifts, but Shadow has a lot of energy."

Dad surveyed me from the front passenger seat. "You and Wren are getting into a rhythm."

It wasn't a question, but it held a gentle probe. My hackles didn't rise like they would've just days ago. What I had told Wren was true—I loved that she'd had my family for all the years I wasn't here and that they were protective of her. That they'd developed a true closeness.

"It's going to take time, but we're getting there."

He nodded but didn't look away. "I'm sorry if how I acted when you came home made you feel like I didn't believe in you.

I love both of you, and there's nothing I want more than seeing you happy."

Instead of hiding behind a mask of indifference, I kept my walls down. I let my dad see everything I normally hid with practiced ease. I let the regret and grief rise to the surface. The pain and self-torture. "I love her, Dad. I never stopped. I really did think I was doing the right thing."

He twisted farther in his seat. "I know that, Holt. I never thought you left for selfish reasons. But relationships are hard. They're work. You have to stick it out even when it seems like running would be easier on everyone."

A muscle flickered in my jaw.

"He's not running, Dad," Nash said from the driver's seat. "He needed time to get his head on straight. Living without Wren has taught him more than any of your lectures ever could."

I studied my brother. He was typically so easygoing, but there was a tension in him now: the way his knuckles bleached white around the wheel, the way his jaw locked tight. And something in his expression said that he knew about regret all too well.

"He's right." I looked at Dad. "I get that you might have reservations. But they aren't going to stop me. I know the agony of living without Wren, of falling asleep thinking about her every night. Of wondering where she is and if she's safe. Happy. Of imagining her falling in love with someone who isn't me. Starting a family."

The brutal pain of all those nights ripped through me. Wren and I had loved dreaming about our future. Thinking up names for our kids. She'd wanted to meet each of them before settling on one because *their little personalities would shine through.* We'd loved drawing up plans for our home. She'd demanded a front porch and swing that could be a couch or bed. Coming up with traditions that would be ours alone: Wren wanted a scavenger hunt for every Easter, and heart-shaped pancakes on

Valentine's Day. Every night at dinner we would share our highs and lows.

My dad's face paled. "Holt—"

I held up a hand. "I'm not trying to make you feel guilty. I just need you to understand. There's no torture I wouldn't live through for her. Because even in that, I thought it was right."

"But now you know it isn't," he said quietly.

"I stole Wren's choice from her. Not just that, I took her voice. I'll hate myself for it for the rest of my days, but I'll never do it again. Wren is the strongest woman I've ever known. And for some reason, she loves me."

"Probably took a hard hit to the head as a baby. It scrambled her good sense," Nash muttered.

I grinned, smacking the back of his head. "I think you were dropped on the head as a baby."

"I know he was," Dad shot back.

Nash scowled at him. "Rude."

A little of the grin slipped from my face as I met Dad's gaze. "I'm never leaving. Not unless she asks me to. And even then, I'd never go far. She has my heart. My soul. Everything that's good in me. She's where I feel peace."

Dad's eyes shone with unshed tears. "That's all I could ever hope to hear. All I could want for her. All I could want for *you*."

I felt the raw truth in his words. And I didn't blame him for the doubt he'd had. Or for wanting to protect Wren—and me. My need to shield the people I cared about had come from my dad. He'd ingrained it in all his kids without even meaning to.

"Good God, I can't take much more of this mushy lovefest," Nash moaned. "I'd almost rather see you and Little Williams making out."

Dad choked on a laugh. "We've really traumatized him today, haven't we?"

I leaned forward, clamping my hands on Nash's shoulders, and giving him a shake. "It's good for you. Gotta work on that emotional intelligence."

Nash cast an affronted look in the rearview mirror. "I have plenty of emotional intelligence, thank you very much."

Dad hid his laugh behind a cough. "Sure, you do."

"How about when he hooked up with Grae and Wren's friend sophomore year?" I said with a grin.

Dad shook his head. "That poor girl."

Nash gaped at us. "Poor girl? What about poor me? After one kiss, she made a photo collage of us by pasting my head on other people's bodies. She basically stalked me!"

I couldn't hold in my laughter now. The girl hadn't been shy about showing her affections, but a person would've had to be blind not to see that she was in love with Nash before he even looked her way. She'd gone to every basketball game, painted his number on her T-shirts, brought him brownies for good luck. It was sweet, but Nash was not a commitment kind of guy, especially not in high school.

The breakup did not go well.

Dad grinned. "You inherited your old man's charm. It's a blessing and a curse."

Nash scoffed. "Katie was off her rocker. I'm pretty sure she's the one who slashed Maddie's tires."

My eyes widened. "Seriously?"

He nodded, the scowl deepening on his face. "What is wrong with people?"

"Broken hearts can lead us all to stupid decisions." Dad's lips twitched. "I don't think Grae ever forgave you for costing her a friend." He glanced at me. "It's a miracle she didn't stand in Holt and Wren's way."

Because Grae knew how I felt about Wren. Knew that I'd been in love with her forever. Before I even recognized the emotion, our friendship slipping into more, into *everything*, so seamlessly it was as easy as breathing. I'd dated before Wren and I got together, but it had never felt *right*, and it had taken that wrong to make me realize what was right in front of me.

"Holt always was her favorite," Nash grumbled as he pulled into the parking lot at the trailhead.

I chuckled. "I don't know about favorite, but I didn't shamelessly flirt with *all* her friends."

"That's because you don't have game."

"It's because there's only one girl who has ever felt right."

Something passed over Nash's face, but he hid it quickly with a grin. "So, what you're saying is that you've basically been whipped since birth."

I shrugged, opening my door. "Happily."

Nash gagged, but my dad gave me an *attaboy*.

Grabbing Shadow's leash, I motioned for her to follow me out of the SUV. "Do you have maps of the area that we can go over?"

Nash nodded. "In the trunk."

I moved around to the back hatch and opened it. There was a cylinder that I knew housed what we needed. It took me a minute to find what I was looking for. "Tell me the range of coordinates her parents gave."

Nash leaned over my shoulder. "Law talked to her dad, and he said she could be anywhere from Mystic Springs to Sage Hollow."

I frowned as I looked at the map. "That's a hell of a range. Even if they hadn't spoken to her in a week, they should have been able to narrow it down more than that."

Nash shrugged. "Maybe she was planning to stop along the way for a couple of nights. There are some beautiful sights around there."

Dad moved in at my other side, running his finger along the path. "Holt's right. We need to see if the parents can narrow it down a little more."

I pulled my sat phone from my pocket and hit Lawson's contact. He answered on the second ring. "Everything okay?"

"I guess we're back to normal if that's how you're answering the phone."

Lawson huffed out a breath. "I could use some normal around here."

Guilt gnawed at me. He'd been through the wringer lately, working crazy hours and still being there for his boys. "We'll be there before too long."

"I know. Did you make it to the trailhead?"

"We're here, but I have a question."

Lawson's chair squeaked as he shifted. "Sure."

"The range of coordinates the parents gave is pretty damn broad. Can you call them and see if they can narrow it down at all? I'm worried we're wasting manpower in areas we won't find her."

Typing came across the line and then a muffled curse. "My head is in a million places. I should've thought about how much ground that would be to cover."

"Don't sweat it."

"Hold on. Let me conference you in with them."

"Perfect." I grabbed my pack, pulling out a small notebook and pencil.

Lawson hit a few keys on his phone, each one letting out a beep. A second later, I heard ringing, and then an automated voice took over. "The number you have called is no longer in service."

Lawson disconnected the third line. "I must've misdialed." He punched in the number again. A single ring and the same message came across the line.

"Maybe I wrote the number down wrong. Let me pull up the dispatch log." The sound of typing filled the air. "No, I've got it right. Who gives a wrong number when their kid is missing?"

The blood drained from my body, replaced by ice sliding through my veins. God, I hoped my instincts were wrong and that my paranoia had taken over and was running away with my good sense. But the overwhelming sense of dread pooling in my gut was too much to take.

"Law, get officers to Wren's house right now."

"What?" he asked, confusion filling his voice.

"Just do it," I barked. "If you wanted me out here, away from Wren, what would you do?"

Lawson went silent for a beat. "Get the SAR team called out."

That and my family were the only things that could take me away from Wren.

Nash's hand tightened on his keys. "Who would want to get you away from Wren? Joe Sullivan is still in custody."

But what if we hadn't caught the right guy? Then Wren was all alone. Unprotected.

Chapter Forty

Wren

THE TAP, TAP, TAP OF WATER AGAINST MY FOREHEAD WOKE me. I groaned and blinked against the low light. My thoughts were jumbled as I tried to assemble them into some coherent narrative. This felt like the worst hangover of my life—or maybe like I'd been mauled by an elk.

My surroundings came to me in snapshots. Packed dirt beneath me. Rough wood walls assembled so haphazardly that light streamed in through the planks. Old machinery in the corner rusted from weather and disuse. *What the hell?*

I started to sit up, but my hands caught, not on anything that held them down but on each other. I blinked at my wrists—wrists that were bound together with rope.

Something about the sight had everything coming back to me in a flash: Amber showing up at my door. The gun.

A door swung open, and light poured in. "Oh, good, you're awake," Amber greeted as if I'd returned a pencil she'd borrowed. "It would've been a real bummer if I'd put you in a coma."

I stared at her, no words coming. My brain was still trying to compute what was happening.

She grinned then. "Payback's a bitch, isn't it?"

"Payback?" I croaked. What had I ever done to her?

The smile slipped from Amber's lips. "You all just kept right on living like nothing had even happened. None of you appreciated how lucky you were. *None* of you know what it's like to lose everything."

Icy claws of dread dug into my chest. "You're the shooter."

The grin was back now. "Uh-uh-uh. Joe's the shooter. They found the rifle in his trunk."

"You framed him."

She studied the gun in her hand, examining it as one might take in freshly painted nails. "It's only fair."

"Fair?" I choked.

Anger blazed in Amber's eyes. "They haven't paid. Not nearly enough."

My heart hammered in my chest. "Who hasn't paid?"

Keep her talking. That was all I could think. I had to keep her talking until help arrived. Because someone would know I was gone. Grae would call Holt when I didn't show up for lunch, and he would check the cameras. He'd know that Amber had me.

The rage in her face only intensified at my question. "None of you! The survivors. Randy and Paul. Who the hell do you think?"

"I've paid, Amber. Over and over again. Excruciating pain. Months of grueling rehab. Endless nightmares."

Her grip on her gun tightened. "My brother *died.* I was always supposed to protect him, and those assholes stole him from me!"

"And they're in prison for the rest of their lives. They'll never breathe freely again. They're paying."

"It's not enough!" Amber screamed. "They need to hurt like I do. This was the only way." A feral smile played at her lips. "Paul's parents were too easy to pick off. Muggings happen all the time in Seattle. They never should've run away to the big city in shame."

Nausea swept through me. Paul's parents had been destroyed

by their son's actions in a way that I knew they would never be the same. But that hadn't been enough for Amber.

"Randy was harder. He doesn't give a damn about his parents. Those wastes of space do more damage alive than dead. I had to get creative. Joe was all Randy ever cared about, so he has to pay for the crime."

There was movement at the door, the sun streaming in behind a large figure I couldn't quite make out. Relief swept through me. Help.

But then the figure spoke. "But you almost ruined everything when you played Rambo outside the police station."

The voice was familiar. Too familiar.

He stepped inside the falling down barn, the light shifting around him and revealing a face I'd seen almost every day for all my life.

"Jude?" I croaked.

"Hey, Little Williams."

Amber sent a scowl in his direction. "I wasn't going to lose my chance to give this bitch a little payback. She almost cost me my job."

A muscle along Jude's jaw fluttered in a staccato rhythm. "And *you* almost fucked our entire plan."

Redness crept up her throat. "Without me, you wouldn't have had access to the police department like you needed. You wouldn't have known where they were searching. Who their suspects were."

"Except I don't have access because you got yourself suspended. Your temper only hurts you, Amber."

She flushed even deeper. "I got suspended because of *her*—"

Jude moved so fast his arm was a blur. One second, Amber was standing. The next, there was a soft pop, and she had crumpled to the ground like a marionette with its strings cut.

My breaths came quicker and quicker as shock took hold, sliding through my system and numbing everything in its wake. "You—you—"

Jude scoffed. "I did you a favor. She had a real hard-on for you. I don't know why. Probably had a crush on Holt like the rest of our class."

He said Holt's name like the worst insult you could level against someone. But I couldn't take my eyes off Amber. The low light of the barn was the only kindness. All I could see was an unmoving form cast in shadows.

Jude snapped his fingers. "Focus, Wren. This won't be any fun if you're catatonic."

"Fun?" The word was just above a whisper.

A grin stretched across Jude's face. "I've been waiting for this for years." His smile morphed into a scowl. "Those idiots just couldn't have a little patience. This all would've been over ten years ago if Randy and Paul were smart enough to follow directions."

My mind spun, the past and the present mixing together in an ugly kaleidoscope of colors. "You. You were there."

The words that had been haunting me forever replayed in my mind. Only this time, they were in Jude's voice. The *right* voice. *"Where the hell is Holt? We need them both."*

His grin was back now, only wider this time, such pride on his face. "People are easily manipulated. You just have to find the right strings to pull. Take our little friend here."

He gestured to Amber, still lying crumpled on the ground. "So much rage in her. She needed a place to channel it. I helped her with that. And she gave me the same thing Randy and Paul did. Cover. The cops never once thought I could have anything to do with this. Any of it. So what if the body count was a little higher because of it?"

The numbness was fading now, replaced by a sickness steadily rolling through me. I'd let this man into my home. Into my *life*. He'd held me as I fell apart, sobbed at the loss of Holt, at my broken body. All of it. And *he* had been the trigger for it all.

"Why?"

It was the only thing I could think to ask. Because I had a deep need to know why he'd been so intent on tearing my life apart, piece by piece.

The fluttering in Jude's jaw was back as his hand tightened around his gun. "He has to feel it."

I blinked up at Jude, trying to make sense of the words falling from his lips. "Who?" But I had a sick feeling I knew the answer.

"Don't play dumb. You know. I'd almost think you'd be grateful. He left us both in the dirt. But no, you just spread your legs for him the second he came back."

The nausea washing through me intensified. "Holt loves you. He always has—"

"He's a traitor! He knew how bad things were for me at home. He knew it, but he still bailed. The second he decided you were the damn love of his life, he didn't have any time for me and Chris."

"That's not true. He—"

Jude's hand shot out, slapping me across the face. "Shut up! You don't know! He had *everything*. And I had nothing. But for a while, I had the Hartleys. Until you came along and stole them all, too."

My head rang, and my vision doubled. The metallic taste of blood filled my mouth. I tried to sit back up, but between Amber's hit and now Jude's, everything swam around me.

"You wanted to kill us both that night. Because we'd hurt you." And now we were all hurting. Lives were being torn apart yet again. Why, for some, was the answer to pain to create more? To pass that burden in an effort to pretend it hadn't scarred them? It never worked. It just left twice the destruction.

Jude's gaze went glacial. "I wanted you both to *suffer*. But Holt most of all. I wanted him to watch the life drain from your body before I took his. Slowly. So he felt it *all*."

Bile surged up my throat, and I struggled to swallow it down. "Jude...don't."

That grin was back. "Sorry, Little Williams."

He pulled a phone from his back pocket. "It might be ten years too late, but we're going to watch him suffer now."

Chapter Forty-One

Holt

SHADOW LET OUT A WHINE FROM THE BACK SEAT AS NASH drove like a bat out of hell down the mountain.

Grae's phone rang for the third time before she picked up. "If you have my best friend in some sort of sexual haze and that's why she's late to lunch, tell her she's being demoted."

"G?" My voice was so raw I barely even recognized it.

Grae's entire demeanor changed in a flash. "What's wrong?"

"Wren isn't with you?"

"No, I've been waiting at Dockside for the past fifteen minutes. I thought she was with you."

My gut twisted in an ugly tangle of fear and rage. The camera feeds at the cabin were dead, and the backlog of video for the past two hours erased. Everything was wrong.

I tried to speak and couldn't. How could I find the words to voice what I feared most in the world? I cleared my throat. "I can't get ahold of her—"

"I'll go to the cabin—"

"No," I barked.

"Holt," Grae whispered.

"I'm sorry, G. I just—Law is on his way there now. Until we know what's going on, just go to the station."

I didn't want Grae anywhere near this if it ended up being my worst nightmare come to life.

"Holt—"

"Please, Grae. Just go to the station."

"Okay." She was quiet for a moment. "Call me the second you find her. And tell her I'm really freaking pissed she missed our lunch. And that she owes me two viewings of *Little Women* and at least three desserts."

I wanted to smile and give my sister the chuckle I knew she was trying for, but I couldn't get there. "I'll tell her."

Grae didn't say anything, but she didn't hang up either.

"Go to the station."

"I'm going."

I hung up. I couldn't even find it in me to say goodbye.

Nash sent a quick look in my direction before taking a sharp curve like a Nascar driver. "G hasn't seen her?"

I swallowed, trying desperately to clear the lump in my throat. "No. She never showed at Dockside."

Dad leaned forward and squeezed my arm. "I'm sure there's an explanation—"

My phone ringing cut off his words. Lawson's name flashed on the screen.

"Do you have her?" I clipped.

"She's not here."

I cursed. "What do you see?"

"Someone's been here. The hub for all your cameras and security system is smashed to hell."

My pulse pounded in my neck. Wren was okay. She had to be. I would know if she weren't. I would feel it. She was still on this planet. Still breathing.

"They would've needed access to her phone to erase the video." Even I could recognize the robotic air to my voice.

A million nightmares played in my mind. All the ways someone could've gotten Wren's phone. How they could've unlocked it.

Dad squeezed my shoulder, hard. "Don't go there. We're gonna find her."

We had to. There wasn't another option. Because I couldn't live another ten years without Wren. I couldn't live another second.

"We'll meet you at the cabin," I told Lawson.

"The crime scene techs are on the way. I put out an APB for her, too."

"Thanks," I said, a gruff edge coating my voice.

I hit end on the call and stared at my phone. It was the same photo background. The one of Wren, her head tipped back, taking in the rise of twilight.

"Dad's right. We're gonna find her. Law will have his people on it and—"

Another incoming call cut Nash off. Jude's name flashed on my screen.

Hope sprang to life in my chest. Maybe he knew something. Had a lead. Anything.

I hit accept and pressed the phone to my ear. "Is Wren with you?"

A dark chuckle cut across the line. One I'd never heard slip from Jude's lips in all our years of friendship. "She is."

Everything around me slowed as dread took root in my gut. But still, some part of me hoped I was wrong. "Can I talk to her?"

"She's a little indisposed at the moment."

"I'm okay," Wren shouted.

Relief swept through me, quickly mixing with sickening fear.

"Shut up," Jude snapped.

I motioned to my dad in the back seat, mouthing words I hoped he could read. *Text Law. Jude has Wren. Track the call to my phone.*

Dad's eyes widened, but he began furiously typing on his phone.

I shoved down the panic threatening to swallow me whole. "Where are you, Jude?"

"I'm going to tell you because it's time for us to have a proper reunion. But I'm gonna need a few things from you first."

"Name them." I would've given him anything, ripped the still-beating heart from my chest if it meant Wren would be okay.

"Lose the cops. I see one sign of a badge, and I blow Wren's pretty little head off and save us all the trouble of a get-together."

Fury swept through me, melting the ice in my veins and turning it to lava. "Done. I'm in Nash's SUV, though." He didn't need to know that Nash was with me, not until it was too late for him.

Jude cursed. "Fine. Park at the start of the access road behind Wren's cabin. I'll give you more instructions once you get there. You've got ten minutes."

"Don't hurt her." The plea was guttural, pulled from the depths of my soul.

He chuckled. "She's already a little hurt. Only time will tell how much worse it gets."

Bile swirled in my gut, and images of Wren flashed in my mind—a slideshow of the worst things I could imagine interspersed with the best memories I had of her. It was a special kind of torture having those two paired together.

My breathing grew ragged as I struggled to keep it under control. "Don't."

"Then you don't want to test my patience. Where are you?"

I searched our surroundings. "Just hitting town now."

Nash blew through the picturesque street, his lights flashing but without the sirens.

"Good. Call me when you get to the access road. Every minute you're late, Wren will pay the price."

Jude hung up before I could get another word out. I slammed my fist into the dashboard.

"Tell me you're not actually doing what this asshole is asking," Nash growled.

My pulse was the only thing I could manage to feel beyond the terror that had me in a vise-grip. "There isn't another option."

"Not going in there alone would be a start," Nash shot back.

My head jerked in his direction. "And what would you do? If it was the woman you loved more than life, what would you do?"

Nash's throat worked as he swallowed, but he didn't say anything.

"We're going to play this smart," Dad said, his voice remarkably calm.

"Jude said any hint of cops and he'd kill her." The words dug the terror in deeper. Because I believed him. The man I'd thought was a friend. A brother. And for half our lives, he'd harbored the kind of hatred that ended in death. Something that had festered, turning into an obsession.

All of this pain… Because I'd brought a monster into our lives.

Dad squeezed my shoulder. "You're going to take my phone and put it on speaker. That way, we can hear everything that's going on. All you have to do is give us enough information to make out the location. Then we'll come for you."

My throat tightened. My dad had always been good in a crisis. Maybe it was the decades of SAR experience. Perhaps it was just an innate calmness that settled in his bones. But all I could think in the moment was that I couldn't imagine facing this without him—without my family at my back.

"It's a good plan."

Dad tried to force a smile. "See, your old man's not so useless, after all."

"No one has ever thought you were useless a day in your life," I said.

He patted my shoulder. "Doesn't hurt to hear that now and again. Lawson and Roan are meeting us at the access road."

"Jude could see—"

"Just them. No one else. But you need backup when it's time. And Roan knows these woods like no one else."

Dad had a point. Roan could've made his way through the forests surrounding the lake blindfolded if he needed to.

I swallowed hard, hoping this was the right move. "Okay."

Nash turned onto the road that would've taken us to the cabin. Home. To where Wren should've been. But instead of veering left toward the lake, he went right and up the hillside toward the access road.

Gravel spit as he pulled to a stop next to Lawson's SUV and Roan's truck. The vehicle wasn't even off before I was out and checking my weapon.

Lawson strode toward me, tension lining his jaw. "You can't go into this alone—"

I held up a hand to halt his words. "Don't. I'm going in. Dad has a plan that should work, though."

Because if Jude wanted me dropped off here without a car, they were within walking distance. My gut tightened as Wren's face flashed in my mind, and I imagined her scared and alone with a monster.

Dad relayed the plan to Lawson and Roan as I slid my weapon back into its holster. Jude would know I'd come armed, and he'd be prepared. But he hadn't spent years working on his marksmanship and reaction time. I'd had nothing but time to hone the skills that would help me keep the people in my care safe.

Roan strode toward me, his expression stony. "This was all Jude?"

I shook my head. "I don't know." There were too many pieces unassembled in my mind. "I'd say it's likely."

Barely restrained fury swept over Roan's expression. There had been a time when the cops had looked for Wren's third shooter. It hadn't lasted long, but they'd circled around one person in particular. Roan.

Maybe because he'd always been a loner and happier with the company of nature than the chatter of people. Maybe because the town was desperate to believe that someone older had been pulling the strings, even if Wren had told them there was no way in hell.

They had questioned Roan twice. And with no alibi other than the fact that he'd been backpacking in the mountains, people looked at him differently—with doubt and suspicion. With fear.

It had broken something in my brother. And now he was the one suspicious of everyone. And his loner tendencies had been intensified to the extreme.

If Jude had been a part of this—all of it—Roan would want him to pay.

Roan's hands clenched and then flexed at his sides. "We'll get him."

Lawson surveyed us both, pressing Dad's phone into my hand. "We'll get him together."

I looked at Roan. "Where are the most likely places Jude could be keeping her within walking distance of here?"

He scrubbed a hand over his face. "There are the caves down by the lake. A couple of vacation homes that might be vacant. An old barn on the property to the west. And if he's not looking for shelter? Just about anywhere."

I replayed the phone call in my mind. I hadn't heard anything that would give away a location. "All right. I need to call him."

Lawson held up a hand. "We need to consider the fact that he could have an accomplice. That you could be walking into an ambush. You talk to Chris lately?"

Nausea swept through me, but I scrolled through the contacts on my phone and hit Chris's name.

It rang twice before he answered. "This is Chris."

A saw sounded in the background, and I heard a few guys yelling.

"It's Holt. You seen Jude lately?"

"No, he went on a supply run. Why?"

"I thought we were supposed to meet up for a beer, but I must've had the wrong day."

"I'm not his damn secretary," Chris muttered.

"Sorry, man."

"Whatever," he clipped and then hung up.

I looked at my brothers and dad. "I don't think he's in on it. He's at a construction site. I could hear that and guys in the background."

Lawson scrubbed a hand over his jaw. "I don't know—"

"It's too late. I'm not leaving her with that monster. If he has help, I'll deal with it." I lifted my phone to call the person I'd once counted among my closest friends.

Roan motioned to Nash. "Conference me in on your call so I can hear an updated location. I'm heading north to swing around. There are a few areas I want to check."

"I said together," Lawson argued.

Roan's eyes flashed. "I know what I'm doing."

"I know you do."

Nash dialed another number on his phone, and a second later, Roan's phone rang. It was a miracle we were getting service at all, but we were up a little higher here, giving us better reception.

"Mute yourselves," I ordered, not giving Lawson a chance to further argue with Roan. "I'm calling Jude."

Roan took that as his signal and took off at a jog into the woods.

I pressed the speakerphone button, and Jude picked up on the first ring. "Just in time. My fingers were getting a little twitchy."

I bit down hard on the inside of my cheek. "Tell me where you want me to go."

"Are you alone, Holt? Don't forget, I know how your voice sounds when you lie."

But he didn't. Jude hadn't spent any real time with me in a decade. He didn't know how my demons had changed me.

"I'm alone. Now tell me where the hell you want me to go."

"Don't, Holt!"

Everything in me seized at the fear in Wren's voice.

"Shut up!" Jude snapped.

A smack sounded, and then a muffled cry.

My fingers tightened around the phone so hard I thought for

sure it would splinter. "Touch a hair on her head and I'll end you," I growled.

Jude's dark laugh was back. "A little too late for that, my friend. Start walking west."

I took one last look at Nash, Lawson, and my dad as I strode in the direction Jude had instructed. I cemented their image in my mind. I didn't want to lose it. Needed to remember how much they cared for me. How they always had my back, even when I hadn't had theirs nearly enough lately.

"I'm walking. What now?"

Jude was quiet for a moment. Waiting, I realized.

"Take the path that veers off the road. In half a mile, you'll come to a barn. Knock real nice, and I might let you in."

"Don't do it, Holt! He's just going to kill us both. Please, don't—"

A sickening sound cut across the line. Not a slap. The sound of a fist meeting flesh.

"Shut the hell up, bitch!"

Another punch sounded, and then a crash. Wren let out an agonized cry.

"You are going to pay every second until he gets here," Jude gritted out.

Then the line went dead.

Chapter Forty-Two

Wren

MY RIBS BLAZED WITH A FIRE I'D NEVER FELT BEFORE. I rolled into a ball, letting out a low moan. But I couldn't regret my words—not if it saved Holt. We might not get our second chance, but he could get his.

Jude shoved his phone into his pocket and chuckled. "You just made lover boy's end that much quicker. He hears one cry from you, and I bet he's running his ass off to get here."

The tiny flicker of hope I'd felt at warning Holt extinguished instantly. Because Jude was right. Holt would never back down. He'd never save himself if I were at risk.

Jude adjusted his grip on his gun, seeming to make sure everything was all in working order after laying waste to Amber. Making sure it was ready for Holt.

Fury burst free, dumping adrenaline into my system—adrenaline that numbed the worst of the pain. This wasn't going to happen.

I moved before I had a chance to think it through. Before I

had the opportunity to realize how dumb my plan was. Shoving up with my elbow, I sprang to my feet and charged at Jude.

Pain flared along my ribs, stealing my breath, but I didn't care. I ran straight for him. I didn't have a weapon to fight with so I would use what I did have: me.

The shock of my movements had Jude's head snapping up, but he wasn't quick enough.

I dipped my shoulder, colliding with Jude like a linebacker would in a football game. He let out a pained grunt and went down, but not before grabbing hold of my hair with a curse.

"Crazy bitch!"

I slammed my bound fists into his face, and Jude howled in pain. The surprise of the hit made him loosen his hold on me for just a moment, and I didn't waste the opportunity.

My body screamed in pain as I ran for the door, but I didn't slow. That light was my goal—my freedom.

A shot sounded behind me, but I didn't stop. I had no idea where Holt was, where I should go, but I knew I needed cover. The bright sunlight had me blinking rapidly, but I kept running.

My surroundings came to me in flashes of images. Trees. A hillside. A tiny glimpse of the lake.

We were close to my cabin. So close to home. But I knew that would be the first place Jude would think I would go. So, instead of heading south, I went north into the trees with a prayer that they would shield me.

A shout sounded behind me, and I knew I was too late to disguise my direction, but not too late to hide.

I pushed my muscles harder as I ducked behind one tree after another. My legs trembled as I ran, fatigue and pain clawing to take hold. Tears stung my eyes—ones of frustration and fear. I just needed a little bit more from my body. Enough to find a place to hide.

My gaze jumped from one thing to the next, desperately searching. But there was nothing I could see. Nothing that would shield me the way I needed.

Footsteps pounded behind me, and twigs snapped.

"I'm gonna make you hurt for this," Jude called.

My heart stuttered in my chest, but it didn't matter if he did. I would take all the pain in the world if it meant keeping him away from Holt.

That little flicker of hope gave me a burst of energy. My muscles carried me farther up the hill and deeper into the neighboring property. I tried to remember what was near here—the other homes and where the road led. But I was moving too quickly to truly get my bearings.

I had to hope that I'd find something—a place to hide until help could find me. Holt wasn't stupid. Lawson knew what was happening, and he had to be right on Holt's heels. I could only hope that he'd bring the entirety of the Cedar Ridge PD with him.

A sharp pain stabbed through my side, and light danced in front of my eyes. Panic seized me as I struggled to suck in air. More tears gathered as I cursed. This couldn't happen. My body couldn't give out when I was so close to escape.

I wheezed out a painful breath as I desperately searched for somewhere to hide. My gaze caught on a cluster of young pines that had sprouted up near some more mature ones. It was all I had because my body was giving out.

My limbs shook as I dove for the trees' cover. Burrowing as deep as I could between them, I wrapped a hand around my ribs.

My breaths came in heavy pants, sounding like my lungs were crunching as they struggled to work. And each one hurt. My chest was so tight it was as if I were breathing with a two-hundred-pound weight on my shoulders.

The pounding footsteps that had been tracking me slowed, and I held my breath, squeezing my eyes closed. I was almost too scared to hope. So, I clung to thoughts of what I always did in my hardest moments. Holt.

I pictured his face. The tender way he looked at me when he told me he loved me. The feel of his stubble beneath my fingertips. The sound of the chuckle I loved so much. I played it over and over in my head, trying to hear each incarnation of it from boy to man.

"I know you're here, Wren..."

Jude singsonged the words in a tone that was too damn happy. I just played Holt's laugh louder in my mind.

"This is just like when we would play Ghost in the Graveyard. Remember that?"

My chest throbbed as I bit the inside of my cheek. We'd played it too many times to count. At least a dozen of us running all over the Hartleys' property in search of the one person hiding. Screaming in laughter as we all raced back to *base* when someone found the person. My first stolen moments with Holt Hartley under the moonlight.

"But who is going to find you first?" Jude snorted. "You were always such a wimp. Holt would hide with you when you were the ghost." His voice grew farther away. "Remember how pathetic you were? How pathetic Holt was for putting up with you?"

My fingernails dug into my palms as I struggled to keep my breathing even. Jude would always see Holt's kind heart and empathy as a weakness because he lacked those things. But I would grab hold of that kindness and never let go.

I swore I could feel Holt with me now, his body huddled next to mine, his voice whispering in my ear. *"Don't worry, Cricket. I'll scare the ghosts away."*

He had a way of taking the fear out of any situation. A way of always making me feel safe. And he had given me a bone-deep knowledge that I was never alone.

Even in the years we'd been apart, I'd carried Holt with me like a brand on my soul. I would hear the whisper of his voice reminding me that I was perfect just as I was. That I didn't need to prove my worth to the world around me, and that those who were meant to love me would see it in me every day.

A twig snapped. Closer now.

My fingernails pierced the skin of my palms in an effort to keep my screams at bay.

A hand dove between the trees and grabbed me by the throat. With a vicious yank, Jude pulled me from my hiding spot. He shoved the gun under my chin.

"I planned on going easy on you. Got a little partial to seeing how wrecked you were by Holt's abandonment. But I changed my mind. Now you're gonna feel it, too. And I can't wait to hear you scream."

Chapter Forty-Three

Holt

MY FEET POUNDED ALONG THE PATH, EACH STRIKE reverberating up my spine. I knew Lawson and Nash had to be behind me. They would've started running the second they had a location. The second they heard Wren's cries.

Because they loved her, too. She was as much of a sister to them as Grae was. And they knew if I lost her, they'd lose me, too.

Trees blurred as I ran faster, pushing my muscles to the breaking point and then begging them for more. Half a mile. How long would it take me to sprint half a mile? Three minutes? Two?

How much damage could Jude inflict in one hundred and twenty seconds? In one hundred and eighty?

Too much.

Flashes of a structure popped into my vision—dark wood falling apart at the seams. The instincts I'd honed over a decade in the military and security screamed that this could be a trap. I didn't even care. I would let Jude kill me a million times over if it meant he'd stop hurting Wren.

My girl. She'd been hurt way too damn much. And I'd been the source of so much of it. I could be the end of it now.

I broke into the clearing and charged for the barn, gun gripped tight and ready. I stayed to the side of the open doors and prayed the dilapidated building would give a chance at cover. Expecting a hail of bullets, I stilled when there wasn't a sound.

My pulse thumped in my neck as I crept along the barn's outer wall and toward the doors. They were wide open. Too welcoming to anyone who might come along.

I strained to hear, and the only thing I picked up was the sound of the breeze in the pines. I ducked inside, dipping low, my gun sweeping the space.

It stilled.

Iron fists wrapped around my chest, squeezing the life out of me. A body lay crumpled on the ground—too slight to be a man.

Bile surged in my throat as my eyes burned. Each step I took was weighed with my failure—my failure then and my failure now.

A strangled sound escaped me as I took in the body. My legs shook and almost buckled.

"Not her."

I said the words over and over, trying to convince myself of their truth. Wren wasn't lying dead in this barn. She didn't have a bullet in her brain.

I stumbled outside, sucking in air and trying not to hurl. Because it could've been her. So easily.

"Where is she?" Lawson barked as he and Nash ran across the clearing, Shadow at their side.

"Not there." I swallowed hard. "Amber Raymond. She's dead."

Nash's eyes widened as he tightened his hold on Shadow's leash. "What the hell is going on?"

I scanned the trees, searching for a hint of anything that might give us a lead. There were no flickers of movement, no hints of sound. We would've all been dead already if this had been a trap.

"She got away."

The words slipped from my mouth without conscious thought.

But I knew in my bones they were true. Wren would fight with everything she had. She was smart. And more than that, she was fierce.

That fierceness was born of all the struggles she'd faced. How strong she'd had to be when the chips were down. I had to believe she'd fight with everything she had now, too.

Lawson started toward the barn. "There could be something here that helps."

My teeth gnashed together, the urge to simply start running through the forests to find Wren so strong. But I had to play it smart—no wasted time.

Shadow let out a low whine. It was a sound I felt in my damn soul.

My fingers sifted through her fur. "We're gonna find her."

I followed Lawson into the barn, Nash at my side. I steeled myself for the sight that greeted us, but Nash cursed. Lawson just stared, his gaze boring into Amber's fallen form as if this were all his fault.

After a few moments, my eyes adjusted to the low light. I scanned the space, searching for anything that might help us. I tracked footprints from one side of the barn to the other, drag marks trailing behind them.

My stomach roiled with acid. Jude had dragged her as if she were nothing more than garbage.

"Looks like there was a struggle."

Nash's voice cut through my thoughts, and I spun around. "What do you mean?"

He pointed to an area closer to the door. "Here."

I surveyed the dirt where he'd indicated. There were deep divots as if someone had taken a hard fall.

Striding over, I crouched. I narrowed my eyes and searched the space for anything. A small patch of earth caught my attention. I crouched, my throat constricting. I reached out and pressed two fingers to the dirt. As I lifted them, a telltale reddish-brown color caught the light.

"Blood." Lawson grimaced.

"It looks like there's some here, too," Nash said, bending and pressing a thumb to the dirt. It too came away red.

As he straightened, Shadow let out a series of loud barks and whines, pulling at the leash.

"It's okay, girl," Nash soothed.

My pulse sped up. "Let her smell the blood."

Nash looked at me like I was crazy. "What?"

"Just do it," I clipped.

He lowered his hand to Shadow, and she sniffed like crazy, then started pulling on the leash.

I hurried to her side. "You want to find Wren?"

Shadow barked.

Lawson sent me a wary look.

"She's got good instincts with scents. Not perfectly trained, but the best option we have," I argued.

Lawson looked down at the dog. "All right."

"Let her sniff your hand again," I ordered Nash. The second she did, I gave her the command. "Find Wren."

Shadow's nose dropped to the ground, and she began to follow a trail we couldn't see. Pain tore at me, knowing the source of it. This wasn't some airborne scent we might get from someone's clothes. This was blood. And it was most likely Wren's.

Shadow pulled us toward the trees, away from the lake and Wren's cabin. I had to hope it was right and that she wasn't taking us farther away. I would've promised anything, given it all if I could just know that Wren would be safe.

Nash kept a firm hold on the leash, letting Shadow pull him along at whatever pace she set. Lawson and I scanned the forest, looking for any signs of a trail.

Shadow began circling, letting out another whine.

Nash's brow furrowed. "I think she's confused."

That little flicker of hope I'd been holding onto burned to ash.

And then a scream split the air.

Chapter Forty-Four

Wren

I COULDN'T HELP THE SCREAM THAT SLIPPED FROM MY LIPS as Jude jammed the gun into my ribs. I didn't want to give him the power that came with knowing that he'd hurt me, but the pain was too great. White-hot, blazing pain ripped along my side and pulsed deeper with each shove Jude gave me.

"Shut up," he snarled. "You ruin everything. I should've known. That's the way it's always been."

His words barely penetrated. I was too focused on trying to breathe through the pain.

"Walk," Jude barked.

I struggled to get my legs to obey, but they shook with the effort. "I can't," I wheezed.

Something was wrong. A rib had to be broken. A punctured lung, maybe. It was too hard to suck in air.

Jude sneered at me. "You can, and you will. I've worked too hard for this to have you screw it up now."

"How long have you been planning this?"

The corner of his mouth kicked up. "Longer than you can imagine."

He shoved me forward, back toward the barn, and I stumbled, the ropes on my wrists digging deeper. A fresh wave of agony swept over me.

"I really didn't think lover boy would be able to stay away from you for as long as he did. Guess he didn't love you that much, after all. Really had to work to get you two back together so he'd feel the pain of losing you all over again."

A few weeks ago, Jude's words would've cut. Now, they simply glanced off me. Because I knew that Holt had fought hard to stay away because of how deeply he loved me. It was misguided and dumb, but Holt had thought he was doing the right thing. And I saw that now.

"I had to get creative to get him back here, too. Couldn't let him get past the ten-year mark."

My steps faltered.

He only grinned wider. "Did you know that monkshood can cause heart attacks and is virtually untraceable in the blood?"

"Nathan." My stomach roiled. He'd given Holt's dad a heart attack, knowing it would likely force Holt back to Cedar Ridge—back to where Holt was within Jude's reach.

"There are all sorts of opportunities to slip something into someone's water bottle while on a search or running drills. Too many to count, really. I was hoping it would be harder, more of a challenge."

I tugged on my ropes, trying to see if they had any give now. Nothing. "He could've died."

Jude shrugged. "Collateral damage." A scowl pulled at his mouth. "But even with his poor dad sick and injured, Holt took his sweet-ass time coming home. Just shows how selfish he is—"

"Might be, but you need to take that out on me, not innocent bystanders."

Holt stepped out from between the trees, and my heart ricocheted around in my chest. The riot of emotions warred with itself: hope and terror, relief and rage. But most of all, love. For this man who would do anything to keep me safe.

Jude tightened his grip on my hair as he used me as a shield. "Hey, best friend. Took you long enough."

Holt's gaze swept over me, assessing the situation in a single breath. "Let her go. I'm the one you want."

He started toward us, gun raised. But there was no good shot, and Jude knew that.

"Uh-uh-uh," Jude clucked. "Stay right there. Wouldn't want my finger to slip."

He tugged me back harder against him, the gun digging into my ribs. I tried to swallow my cry, but a small whimper escaped my lips.

Holt's eyes blazed with fury, but his steps faltered. "You got me here. Now what? You didn't think this through."

Jude's grip on my hair tightened. "That's where you're wrong. We're going to walk back to that barn and end this nice and easy. Everyone will think good ol' Amber lost it, and that you two killed each other in a shootout. But not before she shot poor Wren here."

Holt's knuckles bleached white around his gun. "Gotta admit, that doesn't sound like something I want to do."

Jude shoved the gun harder into my side.

I doubled over in pain, letting out a wheezing cough.

Jude hauled me upright. "You don't, and I'll make her end the most painful we can imagine."

I felt something poke into my hip bone as he forced me up. I'd gotten so used to slipping it into my pocket each day that I rarely remembered I had it on me. Holt's pocketknife. The one I'd given him for his eighteenth birthday. The one he'd wanted me to carry, just in case.

Amber hadn't searched me when she grabbed me. And why would she? I'd been home. No purse. No keys. No phone. Nothing that could help me. Except *this*.

Jude gripped my hair tighter and gave me a shake. "What do you say, Holt?"

I bit the inside of my cheek to keep from crying out, but Holt didn't miss the pain on my face. I gave a slight shake of my head as I tried to slip my fingers into my front pocket. But the ropes made it hard to maneuver, and my ribs made every move agony.

Defeat filled Holt's expression. "Why are you doing this?"

"You left me. You knew my dad was a piece of shit. You knew I needed you. And you just bailed."

I managed to slip two fingers into my front pocket as Jude continued on the same tirade he'd berated me with. About how I'd ruined everything. How Holt had abandoned him. My fingers closed around the knife, and I tugged it free.

Holt stared at Jude, dumbfounded. "I never bailed on you. I had a girlfriend. That didn't mean I stopped caring about you and Chris. We had guys' night every week. You came over for every family dinner."

"You have no idea," Jude growled. "Your place used to be the escape. Instead, I had to go home. To the piece of shit who liked to beat me black and blue."

Holt blanched. "I didn't know."

"You didn't *care*," he spat. "You only cared about *her*."

"I did care about you. But I was sixteen and head over heels in love. I had tunnel vision."

I gritted my teeth as I struggled to work the blade open. It was tiny, no more than an inch and a half, but it was sharp. The bite of it against my finger had me almost weeping with relief.

"How about a little loyalty?" Jude bellowed. "How about not bailing on me for a piece of pussy?"

Holt's nostrils flared as he struggled to rein in his temper.

I flicked my eyes down in rapid movements, hoping he would see what was in my hands. But I didn't even need to do that. Holt had already registered it all. Of course, he had.

Holt gave an almost imperceptible nod.

It was all I needed. I didn't gather my strength. I didn't pause to think about what I was doing or wonder what Holt's move would be. Because I knew that he had me. No matter what happened, Holt would be there.

I slammed the knife into the side of Jude's thigh with all my might. He howled in pain.

Everything happened in flashes. Shouts all around us. Blurs of motion. But I was locked on Holt's eyes. Those deep blue depths that had never left me.

A shot sounded.

Panic streaked across Holt's face. His arms stretched out, reaching for me.

But I was already falling.

Chapter Forty-Five

Holt

MY BROTHERS STORMED JUDE—ROAN FROM BEHIND, Lawson and Nash from the sides after tying Shadow to a tree so she wouldn't get caught in the crossfire. But I only had eyes for Wren.

She crumpled as the sound of the shot still echoed in my ears.

Roan was on Jude, hauling him off her as he kicked and screamed.

I fell to the ground, my hands hovering over Wren, scared to even touch her.

"Holt," she croaked.

I'd never been more relieved to hear a single sound. "Where does it hurt?"

"My ribs," she wheezed.

I frantically searched her for any signs of blood. But the only thing I saw was her split lip. "Did the bullet hit you? Does it hurt anywhere else?"

Gently, I tugged up her shirt and sucked in a breath. Her side was already turning black and blue.

"It wasn't Jude's bullet," Nash called with a grunt as he wrestled Roan away from Jude. "It was Roan's."

Jude howled in pain as Lawson forced him to his stomach and cuffed his hands behind his back. It was then that I saw the blood staining his shirt. Roan had clipped him in the shoulder.

A little of the terror gripping me eased.

"Holt."

Wren's voice was barely audible, and my gaze jerked back to her. Panic streaked her eyes as her hand gripped mine. Her lips were a blue shade that stopped my heart.

"Can't. Breathe."

I counted the linoleum tiles as I paced up and down the hospital hallway. The number never changed. Twenty-three up. Twenty-three back. But I kept counting. It was the only thing I could do.

The burn was back. The one that had lit my sternum every day since Wren's attack ten years ago. It had eased since being back in Cedar Ridge, with every day since seeing Wren for the first time and with every little whisper of her she shared with me.

But it had come back in full force now. As Nash and I had done mouth-to-mouth to keep Wren breathing and carried her to the road on a stretcher. As we'd waited for the helicopter to land. And now, as they were cutting Wren open... The burn was turning me to ash.

A hand landed on my shoulder. I looked up to meet my dad's gaze. He squeezed hard. "She's going to be okay."

But he didn't know that. Not for sure. Wren's lung had collapsed. The tear in it was so bad they needed to stitch her back together. And she hadn't regained consciousness since those last words she'd spoken to me. *"Can't. Breathe."*

Dad squeezed my shoulder again, even harder this time. "Don't go there."

It was the only place I could go. There and to the dark depths of the knowledge that this was all on me. All because I hadn't been the kind of friend someone as sick and twisted as Jude had needed. All because I'd hurt him.

"I don't like that look in your eyes," Dad said, tugging me farther down the hall. "Talk to me."

"How can you even look at me?" The question was low, hoarse. As if sandpaper coated the words.

My dad's eyes flashed. "None of this is on you. Not a damn thing. That boy is sick."

"He poisoned you. You almost died because I was a crap friend."

Dad shook his head vehemently. "I almost died because a disturbed person targeted my son. My family. You did nothing but try to help."

I wanted to hear him. To believe his words. But too much fought against them.

"Holt," Dad said gruffly. "I've seen the change in you over these past couple of weeks. I've seen Wren's love change you. She made you see what no one else could—that this was never on your shoulders."

It was true. Wren had shown me that we had to face things together, no matter what came our way. Because we were our strongest selves when we had the other backing us up. And even in those most difficult moments, life was never sweeter than when she was by my side.

My throat tightened, and tears burned the backs of my eyes. "I just need her to be okay."

My dad took both of my shoulders, dipping his head to meet my gaze. "Wren is going to be just fine. So long as she wakes up to you."

Pain dug its talons into my chest. "I'm not bailing on her."

"I know that," he said. "And it's a good thing because I don't like to think that I raised an idiot. And if you keep blaming yourself for this, that's exactly what you are."

I wanted to laugh. I knew it was what my dad wanted from

me, but I couldn't get my throat to make the sound. "I'll keep that in mind."

Footsteps sounded, and my gaze caught on the man with the tanned skin and warm smile who had introduced himself to us before Wren's surgery. I was already moving toward him.

Dr. Sanchez came to a stop in front of me. "Ms. Williams came through the surgery wonderfully."

I waited for the relief to hit, but it didn't come. It wouldn't. Not until I saw those green flecks sparking in her eyes. Not until I heard that uninhibited laugh.

"You fixed her lung?" I pressed.

He nodded. "The tear was moderate. We were able to repair it using minimally invasive techniques, so her recovery from the surgery itself shouldn't be too bad. But it will take some time for the lung to reinflate."

I frowned at the doctor. "Her lung not working doesn't sound like the surgery went *wonderfully* to me."

Dad stepped forward. "Apologies for my son. He's a bit on edge."

Dr. Sanchez gave me a sympathetic smile. "I get it. Why don't I take you to her? That way you can be there when she wakes up."

I felt a flicker of something in my chest and nodded. "Thank you."

Dad patted my back. "I'll go loop everyone else in."

The waiting room on the surgery floor was jam-packed with people who loved Wren. My mom, Nash, Grae. Lawson's boys: Charlie, Drew, and Luke, even though Lawson had had to stay behind to deal with the aftermath of what had happened. Abel.

I turned, pulling my dad into a hard hug. "Thank you. For everything."

"I love you, Holt. I know I may not always be there for you in the right way—"

"You show up. You love me. Couldn't ask for more."

Tears filled my dad's eyes as he released me. "Go to our girl. Make sure your face is the first one she sees."

I jerked my head in a nod and turned to follow the doctor. He led the way to a bank of elevators. But just before we reached them, a familiar figure stepped into the hallway.

Chris gripped the brim of a ballcap, shaping and reshaping it. "Holt."

My name was a hoarse whisper, more sound than an actual word.

My steps slowed and then halted altogether. I didn't have the first clue what to say. But Chris spoke before I had a chance.

"I didn't know. I swear. God. How could he—?" Chris cut himself off with a shake of his head.

"I know you didn't."

Chris swallowed, his Adam's apple bobbing. "It's why you called earlier, isn't it?"

I let out a breath. "I had to be sure. To know if I was walking into a situation with multiple assailants."

He nodded. "I did that. Being such an asshole to you since you came back. I put that doubt in your head."

"No. I hurt you. I get that."

Chris shook his head. "I'm sorry. Holding onto petty bullshit… Such a waste of time."

At the end of the day, none of us had been the best friends to one another. But every day was a chance to start again. I met Chris's dark gaze and extended a hand. "I think we both deserve a fresh start. What do you say?"

Chris stared down at my palm and then took it. "I'm glad you're back. And I know Wren is, too. She never stopped loving you."

Pain lanced me, a mixture of the good and bad, but I held tight to the good. "Thank you." I released his hand. "I gotta go see her."

Chris bobbed his head. "Tell her we're rooting for her."

"I will." I strode to the bank of elevators where the doctor waited, the same set I'd ridden in countless times after my dad's surgery. If I never saw these fluorescent lights again, it would be too soon.

Dr. Sanchez punched a button for the elevator. "She's strong. Fought her way back to you. She's going to come through this."

"Strongest person I know."

The elevator doors opened, and we stepped inside.

"The best ones always are," he said as if he knew from experience.

We were quiet as the elevator rose, letting us off on the fifth floor. The doctor inclined his head to the left. "This way. Ms. Williams is on a regular floor. If everything goes as planned and her oxygen levels are good, she should be able to go home tomorrow."

My eyes flared at that. "What about her other injuries?"

"She likely has a mild concussion, but none of the bones in her face are broken. Her cracked ribs will be the worst of her recovery. And that will simply take time. You'll have to make sure she doesn't push things too fast."

"Me and what army?" I muttered.

Dr. Sanchez chuckled. "We'll make sure to give her strict orders. And the painkillers should make her sleepy. For the next few weeks, the best thing for Ms. Williams will be rest."

He ushered me into a room. The sun streamed in through the window, illuminating Wren. She looked so damn small in the hospital bed. So fragile.

"She has a heart monitor and IV. The thing on her forefinger helps us track her oxygen."

I nodded but couldn't look away from Wren. But I couldn't move forward either.

The doctor spoke quietly. "Just knowing you're here will be the best medicine."

That was all I needed. I strode forward, sinking into the chair at her bedside. Careful not to dislodge the oxygen monitor, I took her hand in mine.

Her skin was cool, not full of her usual vibrance of life. I bent and pressed my lips to her knuckles as if that would restore it all.

Scooting my chair closer, I brushed my lips against her temple. "I'm right here, Wren. Just need you with me."

So much of her face was bruised and scratched. The anger that seared me nearly stole my breath. I struggled to keep my grip on Wren's hand gentle and keep the rage from my face.

I pictured those hazel eyes in my mind, remembered the feel of her body wrapped around mine. Imagined her laugh.

I lifted her hand to my lips. "Love you, Cricket. Every day. Every minute. Come back to me."

Wren's fingers twitched in my hand, and my gaze flew to hers. Her eyelids fluttered as if trying so desperately to open.

"Come on, Cricket. Open those beautiful eyes. Show me you're with me."

The fluttering intensified, and then Wren's eyes opened. I'd never seen anything more beautiful than that mixture of brown and gold and green.

She stared up at me, the green sparking as I'd hoped. "I'm with you."

Chapter Forty-Six

Wren

MUTED VOICES SIFTED IN FROM THE LIVING ROOM, AND Grae clicked up the volume. "You'd think they could have a little respect. I told them we were watching *Little Women*."

I grinned at her but bit the inside of my cheek to keep from laughing. Over the past three days, I'd learned that laughing and crying were not things I wanted to do if I hoped to keep my pain remotely manageable. Broken ribs sucked big time.

"They have never respected the sacredness of Jo, Beth, Meg, and Amy."

"It's true." Grae adjusted herself against the pillows as she turned toward me, a smile playing on her lips. "Remember when I threw that entire bowl of popcorn at Nash?"

"And then promptly burst into tears," I reminded her.

"He came in singing at the top of his lungs while Beth was *dying*."

I couldn't hold in my chuckle this time and immediately regretted it.

"Shit, Wren. I'm sorry."

I waved her off. "It's okay. I need the happy. It just sucks that it hurts like a B."

Grae paused the movie. "When's the last time you took a pain pill?"

I made a humming noise but didn't answer.

"Wren…"

"I took Tylenol an hour ago."

"That's not what the doctor recommended. He gave you the good stuff so you wouldn't be hurting this much."

I toyed with the edge of the blanket. "I hate the way they make me feel."

I always had. A part of me blamed the pain medication haze for not recognizing how Holt had been pulling away all those years ago.

Grae was quiet for a moment. "Talk to me."

A burn lit the backs of my eyes, and my throat tightened. "I'm okay. Really."

And I was. I had everything to be grateful for. I was alive. So was Holt. We'd gotten out. Instead, I felt like I was one breath away from a nervous breakdown.

"I've known you for my entire life. I know when you're lying." She pulled the blanket up higher around us. "Besties for the resties, remember? What's said here, stays here."

The pressure built in my throat, but I still didn't speak.

Worry etched itself deeper in Grae's face. "If you don't talk to me, promise me you'll talk to *someone*."

It wouldn't be Holt. He'd studiously avoided all talk of what had happened in the time Amber and Jude had held me captive. Lawson had asked me the bare minimum questions, Holt glaring at him the entire time.

"I'm scared this will be too much for him."

The words were out before I could stop them, a softly spoken utterance that ricocheted around the room like a cannon shot.

Empathy instantly filled Grae's expression, blending with the worry. She slipped her hand into mine, squeezing it. "He loves you."

"I know." I didn't doubt that for a second. But Holt had loved me ten years ago, too. Love wasn't always enough.

"Knowing that Jude was behind the attacks ten years ago and the attacks now has been hard for everyone. But he was Holt's best friend."

My chest cracked, another scar to add to the bunch, this one just invisible. And it wasn't just Holt feeling the sting.

Chris had broken down in tears in my hospital room, worried I'd never be able to forgive him for not seeing what was right under his nose. I'd gripped his hand hard and told him that none of it was his fault. Jude's destruction was more than just the physical lives he'd stolen. It was the mental torture he'd inflicted on everyone around him.

I held tight to Grae's hand as I whispered my worst fears aloud. "I'm terrified that Holt will take this all on his shoulders again. That it'll be too much, and he'll leave."

Holt had stayed by my side every moment at the hospital. But he was rarely still. He was always adjusting blankets, ordering food, speaking to doctors, planning for our trip home.

And since we'd arrived back at the cabin, we'd rarely been alone. The Hartley family had all but moved in to make sure we had everything we needed. I was grateful but desperate for some time with just Holt.

Grae nestled in closer to me. "Have you tried talking to him? Telling him you're worried."

"When? We're never alone except at night, and he always insists I need to sleep, not talk."

She rolled her eyes. "Always the bossy one."

I wanted to laugh but couldn't find it in me. "He's not even sleeping with me. He sleeps in that chair." I inclined my head to the piece of furniture that felt more like a nemesis.

Grae's brows rose at that.

"He said he's worried about bumping me in the night."

"That makes sense. He had a scare. The last thing he wants to do is hurt you when you're already in pain."

A tear slipped from my eye. "I'm worried he's just waiting until I'm healed to tell me that he can't do this."

"Wren." Grae squeezed my hand again, harder this time. "Holt was eighteen when you were shot. No one makes wise decisions at that age. But he's lived a lifetime without you. He knows how awful that is. He's not going to leave you now."

"You sound so sure."

A smile pulled at her mouth. "Because I know my brother. And you do, too." She brushed the hair out of my face. "But you have some scars from that time, too. Ones that make you expect the worst when there's no evidence to support it."

I wouldn't have said no evidence. Holt hadn't stopped moving since we'd gotten home. Refortifying the security system, installing new windows, cooking me every favorite meal I'd ever had.

But today was the worst. He'd taken off at first light, giving me a quick kiss and telling me he'd be back by dinner and to call him if I needed anything.

It wasn't about need right now. It was about *want*. I wanted my best friend. The love of my damn life. I wanted his hand in mine, his big body curved around mine, the scent of him soothing all the nightmares away. And he wasn't here.

"You have to keep the faith," Grae urged. "There has to be something you can hold on to right now that reminds you."

My gaze flicked to the dresser. To the photo. The one I'd found in the duffel before my whole world imploded.

Grae followed my line of sight and grinned. She bounded up from the bed and crossed to pick it up. A moment later, she was back, sitting cross-legged on the bed and handing me the photo.

"I asked him about this when you were napping yesterday."

"You did?"

She nodded. "He said he printed it out and had it laminated before boot camp. It's been with him every place he's ever gone."

My fingers ghosted over the spots on the photo where the plastic had worn through.

"He said that he'd slip it into his uniform so you were right next to his heart on every patrol. That he'd tuck it into his bunk or pin it to the tent so he could fall asleep looking at your face."

Tears stung my eyes and slid down my cheeks.

Grae wiped them away. "But then he said that it was nothing like the miracle of watching you sleep now. He loves you, Wren. He'll always come back to you."

Chapter Forty-Seven

Holt

"COULD YOU DRIVE A *LITTLE* FASTER?" I GROWLED.

Jack let out an exasperated sigh as he guided the U-Haul truck down the mountain road. "You're like a little kid asking, '*Are we there yet?*' every two minutes."

"If you weren't driving like a grandma, I wouldn't have to ask the damn question over and over." I checked my watch for the thousandth time. The clock on the dashboard was five minutes slow. I couldn't deny the flicker of annoyance at the inaccuracy, but it didn't tweak me the way it would have a couple of weeks ago.

"I think it's more important that we get there in one piece than at the speed of a racecar driver."

Jack was right. I knew he was. But the twitchiness at being away from Wren for most of the day was driving me out of my skin—even knowing my family would be with her every moment. *I* wanted to be with her. Wanted to make sure that she had everything she needed, and that the cabin was put back just as she wanted it. That she was safe.

Jack glanced in my direction, and the humor fled his face.

"Sorry, man. I know it's hard. But you've checked with your mom every hour on the hour. Wren's fine."

I rolled my shoulders back, trying to alleviate some of the tension there. "It's not the same as being with her."

My obsession with making sure that Wren was okay was one I knew I needed to deal with. But for the first time in forever, I was giving myself grace. It would take time. We'd been through a trauma—one that had opened old wounds.

A little of the tension in my chest eased as we passed the sign for Cedar Ridge. Almost there now.

"You know I'm here if you need to talk," Jack said as he slowed.

"Thanks, man. Sorry I've been in a piss-poor mood this whole drive."

Especially when Jack had dropped everything to help me clear out my condo in record time and drive all my stuff back home.

"No worries. You can repay me in beer."

I chuckled. "I already asked Nash to grab some of the local ales for you to sample."

Jack grinned as he turned onto the gravel road that would take us to the cabin. "See, your grumpy ass is already forgiven."

"Easy amends."

He grunted. "You sure this girl of yours wants your prickly ass living with her?"

"I'm hoping she does because my realtor already has an offer on the condo."

Jack's eyes widened. "You didn't ask Wren if it was okay to move in with her?"

"I told her I was here to stay."

He groaned. "You really do not know your way around women. Some surprises, good. Think flowers, cupcakes, a trip to Hawaii. Some surprises, bad. Any change to home décor, a visit from her in-laws, major life changes…like moving."

A trickle of unease slid through me. "Just park the damn truck."

Jack came to a stop in front of the cabin. "I'm just glad I'm here to witness whatever smackdown she gives you."

I ignored him and jumped out of the U-Haul. I didn't bother to wait for Jack. Instead, I strode straight inside.

Mom, Dad, and Lawson's boys all looked up as I charged in.

"Everything okay?" Mom asked.

I nodded. "Wren in her room?"

"She and Grae are watching a movie," Dad answered.

Safe. She was perfectly fine. But I wouldn't be able to breathe deeply until I locked eyes with her. Opening the bedroom, I stepped inside and froze.

Tears glittered in Wren's eyes, and I saw the remnants of ones having already fallen on her cheeks.

Grae grinned when she saw me. "Told ya."

"What. Happened?" I growled.

Grae hopped up from the bed, patting my chest as she passed me. "You two need to talk." She leaned in closer to me and whispered in my ear. "She's scared of losing you."

My chest constricted as my gaze shot to the woman in the bed—the one who'd had my heart forever and always would. I strode to her, kicking off my boots and climbing onto the bed.

As gently as possible, I curled myself around her. "What are these tears about? I never would've left if I'd known you were upset."

Wren sniffed. "I freaked myself out."

"About?" I asked, brushing a lock of hair away from her face.

"You haven't talked about what happened."

My brows drew together. "You're healing. I didn't want to bring you back to a bad place."

Wren looked up at me, studying my face. "You don't stop moving. Getting food. Fixing things around the house."

"Is that bad?"

Fresh tears welled in her eyes. "You did that before. The trying to *solve* everything."

Understanding dawned. "And then I left."

Wren nodded, wiping at her tears.

Pain lanced deep. "Cricket. I'm so damn sorry. My trying to fix things and make things as easy on you as possible doesn't mean I'm going to bolt."

Her watery gaze lifted to mine. "Do you blame yourself for this?"

I was quiet for a moment, trying to find the words. My first instinct was to shield Wren and soften the edges of how I really felt. But every time I did that, it had gotten us nowhere. So, instead, I went for the complete truth.

My fingers linked with Wren's. I needed that contact and wanted to assure her that I wasn't going anywhere. "When he had you, everything was dark. I had so much rage—at Jude, at myself. I was drowning in it. And when I thought I might lose you...again? I was a wreck."

"That's not an answer."

I squeezed her hand. "It felt like my fault—Jude's obsession. All those innocent people hurt because he used Randy and Paul as a shield to hide what he was really after. Hurting *me*."

Wren lifted a hand to my face, her palm brushing across my stubble. "That's on *Jude*."

"I know that. Dad gave me a good talking to at the hospital and got my head on straight. But I'm not perfect. I can't change the way my brain has worked for the last ten years overnight. Some demons still get at me. But I'm not going to let them win. I'm with you, Wren. Always and forever. No more going it alone because I think it's the right thing to do."

Wren pressed her face to my neck. "We can fight them together. We just have to talk it out. Always."

I tipped her face up to mine. "That goes for you, too. You get scared I'm going to leave, you tell me."

"I was scared. I don't want to lose you. What we have now... It's so much more than I dreamed."

A smile stretched across my face. "I'm glad you think so because I did something today. I thought it would be a good surprise, but Jack informed me I was an idiot and that I should've talked to you about it first."

Wren's brows pulled together. "What did you do?"

"I put my condo on the market last week. Accepted an offer on it yesterday. Cleared it out today."

Her eyes widened. "You have been busy."

I chuckled. "Would it be okay if I moved in with you?"

Tears pooled in Wren's eyes again.

"Shit. Are those good tears or bad?"

"Good," Wren whispered. "Before Amber got me, I was standing in this room, thinking about how amazing it would be for us to make this home *ours*. To meld our things. Pick out art. Put up fresh paint."

The tension that had grabbed hold of me the moment I'd left this morning finally subsided. I pressed my forehead to Wren's. "You know we'll never agree on paint colors."

She let out a huff of air. "Then I can't wait to fight with you over each and every wall."

"Nothing would make me happier. I love you, Wren. This is it." I pulled back to take in her face. "You with me?"

Wren beamed. "I'm with you."

Chapter Forty-Eight

Wren
ONE WEEK LATER

I LEANED BACK AGAINST THE COUCH AND STUDIED THE WALL— or *tried* to study the wall. The sexy-as-sin man standing in front of it proved distracting. What was it about jeans and a simple white tee?

Holt pointed to the first square of color painted on the living room wall. "Sage Meadow."

I made a humming noise.

He pointed to the second, a gray-blue color. "Stormy Sea."

I nodded.

Holt moved to the third. "Newsprint Gray."

I frowned at that one.

Holt didn't miss my expression as he let out an exasperated sigh. "That one's my favorite."

"It's boring."

He strode toward me, gently pulling me to him. "Might be boring, but it'll make whatever art we choose for the walls really pop."

Damn him for having a point.

Holt chuckled, the sound warming me from the inside out.

A hint of annoyance bled into my tone. "What are you laughing at?"

He only laughed harder. "Your expression. You really hate it when I'm right."

I pinched his side. "If you pick the paint, that means I get the final say on the art."

Holt leaned in and swept his mouth across mine. "Deal."

I followed his mouth as he pulled away, hungry for more.

He groaned. "You're killing me."

I huffed. "I think that's the other way around."

Thanks to my ribs, we were on a strict sex ban, and the order was driving us both up the wall. But that didn't stop Holt from showing me just how much he wanted and loved me. Ever since our talk, he'd made sure that I knew just where his head and heart were—with me.

Holt glanced down at his watch. "We should go."

My stomach dipped but I nodded.

"You don't have to do this. I can meet with Law—"

"No, I want to." It was time to put all this to rest. As much as we could until the trial, anyway. I needed some of that closure.

Holt wove his fingers through mine. "I've got a surprise for you afterward."

My brow arched at that. "Didn't Jack warn you off surprises for a while?"

Holt grumbled something under his breath. "This is a good one. Promise."

I stretched up on my tiptoes, ignoring the twinge in my ribs, and pressed a kiss to the underside of Holt's jaw. "I trust you."

He melted into me at that. "How long until the end of the ice age again?"

I laughed. "Two more weeks."

Holt let out some creative expletives at that, and I couldn't help but laugh.

Holt pulled to a stop in front of the police station, and I stared at the building. I hadn't been back since my kidnapping. It looked different somehow. Maybe it was knowing that it had housed a killer. Perhaps it was just that it had been forever since I'd been away from work for this long.

I forced myself to open my door and slide out of Holt's SUV. He was around the vehicle in a flash, taking my hand and squeezing it. I looked up at him. "Thank you. For everything."

His expression softened, and he bent to kiss me. "Love you, Cricket."

I'd never get tired of hearing those words. "Love you, too."

As we started toward the station, the front door swung open, and Nash strode out, a scowl on his face. The downward pull of his lips was so uncharacteristic that my steps faltered.

"Nash Bash?"

His head snapped up from looking at his phone. "Hey."

Little lines appeared between Holt's brows. "What's wrong?"

"Nothing," Nash muttered.

A ball of worry formed in my stomach. "Doesn't look like nothing."

Nash grunted.

"Are you turning into Roan? Single-word answers and grunts are all you're capable of?" Holt asked.

Nash scowled at his brother. "Maddie's back."

"Isn't that a good thing? How long is she here for?" I asked.

A muscle underneath Nash's eye began to twitch. "Apparently, she moved back. But she didn't bother to let me know."

Oh, shit.

Holt winced. "Fiancé make the move with her?"

The muscle that twitched beneath Nash's eye became a full-on tic. "I don't know."

The words were a growl, and I glanced up at Holt in confusion.

He gave a small shake of his head and gripped Nash's shoulder. "Why don't you talk to her before you go getting all pissed off?"

Nash's jaw worked back and forth, but he nodded. "I'm going to talk to her now."

"Good. Tell her I said hi."

"Me, too," I added.

Maddie had always been a good friend when she lived in Cedar Ridge. She and Nash had been attached at the hip for as long as I could remember. Nash was different with her than anyone else. Gentler somehow. More serious.

I glanced up at Holt as Nash strode toward the parking lot. "Is he okay?"

"I'm not sure."

The door opened again, and this time it was Abel. "How's my girl?"

I grinned, letting go of Holt's hand and striding toward my mentor. "I'm good."

He wrapped me in a gentle hug. "It's damn good to see you up and about."

"It feels good to be up and about." Even if my ribs were tender and I looked like I'd gone a few rounds with a heavyweight boxer, the fresh air and getting out of the tiny cabin felt amazing.

"Lawson's waiting for you in his office," Abel informed us.

Holt reached out a hand to Abel. "How've you been?"

Abel harrumphed. "Missing this one like a limb." He leaned closer to Holt conspiratorially. "She's the best dispatcher I got. The other ones are too damn chatty."

I choked on a laugh. "It's called being friendly."

"It's called not being able to shut up," Abel said.

"I heard that," Lucille called from dispatch.

"I wanted you to," Abel shot back.

I sent her a sympathetic look. "I'll be back in a week or two."

She lifted her hands to the heavens. "Praise the good Lord above."

"Oh, shut it, you two," Abel griped.

Holt grinned but gave my hand a gentle tug. "We should go."

He led me through the sea of desks. Officers all stopped what they were doing to say hello and ask how I was doing. I couldn't help that my gaze traveled to the two empty desks. My throat tightened as I took in Amber's space. It had been cleared of all her belongings as if she'd never existed at all.

Holt squeezed my hand, reading me like a book as always. "This is the hardest it'll be. The first time back."

I nodded. "Have you heard how Clint's doing?"

"He asked Law for a week off. I think he's struggling to come to terms with everything that happened."

"I need to go see him."

Holt pressed a kiss to my temple. "Tomorrow. I'll go with you."

"Thanks."

He rapped on Lawson's door, and the chief immediately told us to come in.

As we stepped inside, Lawson smiled. "It's good to have you back here."

"It's good to be back." The words weren't a lie. Because as hard as it had been to walk into this space, it was wonderful, too. It reminded me how much people cared about me. How many I had on my team.

Lawson gestured to the chairs. "Have a seat. You want something to drink?"

We both shook our heads.

Lawson settled back in his desk chair. "I won't beat around the bush. The district attorney has charged Jude with accessory to murder and three counts of first-degree murder."

I swallowed, trying to clear the lump in my throat. "Is he talking?"

"Only to his lawyer. But Randy turned chatty the moment he found out that Jude tried to frame his little brother. Apparently, Jude was the mastermind ten years ago. He got Randy and Paul thinking about payback with all the people who had supposedly wronged them. He was the one who came up with the plan and

311 OF YOU | 311

told them to steal Randy's father's guns. They kept quiet because they got a thrill out of us missing one of them."

Holt's hand tightened around mine. "Jude was using them as cover for what he really wanted."

Lawson nodded slowly. "Looks that way. And we can only guess he did the same with Amber."

"It twisted her, what happened to her brother," I said quietly.

Lawson studied me before he spoke. "Trauma can do that, especially when you don't have the right support around you afterward. No amount of punishment would ever be enough for her. Because it would never take away her pain."

A heaviness settled over me. So much hurt. Destruction. Death. And it was a vicious cycle that never seemed to end.

"It feels hopeless." And I hated that feeling.

A knock sounded on Lawson's door. He straightened in his chair. "Someone has wanted to talk to you. I hope it's okay that I told him to meet us here."

Confusion furrowed my brow, but I nodded. "Sure."

"Come in," Lawson called.

The door opened, and Joe Sullivan hovered in the threshold. He had dark circles under his eyes, but his hair wasn't quite as disheveled as it usually was.

Holt tensed at my side and glared at Lawson.

"Have a seat, Joe," Lawson invited, ignoring Holt's flare of anger.

Joe swallowed hard but moved to the couch Lawson had pushed against the wall in his office. He sat, clasping his hands, his nails digging in.

No one said anything for a few moments.

I shifted in my chair and turned to face Joe. "Are you doing okay?"

His head snapped up at that, his mouth opening and closing a few times before he spoke. "I wasn't there to hurt you." He swallowed again, glancing at Holt. "I'm sorry I shot at you. I couldn't see who was chasing me. I thought it was the shooter."

Holt's jaw was hard, but his tone stayed even. "Why were you there?"

Joe's eyes sought me out. "My brother was good to me. Made sure I had food and that my dad didn't beat the crap out of me."

My heart clenched.

"But he wasn't good to other people. I know that." Unshed tears glistened in his eyes. "You didn't deserve what happened to you. And you were always so...*nice*. It would've been easier if you'd treated me like trash. But you never did. You always said hi and smiled like you were happy to see me." Joe took a deep breath. "I didn't want anything else to happen to you."

My fingers dug into Holt's hand. "You were watching out for me."

He shrugged. "I figured if someone was going after the victims of what happened before, they'd come for you." His face hardened. "I wasn't going to let that happen."

Slowly, I forced myself to release Holt's hand and stood. I moved to the couch and sat next to him. Then, I did the only thing I could think to do. I wrapped my arms around the boy. Because that was what he was...a boy. Not even eighteen and scared out of his mind. Yet he'd tried to do the right thing.

"You're a good person," I whispered.

Joe's shoulders began to shake with silent sobs.

"Thank you for wanting to protect me."

He cried harder. "I'm sorry my brother hurt you."

"Me, too. But that doesn't mean you can't love him. For all he was to you. It's impossible to turn that off. And you shouldn't have to. It just shows the type of person you are—loyal and kind."

"I think you're the only one who thinks that." Joe sniffed.

I pulled back, meeting his eyes. "Other people will see that. You just have to give them a chance."

"He's going to," Lawson said. "Joe's got a scholarship to the University of Washington, and he's gonna live with a friend of mine. Get a fresh start."

Pressure built behind my eyes. "That sounds amazing."

Joe blushed. "It'll be good. I leave right after graduation."

I squeezed his hand. "I'm happy for you."

He studied me for a minute. "Maybe I could email you and tell you how I'm doing? That I'm making something of my life."

"I'd like that," I said hoarsely.

I was quiet as Holt drove us back to the cabin. But I wasn't alone in that silence. Holt's fingers wove through mine, and he had our joined hands resting on his thigh.

"You have the best heart of anyone I've ever known," he said, his voice thick. "What you gave that boy… Never seen a greater gift. He has a chance because of you."

My fingers tightened around Holt's. "You dropping any charges against him didn't hurt either."

The corner of his mouth kicked up. "Like I had a choice after you made him your new best friend."

I chuckled as Holt took the road that led away from the cabin and up the hillside. "Where are you going?"

"You'll see."

My chest tightened as he drove past the turnoff for the barn where Amber and Jude had kept me. The SUV climbed higher until we reached a spot that overlooked the lake. The view was stunning.

Holt turned off the engine and climbed out. He rounded the vehicle and opened my door, leading me toward a small overlook.

"It's beautiful," I said, leaning against him. "I've never been up here."

He pressed his lips to the top of my head. "This land, do you still love it?"

I understood what was beneath the question. So many hard things had happened here—so many terrifying things. But there was so much more to this place. "How could I not? It's where you came back to me. Where we fell in love all over again. It'll always be my favorite place in the world."

Holt's expression filled with such tenderness that it made my heart ache. "Good."

"Now who's turning into Roan with the one-word sentences?"

He chuckled and then took my mouth in a slow kiss, one that poured all that tenderness into my soul. I swore I could feel his love for me in that touch of lips and tongues.

I came away breathless. "I take that back. You can say it all without a word."

Holt framed my face with his hands, the rough pads of his fingers soothing everything in me. "I thought we could build a home here. One that's ours."

My eyes widened. "This property isn't even for sale."

He shrugged. "I had a word with the owner. Made an offer they couldn't ignore. It would mean we owned the land from here to the lake. We could keep the cabin for guests or as a sort of boat-house for days on the lake. But I want a life with you. Children with you. All the things we dreamed of. And I want us to build it from the ground up. Together."

Tears spilled from my eyes. "Holt."

His mouth curved. "Is that a yes? You're with me?"

I threw my arms around him. "I'm with you."

Epilogue

Wren
TWO MONTHS LATER

HOLT SPREAD A BLANKET OUT OVER WHAT I'D COME TO think of as *our spot*. We'd had a lot of them over the years. Hideouts on his parents' property. The massive, overstuffed chair in the house I'd grown up in. The dock we'd spent hours on the moment the weather allowed.

But this one was my favorite. Maybe because of the moments and places that had come before it. Maybe because this was the spot where we would build our lives.

Holt grabbed the picnic basket and gestured for me to sit.

Shadow raced across the blanket and bounded into the field below. Grinning, I lowered myself as a bubble of anticipation floated through me—and perhaps a healthy dose of nerves.

Holt grinned. "You know we can change anything we don't like."

"I know. But we've talked this through with the architects, over and over. I'm hoping it's a slam dunk right out of the gate."

The more tweaks we made, the longer it would take for us to be in our home.

He leaned over and brushed his lips across mine. "Me, too. But better that it's right than us rushing it."

"Why do you always have to make such good points when it comes to house-related things?" I grumbled.

Holt chuckled. The sound had changed in the last two months. It was lighter. Freer somehow. "You don't have to sound so annoyed about it."

"I can't help it. It annoys me when you're right and I'm wrong."

He pressed his lips together to keep from laughing. "This is about Newsprint Gray, isn't it?"

"It looks so freaking good with the photos we hung!"

Holt did laugh then, pulling me onto his lap and kissing me soundly. "I promise to be wrong about at least five things while we're building this house."

I grinned against his mouth. "That would be the gentlemanly thing to do."

"And you know I'm a gentleman."

The husky edge to his voice made heat pool low in my belly. "Please, for the love of all that's holy, do not use that tone right now."

"What tone?" Holt asked innocently, but his eyes had a devilish gleam.

I pinched his side. "You know it makes me want to jump your bones, and if we get arrested for indecent exposure, it really is going to be a long time before we look at these plans."

Holt sighed. "Fine. House plans now, sex later."

My belly clenched at the promise in his words. "Thank you."

Holt kept me on his lap but grabbed the cylindrical case holding the architectural drawings. Carefully, he unrolled them in front of us. There was a stack of pages to go through, but that first page stole my breath.

Tears gathered in my eyes. "It's perfect."

Holt held me tighter against him. "Hey, what's with the waterworks?"

"It's just...I love it." It was everything we'd dreamed of, a blend of rustic mountain lodge and farmhouse with a huge wraparound porch. "They even drew my swing in."

His lips skimmed my neck. "I told them we needed the swing for it to feel right."

"I love you. Have I told you that today?"

"Only ten times, so you've got at least ten more to go."

I laughed and flipped to the next page of the plans. The architects had taken everything we'd told them to the next level. The first floor was open and airy with massive windows. The kitchen spilled into a family room on one side and a dining room on the other. A huge stone fireplace separated the dining room and another living space.

A basement would house a game room with a massive TV on one side and a gym that Holt had said he *needed* on the other. The second story held five bedrooms, including a suite for us with a dream bathroom.

As my fingers trailed over one of the secondary bedrooms, my heart picked up speed. "We could make this one a nursery. It's the closest to ours and has a pretty view of the woods."

Holt grinned, his lips ghosting across my hair. "I love that plan."

I gripped his arms as I breathed deeply. "How would you feel about filling that room a little earlier than we planned?"

Holt's body went rigid beneath mine. "Cricket?"

I twisted in his hold, needing to see his face. Those deep blue eyes held so much as they scanned my face.

He swallowed hard. "Are you?"

"You know how I was on antibiotics last month? I forgot that it can affect birth control. I was late, so I went to the doc this morning. I didn't want to buy a test at the store. It would've been all over town in two seconds. I know we weren't planning—"

Holt cut me off with a searing kiss as his hand came around

to my stomach. "I've never wanted anything more than a family with you."

Tears filled my eyes. "Stop making me cry."

"Sorry, Cricket." He pulled back, his brow furrowing. "Are you feeling okay? You said you were nauseous yesterday."

"That's what tipped me off. But it hasn't been too bad so far."

"You need to rest. We need to get you some prenatal vitamins and get a list of foods that are good to eat and—"

I silenced him with another kiss. "I'm going to be okay."

Holt's thumb swept back and forth across my belly. "We're having a baby," he whispered, and the words had a reverence to them that had emotion clogging my throat.

"I never thought I could be this happy."

"You know, you really stole my thunder."

I looked up at him, eyes dancing. "For what?"

"I got you a present in honor of our house plans. Something to put in the library."

I straightened in his lap. "I like presents."

Holt chuckled and reached into the picnic basket. "Happy new home."

I tore at the pale pink paper with no sign of patience. The book was old, but the cloth binding was still pristine. "Holt…"

Gold lettering stamped *Little Women* across the front. My fingers traced the design etched into the cover as I opened it. "This is…" My head jerked. "A first edition?"

"Our library deserves something special, don't you think?"

"This is amazing. It's so beautiful."

"There's a special bookmark in there, too."

I flipped the pages until my fingers caught on a ribbon, and I tugged it free. My heart hammered against my ribs as a shimmering stone caught the light.

Holt caught the ring. "Never thought I'd get this kind of happiness. This joy." He slid the ring onto my finger, the massive oval diamond glowing in the fading sunlight. "But, somehow, you keep giving me more. Marry me?"

I tilted my head back to take in the beautiful man behind me. "You've given me *everything*. And still, you give me more."

"Is that a yes?"

"Yes," I breathed, my mouth meeting his.

As the sky faded into twilight, I knew all those dreams we'd conjured up years ago were finally coming true. And having them now, we'd appreciate them all the more for everything we'd been through.

The Lost & Found Series continues with
Nash and Maddie's story, *Echoes of You.*

Acknowledgments

Well, we've started a whole new series. It's crazy to think back to 2018 when I published my very first book, that I'd soon have over seventeen books in the world. It has been a rollercoaster of a journey, but I'm incredibly grateful for every moment.

That is one thing that hasn't changed over the past several years. Gratitude. It will forever be a vital part of each and every day for me. And as I end a story, it's wonderful to think back to all the people who were a part of the process. So, let's commence with the thank-yous!

First, in my writerly world. Sam, thank you for being sounding board, support system, and giver of laughs when things get hard. Your feedback on this story was invaluable, and, more than that, your friendship. So grateful to have you in my life. Laura and Willow, our little Love Chain is my safe place in the world. Thank you for your friendship, your hilarity, your support in good times and bad. My Slackers: Amy, Kristy, and Rebecca, what would I do without Team Awesome? It wouldn't be anything good, I can tell you that. Thank you for sprints, accountability, support, and giggles. You make work so much fun, and I'm so thankful for your friendship. Emma and Grahame, I love that we've shared this journey almost since day one. Thank you for riding the rollercoaster alongside me. You guys are the best!

Second, in my non-writer world. My STS soul sisters: Hollis, Jael, and Paige, thank you for the gift of twenty years of your friendship and never-ending support. I love living life with you in every incarnation. Thank you for supporting my dreams and always cheering for each milestone. I love you more than I can say.

And to all my family and friends near and far. Thank you for supporting me on this crazy journey, even if you don't read "kissing books." But you get extra-special bonus points if you picked up one of mine, even if that makes me turn the shade of a tomato when you tell me.

To my fearless beta readers: Crystal, Elle, Kelly, and Trisha, thank you for reading this book in its roughest form and helping me to make it the best it could possibly be!

The crew that helps bring my words to life and gets them out into the world is pretty darn epic. Thank you to Devyn, Margo, Chelle, Jaime, Julie, Hang, Stacey, Jenn, and the rest of my team at Social Butterfly; Katie, Andi, and my Lyric team; and Kimberly, Joy, and my team at Brower Literary. Your hard work is so appreciated!

To all the bloggers who have taken a chance on my words... THANK YOU! Your championing of my stories means more than I can say. And to my launch and ARC teams, thank you for your kindness, support, and sharing my books with the world. And an extra-special thank you to Crystal, who sails that ship so I can focus on the words.

Ladies of the Catherine Cowles Reader Group, you're my favorite place to hang out on the internet! Thank you for your support, encouragement, and willingness to always dish about your latest book boyfriends. You're the freaking best!

Lastly, thank YOU! Yes, YOU. I'm so grateful you're reading this book and making my author dreams come true. I love you for that. A whole lot!

Also Available from
CATHERINE COWLES

The Lost & Found Series
Whispers of You
Echoes of You
More coming soon

The Tattered & Torn Series
Tattered Stars
Falling Embers
Hidden Waters
Shattered Sea
Fractured Sky

The Wrecked Series
Reckless Memories
Perfect Wreckage
Wrecked Palace
Reckless Refuge
Beneath the Wreckage

The Sutter Lake Series
Beautifully Broken Pieces
Beautifully Broken Life
Beautifully Broken Spirit
Beautifully Broken Control
Beautifully Broken Redemption

Stand-alone Novels
Further To Fall

For a full list of up-to-date Catherine Cowles titles,
please visit www.catherinecowles.com.a

About
CATHERINE COWLES

Writer of words. Drinker of Diet Cokes. Lover of all things cute and furry. Catherine has had her nose in a book since the time she could read and finally decided to write down some of her own stories. When she's not writing, she can be found exploring her home state of Oregon, listening to true crime podcasts, or searching for her next book boyfriend.

Stay Connected

You can find Catherine in all the usual bookish places...

Website:
catherinecowles.com

Facebook:
facebook.com/catherinecowlesauthor

Catherine Cowles Facebook Reader Group:
www.facebook.com/groups/CatherineCowlesReaderGroup

Instagram:
instagram.com/catherinecowlesauthor

Goodreads:
goodreads.com/catherinecowlesauthor

BookBub:
bookbub.com/profile/catherine-cowles

Amazon:
www.amazon.com/author/catherinecowles

Twitter:
twitter.com/catherinecowles

Pinterest:
pinterest.com/catherinecowlesauthor

Made in the USA
Middletown, DE
08 March 2024

51001418R00198